THE WINTER FATHER

COLLECTED SHORT STORIES & NOVELLAS   VOLUME 2

By Andre Dubus

The Lieutenant

Separate Flights

Adultery & Other Choices

Finding a Girl in America

The Times Are Never So Bad

Voices from the Moon

The Last Worthless Evening

Selected Stories

Broken Vessels

Dancing After Hours

Meditations from a Moveable Chair

ANDRE DUBUS

The Winter Father

COLLECTED SHORT STORIES & NOVELLAS   VOLUME 2

Introduction by RICHARD RUSSO

Series Editor JOSHUA BODWELL

DAVID R. GODINE · *Publisher*

Boston

LIBRARY OF CONGRESS CATALOGING-IN-PUBLICATION DATA

Names: Dubus, Andre, 1936–1999 author. | Bodwell, Joshua editor.
Title: Collected short stories and novellas / Andre Dubus ;
edited by Joshua Bodwell.
Description: Jaffrey, New Hampshire : David R. Godine, Publisher, 2018. |
Includes bibliographical references and index.
Identifiers: LCCN 2018003815| ISBN 9781567926163 (v. 1 : softcover :
alk. paper) | ISBN 9781567926170 (v. 2 : softcover : alk. paper)
Classification: LCC PS3554.U265 A6 2018 | DDC 813/.54—dc23
LC record available at https://lccn.loc.gov/2018003815

ACKNOWLEDGMENTS

Finding a Girl in America
"Killings" and "The Winter Father" first appeared in *The Sewanee Review*; "The
Dark Men" in *Northwest Review*; "His Lover" in *The William and Mary Review*;
"Townies" in *The Real Paper*; "At St. Croix" in *Ploughshares*; "The Pitcher" in
The North American Review and *Fielder's Choice: An Anthology of Baseball Fiction*; "Waiting" in *The Paris Review*; and "Delivering" in *Harper's*. Dubus
extended his gratitude to the John Simon Guggenheim Memorial
Foundation, The National Endowment for the Arts, and the Artists Foundation
of Massachusetts.

The Times are Never So Bad
"Bless Me, Father" first appeared in *Carleton Miscellany*; "Goodbye" and "The
Captain" in *Ploughshares*; "Leslie in California" in *Redbook*; "The New Boy" in
Harper's; "Anna" in *Playboy*; and "A Father's Story" in *The Black Warrior Review*.

CONTENTS

ORIGINAL RELATIONSHIPS

RICHARD RUSSO

IN VENICE SOME YEARS AGO, my wife and I hired a tour guide to shepherd us through the massive collections at the Accademia and the Scuola San Rocco. In the former he drew our attention to one particular painting that was considered blasphemous at the time because Mary and the infant Jesus were not, as tradition demanded, in the exact center of the painting. To my untutored eye it appeared to be a devout depiction of Madonna and child. But it apparently suggested to contemporary viewers that they might not be at the center of everything that mattered. It's unlikely that I ever would've seen any of that on my own. Still, it put me in mind of an old grad school professor of mine who argued for what he called "an original relationship" between us and the books we were studying, by which he seemed to mean that we should come to our own conclusions about a poem or story before entertaining the opinions of professional critics. When you're told what to look for, he reasoned, you'll likely find it, and having found it you'll be less likely to notice what you otherwise might have. What we're talking about here is context—historical, biographical, cultural, religious—which can either enlighten or blind us, depending. I was grateful for our guide in Venice, but by the end of the two days we spent in his company my wife and I began to sense his blind spots. If we expressed interest in a work he'd already decided was uninteresting, he could be downright dismissive. Did we need a second tour guide as a corrective to the first? Or maybe just return to the exhibits by ourselves in the hopes of arriving at our own conclusions?

In *The Lonely City*, the writer Olivia Laing addresses the issue of context in a chapter on Edward Hopper, whose paintings had for a long time been of enormous personal and aesthetic importance to her, a zeal that was tarnished by reading his wife Jo's unpublished diaries, which reveal that Hopper did everything in his power to stifle her own artistic career. "The revelation of how violently he worked to suppress her," Laing says, "isn't easy to square ... with the image of the suited man in his polished shoes, his stately reticence, his immense reserve." Context that we cannot square with belief has a way of quickly becoming toxic, because once we know something it's impossible to *un*know it or to talk ourselves out of it. We understand, intellectually, that great artists are not always good people, but we still want them to be and somehow manage to feel betrayed when they aren't.

I raise this issue because I was in graduate school, trying to become a writer myself, when I first read Andre Dubus and my relationship to his stories was largely "original" in the sense that I knew very little about him. That said, I did bring a fair amount of personal context to his stories. A lapsed Catholic, I'd been for many years an altar boy and was belatedly discovering that even though I'd successfully flushed most Catholic doctrine from my system, the vocabulary of my former faith—*sin, redemption, grace*—obstinately remained. I admired the serious way Dubus allowed matters of faith to occupy the thematic center of his fiction, like those Renaissance paintings of Madonna and child in Venice. Reading him, I even allowed myself to wonder whether my decision to quit the church had been precipitous, because in truth I missed how warm the church of my youth had been in winter, how cool and dry in summer. The smell of incense, the gentle tinkling of the bell at communion, the sense of an entire community quietly humble in the face of mystery—these were the very elements of faith that Luke Ripley extols in Dubus's "A Father's Story," soothing rituals that nonbelievers throw out with the doctrinal bath water. I probably also sensed that such rituals were not so different from the ones writers use to summon the literary muse; most of us have a favorite time of day to work, a favorite chair to sit in, our favorite pens and writing tablets, favorite coffee cups—objects and habits that help us enter that mysterious world we can never possess but rather are possessed by, to which we gladly surrender ourselves, a state of consciousness that Dubus insisted has less to do with thought than instinct and, yes, feeling. When I first read the stories collected in this volume, I was also struck by their brave, uncompromising honesty. I recognized in Dubus's plain, simple diction his debt to Hemingway, whose style I, like just about every aspiring young male writer, had during my long apprenticeship admired and flirted with, hoping that I might find in such plain speech an honesty I feared my own stories lacked.

Later, after becoming a writer myself, I periodically returned to my favorite Dubus stories ("Killings," "Townies," "The Pretty Girl," "A Father's Story"), finding in them other things to admire, though by then my relationship to his fiction was no longer quite so "original." Over the years I'd crossed paths with writers who'd known Dubus well and who provided additional context. He was by all accounts a brilliant, generous teacher who had, alas, an unfortunate habit of taking as lovers his more attractive female undergraduate students. As a father of daughters I had to squint at this behavior, remind myself that he was of a different generation and that not so long ago such behavior was common and tolerated, perhaps even admired. If he wasn't perfect, well, neither was I. What mattered, I told myself, was the stories, and these I still loved. Which was why, when I heard of the terrible highway accident that put Dubus in a wheelchair for the rest of his life, I grieved, and grieved again a decade later when I heard he had died.

But at that point I had not met and become fast friends with his son, Andre Dubus III. It never occurred to me that reading my friend's heartbreaking memoir *Townie* might radically alter my perception of "Townies" and the rest of his father's fiction.

My friend Andre tells a hilarious story about the genesis of *Townie*. At a Little League baseball game, he witnessed a coach loudly berating the kids on his team. Appalled, Andre decided he would himself coach the following year, thereby protecting his sons, who would be old enough to play, and the other kids on his team from such abuse. He would make sure they concentrated on the fun of the game and on the rules of good sportsmanship. The problem was that these were the only rules with which Andre was familiar. He'd grown up in Newburyport and Haverhill with his mother and his siblings in grinding poverty. Not only had he never played baseball, he'd never even watched it on TV, which meant he was innocent not only of the rules as they applied to professionals, but also of how those were modified for kids. As a result his coaching was unique: he yelled "Run!" to kids on base when they were not allowed to and demanded they remain at bat until they were able to at least make contact with the ball. The kids he was coaching actually had to explain to him it's one, two, three strikes you're out at the old ball game.

Despite *Townie*'s terrifying description of the poverty and violence of Andre's adolescence, the memoir also contains a loving portrait of his famous writer father who, at the time, was living just across the river in Bradford, where he taught creative writing at Bradford College and wrote most of the stories contained in this volume. Baseball plays an important role in many of them. The Red Sox are frequently on the television above the bar at Timmy's, the ubiquitous neighborhood tavern, as well as on TVs at the beachfront New Hampshire restaurants just over the Massachusetts line. Several stories feature seemingly autobiographical protagonists who escape their fic-

tional Haverhill/Bradford with their student girlfriends by
driving to Boston and taking in a game at Fenway Park. One
story, "The Pitcher," showcases the kind of granular detail
about the sport that no casual fan would possess. In still other
stories baseball, a sport steeped (like Catholicism) in soothing
ritual, actually plays a role in offsetting the toxic effects of the
Vietnam War, which often serves as a narrative backdrop. All of
which begs an obvious question: if the author felt so strongly
about the sport, how is it possible that he conveyed none of it
to his son? And asking this question opened the door to others.
How was it possible that this father, who saw his children most
weekends, could be so blind to the poverty they and their
mother were living in? How could he look at the boy who bore
his name and not see that he was constantly being bullied on
the streets of then ungentrified Newburyport, that he lived in a
state of constant terror and deprivation? How could he feel so
little for the woman who'd borne his children and now, as a
single mother lacking the necessary resources to raise them,
had thrown up her hands in defeat?

Unable to square this new context with my "original"
admiration I found myself rereading these stories with a sinking and, yes, ungenerous heart. When the little boy in "The
Winter Father" chases his departing dad's car down the street,
crying, "You bum! You bum!," I saw not a fictional character,
but my friend, and I found myself whole-heartedly concur-
ring with the boy. When the divorced fathers in other stories
lamented not being able to pull up stakes and move to Boston
because that would mean abandoning their children, I smelled
hypocrisy, and in the more Catholic stories, where the protagonists use Original Sin—Man's fallen nature—to excuse shameful, selfish, repetitive behaviors they make no real effort to
change, I sniffed it again. If this weren't bad enough, my
growing disaffection even altered my assessment of the elder
Dubus's style and voice, in particular his debt to Hemingway.
When one character suggests to his young girlfriend that they
go to Boston, "to Casa Romero and have a hell of a dinner,"
I cringed, and cringed again every time one of Dubus's tough

guy protagonists descended into the sort of macho, romantic self-pity for which Hemingway males are so justly famous. Here, I told myself, is a derivative writer who, even in mid-career, is unable to transcend his literary influences. In "Finding a Girl in America," when Hank Allison rhapsodizes about writing as salvation (a soliloquy I'd found thrilling in my late twenties), I winced, and when he describes himself as "an average 260 hitting writer," I saw this as honest, accurate authorial self-evaluation. Just that quickly I'd come to see a man I'd once considered a paragon of honesty as fundamentally *dis*honest. Having saved it for last, I started rereading "A Father's Story" and had to put it down, afraid that it too might have been contaminated by time and context.

And what did all this portend for the introduction (yes, this one) that I'd agreed to write? The choice I seemed to be faced with was writing something dishonest myself, or telling the truth and in so doing risk undermining the reputation of a writer whose work I'd once revered, a betrayal that would not only sadden and anger his many loyal readers but also jeopardize my friendship with his son, who believes—and he's been very clear about this—that his father was one of our very finest storytellers. And in writing *Townie*, he made something else clear: if there was anything to forgive his father for, he'd done it long ago.

What then does one do with unwanted context? Rattled by Jo Hopper's journal entries about her husband's efforts to ruin her career, Olivia Laing found the lens she'd been using to view Hopper had become fogged, her affection for his work undermined. And yet in the end his paintings weren't ruined for her. Why? Unfortunately her chapter on Hopper doesn't answer that question directly, but it's not impossible to make an educated guess. After all, Hopper was, context be damned, such an undeniably great painter, an artist who painted the truth as he saw it. But I suspected there was more to it, and the *more* was personal. Laing, who was at the time terribly lonely herself, found Hopper's paintings "consoling" and, as she put it, a kind of "antidote" to her own dark emotional state.

And so, not long after reading these stories and judging their author harshly, I went back to work, determined, not just to give the stories a more sympathetic reading but also to examine my earlier visceral reaction to them, which was already beginning to feel unfair.

Best to begin, I reasoned, with those matters least likely to raise troublesome context issues—friendship and the temptation to read fiction as autobiography—focusing instead on style, voice, and literary influence. Okay, sure, the debt to Hemingway was undeniable, the sparseness of style and diction, especially in dialogue. But there were other less obvious influences, too, like Faulkner, whose style is lush, expansive and, well, Southern. We think of Dubus as a New England writer because that's where he spent most of his writing life and he set the majority of his stories there, but he grew up in Louisiana and the South is ambiently present in his fiction the way Catholicism is in my own. Dubus's debt to Faulkner, though, has less to do with style than inclination and instinct, a willingness—even a need—to burrow deep into the consciousness of characters who, unlike their creator, are too shy or inarticulate or uneducated or lacking in self-awareness to speak for themselves, and to give such people voice. Take, for instance, the title character of "Anna." In the story's opening paragraphs, long before we learn that she and her boyfriend Wayne will rob a store, Anna Griffin is revealed to us not in terms of what she has, but rather what she lacks. A cashier at the Sunnycorner store, she envies the put-together women who work at the nearby bank and wile away their lunch hours thumbing through the store's magazines. These women don't possess *something* Anna lacks; they possess *everything* she lacks. Her poverty becomes even more clear after the robbery when she and Wayne go shopping at the mall, where they buy many of the things they've longed for (and which the women from the bank no doubt possess): a color TV, a record player, a vacuum cleaner. The story's brilliance lies in the fact that finally owning these things doesn't diminish Anna's sense of poverty but rather deepens it by bringing home to her just how much there is in the world to want; their purchases barely scratch the surface. The story's most heartbreaking detail is the vacuum cleaner, whose cord is longer than it needs to be to clean their tiny apartment. Without being able to articulate it, Anna discovers that their new material wealth doesn't really address the root cause of their poverty. When she confesses to a man at Timmy's that what she'd really like is to tend bar there, his response—"you'd be good at it"—haunts her long after their mall purchases have been unpacked. Her deepest poverty resides in her fear that she'll never be good at anything, never be worthy of what others just assume is their due. It's a revelation worthy of Chekhov, a writer Dubus often taught and clearly revered. Many of Dubus's best stories contain this kind of Chekhovian "pivot."

Take "The Pretty Girl." Here Raymond Yarborough isn't so much inarticulate as baffled. The story's two distinct narrative points of view provide a dramatic contrast between how Ray sees himself and how the world sees him. Much of the story's tension derives from the fact that these two narratives never really align. To his ex-wife Polly and her cop father, Ray is simply crazy and violent, an unhinged thug. Seen through his own eyes, he appears not so much unhinged as confused. He may not understand—himself, his wife, the larger world—but he desperately wants to. "I never know how I feel until I hold that steel," he informs us in the story's haunting first line, and as his narrative unfolds the reader is struck by his honesty and, at times, even generosity. He tenders all sorts of information about himself, much of it intimate, some of it damning, though that's not how he sees it. And while he may not be a gifted thinker, he does possess a surprising moral imagination. For a man who often doesn't know how he himself feels, he has no trouble imagining how Polly's father must feel after he terrorizes her, and given the opportunity to hurt the man (who has come to hurt him) he demurs.

The real tragedy of Raymond's life seems to be that his experiences seldom lead to genuine understanding, and so the more he tries to explain himself—who he is and why he does what he does—the more bewildered he appears. He's unable, for instance, to make the connection between the steel he refers to in the opening line (the bar of his weightlifting rig) and the hunting knife he uses to terrorize Polly. Nor does he suspect, as many readers will, the connection between his own propensity for violence and the Vietnam War, which claimed his brother Kingsley. Indeed, it's Kingsley he's thinking about—imagining his older brother crawling through the jungle in the moments before he trips the land mine—that leads to his decision to assault Polly's new lover and once again terrify her by setting a fire outside the camp in New Hampshire where she's hiding. Despite being a large man ("It helps in this world to be big," he admits), Raymond seems almost child-like, bewildered by the fact that his brother is no longer around to go hunting and fishing and drinking with. In fact, in the story's climactic scene we understand that Raymond's most lethal characteristic may be his innocence. He simply doesn't understand why Polly doesn't love him anymore. "What did I do?" he asks her, because to his way of thinking the fact that he raped her at knife-point is evidence of his depth of feeling, his undying love.

The larger point here is that noting a writer's influences isn't the same as suggesting he lacks originality (as I had done earlier by focusing on Dubus's stylistic debt to Hemingway and ignoring other writers who were equally important to him). Nor should any writer's influences obscure the new uses he puts them to, because Hemingway, Faulkner, and Chekhov aside, Dubus's stories feel as fresh today as they did when I first read them three decades ago. One reason is the delight he takes in wrong-footing readers by playing off their genre expectations. Conventional robbery stories, for example, are almost always concerned with whether the thieves will get caught; if they get away with it, the reader usually breathes a sigh of relief. Here's it's the exact opposite. Dubus couldn't cares less whether Anna and Wayne get caught, because *not* getting caught actually deepens their predicament. Similarly, "Townies," which at first appears to be the story of a murdered college girl, turns out not to be about her at all but rather the unexpected link between the campus cop who finds her body and the boy who kills her, both of whom have been excluded from the privileged girl's world by virtue of their class. Key to conventional stories are clear conflicts that get established early in the narrative so the reader feels oriented and the drama can be heightened. By contrast, Dubus's conflicts are often revealed late in the overall scheme of things and sometimes resolved mere moments later, because he doesn't care much whether we feel oriented or not. He's not here to offer comfort but rather truth.

And what truth is that, exactly? I suspect it's the same one Thomas Hardy insisted we grasp nearly a century earlier—that is, just how small and powerless we are against the forces aligned against us. We read Dubus's stories the same way we read *Jude the Obscure*, not to find out what happens next but rather to watch our deepest fears—about ourselves and a brutal, uncaring world—realized. Dubus's adulterers—adultery is for him the most common and lethal of sins—not only know that what they're doing is wrong but that it will trail harsh consequences. They're simply unable to repress their desires, or even to act in their own self-interest. In "Killings," Frank, the main character's beloved son, knows that his love for another man's wife is dangerous, but love easily trumps both reason and morality. And when Frank's murderer escapes justice to walk the streets of their small town, Matt, the young man's father, has little choice (as he sees it) but to set in motion a murderous plan to put things right. Readers hope against hope that Matt's lifetime of decency will prevail in the end but they also know better. Fate rules here, making a mockery of both free will and chance. Worse, as readers we are made to feel complicit, judging neither father nor son (or even Raymond Yarborough, for that matter, who speaks of Polly as his addiction, something he has no control over), for these men are as God made them. This is the bad news Dubus feels compelled to share with us: that we are, alas, unequal to many of the most important tasks life sets before us. We are too small and the world too large.

I've not said much about "A Father's Story" to this point, but the time has now come, and I won't mince words. It's one of the finest stories ever penned by an American. Any fears I might've had about context diminishing my regard for it did not survive rereading the first page. Art is, after all, its own best defense, although it's probably worth pointing out that in this story context actually worked powerfully in the writer's favor, for I am, as I said earlier, a father of daughters, a man who would without hesitation do what Luke Ripley does on that dark rural road, and for the same reasons. The story's genius resides in its first person narrator, whose voice is so powerful, so hypnotizing, so haunting that the reader either forgets or doesn't really care that for three quarters of the story nothing happens. We're offered no dramatic hook, no clear conflict, no begged question to keep us turning pages. Dubus simply talks to us through Luke, without gimmicks or props, as if our interest in a "big-gutted, gray-haired guy, drinking tea and staring out at the dark woods across the road, listening to a grieving soprano" were a foregone conclusion. As if the unvarying, dogged routine of Luke's everyday life and the crushing loneliness he feels after his wife leaves him were a time-honored, sure-fire method of capturing and holding a reader's attention. As if this old fart's leisurely musings on God and fishing and hunting and baseball and marriage were all any reader had a right to expect from fiction. Because come on, by all rights this story has no business working. By the time something dramatic finally *does* happen the reader is actually surprised, having come to terms with the possibility— no, probability—that if anything were going to happen it would have already.

And then, almost before we know it, the story is over, its conclusion as rich and satisfying as anything in contemporary fiction, leaving us to marvel at the alchemy by which such narrative base metal has been spun into pure gold. What the author has crafted, we realize, a one-trick story, but the trick is, in the end, the only one that really matters. He has made us care. About a big-gutted guy who talks to God because there's nobody else around. Luke Ripley has been instructed, as most of us have, to love God more than the world he gave us, a world that contains our wives and lovers, our sons and daughters, our good work, our pain and loss and struggle. What Luke wants God to understand is that this is simply not possible. Not for him. Probably not for any of us. I was in my twenties and not yet a father the first time I read the story, and at the end when Luke makes his peace with the God he believes he's disappointed, I wept. Thirty some years later—just three weeks ago—I reread it and wept again, for the author I'd once loved and now loved again, for his son and my friend, and, yes, for my own father, who was absent during my young life much as Andre's was. Which is probably why, I now realize, I briefly flirted with disdain and self-righteous disregard for a truly great writer. Because years earlier I'd done exactly what my friend Andre did. I forgave my wayward father. Did so, moreover, for the pleasure of his company and because I could easily imagine doing the exact wrong thing one day and wanting forgiveness myself. I thought I'd forgiven my father completely and without reservation, but apparently not. Some residual resentment apparently remained, and so, without even realizing what I was doing, I offloaded it onto a convenient surrogate.

Edward Hopper once remarked that in all of his paintings, including "Nighthawks," he was really just trying to paint himself. Maybe that's what all artists and writers do, whether they realize it or not. We offer ourselves. *Here I am*, we say, not fully comprehending the nature or value of the offering, only that it's all we have.

FINDING A GIRL IN AMERICA

to Peggy

One is never talking to oneself always one is addressed to someone. Suddenly, without knowing the reason, at different stages in one's life, one is addressing this person or that all the time, even dreams are performed before an audience. I see that. It's well known that people who commit suicide, the most solitary of all acts, are addressing someone.
      NADINE GORDIMER
      Burger's Daughter

PART ONE

KILLINGS

ON THE AUGUST MORNING when Matt Fowler buried his youngest son, Frank, who had lived for twenty-one years, eight months, and four days, Matt's older son, Steve, turned to him as the family left the grave and walked between their friends, and said: 'I should kill him.' He was twenty-eight, his brown hair starting to thin in front where he used to have a cowlick. He bit his lower lip, wiped his eyes, then said it again. Ruth's arm, linked with Matt's, tightened; he looked at her. Beneath her eyes there was swelling from the three days she had suffered. At the limousine Matt stopped and looked back at the grave, the casket, and the Congregationalist minister who he thought had probably had a difficult job with the eulogy though he hadn't seemed to, and the old funeral director who was saying something to the six young pallbearers. The grave was on a hill and overlooked the Merrimack, which he could not see from where he stood; he looked at the opposite bank, at the apple orchard with its symmetrically planted trees going up a hill.

Next day Steve drove with his wife back to Baltimore where he managed the branch office of a bank, and Cathleen, the middle child, drove with her husband back to Syracuse. They had left the grandchildren with friends. A month after the funeral Matt played poker at Willis Trottier's because Ruth, who knew this was the second time he had been invited, told him to go, he couldn't sit home with her for the rest of her life, she was all right. After the game Willis went outside to tell everyone goodnight and, when the others had driven away, he walked with Matt to his car. Willis was a short, silver-haired man who had opened a diner after World War II, his trade then mostly very early breakfast, which he cooked, and then lunch for the men who worked at the leather and shoe factories. He now owned a large restaurant.

'He walks the Goddamn streets,' Matt said.

'I know. He was in my place last night, at the bar. With a girl.'

'I don't see him. I'm in the store all the time. Ruth sees him. She sees him too much. She was at Sunnyhurst today getting cigarettes and aspirin, and there he was. She can't even go out for cigarettes and aspirin. It's killing her.'

'Come back in for a drink.'

Matt looked at his watch. Ruth would be asleep. He walked with Willis back into the house, pausing at the steps to look at the starlit sky. It was a cool summer night; he thought vaguely of the Red Sox, did not even know if they were at home tonight; since it happened he had not been able to think about any of the small pleasures he believed he had earned, as he had earned also what was shattered now forever: the quietly harried and quietly pleasurable days of fatherhood. They went inside. Willis's wife, Martha, had gone to bed hours ago, in the rear of the large house which was rigged with burglar and fire alarms. They went downstairs to the game room: the television set suspended from the ceiling, the pool table, the poker table with beer cans, cards, chips, filled ashtrays, and the six chairs where Matt and his friends had sat, the friends picking up the old banter as though he had only been away on vacation; but he could see the affection and courtesy in their eyes. Willis went behind the bar and mixed them each a Scotch and soda; he stayed behind the bar and looked at Matt sitting on the stool.

'How often have you thought about it?' Willis said.

'Every day since he got out. I didn't think about bail.

I thought I wouldn't have to worry about him for years. She sees him all the time. It makes her cry.'

'He was in my place a long time last night. He'll be back.'

'Maybe he won't.'

'The band. He likes the band.'

'What's he doing now?'

'He's tending bar up to Hampton Beach. For a friend. Ever notice even the worst bastard always has friends? He couldn't get work in town. It's just tourists and kids up to Hampton. Nobody knows him. If they do, they don't care. They drink what he mixes.'

'Nobody tells me about him.'

'I hate him, Matt. My boys went to school with him. He was the same then. Know what he'll do? Five at the most. Remember that woman about seven years ago? Shot her husband and dropped him off the bridge in the Merrimack with a hundred pound sack of cement and said all the way through it that nobody helped her. Know where she is now? She's in Lawrence now, a secretary. And whoever helped her, where the hell is he?'

'I've got a .38 I've had for years. I take it to the store now. I tell Ruth it's for the night deposits. I tell her things have changed: we got junkies here now too. Lots of people without jobs. She knows though.'

'What does she know?'

'She knows I started carrying it after the first time she saw him in town. She knows it's in case I see him, and there's some kind of a situation—'

He stopped, looked at Willis, and finished his drink. Willis mixed him another.

'What kind of a situation?'

'Where he did something to me. Where I could get away with it.'

'How does Ruth feel about that?'

'She doesn't know.'

'You said she does, she's got it figured out.'

He thought of her that afternoon: when she went into

Sunnyhurst, Strout was waiting at the counter while the clerk bagged the things he had bought; she turned down an aisle and looked at soup cans until he left.

'Ruth would shoot him herself, if she thought she could hit him.'

'You got a permit?'

'No.'

'I do. You could get a year for that.'

'Maybe I'll get one. Or maybe I won't. Maybe I'll just stop bringing it to the store.'

Richard Strout was twenty-six years old, a high school athlete, football scholarship to the University of Massachusetts where he lasted for almost two semesters before quitting in advance of the final grades that would have forced him not to return. People then said: Dickie can do the work; he just doesn't want to. He came home and did construction work for his father but refused his father's offer to learn the business; his two older brothers had learned it, so that Strout and Sons trucks going about town, and signs on construction sites, now slashed wounds into Matt Fowler's life. Then Richard married a young girl and became a bartender, his salary and tips augmented and perhaps sometimes matched by his father, who also posted his bond. So his friends, his enemies (he had those: fist fights or, more often, boys and then young men who had not fought him when they thought they should have), and those who simply knew him by face and name, had a series of images of him which they recalled when they heard of the killing: the high school running back, the young drunk in bars, the oblivious hard-hatted young man eating lunch at a counter, the bartender who could perhaps be called courteous but not more than that: as he tended bar, his dark eyes and dark, wide-jawed face appeared less sullen, near blank.

One night he beat Frank. Frank was living at home and waiting for September, for graduate school in economics, and working as a lifeguard at Salisbury Beach, where he met Mary

Ann Strout, in her first month of separation. She spent most days at the beach with her two sons. Before ten o'clock one night Frank came home; he had driven to the hospital first, and he walked into the living room with stitches over his right eye and both lips bright and swollen.

'I'm all right,' he said, when Matt and Ruth stood up, and Matt turned off the television, letting Ruth get to him first: the tall, muscled but slender suntanned boy. Frank tried to smile at them but couldn't because of his lips.

'It was her husband, wasn't it?' Ruth said.

'Ex,' Frank said. 'He dropped in.'

Matt gently held Frank's jaw and turned his face to the light, looked at the stitches, the blood under the white of the eye, the bruised flesh.

'Press charges,' Matt said.

'No.'

'What's to stop him from doing it again? Did you hit him at all? Enough so he won't want to next time?'

'I don't think I touched him.'

'So what are you going to do?'

'Take karate,' Frank said, and tried again to smile.

'That's not the problem,' Ruth said.

'You know you like her,' Frank said.

'I like a lot of people. What about the boys? Did they see it?'

'They were asleep.'

'Did you leave her alone with him?'

'He left first. She was yelling at him. I believe she had a skillet in her hand.'

'Oh for God's sake,' Ruth said.

Matt had been dealing with that too: at the dinner table on evenings when Frank wasn't home, was eating with Mary Ann; or, on the other nights—and Frank was with her every night—he talked with Ruth while they watched television, or lay in bed with the windows open and he smelled the night air and imagined, with both pride and muted sorrow, Frank in Mary Ann's arms. Ruth didn't like it because Mary Ann was in the process of divorce, because she had two children, because she was four years older than Frank, and finally—she told this in bed, where she had during all of their marriage told him of her deepest feelings: of love, of passion, of fears about one of the children, of pain Matt had caused her or she had caused him—she was against it because of what she had heard: that the marriage had gone bad early, and for most of it Richard and Mary Ann had both played around.

'That can't be true,' Matt said. 'Strout wouldn't have stood for it.'

'Maybe he loves her.'

'He's too hot-tempered. He couldn't have taken that.'

But Matt knew Strout had taken it, for he had heard the stories too. He wondered who had told them to Ruth; and he felt vaguely annoyed and isolated: living with her for thirty-one years and still not knowing what she talked about with her friends. On these summer nights he did not so much argue with her as try to comfort her, but finally there was no difference between the two: she had concrete objections, which he tried to overcome. And in his attempt to do this, he neglected his own objections, which were the same as hers, so that as he spoke to her he felt as disembodied as he sometimes did in the store when he helped a man choose a blouse or dress or piece of costume jewelry for his wife.

'The divorce doesn't mean anything,' he said. 'She was young and maybe she liked his looks and then after a while she realized she was living with a bastard. I see it as a positive thing.'

'She's not divorced yet.'

'It's the same thing. Massachusetts has crazy laws, that's all. Her age is no problem. What's it matter when she was born? And that other business: even if it's true, which it probably isn't, it's got nothing to do with Frank, it's in the past. And the kids are no problem. She's been married six years; she ought to have kids. Frank likes them. He plays with them. And he's not going to marry her anyway, so it's not a problem of money.'

'Then what's he doing with her?'

'She probably loves him, Ruth. Girls always have. Why can't we just leave it at that?'

'He got home at six o'clock Tuesday morning.'

'I didn't know you knew. I've already talked to him about it.'

Which he had: since he believed almost nothing he told Ruth, he went to Frank with what he believed. The night before, he had followed Frank to the car after dinner.

'You wouldn't make much of a burglar,' he said.

'How's that?'

Matt was looking up at him; Frank was six feet tall, an inch and a half taller than Matt, who had been proud when Frank at seventeen outgrew him; he had only felt uncomfortable when he had to reprimand or caution him. He touched Frank's bicep, thought of the young taut passionate body, believed he could sense the desire, and again he felt the pride and sorrow and envy too, not knowing whether he was envious of Frank or Mary Ann.

'When you came in yesterday morning, I woke up. One of these mornings your mother will. And I'm the one who'll have to talk to her. She won't interfere with you. Okay? I know it means—' But he stopped, thinking: I know it means getting up and leaving that suntanned girl and going sleepy to the car, I know—

'Okay,' Frank said, and touched Matt's shoulder and got into the car.

There had been other talks, but the only long one was their first one: a night driving to Fenway Park, Matt having ordered the tickets so they could talk, and knowing when Frank said yes, he would go, that he knew the talk was coming too. It took them forty minutes to get to Boston, and they talked about Mary Ann until they joined the city traffic along the Charles River, blue in the late sun. Frank told him all the things that Matt would later pretend to believe when he told them to Ruth.

'It seems like a lot for a young guy to take on,' Matt finally said.

'Sometimes it is. But she's worth it.'

'Are you thinking about getting married?'

'We haven't talked about it. She can't for over a year. I've got school.'

'I *do* like her,' Matt said.

He did. Some evenings, when the long summer sun was still low in the sky, Frank brought her home; they came into the house smelling of suntan lotion and the sea, and Matt gave them gin and tonics and started the charcoal in the backyard, and looked at Mary Ann in the lawn chair: long and very light brown hair (Matt thinking that twenty years ago she would have dyed it blonde), and the long brown legs he loved to look at; her face was pretty; she had probably never in her adult life gone unnoticed into a public place. It was in her wide brown eyes that she looked older than Frank; after a few drinks Matt thought what he saw in her eyes was something erotic, testament to the rumors about her; but he knew it wasn't that, or all that: she had, very young, been through a sort of pain that his children, and he and Ruth, had been spared. In the moments of his recognizing that pain, he wanted to tenderly touch her hair, wanted with some gesture to give her solace and hope. And he would glance at Frank, and hope they would love each other, hope Frank would soothe that pain in her heart, take it from her eyes; and her divorce, her age, and her children did not matter at all. On the first two evenings she did not bring her boys, and then Ruth asked her to bring them next time. In bed that night Ruth said, 'She hasn't brought them because she's embarrassed. She shouldn't feel embarrassed.'

Richard Strout shot Frank in front of the boys. They were sitting on the living room floor watching television, Frank sitting on the couch, and Mary Ann just returning from the kitchen with a tray of sandwiches. Strout came in the front door and shot Frank twice in the chest and once in the face with a 9 mm. automatic. Then he looked at the boys and Mary Ann, and went home to wait for the police.

It seemed to Matt that from the time Mary Ann called weeping to tell him until now, a Saturday night in September, sitting in the car with Willis, parked beside Strout's car, waiting for the bar to close, that he had not so much moved through his life as wandered through it, his spirit like a dazed body bumping into furniture and corners. He had always been a fearful father: when his children were young, at the start of each summer he thought of them drowning in a pond or the sea, and he was relieved when he came home in the evenings and they were there; usually that relief was his only acknowledgment of his fear, which he never spoke of, and which he controlled within his heart. As he had when they were very young and all of them in turn, Cathleen too, were drawn to the high oak in the backyard, and had to climb it. Smiling, he watched them, imagining the fall: and he was poised to catch the small body before it hit the earth. Or his legs were poised; his hands were in his pockets or his arms were folded and, for the child looking down, he appeared relaxed and confident while his heart beat with the two words he wanted to call out but did not: *Don't fall.* In winter he was less afraid: he made sure the ice would hold him before they skated, and he brought or sent them to places where they could sled without ending in the street. So he and his children had survived their childhood, and he only worried about them when he knew they were driving a long distance, and then he lost Frank in a way no father expected to lose his son, and he felt that all the fears he had borne while they were growing up, and all the grief he had been afraid of, had backed up like a huge wave and struck him on the beach and swept him out to sea. Each day he felt the same and when he was able to forget how he felt, when he was able to force himself not to feel that way, the eyes of his clerks and customers defeated him. He wished those eyes were oblivious, even cold; he felt he was withering in their tenderness. And beneath his listless wandering, every day in his soul he shot Richard Strout in the face; while Ruth, going about town on errands, kept seeing him. And at nights in bed she would hold

Matt and cry, or sometimes she was silent and Matt would touch her tightening arm, her clenched fist.

As his own right fist was now, squeezing the butt of the revolver, the last of the drinkers having left the bar, talking to each other, going to their separate cars which were in the lot in front of the bar, out of Matt's vision. He heard their voices, their cars, and then the ocean again, across the street. The tide was in and sometimes it smacked the sea wall. Through the windshield he looked at the dark red side wall of the bar, and then to his left, past Willis, at Strout's car, and through its windows he could see the now-emptied parking lot, the road, the sea wall. He could smell the sea.

The front door of the bar opened and closed again and Willis looked at Matt then at the corner of the building; when Strout came around it alone Matt got out of the car, giving up the hope he had kept all night (and for the past week) that Strout would come out with friends, and Willis would simply drive away; thinking: *All right then. All right*; and he went around the front of Willis's car, and at Strout's he stopped and aimed over the hood at Strout's blue shirt ten feet away. Willis was aiming too, crouched on Matt's left, his elbow resting on the hood.

'Mr. Fowler,' Strout said. He looked at each of them, and at the guns. 'Mr. Trottier.'

Then Matt, watching the parking lot and the road, walked quickly between the car and the building and stood behind Strout. He took one leather glove from his pocket and put it on his left hand.

'Don't talk. Unlock the front and back and get in.'

Strout unlocked the front door, reached in and unlocked the back, then got in, and Matt slid into the back seat, closed the door with his gloved hand, and touched Strout's head once with the muzzle.

'It's cocked. Drive to your house.'

When Strout looked over his shoulder to back the car, Matt aimed at his temple and did not look at his eyes.

'Drive slowly,' he said. 'Don't try to get stopped.'

They drove across the empty front lot and onto the road, Willis's headlights shining into the car; then back through town, the sea wall on the left hiding the beach, though far out Matt could see the ocean; he uncocked the revolver; on the right were the places, most with their neon signs off, that did so much business in summer: the lounges and cafés and pizza houses, the street itself empty of traffic, the way he and Willis had known it would be when they decided to take Strout at the bar rather than knock on his door at two o'clock one morning and risk that one insomniac neighbor. Matt had not told Willis he was afraid he could not be alone with Strout for very long, smell his smells, feel the presence of his flesh, hear his voice, and then shoot him. They left the beach town and then were on the high bridge over the channel: to the left the smacking curling white at the breakwater and beyond that the dark sea and the full moon, and down to his right the small fishing boats bobbing at anchor in the cove. When they left the bridge, the sea was blocked by abandoned beach cottages, and Matt's left hand was sweating in the glove. Out here in the dark in the car he believed Ruth knew. Willis had come to his house at eleven and asked if he wanted a nightcap; Matt went to the bedroom for his wallet, put the gloves in one trouser pocket and the .38 in the other and went back to the living room, his hand in his pocket covering the bulge of the cool cylinder pressed against his fingers, the butt against his palm. When Ruth said goodnight she looked at his face, and he felt she could see in his eyes the gun, and the night he was going to. But he knew he couldn't trust what he saw. Willis's wife had taken her sleeping pill, which gave her eight hours—the reason, Willis had told Matt, he had the alarms installed, for nights when he was late at the restaurant—and when it was all done and Willis got home he would leave ice and a trace of Scotch and soda in two glasses in the game room and tell Martha in the morning that he had left the restaurant early and brought Matt home for a drink.

'He was making it with my wife.' Strout's voice was careful, not pleading.

Matt pressed the muzzle against Strout's head, pressed it harder than he wanted to, feeling through the gun Strout's head flinching and moving forward; then he lowered the gun to his lap.

'Don't talk,' he said.

Strout did not speak again. They turned west, drove past the Dairy Queen closed until spring, and the two lobster restaurants that faced each other and were crowded all summer and were now also closed, onto the short bridge crossing the tidal stream, and over the engine Matt could hear through his open window the water rushing inland under the bridge; looking to his left he saw its swift moonlit current going back into the marsh which, leaving the bridge, they entered: the salt marsh stretching out on both sides, the grass tall in patches but mostly low and leaning earthward as though windblown, a large dark rock sitting as though it rested on nothing but itself, and shallow pools reflecting the bright moon.

Beyond the marsh they drove through woods, Matt thinking now of the hole he and Willis had dug last Sunday afternoon after telling their wives they were going to Fenway Park. They listened to the game on a transistor radio, but heard none of it as they dug into the soft earth on the knoll they had chosen because elms and maples sheltered it. Already some leaves had fallen. When the hole was deep enough they covered it and the piled earth with dead branches, then cleaned their shoes and pants and went to a restaurant farther up in New Hampshire where they ate sandwiches and drank beer and watched the rest of the game on television. Looking at the back of Strout's head he thought of Frank's grave; he had not been back to it; but he would go before winter, and its second burial of snow.

He thought of Frank sitting on the couch and perhaps talking to the children as they watched television, imagined him feeling young and strong, still warmed from the sun at the beach, and feeling loved, hearing Mary Ann moving about in the kitchen, hearing her walking into the living room; maybe he looked up at her and maybe she said something, looking at him over the tray of sandwiches, smiling at him, saying something the way women do when they offer food as a gift, then the front door opening and this son of a bitch coming in and Frank seeing that he meant the gun in his hand, this son of a bitch and his gun the last person and thing Frank saw on earth.

When they drove into town the streets were nearly empty: a few slow cars, a policeman walking his beat past the darkened fronts of stores. Strout and Matt both glanced at him as they drove by. They were on the main street, and all the stoplights were blinking yellow. Willis and Matt had talked about that too: the lights changed at midnight, so there would be no place Strout had to stop and where he might try to run. Strout turned down the block where he lived and Willis's headlights were no longer with Matt in the back seat. They had planned that too, had decided it was best for just the one car to go to the house, and again Matt had said nothing about his fear of being alone with Strout, especially in his house: a duplex, dark as all the houses on the street were, the street itself lit at the corner of each block. As Strout turned into the driveway Matt thought of the one insomniac neighbor, thought of some man or woman sitting alone in the dark living room, watching the all-night channel from Boston. When Strout stopped the car near the front of the house, Matt said: 'Drive it to the back.'

He touched Strout's head with the muzzle.

'You wouldn't have it cocked, would you? For when I put on the brakes.'

Matt cocked it, and said: 'It is now.'

Strout waited a moment; then he eased the car forward, the engine doing little more than idling, and as they approached the garage he gently braked. Matt opened the door, then took off the glove and put it in his pocket. He stepped out and shut the door with his hip and said: 'All right.'

Strout looked at the gun, then got out, and Matt followed him across the grass, and as Strout unlocked the door Matt looked quickly at the row of small backyards on either side, and scattered tall trees, some evergreens, others not, and he thought of the red and yellow leaves on the trees over the hole, saw them falling soon, probably in two weeks, dropping slowly, covering. Strout stepped into the kitchen.

'Turn on the light.'

Strout reached to the wall switch, and in the light Matt looked at his wide back, the dark blue shirt, the white belt, the red plaid pants.

'Where's your suitcase?'

'My suitcase?'

'Where is it.'

'In the bedroom closet.'

'That's where we're going then. When we get to a door you stop and turn on the light.'

They crossed the kitchen, Matt glancing at the sink and stove and refrigerator: no dishes in the sink or even the dish rack beside it, no grease splashings on the stove, the refrigerator door clean and white. He did not want to look at any more but he looked quickly at all he could see: in the living room magazines and newspapers in a wicker basket, clean ashtrays, a record player, the records shelved next to it, then down the hall where, near the bedroom door, hung a color photograph of Mary Ann and the two boys sitting on a lawn—there was no house in the picture—Mary Ann smiling at the camera or Strout or whoever held the camera, smiling as she had on Matt's lawn this summer while he waited for the charcoal and they all talked and he looked at her brown legs and at Frank touching her arm, her shoulder, her hair; he moved down the hall with her smile in his mind, wondering: was that when they were both playing around and she was smiling like that at him and they were happy, even sometimes, making it worth it? He recalled her eyes, the pain in them, and he was conscious of the circles of love he was touching with the hand that held the revolver so tightly now as Strout stopped at the door at the end of the hall.

'There's no wall switch.'

'Where's the light?'

'By the bed.'

'Let's go.'

Matt stayed a pace behind, then Strout leaned over and the room was lighted: the bed, a double one, was neatly made; the ashtray on the bedside table clean, the bureau top dustless, and no photographs; probably so the girl—who *was* she?—would not have to see Mary Ann in the bedroom she believed was theirs. But because Matt was a father and a husband, though never an ex-husband, he knew (and did not want to know) that this bedroom had never been theirs alone. Strout turned around; Matt looked at his lips, his wide jaw, and thought of Frank's doomed and fearful eyes looking up from the couch.

'Where's Mr. Trottier?'

'He's waiting. Pack clothes for warm weather.'

'What's going on?'

'You're jumping bail.'

'Mr. Fowler—'

He pointed the cocked revolver at Strout's face. The barrel trembled but not much, not as much as he had expected. Strout went to the closet and got the suitcase from the floor and opened it on the bed. As he went to the bureau, he said: 'He was making it with my wife. I'd go pick up my kids and he'd be there. Sometimes he spent the night. My boys told me.'

He did not look at Matt as he spoke. He opened the top drawer and Matt stepped closer so he could see Strout's hands: underwear and socks, the socks rolled, the underwear folded and stacked. He took them back to the bed, arranged them neatly in the suitcase, then from the closet he was taking shirts and trousers and a jacket; he laid them on the bed and Matt followed him to the bathroom and watched from the door while he packed his shaving kit; watched in the bedroom as he folded and packed those things a person accumulated and that became part of him so that at times in the store Matt felt he was selling more than clothes.

'I wanted to try to get together with her again.' He was bent over the suitcase. 'I couldn't even talk to her. He was always with her. I'm going to jail for it; if I ever get out I'll be an old man. Isn't that enough?'

'You're not going to jail.'

Strout closed the suitcase and faced Matt, looking at the gun. Matt went to his rear, so Strout was between him and the lighted hall; then using his handkerchief he turned off the lamp and said: 'Let's go.'

They went down the hall, Matt looking again at the photograph, and through the living room and kitchen, Matt turning off the lights and talking, frightened that he was talking, that he was telling this lie he had not planned: 'It's the trial. We can't go through that, my wife and me. So you're leaving. We've got you a ticket, and a job. A friend of Mr. Trottier's. Out west. My wife keeps seeing you. We can't have that anymore.'

Matt turned out the kitchen light and put the handkerchief in his pocket, and they went down the two brick steps and across the lawn. Strout put the suitcase on the floor of the back seat, then got into the front seat and Matt got in the back and put on his glove and shut the door.

'They'll catch me. They'll check passenger lists.'

'We didn't use your name.'

'They'll figure that out too. You think I wouldn't have done it myself if it was that easy?'

He backed into the street, Matt looking down the gun barrel but not at the profiled face beyond it.

'You were alone,' Matt said. 'We've got it worked out.'

'There's no planes this time of night, Mr. Fowler.'

'Go back through town. Then north on 125.'

They came to the corner and turned, and now Willis's headlights were in the car with Matt.

'Why north, Mr. Fowler?'

'Somebody's going to keep you for a while. They'll take you to the airport.' He uncocked the hammer and lowered the revolver to his lap and said wearily: 'No more talking.'

As they drove back through town, Matt's body sagged, going limp with his spirit and its new and false bond with Strout, the hope his lie had given Strout. He had grown up in this town whose streets had become places of apprehension and pain for Ruth as she drove and walked, doing what she had to do; and for him too, if only in his mind as he worked and chatted six days a week in his store; he wondered now if his lie would have worked, if sending Strout away would have been enough; but then he knew that just thinking of Strout in Montana or whatever place lay at the end of the lie he had told, thinking of him walking the streets there, loving a girl there (who *was* she?) would be enough to slowly rot the rest of his days. And Ruth's. Again he was certain that she knew, that she was waiting for him.

They were in New Hampshire now, on the narrow highway, passing the shopping center at the state line, and then houses and small stores and sandwich shops. There were few cars on the road. After ten minutes he raised his trembling hand, touched Strout's neck with the gun, and said: 'Turn in up here. At the dirt road.'

Strout flicked on the indicator and slowed.

'Mr. Fowler?'

'They're waiting here.'

Strout turned very slowly, easing his neck away from the gun. In the moonlight the road was light brown, lighter and yellowed where the headlights shone; weeds and a few trees grew on either side of it, and ahead of them were the woods.

'There's nothing back here, Mr. Fowler.'

'It's for your car. You don't think we'd leave it at the airport, do you?'

He watched Strout's large, big-knuckled hands tighten on the wheel, saw Frank's face that night: not the stitches and bruised eye and swollen lips, but his own hand gently touching Frank's jaw, turning his wounds to the light. They rounded a bend in the road and were out of sight of the highway: tall trees all around them now, hiding the moon. When they reached the abandoned gravel pit on the left, the bare flat earth and steep pale embankment behind it, and the black crowns of trees at its top, Matt said: 'Stop here.'

Strout stopped but did not turn off the engine. Matt

pressed the gun hard against his neck, and he straightened in the seat and looked in the rearview mirror, Matt's eyes meeting his in the glass for an instant before looking at the hair at the end of the gun barrel.

'Turn it off.'

Strout did, then held the wheel with two hands, and looked in the mirror.

'I'll do twenty years, Mr. Fowler; at least. I'll be forty-six years old.'

'That's nine years younger than I am,' Matt said, and got out and took off the glove and kicked the door shut. He aimed at Strout's ear and pulled back the hammer. Willis's headlights were off and Matt heard him walking on the soft thin layer of dust, the hard earth beneath it. Strout opened the door, sat for a moment in the interior light, then stepped out onto the road. Now his face was pleading. Matt did not look at his eyes, but he could see it in the lips.

'Just get the suitcase. They're right up the road.'

Willis was beside him now, to his left. Strout looked at both guns. Then he opened the back door, leaned in, and with a jerk brought the suitcase out. He was turning to face them when Matt said: 'Just walk up the road. Just ahead.'

Strout turned to walk, the suitcase in his right hand, and Matt and Willis followed; as Strout cleared the front of his car he dropped the suitcase and, ducking, took one step that was the beginning of a sprint to his right. The gun kicked in Matt's hand, and the explosion of the shot surrounded him, isolated him in a nimbus of sound that cut him off from all his time, all his history, isolated him standing absolutely still on the dirt road with the gun in his hand, looking down at Richard Strout squirming on his belly, kicking one leg behind him, pushing himself forward, toward the woods. Then Matt went to him and shot him once in the back of the head.

Driving south to Boston, wearing both gloves now, staying in the middle lane and looking often in the rearview mirror at

Willis's headlights, he relived the suitcase dropping, the quick dip and turn of Strout's back, and the kick of the gun, the sound of the shot. When he walked to Strout, he still existed within the first shot, still trembled and breathed with it. The second shot and the burial seemed to be happening to someone else, someone he was watching. He and Willis each held an arm and pulled Strout face-down off the road and into the woods, his bouncing sliding belt white under the trees where it was so dark that when they stopped at the top of the knoll, panting and sweating, Matt could not see where Strout's blue shirt ended and the earth began. They pulled off the branches then dragged Strout to the edge of the hole and went behind him and lifted his legs and pushed him in. They stood still for a moment. The woods were quiet save for their breathing, and Matt remembered hearing the movements of birds and small animals after the first shot. Or maybe he had not heard them. Willis went down to the road. Matt could see him clearly out on the tan dirt, could see the glint of Strout's car and, beyond the road, the gravel pit. Willis came back up the knoll with the suitcase. He dropped it in the hole and took off his gloves and they went down to his car for the spades. They worked quietly. Sometimes they paused to listen to the woods. When they were finished Willis turned on his flashlight and they covered the earth with leaves and branches and then went down to the spot in front of the car, and while Matt held the light Willis crouched and sprinkled dust on the blood, backing up till he reached the grass and leaves, then he used leaves until they had worked up to the grave again. They did not stop. They walked around the grave and through the woods, using the light on the ground, looking up through the trees to where they ended at the lake. Neither of them spoke above the sounds of their heavy and clumsy strides through low brush and over fallen branches. Then they reached it: wide and dark, lapping softly at the bank, pine needles smooth under Matt's feet, moonlight on the lake, a small island near its middle, with black, tall evergreens. He took out the gun and threw for the island: taking two steps back on the pine

needles, striding with the throw and going to one knee as he
followed through, looking up to see the dark shapeless object
arcing downward, splashing.

They left Strout's car in Boston, in front of an apartment
building on Commonwealth Avenue. When they got back to
town Willis drove slowly over the bridge and Matt threw the
keys into the Merrimack. The sky was turning light. Willis let
him out a block from his house, and walking home he listened
for sounds from the houses he passed. They were quiet. A
light was on in his living room. He turned it off and undressed
in there, and went softly toward the bedroom; in the hall he
smelled the smoke, and he stood in the bedroom doorway and
looked at the orange of her cigarette in the dark. The curtains
were closed. He went to the closet and put his shoes on the
floor and felt for a hanger.

'Did you do it?' she said.

He went down the hall to the bathroom and in the dark
he washed his hands and face. Then he went to her, lay on his
back, and pulled the sheet up to his throat.

'Are you all right?' she said.

'I think so.'

Now she touched him, lying on her side, her hand on his
belly, his thigh.

'Tell me,' she said.

He started from the beginning, in the parking lot at the
bar; but soon with his eyes closed and Ruth petting him, he
spoke of Strout's house: the order, the woman presence, the
picture on the wall.

'The way she was smiling,' he said.

'What about it?'

'I don't know. Did you ever see Strout's girl? When you
saw him in town?'

'No.'

'I wonder who she was.'

Then he thought: *not was: is. Sleeping now she is his girl.*

He opened his eyes, then closed them again. There was more light beyond the curtains. With Ruth now he left Strout's house and told again his lie to Strout, gave him again that hope that Strout must have for a while believed, else he would have to believe only the gun pointed at him for the last two hours of his life. And with Ruth he saw again the dropping suitcase, the darting move to the right: and he told of the first shot, feeling her hand on him but his heart isolated still, beating on the road still in that explosion like thunder. He told her the rest, but the words had no images for him, he did not see himself doing what the words said he had done; he only saw himself on that road.

'We can't tell the other kids,' she said. 'It'll hurt them, thinking he got away. But we mustn't.'

'No.'

She was holding him, wanting him, and he wished he could make love with her but he could not. He saw Frank and Mary Ann making love in her bed, their eyes closed, their bodies brown and smelling of the sea; the other girl was faceless, bodiless, but he felt her sleeping now; and he saw Frank and Strout, their faces alive; he saw red and yellow leaves falling to the earth, then snow: falling and freezing and falling; and holding Ruth, his cheek touching her breast, he shuddered with a sob that he kept silent in his heart.

THE DARK MEN

THEIR DARK CIVILIAN CLOTHES defied him. They were from the Office of Naval Intelligence, they sat in his leather chairs in his cabin, they poured coffee from his silver pot, and although they called him Captain and Sir, they denied or out-maneuvered his shoulder boards by refusing to wear their own. He did not know whether they were officers or not, they could even be civilians, and they came aboard his ship and into his cabin, they told him names which he had already for-gotten and, in quiet inflectionless voices, as if they were bring-ing no news at all, they told him that three months ago, during a confession in San Francisco, someone gave them Joe Saldi's name; and they told him what they had been doing for those three months, and what they had discovered. Then for a few moments they were talking but he wasn't listening and there were no images in his mind, not yet; he didn't see their faces either, though he was looking at them. If he was seeing any-thing at all, he was seeing the cold, sinking quickening of his heart. Then he entered their voices again, met their eyes, these men who looked for the dark sides of other men, and then he looked at his watch and said: 'I've forgotten your names.'

They told him. He offered them more coffee and they took it, and as they poured he watched their hands and faces: they appeared to be in their late thirties. Their faces were drained of color, they were men who worked away from the sun. Todd pinched his earlobe; Foster breathed through his mouth. At times it was audible. Foster now had a dispatch case on his lap; the raised top of it concealed his hands, then he lifted a large manila envelope and handed it to Captain Devereaux. The Captain laid it in front of him; then slowly, with a forefinger, pushed it aside, toward the photograph of his wife.

'I wonder how much you've missed,' he said.

'We have enough,' Foster said.

'That's not what I meant. I suppose he doesn't have much of a chance.'

'I wouldn't think so,' Foster said. 'But we don't make recommendations. We only investigate.'

'They always resign,' Todd said.

Captain Devereaux looked at him. Then he picked up the envelope and dropped it across his desk, near Foster.

'I don't want to read it.'

Foster and Todd looked at each other; Todd pinched his ear.

'Very well,' Foster said. 'Then I suppose we could see him now.'

'I suppose you could.' He dialed Joe's stateroom, waited seven rings, then hung up and told them Commander Saldi's plane was ashore and he might have gone flying. He went to the door and opened it and the Marine orderly saluted. The Captain told him to get Commander Saldi on the phone; he told him to try the pilots' wardroom and the commanders' wardroom and the officers' barber shop.

'I'll try the OOD too, sir.'

'Do that last.'

Then he sat at his desk and looked at them. Out of habit he was thinking of a way to make conversation but then he decided he would not. He looked away and tried not to hear Foster breathing.

'He should be flown home tomorrow,' Foster said. 'It's better for everyone that way.'

'Before the word gets out,' Todd said. 'It always gets out.'

'You shouldn't complain.'

'What's that, Captain?'

'It's how you make your living, isn't it? On word that gets out?' Now he looked at them. 'And where do you think he'll be flown to? I mean where do you think he will choose?'

'I don't know where he'll go, Captain,' Foster said. 'Our job is only to make sure he does.'

'You contradict yourself. You said your job was only to investigate.'

'Captain—'

'Yes, Mr. Foster?'

'Never mind, Captain.'

'Have some coffee, Mr. Foster. Don't be disappointed because I'm not making your work easy. Why should it be?'

'We understand you're a friend of his,' Todd said. He was trying to sound gentle. 'We understand that.'

'Do you, Mr. Todd?' The orderly knocked. 'It's strange to talk to you gentlemen; you don't wear ribbons. I have no way of knowing where you've been.'

'It doesn't matter where we've been,' Foster said.

'Maybe that's my point.'

He rose and went to the door. The orderly saluted.

'Sir, the OOD says Commander Saldi went ashore. He'll be back at eighteen hundred.'

'When did the boat leave?' Foster said.

Captain Devereaux looked at him. He was twisted around in his chair.

'What boat is that, Mr. Foster?'

'The one Commander Saldi took.'

Captain Devereaux looked at the orderly.

'Fifteen minutes ago, sir.'

Foster took the envelope from the Captain's desk, put it in his dispatch case, and he and Todd stood up. Captain Devereaux held the door. When they were abreast of him they stopped.

'I don't know what you think you've gained,' Foster said.

'Have a good day in Iwakuni,' the Captain said.

'We'll be back tonight.'

From his door he watched them cross the passageway and start down the ladder. Then he turned to the orderly.

'Have my boat alongside in thirty minutes. Wait: do you know Commander Saldi? What he looks like?'

'Yes sir.'

'Then make it an hour for the boat. Then go eat your lunch. I want you to come with me.'

The carrier was huge, it was anchored far out, and the ride in the launch took twenty minutes. It was a warm blue summer day and, to go ashore, he had changed from khakis to whites. He sat in the rear of the launch, his back against the gunwale, holding his cap so it wouldn't blow off; Corporal Swanson sat opposite him, wearing a white pistol belt and a .45 in a spit-shined holster, his cap chin-strapped to his head, dozing in the warm sun, his chin sinking slowly till it touched his neck-tie, then he snapped his head up and glanced at the Captain who pretended he hadn't seen, and in a few moments the sun did its work again and Swanson—who looked hung over—fought it for a while and then lost until his chin again touched the knot of his tie, and it stayed there; soon his mouth was open. The Captain looked back at the carrier, diminished now but still huge against the sky and the sea beyond; then he turned away and looked up at the blue sky and at the green and rocky shore, his vision broken once by the hull of a British freighter, then shore line again, while in his mind he saw Joe in the orange flight suit, helmet under his arm, crossing the flight deck and turning his face into the wind; sometimes Joe looked up at the bridge and smiled and waved: thinning black hair, a suntanned face that never seemed weary, and the Captain, looking down through glass and lifting his arm in a wave, felt his own weariness, and he yearned for the wind out there, away from the bridge that could make him an admiral, and away from the cabin where he slept little and badly and smoked too much and drank too much coffee and took Maalox after his meals; and Joe would move on to his plane near the catapult and beyond him the Pacific glittered under the sun, and the endless blue sky waited to lift him up; but now images collided in the Captain's mind, images of night and shame, and he actually shook his head to cast them out and to cast out memory too, thinking he must move from one moment to the next and that no matter what he did the day held no hope, and that memory and imagination would only make it worse; he gazed ahead at the white buildings of the Marine air base and he looked at the boat's wake, and kept himself from thinking about what had happened in his heart this morning when, as soon as Foster spoke Joe's name, he had known what was coming next and though he had been Joe's friend for thirteen years this was the first time he knew that he knew it.

As the boat neared the wharf Corporal Swanson was rubbing his neck and blinking his eyes. When the engine slowed, the Captain leaned forward and told him what to do.

'After that,' he said, 'you can sack out till I get back.'

It was early Thursday afternoon, so there weren't many people in the Officers' Club. A commander and his handsome wife were finishing lunch. The commander was a flight surgeon. Three Marine pilots were drinking at the bar. They were loud and happy and the Captain liked being near them. He chose a small polished table with two leather chairs, and he sat facing the door. A Japanese girl took his order. She was pretty and she wore a purple kimono of silk brocade, and as she walked back to the bar he felt an instant's yearning and then it was gone and he was both amused and wistful because either age or responsibility or both had this year kept him clean. He was finishing his second drink when Joe stepped in, wearing whites with short sleeves, four rows of ribbons under the gold wings on his breast, his white cap under his arm like a football; he stood looking about the room while his eyes adjusted and Captain Devereaux raised his hand and Joe saw him and waved and came forward. The Captain stood and took his hand and nodded toward the laughing pilots at the bar.

'It is peacetime and the pilots are happy pretending to make war. I'm about to start my third gimlet. Are you behind?'

'I am.'

They sat, and the Captain signalled to the Japanese girl at the end of the bar, pointed at his glass and at Joe and then himself. Under the table Joe clicked his heels, and briskly raised his hand and held it salute-like at his brow: 'Commander Saldi, sir. Captain Devereaux wishes the Commander to join him at the O Club sir. In the bar sir. He says if the Commander wishes to go back to the ship instead, sir, he is to send me to get the Captain and the Captain will take the Commander back to the ship in the Captain's boat. Sir.' He snapped off the salute. 'Jesus Christ, Ray, I'll drink with you. You don't have to send them out with .45's.'

The girl lowered the drinks and Joe reached for his wallet but the Captain was quicker and paid.

'What about lunch,' Joe said. 'Have you had lunch?'

The girl was waiting.

'I'll buy you a lunch,' the Captain said.

He watched the girl going back to the bar, then he looked at Joe, and Joe raised his glass and the Captain raised his and they touched them over the table.

'Old Captain Devereaux.'

'Old is right. I don't sleep much, out there. My gut's going too.'

'Gimlets'll back up on you.'

'It's the lime, not the gin.'

'Right.'

'How do you know? Is yours on the blink too?'

'Not now. It has been.'

'Not an ulcer.'

'Oh hell no. *You* don't have one, do you?'

'Just acid. I ought to retain the booze and get rid of cigarettes and coffee.'

The girl gave them the menus and then went away.

'You ought to have the lasagna, Joe.'

'Where is it?'

'It's spelled sukiyaki.'

'I don't like lasagna anyway.'

'Really?'

'Too heavy.'

'I'll have the sukiyaki.'

'So will I.'

'Should we have sake too?'

'How's your gut?'

'Fine. I'm going to lay off this lime juice.'

'Then let's have hot sake.'

When they laid down the menus the girl came and took their order and the Captain told her to bring his friend another drink but to leave him out.

'It's my stomach,' he told her. 'It needs gentleness.'

'Oh? I could bring you some nice milk.'

'No, not milk, thanks.'

'What about Asahi?'

'Yes: fine. Bring me a big Asahi.'

She brought Joe's gimlet and his beer, and after a glass of it he quietly belched and felt better but not good enough, so he told Joe he'd be right back and he went to the men's room and took from his pocket the aspirin tin containing six Maalox tablets and chewed two of them. He went back into the bar, approaching the table from Joe's rear and, looking at his shoulders and the back of his head, he felt a power he didn't want but had anyway, and he felt like a traitor for having it.

'You ought to get up more,' Joe said.

'I know.'

'Let's do it then.'

'When?'

'After lunch. We can walk over to the field and go up for an hour.'

'With gin and beer and sake.'

'Oxygen'll fix you up.'

'I can't though. I have things at the ship.'

'Let them wait.'

'They won't.'

'Tomorrow then.'

'Tomorrow?' He frowned, pretending he was trying to

remember what tomorrow held for him, then he said: 'All right. Tomorrow,' and saying the word gave him a sense of plaintive hope that somehow and impossibly this moment with drinks and waiting for lunch would flow into a bright afternoon of tomorrow with Joe off his wing as they climbed from Iwakuni and out over the blue sea. And with that hope came longing: he wanted Foster and Todd to vanish, he wanted to go to sea next week and launch Joe into the wind, he wanted to not know what he knew and, with this longing, fear came shivering into his breast, and he did what he could not recall doing since he was a boy trying to talk to his father, a young boy, before he finally gave up and became silent: he promised himself that when a certain thing happened he would tell Joe: when his cigarette burned down; when he finished his beer; when the girl brought the sukiyaki; when Joe finished telling his story; and as each of these occurred, a third and powerful hand of his clutched his throat and squeezed.

The girl stood smiling and serving them until all the sukiyaki was on their plates and then she left, and he was chilled by her leaving because he had been flirting with her, praising the meal and her kimono and her face and small delicate hands, he had been cocking his head to her and glancing up at her, not up very high because he was a tall man and sat tall and she was barely over five feet and maybe not even that; now she was gone. He started to look at Joe, then poured sake into the china tumbler and carefully pinched rice with his chopsticks and dipped it into raw egg and, leaning forward, quickly raised it to his mouth, and heard over Joe's voice the drinking talk of the Marines at the bar, and he chewed his rice and hated his fear and silence and when he took another swallow of sake the acid rose to his throat and he held his breath for a moment till it went down, and then took another swallow and that one was all right. Joe was laughing: '—and he said I couldn't bail out, Commander. I'm afraid of sharks. You see, he really meant it but the bombardier and the crewman didn't believe him. They thought he believed he had a chance to make it, and he was just being cheerful to help them along. Truth was, he thought he'd go down, but he wasn't going into the water without that plane around him. So he kept telling them: look, you guys better jump, and they'd say what about you, and he'd say not me, I ain't getting down there with no sharks. So they stuck with him and he hit the ship first try, he said if he'd got waved off that time he'd have gone in and too low for anybody to bail out and he was cussing the other two for making him responsible for them going down too. But then he made it and I gave him a shot of rye in my room and he told me, You see, I don't even wade. Not in salt water. I haven't been in salt water for fourteen years. He was shot down, you see, in the Pacific, and he swam to his raft and he was climbing aboard when a shark got his co-pilot. He said the water turned red. He said I heard that scream every night for ten years. He said I ain't been in the water ever since and if any shark's going to get Chuck Thomson he's going to be the most disguised shark you ever saw because he's going to cross two hundred feet of sand walking on his tail and wearing a double-breasted pinstripe suit and some of them reflecting sunglasses—' Then Joe was laughing again, and the Captain was too, his body jerked and made sounds and then he was telling a story too, listening to it as it took shape, just as he had watched and listened to his own laughter: another story of men who had nearly gone into the sea and then had laughed, and after that Joe told one and then he told another, and they kept going. They did not tell stories of valor without humor, as though valor were expected but humor was not, and the man who had both was better. And they did not talk about the dead. Sometimes they spoke a name but that was all. Three o'clock came and the girl brought more tea and Captain Devereaux went to the men's room and chewed two more tablets, standing alone at the mirror, but Joe's ghost was with him, and he went back to the table and looked at Joe and he could not feel the wine now, his heart was quick, his fingers tight on the tumbler of tea, and he said: 'There are two men, Joe. On my ship. Or they were. They're coming back tonight.'

And already Joe's eyes brightened, even before the Captain said: 'They're from ONI, Joe, and it's about you.'

Joe turned in his chair and gazed off toward the bar and shut his eyes and rubbed his forehead and murmured something he couldn't hear and didn't want to, and then it was over, the long bantering friendship between them, he felt it go out of him like dry tears through his ribs and for an instant, watching Joe's profiled face that could never look at him again, he raged at the other face he had never seen, impassioned and vulnerable in the night, then the rage was gone too and he sat watching Joe rubbing his forehead, watched Joe profiled in that place of pain and humiliation where he had fallen and where the Captain could never go. Yet still he kept talking, threw words into the space, bounced them off the silent jaw and shoulder: 'Listen, I hate the bastards. I don't want you to see them. They're going to tell you general court or resign, but I'm going to tell them to get the hell off my ship, and I'll handle it. No one will know anything. Not for a while anyway. Not till you've written your letter and gone. And still they won't know why. I don't care about what they told me, I want you to know that. They brought paperwork and it was sealed and it still is and it'll stay that way. I don't give a good Goddamn and I never *did*. You hear me, Joe?'

He waited. Joe nodded, looking at the bar.

'I hear you, Captain.'

For perhaps a minute they sat that way. Then Captain Devereaux got up and touched Joe's shoulder and walked out.

Corporal Swanson was sleeping in the sun, his cap over his eyes, and he did not wake when the Captain and the coxswain and crew descended into the gently rocking boat, did not wake until Captain Deveraux softly spoke his name. Then he stood quickly and saluted and the Captain smiled and asked if he'd had a good nap. All the way back to the ship he talked to Swanson; or, rather, asked him questions and watched him closely and tried to listen. Swanson was not staying in the Marines; in another year he'd get out and go to college in South Dakota. He wasn't sure yet what he wanted to be. He had a girl in South Dakota and he meant to marry her. The Captain sat smiling and nodding and asking, and sometimes he leaned forward to listen over the sound of the engine, and it wasn't until the launch drew within a hundred yards of the ship that he knew Joe wasn't coming back, and then at once he knew he had already known that too, had known in the Club that Joe's isolation was determined and forever, and now he twisted around and looked back over his shoulder, into the sky above the air base, then looked forward again at the huge ship, at its high grey hull which now rose straight above him, casting a shadow across the launch.

At six-thirty Foster and Todd found him on the flight deck. He had been there for an hour, walking the thousand feet from fore to aft, looking into the sky and out at the sea. When they emerged from the island and moved toward him, walking abreast and leaning into the wind, he was standing at the end of the flight deck. He saw them coming and looked away. The sun was going down. Out there, toward the open sea, a swath of gold lay on the water. When they stopped behind him he did not turn around. He was thinking that, from a distance, a plane flying in the sunset looks like a moving star. Then shutting his eyes he saw the diving silver plane in the sunset, and then he was in it, his heart pounding with the dive, the engine roaring in his blood, and he saw the low red sun out the cockpit and, waiting, the hard and yielding sea.

'Commander Saldi is not here,' he said.

'Not here?' It was Foster. 'Where is he?'

'He's out there.'

Foster stepped around and stood in front of him, and then Todd did, and they stood side by side, facing him, but he continued to stare at the sun on the water.

'Out there?' Foster said. 'You let him fly? In a million dollar—'

Captain Devereaux looked at him, and he stopped.

'Iwakuni lost contact with him an hour ago,' the Captain said.

'You told him,' Foster said. 'You told him and let him go up—'

This time the Captain did not bother to look at him; he stepped through the space between them and stood on the forward edge of the flight deck. He stood there, motionless and quiet, then he heard Foster and Todd going away, only a moment's footsteps on the deck before all sound of them was gone in the wind, and still he watched as the sun went down and under the pale fading light of the sky the sea darkened until finally it was black.

HIS LOVER

When Scotty stopped the police car, Moissant opened the door and put his cane out first. He had both legs out when Scotty said: 'Leo? It's funny you never asked her anything. Where they went at night.'

He did not turn his head; he had been blind for over a year, and it had taken him almost that long to break the habit of looking at people whenever they spoke.

'It didn't matter,' he said.

He got out and shut the door but kept his hand on it. The breeze came from the sea, and he knew from the smell of the salt marsh down the road that the tide was out. He lowered his head to the window so Scotty wouldn't have to talk to his belt buckle, and said: 'She really liked killing those people?'

'She liked talking about it too. I didn't mean you *should* have asked her anything.'

'She was pretty, wasn't she?'

'She's pretty. You give a man something to look forward to.'

'That's what her name means. In Spanish.'

He walked away, touching with his cane the grass and earth ahead of him. He stopped and listened to the car going east, and when he couldn't hear it anymore he went around his trailer to the back lawn, to the hammock Linda had hung from two pines, and he settled into it and took off his sunglasses. He felt shade across his ankles and feet but that was all, and he unbuttoned his shirt and opened it to the sun. Sometimes in the afternoon Linda took him to the hammock; they left his cane inside and she held his hand. She told him the hammock and the van could not be seen from the road, they were hidden by his trailer and the woods, and it was nice to be quiet and secret back there. She sat on the ground beside him. Usually he fell asleep on the hammock and when he woke she was gone to the van where the other girl and the boy were. He could hear their radio music. She always came back to him, soon after he woke.

He rarely spoke to the other two, and they never came to his trailer. It was Linda who had talked to him that first day, had asked if they could park their van in his backyard for a few days. They were from New Mexico and they wanted to spend some time at the Atlantic. He had put on his sunglasses and stepped out of the morning cool of his trailer to talk to her, and he liked her voice coming out of the sun. He almost said no because he knew it was the same van that had gone past his trailer three times in the last two days, once while he was pushing the lawnmower, walking barefooted so he'd know where he had been; he had stopped mowing and turned his face with the van as if he could see it. But he said yes. He had outlived everyone he cared about and now had outlived his eyes too. There was nothing they could take from him.

Then on the first night Linda knocked on his door and he regretted saying yes that morning because now they would want more, it would start with borrowing salt and end with them swarming all over the life he had learned to live. But she did not want to borrow anything. She wanted to cook his dinner. He told her he could do it himself; and while she cooked and he waited to hear the other two coming to move the chairs around and eat with them, he told her how he cooked by smelling and time-guessing and sticking and touching with a fork. She asked how he got his food and he said the grocer's son delivered it. The other girl and the boy did not come, and when she put the plates on the table he thought he should have been able to tell by listening that she had brought and cooked two steaks, not four. For a while they ate quietly, then she asked if he had put on his sunglasses when she knocked on the door. Yes: he didn't wear them when he was alone. Gently she lifted them from his face: it was the first time she touched him. They must be ugly, he said. No: no, they looked like egg whites: like the white of a soft-fried egg, and the eyeballs were like blue marbles under milk.

She washed the dishes while he sat near the screen door and felt the sun going down, the air cooling, and he imagined the long shadows of the pines on the trailer and the lawn and the road. She brought him a beer and sat at the table and asked if she could smoke. Sure, he'd given them up when he was sixty-two and that was eight years ago and if he hadn't gone through such hell to quit he'd have one with her. A smile was in her voice: she didn't mean a cigarette. Oh: marijuana; no, he didn't care. He liked the smell, and he thought her inhaling was funny. Do you have to draw that deep on it? She said mmmm with her breath held. Then she let it out. Is it like booze? Better; quicker; you want to try it? He smiled. He wanted to. But maybe some other time. It took him a while to get around to something new. He had been a boozer. You could say he had been a bad one. But he had retired from whiskey a long time ago, before it caused him any more trouble with either men or women. Only a little beer now at night.

He felt her watching him and then, incredulous and slow to hope, he felt the way she was watching him and he lowered his face to hide his eyes, and basked in her watching. Then her chair slid back and she came lightfooted around the table and stood behind him. Her hands slipped under his shirt and slowly and softly rubbed his chest. She licked his ear and whispered and his body quivered yet his loins were stalled by the question he didn't ask: Why him? Then rising he received her arm around his waist and went with her to his bed. Slowly she took off his clothes while he touched her.

In the morning he listened to her sleeping. Her naked back was against his side. When the trailer warmed she turned to him with her hands and tongue, and he told her he'd thought he would never have a woman again; it had been six years; six years last May. A widow up in Portsmouth. Named Florence. She wasn't as old as he was but she might as well have been. She grew up in Alabama and she still talked like it. It was warm weather, and you could see the girls' legs again. One day Florence saw him watching and she said the young girls come out in spring, like snakes.

On their third night he felt her getting out of bed and he listened to her dress and creep out of the trailer; after a while the van drove slowly out to the road and toward the sea. He lay awake and told himself it was all right, it would be easy enough to start tomorrow without her. Finally he even felt peaceful, and he slept. Then the van came back, and she sneaked into the trailer and undressed and cautiously got into bed. After that he was amused when her leaving waked him; he thought of the night clubs and the beach in the moonlight; he slept until the van returned, and when she was naked in his bed he slept again. Last night he woke because the van did not return; he lay waiting until he knew it was morning, then he dressed and made coffee and was still at the kitchen table when the car came up the road and into the driveway; he put on his glasses and turned his face to the screen door, and then Scotty standing outside told him they had three young people for the murder of a summer couple in a beach house and the one girl who did all the talking said they'd stayed at his place for the past month and if that was true would he mind coming to the station just to make a statement.

She cooked all his meals, and she ate with him. She bought fish and fresh vegetables and fruit in town; she never placed an order with the Peters boy, was never in the trailer when he delivered groceries. One night Moissant said he'd smoke with her. He let her roll it for him but he lit it himself, slowly moving the flame's heat up to his mouth. He laughed and wanted a shower and they stood under the spray till the water turned cold, then went to bed without drying and he pressed his face into her long wet hair. Then all the nights after dinner he smoked with her.

Last night she had blood on her clothes when she talked to Scotty. She couldn't even count the houses they had broken into up and down the coast. She didn't want to talk about that. She wanted to talk about stabbing the man and woman. She said she liked it. She had killed a man they robbed in a motel in Colorado. He was a stupid man. He thought they were junkies and if he gave them money they would go away. He was surprised when she stuck her knife in his fat stomach. She would like to stab the chief of police and his two cops. She would save the chief for last. It was nothing personal. She would just like to do it. The other girl was waiting in the van and she and the boy were in the bedroom looking for the money. They were very quiet; they were quieter than the sea. She could hear the waves outside. But the man woke up. She was near the bed when she heard him move. Before he could get his feet on the floor she stabbed him. She stabbed him again while the boy grabbed the woman and put his hand over her mouth. The woman was on her stomach and he was sitting on her back and holding her arms behind her and she was moaning into his hand. He told Linda to look for something to tie her with. Linda said okay and reached across the man and stabbed her in the back. The boy ran out of the house but she kept stabbing till the moaning and jerking stopped.

Lying in the hammock Moissant loved her hands: going down his shirt that first night and combing the hair of his chest while her tongue wet his ear and she whispered; her hands taking off his clothes; her small soft hand stroking slow and patient until she could not close it. In the long nights he kneeled astride her legs and his hands caressed her body, like a child on the beach smoothing a figure made of sand. Under the high sun he was sleepy, was going, a dream starting, pines and fetid marsh breath and sea wind in the dream; her smell; her breathing; he was swelling, then erect, and the dream was gone like fog burned away by the sun on his face. Then he slept.

TOWNIES

THE CAMPUS SECURITY GUARD found her. She wore a parka and she lay on the footbridge over the pond. Her left cheek lay on the frozen snow. The college was a small one, he was the only guard on duty, and in winter he made his rounds in the car. But partly because he was sleepy in the heated car, and mostly because he wanted to get out of the car and walk in the cold dry air, wanted a pleasurable solitude within the imposed solitude of his job, he had gone to the bridge.

He was sixty-one years old, a tall broad man, but his shoulders slumped and he was wide in the hips and he walked with his toes pointed outward, with a long stride which appeared slow. His body, whether at rest or in motion, seemed the result of sixty-one years of erosion, as though all his life he had been acted upon and, with just enough struggle to keep going, he had conceded; fifty years earlier he would have sat quietly at the rear of a classroom, scraped dirt with his shoe on the periphery of a playground. In a way, he was the best man to find her. He was not excitable, he was not given to anger, he was not a man of action: when he realized the girl was dead he did not think immediately of what he ought to do, of what acts and words his uniform and wages required of him. He did not think of phoning the police. He knelt on the snow, so close to her that his knee touched her shoulder, and he stroked her cold cheek, her cold blonde hair.

He did not know her name. He had seen her about the campus. He believed she had died of an overdose of drugs or a mixture of drugs and liquor. This deepened his sorrow. Often when he thought of what young people were doing to themselves, he felt confused and sad, as though in the country he loved there were a civil war whose causes baffled him, whose victims seemed wounded and dead without reason. Especially the girls, and especially these girls. He had lived all his life in this town, a small city in northeastern Massachusetts; once there had been a shoe industry. Now that was over, only three factories were open, and the others sat empty along the bank of the Merrimack. Their closed windows and the dark empty rooms beyond them stared at the street, like the faces of the old and poor who on summer Sundays sat on the stoops of the old houses farther upriver and stared at the street, the river, the air before their eyes. He had worked in a factory, as a stitcher. When the factory closed he got a job driving a truck, delivering fresh loaves of bread to families in time for their breakfast. Then people stopped having their bread delivered. It was a change he did not understand. He had loved the smell of bread in the morning and its warmth in his hands. He did not know why the people he had delivered to would choose to buy bread in a supermarket. He did not believe that the pennies and nickels saved on one expense ever showed up in your pocket.

When they stopped eating fresh bread in the morning he was out of work for a while, but his children were grown and his wife did not worry, and then he got his last and strangest job. He was not an authorized constable, he carried no weapons, and he needed only one qualification other than the usual ones of punctuality and subservience: a willingness to work for very little money. He was so accustomed to all three that none of them required an act of will, not even a moment's pause while he made the decision to take and do the job. When he worked a daylight shift he spent some time ordering possible vandals off the campus: they were usually children on bicycles; sometimes they made him chase them away, and he did this in his long stride, watching the distance lengthen between him and the children, the bicycles. Mostly during the day he chatted with the maintenance men and students and some of the teachers; and he walked the campus, which was contained by an iron fence and four streets, and he looked at the trees. There were trees he recognized, and more that he did not. One of the maintenance men had told him that every kind of New England tree grew here. There was one with thick, low, spreading branches and, in the fall, dark red leaves; sometimes students sat on the branches.

The time he saw three girls in the tree he was fooled: they were pretty and they wore sweaters in the warm autumn afternoon. They looked like the girls he had grown up knowing about: the rich girls who came from all parts of the country to the school, and who were rarely seen in town. From time to time some of them walked the three blocks from the campus to the first row of stores where the commercial part of the town began. But most of them only walked the one block, to the corner where they waited for the bus to Boston. He had smelled them once, as a young man. It was a winter day. When he saw them waiting for the bus he crossed the street so he could walk near them. There were perhaps six of them. As he approached, he looked at their faces, their hair. They did not look at him. He walked by them. He could smell them and he could feel their eyes seeing him and not seeing him. Their smells were of perfume, cold fur, leather gloves, leather suitcases. Their voices had no accents he could recognize. They seemed the voices of mansions, resorts, travel. He was too conscious of himself to hear what they were saying. He knew it was idle talk; but its tone seemed peremptory; he would not have been surprised if one of them had suddenly given him a command. Then he was away from them. He smelled only the cold air now; he longed for their smells again: erotic, unattainable, a world that would never be open to him. But he did not think about its availability, any more than he would wish for an African safari. He knew people who hated them because they were rich. But he did not. In the late sixties more of them began appearing in town and they wore blue jeans and smoked on the street. In the early seventies, when the drinking age was lowered, he heard they were going to the bars at night, and some of them got into trouble with the local boys. Also, the college started accepting boys, and they lived in the dormitories with the girls. He wished all this were not so; but by then he wished much that was happening was not so.

When he saw the three girls in the tree with low spreading branches and red leaves, he stopped and looked across the lawn at them, stood for a moment that was redolent of his past, of the way he had always seen the college girls, and still tried to see them: lovely and nubile, existing in an ambience of benign royalty. Their sweaters and hair seemed bright as the autumn sky. He walked toward them, his hands in his back pockets. They watched him. Then he stood under the tree, his eyes level with their legs. They were all biting silenced giggles. He said it was a pretty day. Then the giggles came, shrill and relentless; they could have been monkeys in the tree. There was an impunity about the giggling that was different from the other graceful impunity they carried with them as they carried the checkbooks that were its source. He was accustomed to that. He looked at their faces, at their vacant eyes and flushed cheeks; then his own cheeks flushed with shame. It was marijuana. He lifted a hand in goodbye.

He was not angry. He walked with lowered eyes away from the giggling tree, walked impuissant and slow across the lawn and around the snack bar, toward the library; then he shifted direction and with raised eyes went toward the ginkgo tree near the chapel. There was no one around. He stood looking at the yellow leaves, then he moved around the tree and stopped to read again the bronze plaque he had first read and marvelled at his second day on the job. It said the tree was a gift of the class of 1941. He stood now as he had stood on that first day, in a reverie which refreshed his bruised heart, then healed it. He imagined the girls of 1941 standing in a circle as one of the maintenance men dug a hole and planted the small tree. The girls were pretty and hopeful and had sweethearts. He thought of them later in that year, in winter; perhaps skiing while the *Arizona* took the bombs. He was certain that some of them lost sweethearts in that war, which at first he had followed in the newspapers as he now followed the Red Sox and Patriots and Celtics and Bruins. Then he was drafted. They made him a truck driver and he saw England while the war was still on, and France when it was over. He was glad that he missed combat and when he returned he did not pretend to his wife and family and friends that he wished he had been shot at. Going over, he had worried about submarines; other than that, he had enjoyed his friends and England and France, and he had saved money. He still remembered it as a pleasurable interlude in his life. Looking at the ginkgo tree and the plaque he happily felt their presence like remembered music: the girls then, standing in a circle around the small tree on that spring day in 1941; those who were in love and would grieve; and he stood in the warmth of the afternoon staring at the yellow leaves strewn on the ground like deciduous sunshine.

So this last one was his strangest job: he was finally among them, not quite their servant like the cleaning women and not their protector either: an unarmed watchman and patrolman whose job consisted mostly of being present, of strolling and chatting in daylight and, when he drew the night shift, of driving or walking, depending on the weather, and of daydreaming and remembering and talking to himself. He enjoyed the job. He would not call it work, but that did not bother him. He had long ago ceased believing in work: the word and its connotation of fulfillment as a man. Life was cluttered with these ideas which he neither believed nor disputed. He merely ignored them. He liked wandering about in this job, as he had liked delivering bread and had liked the Army; only the stitching had been tedious. He liked coming home and drinking coffee in the kitchen with his wife: the daily chatting which seemed eternal. He liked his children and his grandchildren. He accepted the rest of his life as a different man might accept commuting: a tolerable inconvenience. He knew he was not lazy. That was another word he did not believe in.

He kneeled on the snow and with his ungloved hand he touched her cold blonde hair. In sorrow his flesh mingled like death-ash with the pierced serenity of the night air and the trees on the banks of the pond and the stars. He felt her spirit everywhere, fog-like across the pond and the bridge, spreading and rising in silent weeping above him into the black visible night and the invisible space beyond his ken and the cold silver truth of the stars.

On the bridge Mike slipped and cursed, catching himself on the wooden guard rail, but still she did not look back. He was about to speak her name but he did not: he knew if his voice was angry she would not stop and if his voice was pleading she might stop and even turn to wait for him but he could not bear to plead. He walked faster. He had the singular focus that came from being drunk and sad at the same time: he saw nothing but her parka and blonde hair. All evening, as they drank, he had been waiting to lie with her in her bright clean room. Now there would be no room. He caught up with her and grabbed her arm and spun her around; both her feet slipped but he held her up.

'You asshole,' she said, and he struck her with his fist, saw the surprise and pain in her eyes, and she started to speak but he struck her before she could; and when now she only moaned he swung again and again, holding her up with his left hand, her parka bunched and twisted in his grip; when he released her she fell forward. He kicked her side. He knew he should stop but he could not. Kicking, he saw her naked in the bed in her room. She was slender. She moaned and gasped while they made love; sometimes she came so hard she cried. He stopped kicking. He knew she had died while he was kicking her. Something about the silence of the night, and the way her body yielded to his boot.

He looked around him: the frozen pond, the tall trees, the darkened library. He squatted down and looked at her red-splotched cheek. He lifted her head and turned it and lowered it to the snow. Her right cheek was untouched; now she looked asleep. In the mornings he usually woke first, hung over and hard, listening to students passing in the hall. Now on the snow she looked like that: in bed, on her pillow. Under the blanket he took her hand and put it around him and she woke and they smoked a joint; then she kneeled between his legs and he watched her hair going up and down.

He stood and walked off the bridge and around the library. His body was weak and sober and it weaved; he did not feel part of it, and he felt no need to hurry away from the campus and the bridge and Robin. What waited for him was home, and a two-mile walk to get there: the room he hated though he tried to believe he did not. For he lived there, his clothes hung there, most of all he slept there, the old vulnerable breathing of night and dreams; and if he allowed himself to hate it then he would have to hate his life too, and himself.

He walked without stealth across the campus, then up the road to town. He passed Timmy's, where he and Robin had drunk and where now the girls who would send him to prison were probably still drinking. He and Robin had sat in a booth on the restaurant side. She drank tequila sunrises and paid for those and for his Comfort and ginger, and she told him that all day she had been talking to people, and now she had to talk to him, her mind was blown, her father called her about her grades and he called the dean too so she had to go to the counselor's office and she was in there three hours, they talked about everything, they even got back to the year she was fifteen and she told the counselor she didn't remember much of it, that was her year on acid, and she had done a lot of balling, and she said she had never talked like that with anybody before, had never just sat down and *list*ed what she had done for the last four years, and the counselor told her in all that time she had never felt what she was doing or done what she felt. She was talking gently to Mike, but in her eyes she was already gone: back in her room; home in Darien; Bermuda at Easter; the year in Europe she had talked about before, the year her father would give her when she got out of school. He could not remember her loins, and he felt he could not remember himself either, that his life had begun a few minutes earlier in this booth. He watched her hands as she stirred her tequila sunrise and the grenadine rose from the bottom in a menstrual cloud, and she said the counselor had gotten her an appointment in town with a psychiatrist tomorrow, a woman psychiatrist, and she wanted to go, she wanted to talk again, because now she had admitted it, that she wasn't happy, hadn't been happy, had figured nobody ever could be.

Then he looked at her eyes. She liked to watch him when they made love, and sometimes he opened his eyes and saw on her face that eerie look of a woman making love: as if her eyes, while watching him, were turned inward as well, were indeed watching his thrusting from within her womb. Her eyes now were of the counselor's office, the psychiatrist's office tomorrow, they held no light for him; and in his mind, as she told him she had to stop dope and alcohol and balling, he saw the school: the old brick and the iron fence with its points like spears and the serene trees. All his life this town had been dying. His father had died with it, killing himself with one of the last things he owned: they did not have a garage so he drove the car into a woods and used the vacuum cleaner hose. She said she had never come, not with anybody all these years, she had always faked it; he finished his drink in a swallow and immediately wished he had not, for he wanted another but she didn't offer him one and he only had three dollars which he knew now he would need for the rest of the night; then he refused to imagine the rest of the night. He smiled.

'Only with my finger,' she said.

'I hope it falls off.'

She slid out of the booth; his hand started to reach for her but he stopped it; she was saying something that didn't matter now, that he could not feel: her eyes were suddenly damp as standing she put on her parka, saying she had wanted to talk to him, she thought at least they could talk; then she walked out. He drank her tequila sunrise as he was getting out of the booth. Outside, he stood looking up the street; she was a block away, almost at the drugstore. Then she was gone around the bend in the street. He started after her, watching his boots on the shovelled sidewalk.

Now he walked on the bridge over the river and thought of her lying on the small one over the pond. The wind came blowing down freezing over the Merrimack; his moustache stiffened, and he lowered his head. But he did not hurry. Seeing Robin on the bridge over the pond he saw the dormitory beyond it, just a dormitory for them, rooms which they crowded with their things, but the best place he had ever slept in. The things that crowded their rooms were more than he had ever owned, yet he knew for the girls these were only selected and favorite or what they thought necessary things, only a transportable bit of what filled large rooms of huge houses at home. For four or five years now he had made his way into the dormitory; he met them at Timmy's and they took him back to the dormitory to drink and smoke dope and when the party dissolved one of them usually took him to bed.

One night in the fall before Robin he was at a party there and toward three in the morning nearly all the girls were gone and no one had given him a sign and there were only two girls left and the one college fag, a smooth-shaven, razor-cut boy who dressed better than the girls, went to Timmy's, and even to the bar side of it, the long, narrow room without booths or bar stools where only men drank; he wore a variety of costumes: heels and yellow and rust and gold and red, and drank sloe gin fizzes and smoked like a girl. And Mike, who rarely thought one way or another about fags but disliked them on sight, liked this one because he went into town like that and once a man poured a beer over his head, but he kept going and joking, his necklaces tapping on his chest as he swayed back and forth laughing. That night he came over and sat beside Mike just at the right time, when Mike had understood that the two remaining girls not only weren't interested in him, but they despised him, and he was thinking of the walk home to his room when the fag said he had some Colombian and Mike nodded and rose and left with him. In the room the fag touched him and Mike said twenty-five bucks and put it in his pocket, then removed the fag's fingers from his belt buckle and turned away and undressed. He would not let the fag kiss him but the rest was all right, a mouth was a mouth, except when he woke sober in the morning, woke early, earlier than he ever woke when he slept there with a girl. A presence woke him, as though a large bird had flown inches above his chest. He got up quickly and glanced at the sleeping fag, lying on his back, his bare, smooth shoulders and slender arms above the blanket, his face turned toward Mike, the mouth open, and Mike wanted to kill him or himself or both of them, looking away from the mouth which had consumed forever part of his soul, and with his back turned he dressed. Then quietly opening the door he was aware of his height and broad shoulders and he squared them as glaring he stepped into the corridor; but it was empty, and he got out of the dormitory without anyone seeing him and ate breakfast in town and at ten o'clock went to the employment office for his check.

Through the years he had stolen from them: usually cash from the girls he slept with, taking just enough so they would believe or make themselves believe that while they were drunk at Timmy's they had spent it. Twice he had stolen with the collusion of girls. One had gone ahead of him in the corridor, then down the stairs, as he rolled and carried a ten-speed bicycle. He rode it home and the next day sold it to three young men who rented a house down the street; they sold dope, and things other people stole, mostly things that kids stole, and Mike felt like a kid when he went to them and said he had a ten-speed. A year later, when a second girl helped him steal a stereo, he sold it at the same house. The girl was drunk and she went with him into the room one of her friends had left unlocked, and in the dark she got the speakers and asked if he wanted any records while he hushed her and took the ampli-

fier and turntable. They carried everything out to her Volvo.
In the car he was relieved but only for a moment, only until
she started the engine, then he thought of the street and the
building where he lived, and by the time she turned on the
heater he was trying to think of a way to keep her from taking
him home.

All the time she was talking. It was the first time she had
stolen anything. Or anything worth a lot of money. He made
himself smile by thinking of selling her to the men in the
house; he thought of her sitting amid the stereos and television sets and bicycles. Then he heard her say something. She
had asked if he was going to sell his old set so he could get
some bucks out of the night too. He said he'd give the old one
to a friend, and when she asked for directions he pointed
ahead in despair. He meant to get out at the corner but when
she said Here? and slowed for the turn he was awash in the
loss of control which he fought so often and overcame so little, though he knew most people couldn't tell by looking at
him or even talking to him. She turned and climbed up the
street, talking all the time, not about the street, the buildings,
but about the stereo: or the stealing of it, and he knew from
her voice she was repeating herself so she would not have to
talk about what she saw. Or he felt she was. But that was not
the worst. The worst was that he was so humiliated he could
not trust what he felt, could not know if this dumb rich drunk
girl was even aware of the street, and he knew there was no
way out of this except to sleep and wake tomorrow in the bed
that held his scent. He had been too long in that room (this
was his third year), too long in the building: there were six
apartments; families lived in the five larger ones; one family
had a man: a pumper of gasoline, checker of oil and water,
wiper of windshields. Mike thought of his apartment as a room,
although there was a kitchen he rarely used, a bathroom, and
a second room that for weeks at a time he did not enter. Some
mornings when he woke he felt he had lived too long in his
body. He smoked a joint in bed and showered and shaved and
left the room, the building, the street of these buildings. Once

free of the street he felt better: he liked feeling and smelling
clean; he walked into town. The girl stopped the Volvo at
another of his sighed directions and touched his thigh and
said she would help him bring the stuff in. He said no and
loaded everything in his arms and left her.

Robin had wanted to go to his room too and he had never
let her and now for the first time grieving for her lost flesh, he
wished he had taken her there. Saw her there at nights and
on the weekends, the room—rooms: he saw even the second
room—smelling of paint; saw buckets and brushes on newspaper awaiting her night and weekend hand, his hand too: the
two of them painting while music played not from his tinny-
sounding transistor but a stereo that was simply there in his
apartment with the certainty of something casually purchased
with cash neither from the employment office nor his occasional and tense forays into the world of jobs: dishwashing at
Timmy's, the quick and harried waitresses bringing the trays
of plates which he scraped and racked and hosed and slid into
the washer, hot water in the hot kitchen wetting his clothes;
he scrubbed the pots by hand and at the night's end he mopped
the floor and the bartender sent him a bottle of beer; but he
only worked there in summers, when the students were gone.
He saw Robin painting the walls beside him, their brushstrokes
as uniform as the beating of their hearts. He was approaching
the bar next to the bus station. He did not like it because the
band was too loud, and the people were losers, but he often
went there anyway, because he could sit and drink and watch
the losers dancing without having to make one gesture he had
to think about, the way he did at Timmy's when he sat with
the girls and was conscious of his shoulders and arms and
hands, of his eyes and mouth as if he could see them, so that
he smiled—and coolly, he knew—when girl after girl year after
year touched his flesh and sometimes his heart and told him
he was cool.

He went into the bar, feeling the bass drum beat as though
it came from the floor and walls, and took the one untaken
stool and ordered a shot of Comfort, out of habit checking his

pocket although he knew he had three ones and some change. Everyone he saw was drunk, and the bartender was drinking. Vic was at the end of the bar, wearing a bandana on his head, earring on one ear, big fat arms on the bar; Mike nodded at him. He drank the shot and pushed the glass toward the bartender. His fingers trembled. He sipped the Comfort and lit a cigarette, cold sweat on his brow, and he thought he would have to go outside into the cold air or vomit.

He finished the shot then moved through the crowd to Vic and spoke close to his ear and the gold earring. 'I need some downs.' Vic wanted a dollar apiece. 'Come on,' Mike said. 'Two.' Vic's arm left the bar and he put two in Mike's hand; Mike gave him the dollar and left, out onto the cold street, heading uphill, swallowing, but his throat was dry and the second one lodged; he took a handful of snow from a mound at the base of a parking meter and ate it. He walked on the lee side of buildings now. He was dead with her. He lay on the bridge, his arm around her, his face in her hair. At the dormitory the night shift detectives would talk to the girls inside, out of the cold; they would sit in the big glassed-in room downstairs where drunk one night he had pissed on the carpet while Robin laughed before they went up to her room. The girls would speak his name. His name was in that room, back there in the dormitory; it was not walking up the hill in his clothing. He had two joints in his room and he would smoke those while he waited, lying dressed on his bed. When he heard their footsteps in the hall he would put on his jacket and open the door before they knocked and walk with them to the cruiser. He walked faster up the hill.

PART TWO

THE MISOGAMIST

IN THE SUMMER OF 1944 Roy Hodges was back from the Pacific. He was a staff sergeant, a drill instructor at the Recruit Depot at San Diego. He was twenty-six years old, and he was training eighteen-year-old boys. He was also engaged to marry Sheila Russell, who was twenty-six and had been waiting for eight years in Marshall, Texas, to marry him. At eighteen, and still a virgin, her goodbye kiss was sad, loving, and hopeful. She told him she would not go out with other boys while he was gone. After boot camp he went home on leave, and on the first night he took her virginity. She believed he was giving his too; he had bought out of it with a middle-aged whore when he was fifteen. He took her much more easily than he had expected. Every night and sometimes the afternoons for three weeks he made love with her, and she aroused in him an excitement he had never felt before with a woman; nor did he ever feel it again. In the evening she drank beer with him and learned to smoke his cigarettes, and he liked that too. Then they drove in his father's Ford out into the country, the woods. It was early spring and there were no mosquitoes. Gently with her on the blanket he sometimes remembered with a heart's grin the attacking mosquitoes as he lay with Betty Jean Simpson in high school; with her, he had often thought of Sheila at home, and thinking of that pure side of his life had increased his passion for Betty Jean. Now, memory of Betty Jean and the mosquitoes on his rump waxed his passion with Sheila. And he finally felt in control of her: she was both his sweet, auburn-haired brown-eyed girl and his lustful woman. When he left her again, her goodbye kiss was erotic, fearful, and demanding.

He had told her, the night before leaving, that they would get married when his tour was up. She could tell her family and friends; he would write to his parents. Which he did: from sea duty, on a battleship. But most of the letter was about the sea. He had never in his life been out of sight of land: a sailor had told him the horizon was always twelve miles away; he wrote that to his parents, and told them to think of him seeing forty-eight miles of the Pacific by standing in one spot and turning in a circle. He wrote that he had won the heavyweight boxing championship in intramurals aboard ship; that in the final match he had won by jabbing and hooking the charging face of a slugging, body-punching sailor from Pittsburgh; that his commanding officer, a captain, had been a corporal in the Banana Wars, was tough and hard, and would throw you in the brig on bread and water if you looked at him wrong. He wrote of inspections, of gunnery, of Honolulu: the strange city and people and food.

His letters to Sheila were the same. He thought he should write love letters, write of their love on the blanket, but even while a sentence took shape in his mind it seemed false; the abstract words had little to do with what had occurred on the blanket; they had even less to do with how he felt about it. So finally he simply wrote that he loved and missed her. Both were true; but he did not know the extent of their truth.

He found it even more difficult to write of their future life together. Again, the words in his mind were abstract, for he could not imagine himself performing the concrete rituals of marriage. He did not know what work he would do as a civilian; he did not even want to know; sitting on his foot locker and feeling the roll of the sea, he could not imagine himself as a civilian in Marshall, Texas. And he could not see himself at night and on the weekends with Sheila. His days now were filled: in the normal pattern of the service, on some days he did very little, but because he did it in uniform it seemed worthwhile; on other days, when they practiced gunnery and he imagined actual combat, the work was intense. Either way, during the hours of his work he did not need Sheila, or anyone female. It was at night that he missed her, in the compartment smelling of male sweat and shoe polish and leather; that was when he wrote to her. When he was in port, on liberty, he did not miss her at all; he thought of her, usually after drinking and whoring, with paternal tenderness; and he sent her gifts, knowing they were junk, knowing he was incapable of buying gifts for a woman anyway, incapable of understanding their affinity for things which couldn't be used.

She wrote him love letters. They were not scented but they might as well have been; on their pages he felt the summer evening quiet of her front porch, heard the creaking of the chain that held the swing where she sat, where perhaps she had even written the letter; and he smelled her washed flesh and hair, and the lilac bush beside the porch. Reading these letters, touching them, sometimes after reading them just looking at each page as if they were pictures, he deeply loved her. He could have wept. He wanted to hold her. Yet he also felt, and with fear, the great division between them.

He was afraid because there was nothing wrong with Sheila. There was nothing he could hold against her, nothing he could point to and say: That's it; that's why I feel this way. She was pure in a way that excited his love: a good Methodist, she believed that making love with him was a sin. Yet she had sinned with him anyway, and he felt blessed. Betty Jean Simpson was the town punch: anyone who could move suitably as a boy in the world had a shot at her. The only element of challenge was finding a location where he thought she had never been, a fresh spot on the earth's surface, free of the memory of past and present boys; while at the same time the knowledge of those boys gave him advance acquittal in case she got pregnant. Sheila's sin was as secret as her parts were; each spot of earth and sheltering tree and concealing bush were new; as her breasts and loins were, eighteen years old and for the first time stroked and plunged into action. He would never forget that. (Nor would he ever make love with a virgin again, nor anyone who loved him, and when it was over with Sheila, when he had broken her heart, he wondered—this on the drill field one day at San Diego, while calling cadence to a marching platoon—if she had ever had an orgasm with him; saddened, he realized she had not, and he knew someone else would take her there, someone strong and gentle who could be for her what he could not, and that was almost enough to make him write to her again, to seek forgiveness and to return to her and nail down once and for all, with marriage, what he had started that first night he so easily unclothed her and shaped her into his sweet and sinful lover.) She was a cheerful girl. He had dated her for three years before joining the Marines, and he knew he had not been fooled. She was undemanding, acquiescent (a quality, strangely, that Betty Jean did not share, as though compensating for her round heels with trifling demands that were nevertheless rigid); there was nothing wrong with her.

It followed then, in his mind, that something was wrong with him: to prefer a life with men, broken periodically by forgettable transactions with whores. He began to believe that he was reaching a pivotal point in his life: either Sheila, who at times seemed to live in a fairy tale rather than in the world he knew; or whores, threats of VD, promises of nothing. Then he saw it wasn't that at all. In Marshall he would not miss the whores; he would long for the men. Now he knew what the pride in performing his duties and the immediate camaraderie of the Corps, as well as the deeper one—the sense that he belonged to a recognized group of men, past and present, dead and living—had been bringing him to: he had, as the troops said, found a home. He was a career man.

He wrote to her, asking how she felt about leaving Marshall and living with him on or near Marine bases until he retired. She answered his letter on the day she got it. Again her stationery in his fingers brought to him her smells, her lowered face as she talked to him, strolling with him. In a voice whose sweet compliance he could almost hear, she told him of course she would miss Marshall, she had never thought she would live any place else, but she loved him and would marry him and go with him wherever he had to go; and she looked forward to those new places.

His next leave was in summer and they made love with sweat and mosquitoes and he told her he must now work hard to get promoted so they could afford to be married. He did not name a rank. Now he could sense a brooding quality in her lovemaking, as though resigning herself to annual trysts granted by the Marine Corps which would someday grant the promotion and money that would allow them to live as they should; and he felt her trying to possess him. For the first time she asked what he did on liberty; she asked if he did this with other girls. He lied. He had lied about Betty Jean Simpson too, but in a different way: he had simply told her nothing about where he was going on a particular night. Now telling her a direct lie made him feel diminished as a man, and he held that against her. At the train station her goodbye kiss was both vulnerable and sternly possessive.

And so it went on: every year with a mingling of reluctance, fear, and passionate anticipation—all blurring his deeper and true feeling of love for her, his knowledge that for his own good he ought to marry her—he returned to Marshall. By the time she was twenty-two he was in the first year of his second enlistment, he was a corporal, and he had promised her that sergeant was the rank. He spoke to her father about it; he even spoke quite easily to her father, who had a small farm and believed in hard work and bad luck and little else, and who liked Roy's having man's work which was based on skill yet had nothing to do with rain or dry seasons or prices. In her father's eyes Roy saw neither suspicion nor misgivings, and he felt that his decision to wait until he made sergeant was that of a worldly, responsible man. Roy also suspected that Mr. Russell knew what he and Sheila did after they left the house for what they called a ride and a talk, and that further, Mr. Russell didn't care about it as long as he wasn't forced to.

Not so with Mrs. Russell: thin and nearly as wiry as her husband, beauty long gone from her strong face which had kept its humor and cheer in the eyes and their crinkled corners and the quick grin above the body which had waked so early and worked so hard for so long. She did not look at Roy with suspicion either; it was worse than that: at times, when her eyes met his, there was a flicker of pain: *Why did you do it to us?* Or that was the question and the pain he saw before she looked away or, more often, started talking and her eyes brightened again, as if the question had come against her will, like a sad, irrelevant memory while talking with a friend. *Why did you do it to us?* Not: Why have you taken my daughter's virginity and left her single? Not even: Why have you brought a secret sin between my daughter and me? But more than that, a vaster accusation, as if she represented in those moments—and, thankfully, they were sparse—all the women who lived on one side of the line he had drawn between them and the others: the forgotten sensations and names, the remembered faces and prices. And when she looked at him that way he felt that God and time, life and death, were on her side; that he was a puny and defenseless man who had committed a sin of Old Testament proportion, the kind of sin you never escaped from, no matter where you went, or how long you stayed there. So that at times, drinking and talking with Mr. Russell, sounding to himself like a reasonable, ambitious, and absolutely trustworthy man, he suddenly felt the judgmental presence of the mother and daughter in the room, as if in concert they had focused on him a knowing glare, and all his talk of money and promotion and career seemed no more than a boy's chatter about what he'd be when he grew up.

He was promoted to sergeant on the second of December, 1941. On the seventh he had still not written to tell her. He woke up that morning in a cheap two-room apartment in Los Angeles; woke tasting last night's beer and smelling traces of perfume and lovemaking. He had gone to the city with three friends, and had left them at a bar and walked home with the girl. She was not in bed with him. Then he remembered her name was Lisa. He wanted to make love to clear his hung-over head. He heard the radio in the kitchen, not music but a man's voice, and he imagined her making coffee and bringing him a cup, bringing him herself too, and he thought of that and then breakfast and the afternoon left to hitchhike back to the base. He took his wallet from the bedside table and was looking in it to see if there was another condom (there was) when she came to the door in an old blue robe, with her black hair unbrushed, last night's lipstick faint on her lips. She stood quietly in the doorway, looking at him, knowing she was about to tell him the most important news he had ever heard, and then she said: 'I think you better come to the kitchen. I think you better come hear what's on the radio.'

He didn't want to go; he was put off by her dramatics, and wanted her in bed. But looking at her face he suddenly knew with both fear and eagerness that somehow the news of the nation or even the world was affecting him; and since his only involvement with the world was as a Marine he knew by the time he reached the kitchen that, while he had been in bed with a strange girl, America had gotten into the war. He listened to the radio for perhaps thirty minutes, then he borrowed her leg-dulled razor and shaved and put on his uniform; for a moment he wanted to take Lisa to bed again, but as the desire struck him he tossed it aside as a foolish indulgence.

The man who picked him up was a Lutheran minister who was returning home from services and going only a few miles south of the city; but he drove Roy all the way to Camp Pendleton, called him Sergeant, wondered aloud about the damages to the fleet and if the Japs were going to keep on coming, to California; he spoke of coastal defense, of going into the Navy as a chaplain (he was thirty-six), and at the main gate he firmly shook Roy's hand, and said: 'Good luck, and God bless you, Sergeant.' Roy nearly smiled. He thought of the man in uniform, the cross on his lapel. Roy had heard little of what the minister had said: on the drive south he had been thinking about his gear waiting for him, clean and ready, and trying to imagine what was happening in the barracks, and he knew he was late for something, but for what? What was the platoon doing? The company? He thought of them digging foxholes in the hills overlooking the beach; saw them marching to trucks which would drive them to ships. What happened when a war started? How did you finally get to where the war was? He could not imagine it. It was all too big.

Later that week he wrote his last lie to Sheila: told her his promotion had come through the day after the war started. He never saw her again. Exactly eight months after Pearl Harbor he followed Lieutenant DiMeo through the surf and across the beach at Guadalcanal. The Japanese were not there; that came two weeks later, farther inland.

In the summer of 1944, when he was certain as he could be that he would spend the rest of the war as a drill instructor, he applied for leave to get married, took some obscene harassment from the First Sergeant (and enjoyed it), and phoned Sheila, telling her to go ahead with the plans for the wedding. He felt no sense of duty. He wanted to hold her and tell her about the war. He had written about it, but not much: except for a few words his letters could have been written by any man doing work away from home. He had left out the details he now wanted to share with her because he had not wanted her to know them until he was with her.

The truth had not occurred to him: that because of newsreels and newspapers and magazines there was nothing he could tell her that would be as terrifying as what she had already imagined. She never wrote of this in her letters. Also, Marshall had its dead and its maimed (she never wrote of this either), and one—a victim of shell shock—who daily walked the streets, though his mind was permanently somewhere else; people treated him kindly, spoke to him as though he were sane; he liked to imitate the sound of a train whistle, did it often, and was very good at it. So Roy had protected her from nothing.

From nothing at all, so that when he did not get off the

train the morning before the wedding she was heartbroken and humiliated (already thinking of the phone calls she would have to make), but she was not absolutely surprised. She did not phone the Recruit Depot. That night her father got quietly drunk and finally said: 'I should have put a shotgun to his butt eight years ago and marched him down to the church.' Sheila moved to the sofa and sat beside him and held his hand to shut him up; she told him she was all right, it was better to learn this about Roy now than find it out later when they were married and maybe even had children. Though she was afraid he would start to mutter about seduction and damaged goods, she also felt loved because he knew, and she wished things were different between them and that she could take him out on the porch, away from her mother, and ask him how, all those years, from the very beginning, he had known. She promised herself that someday when she was older (and at this moment she knew she would leave Marshall soon, and would, yes, marry) she would take him aside, out in her backyard in Houston or Dallas (yes, it would have to be a city now, after this) and she would ask him how he had known. But she never did.

Yet out of that promise to herself came the vision of her future. A month later she moved to Houston and got a job as a dentist's receptionist. The dentist was single and was soon dating her. He was forty-two years old; she found that interesting, but little more. At one of his parties she met a geologist who had just returned to his job with an oil company after flying Corsairs from an aircraft carrier; his left arm was gone. At first when they made love and the stump moved above her right breast and shoulder she remembered Roy's arm: both arms on the earth in the woods. And sometimes she felt that the spirit of the arm extended from the stump and held her. When she told him, he said he could feel it too. Lying with him at night she listened to his war stories; a year later they drove to Marshall and got married.

On the night before he was supposed to pick up his leave papers and catch the train, Roy could not have predicted any of this. A half dozen sergeants took him out in San Diego.

When they got drunk one of them joked about getting Roy laid. Roy blinked at him and was suddenly, drunkenly, depressed. He had forgotten why they were drinking. He had not forgotten the facts: that he was going on leave tomorrow, that he was going to Marshall, going to marry Sheila. But he had forgotten her presence. She seemed as far away as she had when he was younger, before the war. The friend who had suggested a whorehouse was watching him.

'Cheer up,' the friend said. The others looked at Roy, stopped talking.

'The troops,' Roy said. 'You've got to train the fucking troops.'

Someone nodded, motioned to the waitress, ordered Roy a shot. Roy didn't want it, but said nothing; then he did want it, waited with anticipation for it, felt his drunkenness taking him somewhere, somewhere he had been, somewhere he was going.

'You got to kick ass. At the Canal we weren't ready. Fucking Japs were ready.'

'Peleliu,' someone murmured, and Roy's shot came.

'We learned from them. We weren't ready.' He held the shot glass, looked at it; then he gulped it dry, seeing as clearly as the moment it happened the death of Lieutenant DiMeo walking into the jungle on Guadalcanal when they were still learning about the Japanese and camouflage; when DiMeo was ten feet from an antitank gun, looking directly at the brush that concealed it, they fired and took his head off. Roy saw himself on his belly firing into the brush, through the image of blood spurting out of DiMeo's body that twitched and seemed to try to speak; from that moment on he had been certain he would not leave Guadalcanal. When they left the island four months later he led the platoon up the landing net, onto the ship. At the top he looked down: the troops were spread beneath him; most were not halfway up the net; several stopped to rest after each climbing step. He climbed onto the deck and looked down at their helmets and the gear on their backs and their toiling arms and legs. He had not known

until then how tired they were; then he realized they hadn't
known either. 'We were ready in here,' he said, pointing to his
heart. 'Not here.' He pointed to his head. 'We had to learn.
When I write to—' He paused, waited, a moment's blank in
his mind, the moment seeming to him longer, fearfully longer,
until her name floated up to him out of some region of need
for women, needs satisfied and needs not—'Sheila,' he said.
'When I write to her all I can write about is the troops. It's all
I know.' He looked around at the six faces. 'It's all I fucking
want to know. She answers the letters. She says, I'm glad your
men are learning. But it's all I write to her about: the fucking
troops. You know what I mean?'

He looked at the friend who wanted to go to a whorehouse.

'No,' the friend said.

'I mean I love the fucking troops. You got to train them.
You got to put it in here—' again he touched his breast '—and it
gets there through the ass end. That's all I write to her about.
The fucking Corps. All I want to do is train troops and kick
their ass and go out and drink with my Goddamn friends.
I don't want a Goddamn house full of gear. I don't want to go
home to that shit. If a man—' he picked up his empty shot
glass, looked in it; someone ordered him another '—if a man
could have his Goddamn quarters on the base, with his bunk
and his gear squared away and go home to his woman—' He
stopped again: the word woman drove Sheila's name from his
mind, replaced the image of her in a San Diego kitchen with
no image at all but merely with a nebulous and designated
emotion; and he glimpsed the concrete details of his life as
male and military, uniforms and gear and troops, and his
needs for a woman had no surrounding details at all, they all
ended in something abstract. He could not see himself in a
house with one of them, could not see himself taking all but
his noon meals with one of them, and could not imagine what
he would do with one of them on ordinary Saturdays and the
old useless Sundays: saw the two of them smoking cigarettes
and listening to the radio; and the woman he saw was not

Sheila, was not any woman at all, a face and body vague as the
people in the far background of a newspaper photograph.

'Fuck it,' he said.

His curse was decisive. And he kept himself from feeling
Sheila's pain by making her generic, placing her with all the
good women who had no real part in his life, so that it wasn't
Sheila he was rejecting but cohabitation, and in this brief and
cathartic vision he was able to feel as guiltless and purposeful
as a monk choosing prayers and a cell. Yet he wasn't happy
either. He felt despair at his limitations, and he raised his
glass in an unspoken toast to the grave forecast of loneliness,
and repeated his curse.

Which followed him through the years, the years which
began next morning when he reported in uniform to the burly
First Sergeant who had Roy's leave papers waiting, along with
a speech about women and marriage. Roy told him he was not
going on leave, he was not getting married, and he wanted a
platoon of recruits as soon as the next shitload of them came
in. The First Sergeant glared at him; he did not like to show
surprise but he knew it was in his face, so he exaggerated it,
made it look like it wasn't surprise at all.

'What manner of coo-coo juice were you drinking last
night, Hodges?'

'Most of San Diego.'

'And who called off this Texas altar-fuck?'

'I did.'

The First Sergeant leaned back in his chair.

'Sergeant Hodges, there are two holes a man doesn't want
to get into. One of them he can't stay out of unless he's buried
at sea, cremated, or set upon by a tribe of bone-licking canni-
bals. The other is the hole between the legs of a woman who's
wearing the fuck-ring. Unless it has been placed on her finger
by some other dumb son of a bitch who figured in order to
fuck self-same lady he had to get a job and buy a house to do it
in. I've had many adventures in the fuck-houses of others.
You are a fortunate man: when you were seagoing I'm sure
you heard many tales of woe from sailors who were unable to

forgive the trespassers who entered their fuck-houses while
the ship was out to sea. So I'm sure you have learned that the
best duty in the Marine Corps is with the infantry, and the
second best is to serve at a barracks on a naval base, so as to be
available to those lonesome wives when the ships go do their
merry shit at sea. I have no doubts that there are several U.S.
Navy dependents who bear a resemblance to the First Sergeant who talks to you now, but who step on the toes of a
sailor they call Daddy. This may also be true of certain Marine
dependents. I have never known a woman who gave a fart
whether she was married or not once it came upon her that
what she wanted to do was fuck. But it could be that, as well-
travelled as I am, my experience is still limited. For instance I
have never fucked in the state of Nebraska, partly because
I've heard it's considered a felony there. Then again, it could
be I have only known bad women, because like a pointer I
smell out the pheasant and ignore the dove. You will find that
sailors have the worst wives of all military men. One reason is
your average sailor is a dumb shit once he sets foot on land.
They spend too much time on boats. They all turn into country hicks, doesn't matter where they came from to begin with.
They get into port and they either believe everything they see,
or they don't understand it; worse than that, they believe
everything they hear. Which brings us to the next point: it's a
rare sailor that gets more than six blocks from the pier. So
what they do is meet the women that hang out in sailors' bars.
There you have it. What they meet is semi-pro whores. I am
right now, Sergeant Hodges—though not at the moment, since
you can see I'm here at my desk about to tear up your leave
papers and lend a helping hand in saving your young ass from
bad watering hole number two—fucking the sweet wife of a
gunner's mate, said gunner's mate stationed on a destroyer.
I hope he comes back alive. She does not talk about him, nor
has she told me his name. There is a color photograph of him
in uniform; it sits on the bureau in the bedroom, which allows
him to watch my ass-end doing its humble work on his wife.
While I am thus at labor I do believe I think about him more

than she does. Sergeant Hodges, I do not mean to piss you off when I say I assume you fucked this girl who lives and reigns in Marshall, Texas. It could even be that you were the first to do the old prone dance with her—' Roy nodded, and then was ashamed, and then he was sad, thinking of her eight years ago on the blanket in the woods. The phrase ran through his weary hung-over mind: *on the blanket in the woods.* 'Ah: a virgin. I have noticed that women can be compared to shooters. The virgin—and I have only had two of them, very long ago, and will never have another unless I come across some horny old nun—the virgin uses Kentucky windage. She moves her weapon this way and that, adjusting to the wind. And you are the wind. And the wind must go. But not to Nebraska, where it's frowned upon. I have no doubt the lady in Marshall is pretty, else you would not have spent such time and money crossing the state of Texas. So you can be assured that your place will soon be taken, and she'll be better at it this time around, and thus you will have two people who will be thankful to you. It behooves—'

'First Sergeant.'

'Speak.'

'Can I have the day off to get rid of this fucking hangover?'

'I recommend a shot of booze, a piece of ass, and a long sleep. Here—' He wrote on the note pad on his desk, tore the page out, and gave it to Roy.

'Her name is Meg. Tell her you're an old buddy of mine, just back from the wars. Don't let her get you out of the house, or she'll spend all your money.'

Roy neither liked nor understood the collusive look in the First Sergeant's eyes, the softening of his mouth and jaw. But he put the paper in his pocket, borrowed a friend's car, and drove into town and to her apartment where, after coffee and pretense at talk, he spent the day in bed, from time to time looking at the gunner's mate watching from the bureau. Just after sundown he was lying on his back and she was lick-

ing his chest and belly, moving down, when she stopped and
said: 'He'll ask about this too.'

'Who?'

'Johnny.'

It took him a moment to think of the First Sergeant as
Johnny.

'What do you mean?'

'He likes to hear about it. While we're screwing he likes
to hear about it with somebody else.'

'You tell him?'

'Yes.'

'You like to tell him?'

'Yes.'

'Jesus.'

But he was not really disturbed. Scornfully he thought of
Sheila. Then Meg moved down again and he stroked her hair
and thought of nothing. His curse of the night before had
taken flesh, and he came in its mouth.

Two nights later he wrote to Sheila. He wrote that he loved
his career and he had no place for a wife. It took him one page,
and seeing his life so compressed saddened him. He dropped
the page to the floor. On another page he told her how sorry
he was, and how he hated himself. He thought of her standing
at the train station, waiting after the last passenger had gone
by. She would have been dressed up. He picked up the first
letter and tore both of them in half and wadded them in his
fist. Better to slash a wrist and send her a page soaked in his
blood. The phone wouldn't do either. What he needed was to
see her, to be there now without transition, to deliver to her
some immortal touch that was neither erotic nor comforting
but something new and final between them: to firmly and lovingly squeeze her hand and look into her eyes and then disappear, like a love-rooted ghost making its farewell.

AT ST. CROIX

Peter Jackman and Jo Morrison were both divorced, and
had been lovers since winter. She knew much about his marriage, as he did about hers, and at times it seemed to Peter
that their love had grown only from shared pain. His ex-wife,
Norma, had married and moved to Colorado last summer, and
he had not seen David and Kathi since then. They were eleven
and nine, and in June they were coming to Massachusetts to
spend the summer with him. In May, Peter and Jo went to St.
Croix to recover, as they said, from the winter. They did not
mean simply the cold, but their nights tangled with the sorrow of divorce, with euphoric leaps away from it, with Peter's
creeping out of the house while Jo's two girls slept, with his
grieving for his children, and with both of them drinking too
much, talking too much, needing too much.

The hotel at St. Croix was a crescent of separate buildings facing the sea. The beach was short and narrow, bounded
by rocks that hid the rest of the coastline. About thirty yards
out, a reef broke the surf, and the water came gently and
foamless, and lapped at the beach. Peter could have walked to
the reef without wetting his shoulders, but he stayed close to
shore, swimming in water so shallow that sometimes his
hands touched rocks and pebbles and sand. Jo was curious
about him in that warmly possessive way that occurs when
people become lovers before they are friends, and on the first

day she asked him about the water. They were in lounge chairs near a palm tree on the beach, and she was watching his face. He looked beyond the reef at the blue sea and sky.

'I don't know. I've always been afraid of it.'

'What about the beach at home. You said you liked it.'

'I do. But I don't go out over my chest.'

'Maybe you just went for your children.'

'No. I love it. And this.' He waved a hand seaward. 'And bodysurfing. The worst about that is when I turn my back. I don't like turning my back on the sea.'

'Let's leave Buck Island to the fish.'

She was smiling at him, and there was no disappointment in her face or voice.

'You'd enjoy it,' he said.

'It's not important.'

Each morning after breakfast he went alone to the hotel lobby and chose a postcard for David and Kathi from the racked pictures of the sea, beaches, a black fisherman squatting beside a dead shark on the wharf, scarlet-flowered trees, coconut palms, steep green hills, tall trees of the rain forest. He had not told them he was going to St. Croix with a woman, nor had he told them he was going alone, and on the postcards he wrote crowded notes about the island. On one he wrote that mongooses lived here but there were no snakes, so they ate lizards and frogs, and some of the young men killed them and soaked their tails in rum for two weeks, then wore them stiff like feathers in their hatbands. Then he realized that David would want a tail, so he tore up the card and threw it away, and began watching from taxi windows for a dead mongoose on the road. He also wrote that he wished they were with him, and next year he would wait until June, when they were out of school, and he would bring them here. He did not send them a picture of the hotel. The wound he had opened in himself when he left them had not healed, and it never would; now going to St. Croix was like leaving them again. Jo was glad to be away from her daughters for a week, so Peter did not talk to her about his children.

Always the trade winds were blowing across the island, and Peter only felt the heat when he walked on the lee side of a building. The breeze cooled the town of Christiansted too, where they went by taxi in late afternoons, and walked the narrow streets of tourist shops and restaurants, and looked at the boats in the harbor. On the third day, they went sailing at sunset on a boat owned by Don Jensen, a young blond man with a deep tan, who charged them twelve dollars and kept their paper cups filled with rum punch from the ice chest in the cabin, and told them he and his wife had come from California six years ago, that she taught painting at a private school on the island and, when the sun was low, he told them if they were lucky they'd see the green ball when it sank under the horizon, though he had rarely seen it. But he had seen dust in the sky, blown from Africa, hanging red in the sunset. And he asked if they were going to Buck Island. Peter and Jo were sitting on benches on opposite sides of the boat. Peter looked at the glittering water near the sun and said: 'I'm afraid of it.'

'Can you swim?'

'Yes.'

'It's something you ought to see.'

'I know.'

'Nobody's ever drowned there. With the snorkel and fins, you just can't. I even take nonswimmers: kids who just hold onto a float and kick.'

'I want to see it. I don't want to get home, and then wish I had.'

'Are you sure?' Jo said.

'I think I'd like it when it's over.'

They watched the sun go down, did not see the green ball, then sailed back to Christiansted in the twilight. That night Peter and Jo got drinks from the hotel bar and took them to the beach and sat in upright chairs. He watched the gentle white breakers at the reef, and looked out at the dark sea, listened to it, smelled it. Next morning at breakfast he told the waitress where they were going, and she said: 'I never go in the water. We have a saying: The sea has no back door.' At eight-thirty he was on it, Don standing at the wheel next to the cabin door and working the sail, the long boat heeling so that when it rocked his way, to starboard, he could have touched the water with his hand, and the spray smacked his face and bare shoulders and chest, and when he looked up at Jo sitting on the port bench he could see only the sky behind her; when the boat heeled her way, he held onto his bench, and the sky was gone, and he was looking past her face, down at the sea. She bowed her head and cupped her hands to light a cigarette. When she straightened, Peter shaped his lips in a kiss. She returned it. He tried to care whether she was getting seasick or sunburned or was uncomfortable in the sea-spray, but he could not: his effort seemed physical, as though he were trying to push an interior part of his body out of himself and across the boat to Jo. With a slapping of sail Don brought the boat about and it steadied and now when it rocked, Peter could see both sky and water behind Jo. The spray was not hitting them. He half turned and watched the shore of St. Croix and the hills rising up from it, dirt roads climbing them and disappearing into green swells of trees. A tern hovered near the boat. Beyond Jo, toward the open sea, two black fishermen sat in a small pink sailboat. Peter crossed the boat, his feet spread and body swaying, and took one of Jo's cigarettes, his first since leaving home. She smiled and pressed his hand. He went back to the bench and watched the horizon and thought of shopping this afternoon for David and Kathi, then drinking at the roofed veranda of the Paris Café, where the breeze came with scents of cooking and sweet flowers.

He looked ahead of the boat at Buck Island, and sailboats anchored around a boatless surface that he knew covered the reef. The island was a mile long, and steep and narrow, and stood now between them and the open sea. On this side of it the water and wind were calm. Beyond the uneven curve of anchored boats, people were swimming the trail, a waving line of them with snorkels sticking out of the water; most wore shirts to protect their backs from the sun. While Don dropped the anchor, Peter found children swimming in the line. He looked into the water beside the boat and saw the sand bottom. Don came up from the cabin, carrying masks and snorkels and fins.

'It's about a hundred yards, there and back. Maybe a little more. How are you?'

'All right, I think.'

'Keep letting me know.'

Don gave them fins and, when they had put them on, he showed them how to use the mask and snorkel. Peter took a snorkel from him and put it in his mouth and breathed through it, then took the mask and looked at the green island and up at the sky, then pulled the mask over the snorkel tube and his face, and went to the ladder, feeling nothing that he could recognize of himself, feeling only the fins on his feet, and the mask over his nose and eyes, and the mouthpiece against his gums and teeth.

Don told them to swim near the boat until they were used to the snorkel, then he went down the ladder. Jo went next, and Peter looked at Don treading water, then watched her climbing down; when she pushed away from the ladder he turned and backed onto it, and down: legs into the water, then his waist, and when his feet were beneath the last rung he still worked down the ladder with his hands until his arms were in the water, then he turned, swimming a breast stroke, his face in it now, his breathing loud in the tube, and he looked through the mask at the sand bottom and the anchor resting on it. When he saw to his left the keel and white hull of the boat, he jerked his head from the water and swam overhand to the ladder and grasped it with one hand while he took the snorkel from his mouth. Then Don and Jo were on either side of him, snorkels twisted away from their lips. He shook his head at Don.

'It's worse than I thought,' he said.

'I was watching you. You looked all right.'

'No. I can't do it.'

Jo moved to Don's side, treading.

'I panicked a little at first,' she said. 'You just have to get used to breathing.'

'No. You two go on, and I'll wait on the boat. I'll drink beer in the sun.'

Their faces were tender, encouraging.

'I've got some floats aboard,' Don said. 'What about trying that?'

'Me and the kids who can't swim. All right.'

He moved one hand from the ladder until Don climbed past him, then he held on with both again.

'I wish you'd go without me,' he said to Jo.

'I wouldn't want to think of you alone on the boat.'

'If you knew how I felt in the water you'd rather think of me alone on the boat.'

'We could just go back.'

He shook his head, and moved a hand from the ladder as Don came down with a small white float. Peter blew into the snorkel, placed it in his mouth, and took the float. Kicking, he stretched out behind it, and lowered his face into the water, into the sound of his breath moving through the tube past his ear; he looked once at the sand bottom, then raised his head and took out the mouthpiece. Don was beside him. He knew Jo was behind him, but he felt only water there.

'That's it. I drink beer.'

'How about this: you just hold onto the float and I'll pull you.'

Now Jo was with them.

'That's a lot of trouble, just so I can see some fish and a reef.'

'It's easy. I just hold the strap.'

'Everybody's so kind around here, I don't have much choice. You won't let go?'

'No. Just relax and look. You'll be glad you saw it.'

Peter grasped the corners of the float and watched Don's kicking legs which were his only hold on air, on earth, on returning to the day itself; and he concentrated on the act of breathing: in the tube it sounded as though it would stop and he would not be able to start it again; he emptied and filled his lungs with a sense that he was breathing life into the Peter

Jackman who had vanished somewhere in the water behind him. He had no picture of himself in the water. He floated without thoughts or dreams, and when he entered the trail he saw the coral reef, and growing things waving like tall grass in the wind; he saw fish pause and dart; fish that were black, golden, scarlet, silver; fish in schools, fish alone, and he could not remember anything he saw. He recognized one fish as it swam into a tiny cave and three breaths later he could not remember its name and shape and color. Scattered along the trail were signs, driven into the bottom. They welcomed him to Buck Island National Park, quizzed him on the shapes of fish drawn on a signboard, told him what was growing near a sign … He found that he could remember the words longer than he could a fish or plant or part of the reef. He read each sign, and as he moved away from one he tried to hold its words in his mind; then the words were gone, and all he knew was the fluid snore of his breath, and the water: as though he were fathoms deep, he could not imagine the sky, nor the sun on his back; his mind was the sea bottom, and was covered too with that blue-green dispersal of his soul.

Then he saw only water and sand. He watched Don's legs, and waited for the reef again; he looked for fish, for signs, but the water now was empty and boundless and he wanted to look up but he did not, for he knew he would see miles of water to the horizon, and his breathing would stop. Then he saw a white hull. He was moving toward it, and the legs were gone; he looked up at the boat and sky, took the snorkel from his mouth, let go of the float, and grabbed the ladder. He did not look behind him. He climbed and stepped over the side and pulled off the mask and sat on the bench and took off the fins before Jo's hands, then masked face, appeared on the ladder. She was smiling. He looked at the deck. He watched the black fins on her feet as she crossed it, then she stood over him, smelling of the sea, and placed her hands on his cheeks. Don came over the side, carrying the float.

'You seemed all right,' he said. 'How was it?'

'Bad.'

Jo lifted his face.

'You didn't like any of it?'

'I didn't see any of it.' He looked at Don. 'You know something? I didn't even know you had turned and headed back. Not till you let me go at the boat.'

'You'd better have that beer now. Jo?'

'Please.'

He went down into the cabin.

'I want you to tell me about the fish,' Peter said.

'But you saw them.'

'No I didn't.'

'Maybe you'd better tell me about that.'

'I want you to tell me about the fish,' he said.

On the ride back he drank beer and smoked her cigarettes and listened to her talking about the fish and the reef. For a while her voice sounded as it did on those nights when they fought and, the fight ended, they talked about other things, past their wounds and over the space between them. He did not watch her face. St. Croix was beyond her, and he looked at the sky touching the hills, and listened to Jo and Don talking about the reef. But he could not remember it. Sometimes he looked over his shoulder at the horizon and the dark blue swelling sea.

That night, after Jo was asleep, he dressed and crept out of the room and went to the beach. Lying sunburned in a chair he shuddered as the sea came at him over the reef, and he looked beyond the breakers at the endless dark surface of it, and watched the lights and silhouette of a passing ship, fixed on it as though on a piece of solid and arid earth, and remembered the summer evening four years ago when he and Ryan, both drunk, had left their wives and children in the last of the charcoal smoke on Ryan's sundeck and had rowed an aluminum boat in a twilight fog out to the middle of the lake where they could drink beer and complain about marriage, and Ryan had stood in the bow to piss, and the boat had turned over; Peter hit the water swimming to the shore he could not see. He heard Ryan calling him back to the boat but he swam on into the fog, and when he tired he four times lowered his legs to nothing but water, and finally the evergreens appeared above the fog; he swam until he was in reeds and touching mud, then he crawled out of the water and lay on mud until Ryan came in, kicking alongside the overturned boat. When he and Norma and David and Kathi got home and he stepped into the shower and was enclosed by water he started to scream.

Yet in the summer of 1960 he was a Marine lieutenant at Camp Pendleton, California. One July afternoon his company boarded landing crafts and went a mile out to sea and then, wearing life jackets, floated to shore. Peter and his platoon were in one boat. He waited while his men, barefoot and free of helmets, cartridge belts, and weapons, climbed over the side and dropped into the sea. Then Peter went over and, floating on his back, he paddled and kicked into the cluster of his troops. Slowly, bantering, they formed a line parallel to the coast. With their heads toward shore, they started float-ing in on their backs. Peter kept watching them, counting them, twenty to his right, twenty-one to his left. He looked past their faces and green wet uniforms and orange jackets at the bobbing lines of the other platoons on his flanks. Some-times he looked at his feet trailing white as soap in the water, then out beyond the landing crafts at the horizon. Always he saw himself as his troops did: calm, smiling, talking to them; their eyes drew him out of the narrow space where he floated, as though he were spread over the breadth of forty-one men.

Wind blew the palm leaves behind his chair. The ship's lights were fading; its silhouette started to blend with the sea and sky; then it was gone, and he saw Kathi one night two years ago, perhaps a month after he had left them. She was seven, and it was Wednesday night, the night he was with them during the week; they ate at a restaurant and planned their weekend and when he drove them home she said, as she always did that first year, 'Do you want to come in?' And he did, and drank one cup of coffee with Norma, and they both talked to Kathi and David. But when he got his coat from the hall and went back to the kitchen Kathi was gone. He went from room to room, not calling her name, unable to call her name, until he found her in the den lying face down on the couch. She was not crying. He went to her, and leaning forward petted her long red hair; then he lifted her to his chest, held her while her arms went suddenly and tightly around his neck. Then she kissed him. Her lips on his were soft, cool, parted like a woman's.

Now, for the first time since going into the water that morning, he felt the scattered parts of his soul returning, as if they were in the salt air he breathed, filling his lungs, coursing with his blood. Behind his eyes the dark sea and sky were transformed: the sky blue and cloudless with a low hot sun, the sea the cold blue Atlantic off the coast at home, waves coming high and breaking with a crack and a roar, and he was between Kathi and David, holding their hands; they walked out against the surf and beyond it and let go of each other and waited for a wave, watched it coming, then dived in front of it as it broke, rode it in until their bodies scraped sand. Then they walked out again, but now sand shifted under their feet, water rushed seaward against their legs, then she was gone, her hand slipping out of his quick squeeze, she was tumbling and rolling out to sea, and he dived through a breaking wave and swam toward her face, her hair, her hands clutching air and water; swam out and held her against him, spoke to her as he kicked and stroked back through the waves, into the rush of surf, then he stood and walked toward David waiting in foam, and he spoke to her again, pressing her flesh against his. Lying in the chair on the beach at St. Croix, he received that vision with a certainty as incarnate as his sunburned flesh. He looked up at the stars. He was waiting for June: their faces at the airport, their voices in the car, their bodies with his in the sea.

THE PITCHER

for Philip

THEY CHEERED AND CLAPPED when he and Lucky Ferris came out of the dugout, and when the cheering and clapping settled to sporadic shouts he had already stopped hearing it, because he was feeling the pitches in his right arm and watching them the way he always did in the first few minutes of his warm-up. Some nights the fast ball was fat or the curve hung or the ball stayed up around Lucky's head where even the hitters in this Class C league would hit it hard. It was a mystery that frightened him. He threw the first hard one and watched it streak and rise into Lucky's mitt; and the next one; and the next one; then he wasn't watching the ball anymore, as though it had the power to betray him. He wasn't watching anything except Lucky's target, hardly conscious of that either, or of anything else but the rhythm of his high-kicking wind-up, and the ball not thrown but released out of all his motion; and now he felt himself approaching that moment he could not achieve alone: a moment that each time was granted to him. Then it came: the ball was part of him, as if his arm stretched sixty feet six inches to Lucky's mitt and slammed the ball into leather and sponge and Lucky's hand. Or he was part of the ball.

Now all he had to do for the rest of the night was concen-

trate on prolonging that moment. He had trained himself to
do that, and while people talked about his speed and curve
and change of pace and control, he knew that without his
concentration they would be only separate and useless parts;
and instead of nineteen and five on the year with an earned
run average of two point one five and two hundred and six
strikeouts, going for his twentieth win on the last day of the
season, his first year in professional ball, three months short
of his twentieth birthday, he'd be five and nineteen and on his
way home to nothing. He was going for the pennant too, one
half game behind the New Iberia Pelicans who had come to
town four nights ago with a game and a half lead, and the
Bulls beat them Friday and Saturday, lost Sunday, so that now
on Monday in this small Louisiana town, Billy's name was on
the front page of the local paper alongside the news of the
war that had started in Korea a little over a month ago. He
was ready. He caught Lucky's throw, nodded to him, and
walked with head down toward the dugout and the cheers
growing louder behind it, looking down at the bright grass,
holding the ball loosely in his hand.

He spoke to no one. He went to the far end of the dugout
that they left empty for him when he was pitching. He was
too young to ask for that, but he was good enough to get it
without asking; they gave it to him early in the year, when
they saw he needed it, this young pitcher Billy Wells who
talked and joked and yelled at the field and the other dugout
for nine innings of the three nights he didn't pitch, but on his
pitching night sat quietly, looking neither relaxed nor tense,
and only spoke when politeness required it. Always he was
polite. Soon they made a space for him on the bench, where
he sat now knowing he would be all right. He did not think
about it, for he knew as the insomniac does that to give it
words summons it up to dance; he knew that the pain he had
brought with him to the park was still there; he even knew it
would probably always be there; but for a good while now it
was gone. It would lie in wait for him and strike him again
when he was drained and had a heart full of room for it. But

that was a long time from now, in the shower or back in the hotel, longer than the two and a half hours or whatever he would use pitching the game; longer than a clock could measure. Right now it seemed a great deal of his life would pass before the shower. When he trotted out to the mound they stood and cheered and, before he threw his first warm-up pitch, he tipped his cap.

He did not make love to Leslie the night before the game. All season, he had not made love to her on the night before he pitched. He did not believe, as some ballplayers did, that it hurt you the next day. *It's why they call it the box score anyway,* Hap Thomas had said on the bus one night after going hitless; *I left me at least two base hits in that whorehouse last night.* Like most ballplayers in the Evangeline League, Thomas had been finished for a long time: a thirty-six-year-old outfielder who had played three seasons—not consecutively—in Triple A ball, when he was in his twenties. Billy didn't make love the night before a game because he still wasn't used to night baseball; he still had the same ritual that he'd had in San Antonio, playing high school and American Legion ball: he drank a glass of buttermilk then went to bed, where for an hour or more he imagined tomorrow's game, although it seemed the game already existed somewhere in the night beyond his window and was imagining him. When finally he slept, the game was still there with him, and in the morning he woke to it, remembered pitching somewhere between daydream and nightdream; and until time for the game he felt like a shadow cast by the memory and the morning's light, a shadow that extended from his pillow to the locker room, when he took off the clothes which had not felt like his all day and put on the uniform which in his mind he had been wearing since he went to bed the night before. In high school, his classes interfered with those days of being a shadow. He felt that he was not so much going to classes as bumping into them on his way to the field. But in summer when he played American Legion ball, there was nothing to bump into, there was only the morning's wait which wasn't really waiting because waiting was watching time, watching it win usually, while on those mornings he joined time and flowed with it, so that sitting before the breakfast his mother cooked for him he felt he was in motion toward the mound.

And he had played a full season less one game of pro ball and still had not been able to convince his mind and body that the night before a game was far too early to enter the rhythm and concentration that would work for him when he actually had the ball in his hand. Perhaps his mind and body weren't the ones who needed convincing; perhaps he was right when he thought he was not imagining the games, but they were imagining him: benevolent and slow-witted angels who had followed him to take care of him, who couldn't understand they could rest now, lie quietly the night before, because they and Billy had all next day to spend with each other. If he had known Leslie was hurt he could have told her, as simply as a man saying he was beset by the swollen agony of mumps, that he could not make love on those nights, and it wasn't because he preferred thinking about tomorrow's game, but because those angels had followed him all the way to Lafayette, Louisiana. Perhaps he and Leslie could even have laughed about it, for finally it was funny, as funny as the story about Billy's Uncle Johnny whose two hounds had jumped the fence and faithfully tracked or followed him to a bedroom a few blocks from his house, and bayed outside the window: a bedroom Uncle Johnny wasn't supposed to be in, and more trouble than that, because to get there he had left a bedroom he wasn't supposed to leave.

Lafayette was funny too: a lowland of bayous and swamps and Cajuns. The Cajuns were good fans. They were so good that in early season Billy felt like he was barnstorming in some strange country, where everybody loved the Americans and decided to love baseball too since the Americans were playing it for them. They knew the game, but often when they yelled about it, they yelled in French, and when they yelled in

English it sounded like a Frenchman's English. This came from the colored section too. The stands did not extend far beyond third and first base, and where the first base stands ended there was a space of about fifty feet and, after that, shoved against each other, were two sections of folding wooden bleachers. The Negroes filled them, hardly noticed beyond the fifty feet of air and trampled earth. They were not too far down the right field line: sometimes when Billy ran out a ground ball he ended his sprint close enough to the bleachers to hear the Negroes calling to him in French, or in the English that sounded like French.

Two Cajuns played for the Bulls. The team's full name was the Lafayette Brahma Bulls, and when the fans said all of it, they said Bremabulls. The owner was a rancher who raised these bulls, and one of his prizes was a huge and danger-ous-looking hump-necked bull whose grey coat was nearly white; it was named Huey for their governor who was shot and killed in the state capitol building. Huey was led to home plate for opening day ceremonies, and after that he attended every game in a pen in foul territory against the right field fence. During batting practice the left handers tried to pull the ball into the pen. Nobody hit him, but when the owner heard about it he had the bull brought to the park when bat-ting practice was over. By then the stands were filling. Huey was brought in a truck that entered through a gate behind the colored bleachers, and the Negroes would turn and look behind them at the bull going by. The two men in the truck wore straw cowboy hats. So did the owner, Charlie Breaux. When the Cajuns said his first and last names together they weren't his name anymore. And since it was the Cajun third baseman, E. J. Primeaux, a wiry thirty-year-old who owned a small grocery store which his wife ran during the season, who first introduced Billy to the owner, Billy had believed for the first few days after reporting to the club that he pitched for a man named Mr. Chollibro.

One night someone did hit Huey: during a game, with two outs, a high fly ball that Hap Thomas could have reached for and caught; he was there in plenty of time, glancing down at the pen's fence as he moved with the flight of the ball, was waiting safe from collision beside the pen, looking now from the ball to Huey who stood just on the other side of the fence, watching him; Hap stuck his arm out over the fence and Huey's head; then he looked at Huey again and withdrew his arm and stepped back to watch the ball strike Huey's head with a sound the fans heard behind third base. The ball bounced up and out and Hap barehanded it as Huey trotted once around the pen. Hap ran toward the dugout, holding the ball up, until he reached the first base umpire who was alternately signalling safe and pointing Hap back to right field. Then Hap flipped him the ball and, grinning, raised both arms to the fans behind the first base line, kept them raised to the Negroes as he ran past their bleachers and back to Huey's pen, taking off his cap as he approached the fence where Huey stood again watching, waved his cap once over the fence and horns, then trotted to his position, thumped his glove twice, then lowered it to his knee, and his bare hand to the other, and crouched. The fans were still laughing and cheering and calling to Hap and Huey and Chollibro when two pitches later the batter popped up to Caldwell at short.

In the dugout Primeaux said: 'Hap, I seen many a outfielder miss a fly ball because he's wall-shy, but that's the first time I ever seen one miss because he's *bull*-horn shy.' And Hap said: 'In this league? That's nothing. No doubt about it, one of these nights I'll go out to right field and get bit by a cottonmouth so big he'll chop my leg in two.' 'Or get hit by lightning,' Shep Caldwell said. In June lightning had struck a centerfielder for the Abbeville Athletics; struck the metal peak of his cap and exited into the earth through his spikes. When the Bulls heard the announcement over their public address system, their own sky was cloudy and there were distant flashes; perhaps they had even seen the flash that killed Tommy Lyons thirty miles away. The announcement came between innings when the Bulls were coming to bat; the players and fans stood for a minute of silent prayer. Billy was sitting beside Hap. Hap went to the cooler and came back with a paper cup and sat looking at it but not drinking, then said: 'He broke a leg, Lyons did. I played in the Pacific Coast League with him one year. Forty-one. He was hitting three-thirty; thirty-something home runs; stole about forty bases. Late in the season he broke his leg sliding. He never got his hitting back. Nobody knew why. Tommy didn't know why. He went to spring training with the Yankees, then back to the Pacific Coast League, and he kept going down. I was drafted by then, and next time I saw him was two years ago when he came to Abbeville. We had a beer one night and I told him he was headed for the major leagues when he broke his leg. No doubt about it. He said he knew that. And he still didn't understand it. Lost something: swing; timing. Jesus, he used to hit the ball. Now they fried him in front of a bunch of assholes in Abbeville. How's that for shit.' For the rest of the game most of the players watched their sky; those who didn't were refusing to. They would not know until next day about the metal peak on Lyons's cap; but two innings after the announcement, Lucky went into the locker room and cut his off. When he came back to the dugout holding the blue cap and looking at the hole where the peak had been, Shep said: 'Hell, Lucky, it never strikes twice.' Lucky said: 'That's because it don't have to,' and sat down, stroking the hole.

Lafayette was only a town on the way to Detroit, to the Tigers; unless he got drafted, which he refused to think about, and thought about daily when he read of the war. Already the Tiger scout had watched Billy pitch three games and talked to him after each one, told him all he needed was time, seasoning; told him to stay in shape in the off-season; told him next year he would go to Flint, Michigan, to Class A ball. He was the only one on the club who had a chance for the major leagues, though Billy Joe Baron would probably go up, but not very far; he was a good first baseman and very fast, led the league in stolen bases, but he had to struggle and beat out drag bunts and ground balls to keep his average in the two-nineties and low three hundreds, and he would not go higher than Class A unless they outlawed the curve ball. The others would stay with the Bulls, or a team like the Bulls. And now Leslie was staying in this little town that she wasn't supposed to see as a town to live in longer than a season, and staying too in the little furnished house they were renting, with its rusted screen doors and its yard that ended in the back at a woods which farther on became a swamp, so that Billy never went off the back porch at night and if he peered through the dark at the grass long enough he was sure he saw cottonmouths.

She came into the kitchen that morning of the final game, late morning after a late breakfast so he would eat only twice before pitching, when he was already—or still, from the night before—concentrating on his twentieth win; and the pennant too. He wanted that: wanted to be the pitcher who had come to a third-place club and after one season had ridden away from a pennant winner. She came into the kitchen and looked at him more seriously than he'd ever seen her, and said: 'Billy, it's a terrible day to tell you this but you said today was the day I should pack.'

He looked at her from his long distance then focused in closer, forced himself to hear what she was saying, felt like he was even forcing himself to see her in three dimensions instead of two, and said: 'What's the matter, baby?'

'I'm not going.'

'Not going where?'

'San Antonio. Flint. I'm staying here.'

Her perspiring face looked so afraid and sorry for him and determined all at once that he knew he was finished, that he didn't even know what was happening but there would never be enough words he could say. Her eyes were brimming with tears, and he knew they were for herself, for having come to this moment in the kitchen, so far from everything she could have known and predicted; deep in her eyes, as visible as stars, was the hard light of something else, and he knew that she had hated him too, and he imagined her hating him for days while he was on the road: saw her standing in this kitchen and staring out the screen door at the lawn and woods, hating him. Then the picture completed itself: a man, his back to Billy, stood beside her and put his arm around her waist.

'Leslie?' and he had to clear his throat, clear his voice of the fear in it: 'Baby, have you been playing around?'

She looked at him for such a long time that he was both afraid of what she would say, and afraid she wouldn't speak at all.

'I'm in love, Billy.'

Then she turned and went to the back door, hugging her breasts and staring through the screen. He gripped the corners of the table, pushed his chair back, started to rise, but did not; there was nothing to stand for. He rubbed his eyes, then briskly shook his head.

'It wasn't just that you were on the road so much. I was ready for that. I used to tell myself it'd be exciting a lot of the time, especially in the big leagues. And I'd tell myself in ten years it'd be over anyway, some women have to—'

'*Ten?*' Thinking of the running he did, in the outfield on the days he wasn't pitching, and every day at home between seasons, having known long ago that his arm was a gift and it would last until one spring when it couldn't do the work anymore, would become for the first time since it started throwing a baseball just an ordinary arm; and what he could and must do was keep his lungs and legs strong so they wouldn't give out before it did. He surprised himself: he had not known that, while his wife was leaving him, he could proudly and defensively think of pitching in his early thirties. He had a glimpse of the way she saw him, and he was frightened and ashamed.

'All right: fifteen,' she said. 'Some women are married to sailors and soldiers and it's longer. It wasn't the road trips. It was when you were home: you weren't here. You weren't here, with me.'

'I was here all day. Six, seven hours at the park at night. I don't know what that means.'

'It means I'm not what you want.'

'How can you tell me what I want?'

'You want to be better than Walter Johnson.'

From his angle he saw very little of her face. He waited. But this time she didn't speak.

'Leslie, can't a man try to be the best at what he's got to do and still love his wife?' Then he stood: 'Goddamnit who *is* he?'

'George Lemoine,' she said through the screen.

'George Le*moine*. Who's George Le*moine*?'

'The dentist I went to.'

'What dentist you went to?'

She turned and looked at his face and down the length of his arms to his fists, then sat at the opposite end of the table.

'When I lost the filling. In June.'

'*June?*'

'We didn't start then.' Her face was slightly lowered, but her eyes were raised to his, and there was another light in them: she was ashamed but not remorseful, and her voice had the unmistakable tone of a woman in love; they were never so serious as this, never so threatening, and he was assaulted by images of Leslie making love with another man. 'He went to the games alone. Sometimes we talked down at the concession stand. We—' Now she looked down, hid her eyes from him, and he felt shut out forever from the mysteries of her heart.

All his life he had been confident. In his teens his confidence and hope were concrete: the baseball season at hand, the season ahead, professional ball, the major leagues. But even as a child he had been confident and hopeful, in an abstract way. He had barely suffered at all, and he had survived that without becoming either callous or naive. He was not without compassion when his life involved him with the homely, the clumsy, the losers. He simply considered himself lucky. Now his body felt like someone else's, weak and trembling. His urge was to lie down.

'And all those times on the road I never went near a whorehouse.'

'It's not the same.'

He was looking at the beige wall over the sink, but he felt that her eyes were lowered still. He was about to ask what she meant, but then he knew.

'So I guess when I go out to the mound tonight he'll be moving in, is that right?'

Now he looked at her, and when she lifted her face, it had changed: she was only vulnerable.

'He has to get a divorce first. He has a wife and two kids.'

'Wait a minute. *Wait* a minute. He's got a wife and two *kids?* How *old* is this son of a bitch?'

'Thirty-four.'

'God*damn* it Leslie! How dumb can you be? He's getting what he wants from you, what makes you think he won't be smart enough to leave it at that? God*damn*.'

'I believe him.'

'You believe him. A dentist anyhow. How can you be married to a ballplayer and fall for a dentist anyhow? And what'll you do for money? You got that one figured out?'

'I don't need much. I'll get a job.'

'Well, you won't have much either, because I'm going over there and kill him.'

'Billy.' She stood, her face as admonitory as his mother's. 'He's got enough troubles. All summer I've been in trouble too. I've been sad and lonesome. That's the only way this could ever happen. You know that. All summer I've been feeling like I was running alongside the players' bus waving at you. Then he came along.'

'And picked you up.'

He glared at her until she blushed and lowered her eyes. Then he went to the bedroom to pack. But she had already done it: the suitcase and overnight bag stood at the foot of the bed. He picked them up and walked fast to the front door. Before he reached it she came out of the kitchen, and he stopped.

'Billy. I don't want you to be hurt; and I know you won't be for long. I hope someday you can forgive me. Maybe write and tell me how you're doing.'

His urge to drop the suitcase and overnight bag and hold

her and ask her to change her mind was so great that he could only fight it with anger; and with the clarity of anger he saw a truth which got him out the door.

'You want it all, don't you? Well, forget it. You just settle for what you chose.'

Scornfully he scanned the walls of the living room, then Leslie from feet to head; then he left, out into the sun and the hot still air, and drove into town and registered at a hotel. The old desk clerk recognized him and looked puzzled but quickly hid it and said: 'Y'all going to beat them New Iberia boys tonight?'

'Damn right.'

The natural thing to do now was go to Lemoine's office, walk in while he was looking in somebody's mouth: *It's me you son of a bitch*, and work him over with the left hand, cancel his afternoon for him, send him off to another dentist. What he had to do was unnatural. And as he climbed the stairs to his room he thought there was much about his profession that was unnatural. In the room he turned off the air conditioning and opened the windows, because he didn't want his arm to be in the cool air, then lay on the bed and closed his eyes and began pitching to the batting order. He knew them all perfectly; but he did not trust that sort of perfection, for it was too much like confidence, which was too much like complacency. So he started with Vidrine, the lead-off man. Left-handed. Went with the pitch, hit to all fields; good drag-bunter but only fair speed and Primeaux would be crowding him at third; choke-hitter, usually got a piece of the ball, but not that quick with the bat either; couldn't hit good speed. Fastballs low and tight. Change on him. Good base-runner but he had to get a jump. Just hold him close to the bag. Then Billy stopped thinking about Vidrine on base. Thing was to concentrate now on seeing his stance and the high-cocked bat and the inside of the plate and Lucky's glove. He pushed aside the image of Vidrine crouching in a lead off first, and at the same time he pushed from his mind Leslie in the kitchen telling him; he saw Vidrine at the plate and, beyond him, he saw Leslie going away. She had been sitting in the box seat but now she walked alone down the ramp. Poor little Texas girl. She even sounded like a small town in Texas: Leslie Wells. Then she was gone.

The home run came with one out and nobody on in the top of the third inning after he had retired the first seven batters. Rick Stanley hit it, the eighth man in the order, a good-field no-hit third baseman in his mid-twenties. He had been in the minors for seven years and looked like it: though trimly built, and the best third baseman Billy had ever seen, he had a look about him of age, of resignation, of having been forced—when he was too young to bear it well—to compromise what he wanted with what he could do. At the plate he looked afraid, and early in the season Billy thought Stanley had been beaned and wasn't able to forget it. Later he realized it wasn't fear of beaning, not fear at all, but the strain of living so long with what he knew. It showed in the field too. Not during a play, but when it was over and Stanley threw the ball to the pitcher and returned to his position, his face looking as though it were adjusting itself to the truth he had forgotten when he backhanded the ball over the bag and turned and set and threw his mitt-popping peg to first; his face then was intense, reflexive as his legs and hands and arm; then the play was over and his face settled again into the resignation that was still new enough to be terrible. It spread downward to his shoulders and then to the rest of him and he looked old again. Billy wished he had seen Stanley play third when he was younger and still believed there was a patch of dirt and a bag and a foul line waiting for him in the major leagues.

One of Billy's rules was never to let up on the bottom of the batting order, because when one of them got a hit it hurt more. The pitch to Stanley was a good one. Like many players, Stanley was a poor hitter because he could not consistently be a good hitter; he was only a good hitter for one swing out of every twelve or so; the other swings had changed his life for him. The occasional good one gave the fans, and Stanley too by now, a surprise that always remained a surprise and so never engendered hope. His home run was a matter of numbers and time, for on this one pitch his concentration and timing and swing all flowed together, making him for that instant the hitter of his destroyed dream. It would happen again, in other ball parks, in other seasons; and if Stanley had been able to cause it instead of having it happen to him, he would be in the major leagues.

Billy's first pitch to him was a fast ball, waist high, inside corner. Stanley took it for a strike, with that look on his face. Lucky called for the same pitch. Billy nodded and played with the rosin bag to keep Stanley waiting longer; then Stanley stepped out of the box and scooped up dust and rubbed it on his hands and the bat handle; when he moved to the plate again he looked just as tense and Billy threw the fast ball; Stanley swung late and under it. Lucky called for the curve, the pitch that was sweet tonight, and Billy went right into the wind-up, figuring Stanley was tied up tightly now, best time to throw a pitch into all that: he watched the ball go in fast and groin-high, then fall to the left, and it would have cut the outside corner of the plate just above Stanley's knees; but it was gone. Stanley not only hit it so solidly that Billy knew it was gone before looking, but he got around on it, pulled it, and when Billy found it in the left-centerfield sky it was still climbing above James running from left and LeBlanc from center. At the top of its arc, there was something final about its floodlit surface against the real sky, dark up there above the lighted one they played under.

He turned his back to the plate. He never watched a home run hitter cross it. He looked out at LeBlanc in center; then he looked at Harry Burke at second, old Harry, the manager, forty-one years old and he could still cover the ground, mostly through cunning; make the pivot—how many double plays had he turned in his life?—and when somebody took him out with a slide Billy waited for the cracking sound, not just of bone but the whole body, like a dried tree limb. Hap told him not to worry, old Harry was made of oiled leather. His face looked as if it had already outlived two bodies like the one it commanded now. Never higher than Triple A, and that was long ago; when the Bulls hired him and then the fans loved him he moved his family to Lafayette and made it his home, and between seasons worked for an insurance company, easy money for him, because he went to see men and they drank coffee and talked baseball. He had the gentlest eyes Billy had ever seen on a man. Now Harry trotted over to him.

'We got twenty-one outs to get that back for you.'

'The little bastard hit that pitch.'

'Somebody did. Did you get a close look at him?'

Billy shook his head and went to the rubber. He walked the fat pitcher Talieferro on four pitches and Vidrine on six, and Lucky came to the mound. They called him Lucky because he wasn't.

'One run's one thing,' Lucky said. 'Let's don't make it three.'

'The way y'all are swinging tonight, one's as good as nine.' For the first time since he stepped onto the field, Leslie that morning rose up from wherever he had locked her, and struck him.

'Hey,' Lucky said. 'Hey, it's early.'

'Can't y'all hit that fat son of a bitch?'

'We'll hit him. Now you going to pitch or cry?'

He threw Jackson a curve ball and got a double play around the horn, Primeaux to Harry to Baron, who did a split stretching and got Jackson by a half stride.

He went to his end of the bench and watched Talieferro, who for some reason pronounced his name Tolliver: a young big left-handed pitcher with the kind of belly that belonged on a much older man, in bars on weekend afternoons; he had pitched four years at the local college, this was his first season of pro ball, he was sixteen and nine and usually lost only when his control was off. He did not want to be a professional ballplayer. He had a job with an oil company at the end of the season, and was only pitching and eating his way through a Louisiana summer. Billy watched Lucky adjust his peakless

cap and dust his hands and step to the plate, and he pushed
Leslie back down, for she was about to burst out of him and
explode in his face. He looked down at the toe plate on his
right shoe, and began working the next inning, the middle of
the order, starting with their big hitter, the centerfielder Remy
Gauthreaux, who was finished too, thirty years old, but smart
and dangerous and he'd knock a mistake out of the park. Low
and away to Gauthreaux. Lucky popped out to Stanley in foul
territory and came back to the dugout shaking his head.

Billy could sense it in all the hitters in the dugout, and
see it when they went to the plate: Talieferro was on, and they
were off. It could be anything: the pennant game, when every
move counted; the last game of the season, so the will to be a
ballplayer was losing to that other part of them which insisted
that when they woke tomorrow nothing they felt tonight
would be true; they would drive home to the jobs and other
lives that waited for them; most would go to places where
people had not even heard of the team, the league. All of that
would apply to the Pelicans too; it could be that none of it
applied to Talieferro: that rarely feeling much of anything
except digestion, hunger, and gorging, he had no conflict
between what he felt now and would start feeling tomorrow.
And it could be that he simply had his best stuff tonight, that
he was throwing nearly every pitch the way Stanley had
swung that one time.

Billy went to the on-deck circle and kneeled and watched
Harry at the plate, then looked out at Simmons, their big first
baseman: followed Gauthreaux in the order, a power hitter
but struck out about a hundred times a year: keep him off balance, in and out, and throw the fast one right into his power,
and right past him too. Harry, choking high on the bat, fouled
off everything close to the plate then grounded out to short,
and Billy handed his jacket to the batboy and went through
cheers to the plate. When he stepped in Talieferro didn't look
at him, so Billy stepped out and stared until he did, then dug
in and cocked the bat, a good hitter so he had played right
field in high school and American Legion when he wasn't

pitching. He watched the slow, easy fat man's wind-up and the fast ball coming out of it: swung for the fence and popped it to second, sprinting down the line and crossing the bag before the ball came down. When he turned he saw Talieferro already walking in, almost at the third base line. Harry brought Billy's glove out to the mound and patted his rump.

'I thought you were running all the way to Flint.'

In the next three innings he pitched to nine men. He ended the fifth by striking out Stanley on curve balls; and when Talieferro led off the sixth Billy threw a fast ball at his belly that made him spin away and fall into the dust. Between innings he forced himself to believe in the hope of numbers: the zeros and the one on the scoreboard in right center, the inning number, the outs remaining for the Bulls; watched them starting to hit, but only one an inning, and nobody as far as second base. He sat sweating under his jacket and in his mind pitched to the next three Pelicans, then the next three just to be sure, although he didn't believe he would face six of them next inning, or any inning, and he thought of eighteen then fifteen then twelve outs to get the one run, the only one he needed, because if it came to that, Talieferro would tire first. When Primeaux struck out leading off the sixth, Billy looked at Hap at the other end of the bench, and he wanted to be down there with him. He leaned forward and stared at his shoes. Then the inning was over and he gave in to the truth he had known anyway since that white vision of loss just before the ball fell.

Gauthreaux started the seventh with a single to right, doing what he almost never did: laid off pulling and went with the outside pitch. Billy worked Simmons low and got the double play he needed, then he struck out the catcher Lantrip, and trotted off the field with his string still going, thirteen batters since the one-out walk to Vidrine in the third. He got the next six. Three of them grounded out, and the other three struck out on the curve, Billy watching it break under the shiny blur of the bat as it would in Flint and wherever after that and Detroit too: his leg kicking and body wheeling and arm whipping around in rhythm again with his history which had begun with a baseball and a friend to throw it to, and had excluded all else, or nearly all else, and had included the rest somewhere alongside him, almost out of his vision (once between innings he allowed himself to think about Leslie, just long enough to forgive her); his history was his future too and the two of them together were twenty-five years at most until the time when the pitches that created him would lose their speed, hang at the plate, become hits in other men's lives instead of the heart of his; they would discard him then, the pitches would. But he loved them for that too, and right now they made his breath singular out of the entire world, so singular that there was no other world: the war would not call him because it couldn't know his name; and he would refuse the grief that lurked behind him. He watched the final curve going inside, then breaking down and over, and Lucky's mitt popped and the umpire twisted and roared and pointed his right fist to the sky.

He ran to the dugout, tipping his cap to the yelling Cajuns, and sat between Hap and Lucky until Baron flied out to end the game. After the showers and goodbyes he drove to the hotel and got his still-packed bags and paid the night clerk and started home, out of the lush flatland of marsh and trees, toward Texas. Her space on the front seat was filled as with voice and touch. He turned on the radio. He was not sleepy, and he was driving straight through to San Antonio.

WAITING

JUANITA CREEHAN was a waitress in a piano bar near Camp Pendleton, California. She had been a widow for twelve years, and her most intense memory of her marriage was an imagined one: Patrick's death in the Chosin Reservoir. After Starkey got back from Korea, he and Mary came to her apartment, and he told Juanita how it happened: they were attacking a hill, and when they cleared it they went down to the road and heard that Patrick had caught it. Starkey went over to the second platoon to look at him.

'What did they do to him?' Juanita said.

'They wrapped him in a shelter half and put him in a truck.'

She thought of the road of frozen mud and snow; she had never seen snow but now when it fell or lay white in her mind it was always death. Many nights she drank and talked with Starkey and Mary, and she asked Starkey for more details of the Reservoir, and sometimes she disliked him for being alive, or disliked Mary for having him alive. She had been tolerant of Mary's infidelity while Starkey was gone, for she understood her loneliness and dread; but now she could not forgive her, and often she looked quickly into Mary's eyes, and knew that her look was unforgiving. Years later, when she heard they were divorced, she was both pleased and angry. At the end of those nights of listening to Starkey, she went to bed and saw the hills and sky, and howitzers and trucks and troops on the road. She saw Patrick lying in the snow while the platoon moved up the hill; she saw them wrap him in the shelter half and lift him to the bed of the truck.

Some nights she descended further into the images. First she saw Patrick walking. He was the platoon sergeant, twenty-six years old. He walked on the side of the road, watching his troops and the hills. He had lost weight, was thinner than ever (my little bantam rooster, she had called him), his cheeks were sunken, and on them was a thin red beard. She no longer felt her own body. She was inside his: she felt the weight of helmet and rifle and parka; the cold feet; and the will to keep the body going, to believe that each step took him and his men closer to the sea. Through his green eyes and fever-warmth she looked up the road: a howitzer bounced behind a truck; Lieutenant Dobson, walking ahead on the road, wore a parka hood under his helmet; she could see none of his flesh as he looked once up at the sky. She heard boots on the hard earth, the breathing and coughing of troops, saw their breath-plumes in the air. She scanned the hills on both sides of the road, looked down at her boots moving toward the sea; glanced to her left at the files of young troops, then looked to the right again, at a snow-covered hill without trees, and then her chest and belly were struck and she was suddenly ill: she felt not pain but nausea, and a sense of futility at living this long and walking this far as her body seemed to melt into the snow ...

On a summer night in 1962, for the first time in her life, she woke with a man and had to remember his name. She lay beside the strange weight of his body and listened to his breath, then remembered who he was: Roy Hodges, a sergeant major, who last night had talked with her when she brought his drinks, and the rest of the time he watched her, and when she went to the restroom she looked at her tan face and blonde hair; near the end of the evening he asked if he could take her home; she said she had a car but he could follow her, she'd like to have a drink, and they drank vodka at her kitchen table. Now she did not want to touch him, or wake him and tell him to go. She got up, found her clothes on the floor and dressed; quietly she opened a drawer and took a sweater and put it on her shoulders like a cape. Her purse was in the kitchen. She found it in the dark, on the floor beside her chair, and went out of the apartment and crossed the cool damp grass to her car. With the windshield wipers sweeping dew, she drove down a hill and through town to the beach. She locked her purse in the car and sat on loose sand and watched the sea. Black waves broke with a white slap, then a roar. She sat huddled in the cool air.

Then she walked. To her left the sea was loud and dark, and she thought of Vicente Torrez with the pistol in his lap: a slender Mexican boy who in high school had teased her about being named Juanita, when she had no Mexican blood. Blonde gringita, he called her, and his eyes looked curiously at her, as if her name were an invitation to him, but he didn't know how to answer it. Five years after high school, while she was married to Patrick, she read in the paper that he had shot himself. There was no photograph, so she read the story to know if this were the same Vicente, and she wanted it to be him. He had been a cab driver in San Diego, and had lived alone. The second and final paragraph told of the year he was graduated from the high school in San Diego, and listed his survivors: his parents, brothers, sisters. So it was Vicente, with the tight pants and teasing face and that question in his eyes: Could you be my girl? Love me? Someone she once knew had sat alone in his apartment and shot himself; yet her feeling was so close to erotic that she was frightened. Patrick came home in late afternoon and she watched through the window as he walked uniformed across the lawn (it was winter: he was wearing green) and when he came inside she held him and told him and then she was crying, seeing Vicente sitting in a dirty and disorderly room, sitting on the edge of his bed and reaching that moment when he wanted more than anything else not to be Vicente, and crying into Patrick's chest she said: 'I wonder if he knew somebody would cry; I wonder if he wouldn't have done it; if that would have seen him through till tomorrow—' The word tomorrow stayed in her heart. She saw it in her mind, its letters printed across the black and white image of Vicente sitting on the bed with the pistol, and she loosened Patrick's tie and began to unbutton his green blouse.

She was looking out at the sea as she walked, and she stepped into a shallow pool left by the tide; the water covered her sandaled feet and was cool and she stood in it. Then she stepped out and walked on. For a year after Patrick was killed she took sleeping pills. She remembered lying in bed and waiting for the pill to work, and the first signals in her fingers, her hands: the slow-coming dullness, and she would touch her face, its skin faintly tingling, going numb, then she was aware only of the shallow sound and peaceful act of her slow breathing.

Juanita Jody Noury Creehan. Her mother had named her, given her a choice that would not change her initials if later she called herself Jody. Her mother's maiden name had been Miller. She looked up at the sky: it was clear, stars and a quarter-moon. Noury Creehan: both names from men. She stepped out of her sandals, toe against heel, toe against heel, heart beating as though unclothing for yet another man, remembering the confessions when she was in high school, remembering tenderly as if she were mother to herself as a young girl. Petting: always she called it that, whispering through lattice and veil, because that was the word the priests used in the confessional and when they came to the Saturday morning catechism classes for talks with the junior and senior girls; and the word the nuns used too on Saturday mornings, black-robed and looking never-petted themselves, so the word seemed strange on their tongues. The priests looked as if they had petted, or some of them did, probably only because they were men, they had hands and faces she liked to watch, voices she liked to hear.

Petting, for the bared and handled and suckled breasts,

her blouse unbuttoned, and her pants off and skirt pulled up for the finger; the boys' pants on and unzipped as they gasped, thick warmth on her hand, white faint thumping on the dashboard. She confessed her own finger too, and while petting was a vague word and kept her secrets, masturbation was stark and hid nothing, exposed her in the confessional like the woman in the photograph that Ruth had shown her: a Mexican woman of about thirty, sitting naked in an armchair, legs spread, hand on her mound, and her face caught forever in passion real or posed.

Then finally in high school it was Billy Campbell in the spring of her junior year, quick-coming Billy dropping the Trojan out of the car window, the last of her guilt dropping with it, so that after one more confession she knew she had kneeled and whispered to a priest for the last time. Young and hot and pretty, she could not imagine committing any sin that was not sexual. When she was thirty there was no one to tell that sometimes she could not bear knowing what she knew: that no one would help her, not ever again. That was the year she gained weight and changed sizes and did not replace her black dress, though she liked herself in black, liked her blonde hair touching it. She began selecting colors which in the store were merely colors; but when she thought of them on her body and bed, they seemed to hold possibilities: sheets and pillowcases of yellow and pink and pale blue, and all her underwear was pastel, so she could start each day by stepping into color. Many of those days she spent at the beach, body-surfing and swimming beyond the breakers and sleeping in the sun, or walking there in cool months. Once a bartender told her that waitresses and bartenders should have a month off every year and go to a cabin in the mountains and not smile once. Just to relax the facial muscles, he said; maybe they go, like pitchers' arms. Her days were short, for she slept late, and her evenings long; and most days she was relieved when it was time to go to work, to the costume-smile and chatter that some nights she brought home with a gentle man, and next day she had that warmth to remember as she lay on the beach.

She unbuttoned and unzipped her skirt, let it fall to the sand; pulled down her pants and stepped out of them. She took off the sweater and blouse and shivering dropped them, then reached around for the clasp of her brassiere. She walked across wet sand, into the rushing touch of sea. She walked through a breaking wave, sand moving under her feet, current pulling and pushing her farther out, and she walked with it and stood breast-deep, watching the surface coming from the lighter dome of the sky. A black swell rose toward her and curled, foam skimming its crest like quick smoke; she turned to the beach, watched the wave over her shoulder: breaking it took her with head down and outstretched arms pointing, eyes open to dark and fast white foam, then she scraped sand with breasts and feet, belly and thighs, and lay breathing salt-taste as water hissed away from her legs. She stood and crossed the beach, toward her clothes.

He was sleeping. In the dark she undressed and left her clothes on the floor and took a nightgown to the bathroom. She showered and washed her hair and when she went to the bedroom he said: 'Do you always get up when it's still night?'

'I couldn't sleep.'

She got into bed; he placed a hand on her leg and she shifted away and he did not touch her again.

'In three months I'll be thirty-nine.'

'Thirty-nine's not bad.'

'I was born in the afternoon. They didn't have any others.'

'What time is it?'

'Almost five.'

'It's going to be a long day.'

'Not for me. I'll sleep.'

'Night worker.'

'They were Catholics, but they probably used something anyway. Maybe I was a diaphragm baby. I feel like one a lot of the time.'

'What's that supposed to mean?'

'Like I sneaked into the movie and I'm waiting for the usher to come get me.'

'Tell him to shove off.'

'Not this usher.'

'You talking about dying?'

'No.'

'What then?'

'I don't know. But he's one shit of an usher.'

She believed she could not sleep until he left. But when she closed her eyes she felt it coming in her legs and arms and breath, and gratefully she yielded to it: near-dreaming, she saw herself standing naked in the dark waves. One struck her breast and she wheeled slow and graceful, salt water black in her eyes and lovely in her mouth, hair touching sand as she turned then rose and floated in swift tenderness out to sea.

PART THREE

DELIVERING

JIMMY WOKE BEFORE the alarm, his parents' sounds coming back to him as he had known they would when finally three hours ago he knew he was about to sleep: their last fight in the kitchen, and Chris sleeping through it on the top bunk, grinding his teeth. It was nearly five now, the room sunlit; in the dark while they fought Jimmy had waited for the sound of his father's slap, and when it came he felt like he was slapping her and he waited for it again, wished for it again, but there was only the one clap of hand on face. Soon after that, she drove away.

Now he was ashamed of the slap. He reached down to his morning hardness which always he had brought to the bathroom so she wouldn't see the stain; he stopped once to turn off the alarm when he remembered it was about to ring into his quick breath. Then he stood and gently shook Chris's shoulder. He could smell the ocean. He shook Chris harder: twelve years old and chubby and still clumsy about some things. Maybe somebody else was Chris's father. No. He would stay with what he heard last night; he would not start making up more. Somewhere his mother was naked with that son of a bitch, and he squeezed Chris's shoulder and said: 'Wake up.' Besides, their faces looked alike: his and Chris's and his father's. Everybody said that. Chris stared at him.

'Come with me.'

'You're crazy.'

'I need you to.'

'You didn't say anything last night.'

'Come on.'

'You buying the doughnuts?'

'After we swim.'

In the cool room they dressed for the warm sun, in cut-off jeans and T-shirts and sneakers, and went quietly down the hall, past the closed door where Jimmy stopped and waited until he could hear his father's breath. Last night after she left, his father cried in the kitchen. Chris stood in the doorway, looking into the kitchen; Jimmy looked over his head at the table, the beer cans, his father's bent and hers straight, the ashtray filled, ashes on the table and, on the counter near the sink, bent cans and a Seagram's Seven bottle.

'Holy shit,' Chris said.

'You'd sleep through World War III.'

He got two glasses from the cupboard, reaching over the cans and bottle, holding his breath against their smell; he looked at the two glasses in the sink, her lipstick on the rim of one, and Chris said: 'What's the matter?'

'Makes me sick to smell booze in the morning.'

Chris poured the orange juice and they drank with their backs to the table. Jimmy picked up her Winston pack. Empty. Shit. He took a Pall Mall. He had learned to smoke by watching her, had started three years ago by stealing hers. He was twelve then. Would he and Chris see her alone now, or would they have to go visit her at that son of a bitch's house, wherever it was? They went out the back door and around to the front porch where the stacked papers waited, folded and tied, sixty-two of them, and a note on top saying Mr. Thompson didn't get his paper yesterday. 'It's his Goddamn dog,' he said, and cut the string and gave Chris a handful of rubber bands. Chris rolled and banded the papers while Jimmy stood on the lawn, smoking; he looked up the road at the small houses, yellow and brown and grey, all of them quiet with sleeping families, and the tall woods beyond them and, across the road, houses whose back lawns ended at the salt marsh that spread out to the northeast where the breeze came from. When he heard the rolling papers stop, he turned to Chris sitting on the porch and looking at him.

'Where's the car?'

'Mom took it.'

'This early?'

He flicked the cigarette toward the road and kneeled on the porch and started rolling.

'Where'd she go so early?'

'Late. Let's go.'

He trotted around the lawn and pushed up the garage door and went around the pickup; he did not look at Chris until he had unlocked the chain and pulled it from around the post, coiled it under his bicycle seat, and locked it there. His hands were ink-stained.

'You can leave your chain. We'll use mine at the beach.'

He took the canvas sack from its nail on the post and hung it from his right side, its strap over his left shoulder, and walked his bicycle past the truck and out into the sun. At the front porch he stuffed the papers into the sack. Then he looked at Chris.

'We're not late,' Chris said.

'She left late. Late last night.' He pushed down his kick-stand. 'Hold on. Let's get these papers out.'

'She left?'

'Don't you start crying on me. Goddamnit, don't.'

Chris looked down at his handlebar.

'They had a fight,' Jimmy said.

'Then she'll be back.'

'Not this time. She's fucking somebody.'

Chris looked up, shaking his head. Shaking it, he said: 'No.'

'You want to hear about it or you just going to stand there and tell me I didn't hear what I heard.'

'Okay, tell me.'

'Shit. I was going to tell you at the beach. Wait, okay?'

'Sixty-two papers?'

'You know she's gone. Isn't that enough for a while?' He kicked up his stand. 'Look. We've hardly ever lived with both of them. It'll be like Pop's aboard ship. Only it'll be her.'

'That's not true.'

'What's not.'

'About hardly ever living with both of them.'

'It almost is. Let's go.'

Slowly across the grass, then onto the road, pumping hard, shifting gears, heading into the breeze and sun, listening for cars to their rear, sometimes looking over his shoulder at the road and Chris's face, the sack bumping his right thigh and sliding forward but he kept shoving it back, keeping the rhythm of his pedalling and his throws: the easy ones to the left, a smooth motion across his chest like second to first, snapping the paper hard and watching it drop on the lawn; except for the people who didn't always pay on time or who bitched at him, and he hit their porches or front doors, a good hard sound in the morning quiet. He liked throwing to his right better. The first week or so he had cheated, had angled his bicycle toward the houses and thrown overhand; but then he stopped that, and rode straight, leaning back and throwing to his right, sometimes having to stop and leave his bicycle and get a paper from under a bush or a parked car in the driveway, but soon he was hitting the grass just before the porch, unless it was a house that had a door or wall shot coming, and he could do that with velocity too. Second to short. He finished his road by scaring himself, hitting Reilly's big front window instead of the wall beside it, and it shook but didn't break and when he turned his bicycle and headed back he grinned at Chris, who still looked like someone had just punched him in the mouth.

He went left up a climbing road past a pine grove, out of its shade into the warmth on his face: a long road short on customers, twelve of them scattered, and he rode faster, thinking of Chris behind him, pink-cheeked, breathing hard. Ahead on the right he saw Thompson's collie waiting on the lawn, and he pulled out a paper and pushed the sack behind his leg, then rose from the seat pumping toward the house, sitting as he left the road and bounced on earth and grass: he threw the paper thumping against the open jaws, his front tire grazing the yelping dog as it scrambled away, and he lightly hand-braked for his turn then sped out to the road again. He threw two more to his left and started up a long steep hill for the last of the route: the road cut through woods, in shade now, stand-ing, the bicycle slowing as the hill steepened near the hardest house of all: the Claytons' at the top of the hill, a pale green house with a deep front lawn: riding on the shoulder, holding a paper against the handlebar, standing, his legs hot and tight, then at the top he sat to throw, the bicycle slowing, leaning, and with his left hand he moved the front wheel from side to side while he twisted to his right and cocked his arm and threw; he stood on the pedals and gained balance and speed before the paper landed sliding on the walk. The road wound past trees and fifteen customers and twice that many houses. He finished quickly. Then he got off his bicycle, sweating, and folded the sack and put it in his orange nylon saddlebag, and they started back, Chris riding beside him.

From one house near the road he smelled bacon. At another he saw a woman at the kitchen window, her head down, and he looked away. Some of the papers were inside now. At Clay-ton's house he let the hill take him down into the shade to flat land and, Chris behind him now, he rode past the wide green and brown salt marsh, its grass leaning with the breeze that was cool and sea-tanged on his face, moving the hair at his ears. There were no houses. A fruit and vegetable stand, then the bridge over the tidal stream: a quick blue flow, the tide com-ing in from the channel and cove beyond a bend to the north, so he could not see them, but he knew how the cove looked this early, with green and orange charter boats tied at the wharves. An hour from now, the people would come. He and Chris and his father went a few afternoons each summer, with sandwiches and soft drinks and beer in the ice chest, and his father drank steadily but only a six-pack the whole after-noon, and they stood abreast at the rail, always near the bow, the boat anchored a mile or two out, and on lucky days filled a plastic bag with mackerel slapping tails till they died, and on unlucky ones he still loved the gentle rocking of the boat and the blue sea and the sun warmly and slowly burning him. Twice in late summer they had bottom-fished and pulled up cusks from three hundred feet, tired arm turning the reel, cusk breaking the surface with eyes pushed outward and guts in its mouth. His mother had gone once. She had not complained, had pretended to like it, but next time she told them it was too much sun, too smelly, too long. Had she been with that son of a bitch when they went fishing again? The boats headed in at five and his father inserted a cleaning board into a slot in the gunwale and handed them slick cool mackerel and he and Chris cleaned them and threw their guts and heads to the sea gulls that hovered and cried and dived until the boat reached the wharf. Sometimes they could make a gull come down and take a head from their fingers.

They rode past beach cottages and up a one-block street to the long dune that hid the sea, chained their bicycles to a telephone pole, and sprinted over loose sand and up the dune; then walking, looking at the empty beach and sea and breakers, stopping to take off sneakers and shirts, Jimmy stuffing his three bills into a sneaker, then running onto wet hard sand, into the surf cold on his feet and ankles, Chris beside him, and they both shouted at once, at the cold but to the sea as well, and ran until the water pushed at their hips and they walked out toward the sea and low sun, his feet hurting in the cold. A wave came and they turned their backs to it and he watched over his shoulder as it rose; when it broke they dived and he was riding it fast, swallowing water, and in that instant of old sea-panic he saw his father crying; he opened his eyes to the sting, his arms stretched before him, hands joined, then he was lying on the sand and the wave was gone and he stood shouting: 'All *right*.' They ran back into the sea and body-surfed until they were too cold, then walked stiffly up to higher sand. He lay on his back beside his clothes, looked at the sky; soon people would come with blankets and ice chests. Chris lay beside him. He shut his eyes.

'I was listening to the ball game when they came home. With the ear plug. They won, three to two. Lee went all the way. Rice drove in two with a double—' Bright field and uniforms under the lights in Oakland, him there too while he lay on his bunk, watching Lee working fast, Remy going to his left and diving to knock it down, on his knees for the throw in time when they came in talking past the door and down the hall to the kitchen—'They talked low for a long time; that's when they were drinking whiskey and mostly I just heard Pop getting ice, then I don't know why but after a while I knew it was trouble, all that ice and quiet talk and when they popped cans I figured they'd finished the whiskey and they were still talking that way so I started listening. She had already told him. That's what they were talking about. Maybe she told him at the Chief's Club. She was talking nice to him—'

'What did she say?'

'She said—shit—' He opened his eyes to the blue sky, closed them again, pressed his legs into the warm sand, listened to the surf. 'She said I've tried to stop seeing him. She said Don't you believe I've tried? You think I want to hurt you? You know what it's like. I can't stop. I've tried and I can't. I wish I'd never met him. But I can't keep lying and sneaking around. And Pop said Bullshit: you mean you can't keep living here when you want to be fucking him. They didn't say anything for a minute and they popped two more cans, then she said You're right. But maybe I don't have to leave. Maybe if you'd just let me go to him when I wanted to. That's when he started yelling at her. They went at it for a long time, and I thought you'd wake up. I turned the game up loud as I could take it but it was already the ninth, then it was over, and I couldn't stop hearing them anyway. She said Jason would never say those things to her, that's all I know about that son of a bitch, his name is Jason and he's a civilian somewhere and she started yelling about all the times Pop was aboard ship he must have had a lot of women and who did he think he was anyway and she'd miss you and me and it broke her heart how much she'd miss you and me but she had to get out from under his shit, and he was yelling about she was probably fucking every day he was at sea for the whole twenty years and she said You'll never know you bastard you can just think about it for another twenty. That's when he slapped her.'

'Good.'

'Then she cried a little, not much, then they drank some more beer and talked quiet again. He was trying to make up to her, saying he was sorry he hit her and she said it was her fault, she shouldn't have said that, and she hadn't fucked anybody till Jason—'

'She said that?'

'What.'

'Fuck.'

'Yes. She was talking nice to him again, like he was a little kid, then she went to their room and packed a suitcase and he went to the front door with her, and I couldn't hear what they said. She went outside and he did too and after she drove off he came back to the kitchen and drank beer.' He raised his head and looked past his feet at a sea gull bobbing on the water beyond the breakers. 'Then he cried for a while. Then he went to bed.'

'He did?'

'Yes.'

'I've never heard him cry.'

'Me neither.'

'Why didn't you wake me up?'

'What for?'

'I don't know. I wish you had.'

'I did. This morning.'

'What's going to happen?'

'I guess she'll visit us or something.'

'What if they send Pop to sea again and we have to go live with her and that guy?'

'Don't be an asshole. He's retiring and he's going to buy that boat and we'll fish like bastards. I'm going to catch a big fucking tuna and sell it to the Japanese and buy you some weights.'

He squeezed Chris's bicep and rose, pulling him up. Chris turned his face, looking up the beach. Jimmy stepped in front of him, still holding his arm.

'Look: I heard Pop cry last night. For a long time. Loud. That's all the fucking crying I want to hear. Now let's take another wave and get some doughnuts.'

They ran into the surf, wading coldly to the wave that rose until there was no horizon, no sea, only the sky beyond it.

Dottie from tenth grade was working the counter, small and summer-brown.

'Wakefield boys are here,' Jimmy said. 'Six honey dip to go.'

He only knew her from math and talking in the halls, but the way she smiled at him, if it were any other morning, he would stay and talk, and any other day he would ask her to meet him in town tonight and go on some of the rides, squeeze her on the roller coaster, eat pizza and egg rolls at the stands, get somebody to buy them a six-pack, take it to the beach. He told her she was foxy, and got a Kool from her. Cars were on the roads now, but so many that they were slow and safe, and he and Chris rode side by side on the shoulder; Chris held the doughnut bag against the handlebar and ate while Jimmy smoked, then he reached over for the bag and ate his three. When they got near the house it looked quiet. They chained their bicycles in the garage and crept into the kitchen and past the closed door, to the bathroom. In the shower he pinched Chris's gut and said: 'No shit, we got to work on that.'

They put on gym shorts and sneakers and took their gloves and ball to the backyard.

'When we get warmed up I'm going to throw at your face, okay?'

'Okay.'

'You're still scared of it there and you're ducking and you'll get hurt that way.'

The new baseball smooth in his hand and bright in the sun, smacking in Chris's glove, coming back at him, squeezed high in the pocket and webbing; then he heard the back door and held the ball and watched his father walking out of the shade into the light. He squinted at his father's stocky body and sunburned face and arms, his rumpled hair, and motioned to Chris and heard him trotting on the grass. He was nearly as tall as his father, barely had to tilt his head to look into his eyes. He breathed the smell of last night's booze, this morning's sleep.

'I heard you guys last night,' he said. 'I already told him.'

His father's eyes shifted to Chris, then back.

'She'll come by tomorrow, take you boys to lunch.' He scratched his rump, looked over his shoulder at the house, then at Jimmy. 'Maybe later we'll go eat some lobsters. Have a talk.'

'We could cook them here,' Chris said.

'Sure. Steamers too. Okay: I'll be out in a minute.'

They watched him walk back to the house, then Jimmy touched Chris, gently pushed him, and he trotted across the lawn. They threw fly balls and grounders and one-hop throws from the outfield and straight ones to their bare chests, calling to each other, Jimmy listening to the quiet house too, seeing it darker in there, cooler, his father's closet where in a corner behind blue and khaki uniforms the shotgun leaned. He said, 'Here we go,' and threw at Chris's throat, then face, and heard the back door; his breath quickened, and he threw hard: the ball grazed the top of Chris's glove and struck his forehead and he bent over, his bare hand rubbing above his eye, then he was crying deeply and Jimmy turned to his running father, wearing his old glove, hair wet and combed, smelling of after-shave lotion, and said: 'He's all right, Pop. He's all right.'

THE WINTER FATHER

for Pat

THE JACKMAN'S MARRIAGE had been adulterous and violent, but in its last days, they became a couple again, as they might have if one of them were slowly dying. They wept together, looked into each other's eyes without guile, distrust, or hatred, and they planned Peter's time with the children. On his last night at home, he and Norma, tenderly, without a word, made love. Next evening, when he got home from Boston, they called David and Kathi in from the snow and brought them to the kitchen.

David was eight, slender, with light brown hair nearly to his shoulders, a face that was still pretty; he seemed always hungry, and Peter liked watching him eat. Kathi was six, had long red hair and a face that Peter had fallen in love with, a face that had once been pierced by glass the shape of a long dagger blade. In early spring a year ago: he still had not taken the storm windows off the screen doors; he was bringing his lunch to the patio, he did not know Kathi was following him, and holding his plate and mug he had pushed the door open with his shoulder, stepped outside, heard the crash and her scream, and turned to see her gripping then pulling the long shard from her cheek. She got it out before he reached her.

He picked her up and pressed his handkerchief to the wound, midway between her eye and throat, and held her as he phoned his doctor who said he would meet them at the hospital and do the stitching himself because it was cosmetic and that beautiful face should not be touched by residents. Norma was not at home. Kathi lay on the car seat beside him and he held his handkerchief on her cheek, and in the hospital he held her hands while she lay on the table. The doctor said it would only take about four stitches and it would be better without anesthetic, because sometimes that puffed the skin, and he wanted to fit the cut together perfectly, for the scar; he told this very gently to Kathi, and he said as she grew, the scar would move down her face and finally would be under her jaw. Then she and Peter squeezed each other's hands as the doctor stitched and she gritted her teeth and stared at pain.

She was like that when he and Norma told them. It was David who suddenly cried, begged them not to get a divorce, and then fled to his room and would not come out, would not help Peter load his car, and only emerged from the house as Peter was driving away: a small running shape in the dark, charging the car, picking up something and throwing it, missing, crying *You bum You bum You bum ...*

Drunk that night in his apartment whose rent he had paid and keys received yesterday morning before last night's grave lovemaking with Norma, he gained through the blur of bourbon an intense focus on his children's faces as he and Norma spoke: We fight too much, we've tried to live together but can't; you'll see, you'll be better off too, you'll be with Daddy for dinner on Wednesday nights, and on Saturdays and Sundays you'll do things with him. In his kitchen he watched their faces.

Next day he went to the radio station. After the news at noon he was on; often, as the records played, he imagined his children last night, while he and Norma were talking, and after he was gone. Perhaps she took them out to dinner, let them stay up late, flanking her on the couch in front of the television. When he talked he listened to his voice: it sounded as it did every weekday afternoon. At four he was finished. In the parking lot he felt as though, with stooped shoulders, he were limping. He started the forty-minute drive northward, for the first time in twelve years going home to empty rooms. When he reached the town where he lived he stopped at a small store and bought two lamb chops and a package of frozen peas. *I will take one thing at a time*, he told himself. Crossing the sidewalk to his car, in that short space, he felt the limp again, the stooped shoulders. He wondered if he looked like a man who had survived an accident which had killed others.

That was on a Thursday. When he woke Saturday morning, his first thought was a wish: that Norma would phone and tell him they were sick, and he should wait to see them Wednesday. He amended his wish, lay waiting for his own body to let him know it was sick, out for the weekend. In late morning he drove to their coastal town; he had moved fifteen miles inland. Already the snow-ploughed streets and country roads leading to their house felt like parts of his body: intestines, lung, heart-fiber lying from his door to theirs. When they were born he had smoked in the waiting room with the others. Now he was giving birth: stirruped, on his back, waves of pain. There would be no release, no cutting of the cord. Nor did he want it. He wanted to grow a cord.

Walking up their shovelled walk and ringing the doorbell, he felt at the same time like an inept salesman and a con man. He heard their voices, watched the door as though watching the sounds he heard, looking at the point where their faces would appear, but when the door opened he was looking at Norma's waist; then up to her face, lipsticked, her short brown hair soft from that morning's washing. For years she had not looked this way on a Saturday morning. Her eyes held him: the nest of pain was there, the shyness, the coiled anger; but there was another shimmer: she was taking a new marriage vow: This is the way we shall love our children now; watch how well I can do it. She smiled and said: 'Come in out of the cold and have a cup of coffee.'

In the living room he crouched to embrace the hesitant children. Only their faces were hesitant. In his arms they squeezed, pressed, kissed. David's hard arms absolved them both of Wednesday night. Through their hair Peter said pleasantly to Norma that he'd skip the coffee this time. Grabbing caps and unfurling coats, they left the house, holding hands to the car.

He showed them his apartment: they had never showered behind glass; they slid the doors back and forth. Sand washing down the drain, their flesh sunburned, a watermelon waiting in the refrigerator ...

'This summer—'

They turned from the glass, looked up at him.

'When we go to the beach. We can come back here and shower.'

Their faces reflected his bright promise, and they followed him to the kitchen; on the counter were two cans of kidney beans, Jalapeño peppers, seasonings. Norma kept her seasonings in small jars, and two years ago when David was six and came home bullied and afraid of next day at school, Peter asked him if the boy was bigger than he was, and when David said 'A lot,' and showed him the boy's height with one hand, his breadth with two, Peter took the glass stopper from the cinnamon jar, tied it in a handkerchief corner, and struck his palm with it, so David would know how hard it was, would believe in it. Next morning David took it with him. On the schoolground, when the bully shoved him, he swung it up from his back pocket and down on the boy's forehead. The boy cried and went away. After school David found him on the sidewalk and hit his jaw with the weapon he had sat on all day, chased him two blocks swinging at his head, and came home with delighted eyes, no damp traces of yesterday's shame and fright, and Peter's own pain and rage turned to pride, then caution, and he spoke gently, told David to carry it for a week or so more, but not to use it unless the bully attacked; told him we must control our pleasure in giving pain.

Now reaching into the refrigerator he felt the children behind him; then he knew it was not them he felt, for in the bathroom when he spoke to their faces he had also felt a presence to his rear, watching, listening. It was the walls, it was fatherhood, it was himself. He was not an early drinker but he wanted an ale now; looked at the brown bottles long enough to fear and dislike his reason for wanting one, then he poured two glasses of apple cider and, for himself, cider and club soda. He sat at the table and watched David slice a Jalapeño over the beans, and said: 'Don't ever touch one of those and take a leak without washing your hands first.'

'Why?'

'I did it once. Think about it.'

'Wow.'

They talked of flavors as Kathi, with her eyes just above rim-level of the pot, her wrists in the steam, poured honey, and shook paprika, basil, parsley, Worcestershire, wine vinegar. In a bowl they mixed ground meat with a raw egg: jammed their hands into it, fingers touching; scooped and squeezed meat and onion and celery between their fingers; the kitchen smelled of bay leaf in the simmering beans, and then of broiling meat. They talked about the food as they ate, pressing thick hamburgers to fit their mouths, and only then Peter heard the white silence coming at them like afternoon snow. They cleaned the counter and table and what they had used; and they spoke briefly, quietly, they smoothly passed things; and when Peter turned off the faucet, all sound stopped, the kitchen was multiplied by silence, the apartment's walls grew longer, the floors wider, the ceilings higher. Peter walked the distance to his bedroom, looked at his watch, then quickly turned to the morning paper's television listing, and called: 'Hey! *The Magnificent Seven*'s coming on.'

'All *right*,' David said, and they hurried down the short hall, light footsteps whose sounds he could name: Kathi's, David's, Kathi's. He lay between them, bellies down, on the bed.

'Is this our third time or fourth?' Kathi said.

'I think our fourth. We saw it in a theater once.'

'I could see it every week,' David said.

'Except when Charles Bronson dies,' Kathi said. 'But I like when the little kids put flowers on his grave. And when he spanks them.'

The winter sunlight beamed through the bedroom window, the afternoon moving past him and his children. Driving them home he imitated Yul Brynner, Eli Wallach, Charles Bronson; the children praised his voices, laughed, and in front of their house they kissed him and asked what they were going to do tomorrow. He said he didn't know yet; he would call in the morning, and he watched them go up the walk between snow as high as Kathi's waist. At the door they turned and waved; he tapped the horn twice, and drove away.

That night he could not sleep. He read *Macbeth*, woke propped against the pillows, the bedside lamp on, the small book at his side. He put it on the table, turned out the light, moved the pillows down, and slept. Next afternoon he took David and Kathi to a movie.

He did not bring them to his apartment again, unless they were on the way to another place, and their time in the apartment was purposeful and short: Saturday morning cartoons, then lunch before going to a movie or museum. Early in the week he began reading the movie section of the paper, looking for matinees. Every weekend they went to a movie, and sometimes two, in their towns and other small towns and in Boston. On the third Saturday he took them to a PG movie which was bloody and erotic enough to make him feel ashamed and irresponsible as he sat between his children in the theater. Driving home, he asked them about the movie until he believed it had not frightened them, or made them curious about bodies and urges they did not yet have. After that, he saw all PG movies before taking them, and he was angry at mothers who left their children at the theater and picked them up when the movie was over; and left him to listen to their children exclaiming at death, laughing at love; and often they roamed the aisles going to the concession stand, and distracted him from this weekly entertainment which he suspected he waited for and enjoyed more than David and Kathi. He had not been an indiscriminate moviegoer since he was a child. Now what had started as a duty was pleasurable, relaxing. He knew that beneath this lay a base of cowardice. But he told himself it would pass. A time would come when he and Kathi and David could sit in his living room, talking like three friends who had known each other for eight and six years.

Most of his listeners on weekday afternoons were women. Between love songs he began talking to them about movie ratings. He said not to trust them. He asked what they felt about violence and sex in movies, whether or not they were bad for children. He told them he didn't know; that many of the fairy tales and all the comic books of his boyhood were violent; and so were the westerns and serials on Saturday afternoons. But there was no blood. And he chided the women about letting their children go to the movies alone.

He got letters and read them in his apartment at night. Some thanked him for his advice about ratings. Many told him it was all right for him to talk, he wasn't with the kids every afternoon after school and all weekends and holidays and summer; the management of the theater was responsible for quiet and order during the movies; they were showing the movies to attract children and they were glad to take the money. The children came home happy and did not complain about other children being noisy. Maybe he should stop going to matinees, should leave his kids there and pick them up when it was over. *It's almost what I'm doing*, he thought; and he stopped talking about movies to the afternoon women.

He found a sledding hill: steep and long, and at its base a large frozen pond. David and Kathi went with him to buy his sled, and with a thermos of hot chocolate they drove to the hill near his apartment. Parked cars lined the road, and children and some parents were on the hill's broad top. Red-faced children climbed back, pulling their sleds with ropes. Peter sledded first; he knew the ice on the pond was safe, but he was beginning to handle fatherhood as he did guns: always as if they were loaded, when he knew they were not. There was a satisfaction in preventing even dangers which did not exist.

The snow was hard and slick, rushed beneath him; he went over a bump, rose from the sled, nearly lost it, slammed down on it, legs outstretched, gloved hands steering around the next bump but not the next one suddenly rising toward his face, and he pressed against the sled, hugged the woodshock to his chest, yelled with delight at children moving slowly upward, hit the edge of the pond and sledded straight out, looking at the evergreens on its far bank. The sled stopped near the middle of the pond; he stood and waved to the top of the hill, squinting at sun and bright snow, then two silhouettes waved back and he saw Kathi's long red hair. Holding the sled's rope he walked on ice, moving to his left as David started down and Kathi stood waiting, leaning on her sled. He told himself he was a fool: had lived winters with his children, yet this was the first sled he had bought for himself; sometimes he had gone with them because they asked him to, and he had used their sleds. But he had never found a sledding hill. He had driven past them, seen the small figures on their crests and slopes, but no more. Watching David swerve around a bump and Kathi, at the top, pushing her sled, then dropping onto it, he forgave himself; there was still time; already it had begun.

But on that first afternoon of sledding he made a mistake: within an hour his feet were painfully cold, his trousers wet and his legs cold; David and Kathi wore snow pants. Beneath his parka he was sweating. Then he knew they felt the same, yet they would sled as long as he did, because of the point and edges of divorce that pierced and cut all their time together.

'I'm freezing,' he said. 'I can't move my toes.'

'Me too,' David said.

'Let's go down one more time,' Kathi said.

Then he took them home. It was only three o'clock.

After that he took them sledding on weekend mornings. They brought clothes with them, and after sledding they went to his apartment and showered. They loved the glass doors. On the first day they argued about who would shower first, until Peter flipped a coin and David won and Peter said Kathi would have the first shower next time and they would take turns that way. They showered long and when Peter's turn came the water was barely warm and he was quickly in and out. Then in dry clothes they ate lunch and went to a movie.

Or to another place, and one night drinking bourbon in his living room, lights off so he could watch the snow falling, the yellowed, gentle swirl at the corner streetlight, the quick flakes at his window, banking on the sill, and across the street the grey-white motion lowering the sky and making the evergreens look distant, he thought of owning a huge building to save divorced fathers. Free admission. A place of swimming pool, badminton and tennis courts, movie theaters, restaurants, soda fountains, batting cages, a zoo, an art gallery, a circus, aquarium, science museum, hundreds of restrooms, two always in sight, everything in the tender charge of women trained in first aid and Montessori, no uniforms, their only style warmth and cheer. A father could spend entire days there, weekend after weekend, so in winter there would not be all this planning and driving. He had made his cowardice urbane, mobile, and sophisticated; but perhaps at its essence cowardice knows it is apparent: he believed David and Kathi knew that their afternoons at the aquarium, the Museum of Fine Arts, the Science Museum, were houses Peter had built, where they could be together as they were before, with one difference: there was always entertainment.

Frenetic as they were, he preferred weekends to the Wednesday nights when they ate together. At first he thought it was shyness. Yet they talked easily, often about their work, theirs at school, his as a disc jockey. When he was not with the children he spent much time thinking about what they said to each other. And he saw that, in his eight years as a father, he had been attentive, respectful, amusing; he had taught and disciplined. But no: not now: when they were too loud in the car or they fought, he held onto his anger, his heart buffeted with it, and spoke calmly, as though to another man's children, for he was afraid that if he scolded as he had before, the day would be spoiled, they would not have the evening at home, the sleeping in the same house, to heal them; and they might not want to go with him next day or two nights from now or two days. During their eight and six years with him, he had shown them love, and made them laugh. But now he knew that he had remained a secret from them. What did they know about him? What did he know about them?

He would tell them about his loneliness, and what he had learned about himself. When he wasn't with them, he was lonely all the time, except while he was running or working, and sometimes at the station he felt it waiting for him in the parking lot, on the highway, in his apartment. He thought much about it, like an athletic man considering a sprained ligament, changing his exercises to include it. He separated his days into parts, thought about each one, and learned that all of them were not bad. When the alarm woke him in the winter dark, the new day and waiting night were the grey of the room, and they pressed down on him, fetid repetitions bent on smothering his spirit before he rose from the bed. But he got up quickly, made the bed while the sheets still held his warmth, and once in the kitchen with coffee and newspaper he moved into the first part of the day: bacon smell and solemn disc jockeys with classical music, an hour or more at the kitchen table, as near-peaceful as he dared hope for; and was grateful for too, as it went with him to the living room, to the chair at the southeast window where, pausing to watch traffic and look at the snow and winter branches of elms and maples in the park across the street, he sat in sun-warmth and entered the cadence of Shakespeare. In midmorning, he Vaselined his face and genitals and, wearing layers of nylon, he ran two and a half miles down the road which, at his corner, was a town road of close houses but soon was climbing and dropping past farms and meadows; at the crest of a hill, where he could see the curves of trees on the banks of the Merrimack, he turned and ran back.

The second part began with ignition and seat belt, driving forty minutes on the highway, no buildings or billboards, low icicled cliffs and long white hills, and fields and woods in the angled winter sun, and in the silent car he received his afternoon self: heard the music he had chosen, popular music he would not listen to at home but had come to accept and barely listen to at work, heard his voice in mime and jest and remark, often merry, sometimes showing off and knowing it, but not much, no more than he had earned. That part of his day behind glass and microphone, with its comfort drawn from combining the familiar with the spontaneous, took him to four o'clock.

The next four hours, he learned, were not only the time he had to prepare for, but also the lair of his loneliness, the source of every quick chill of loss, each sudden whisper of dread and futility: for if he could spend them with a woman he loved, drink and cook and eat with her while day changed to night (though now, in winter, night came as he drove home), he and this woman huddled in the light and warmth of living room and kitchen, gin and meat, then his days until four and nights after eight would demand less from him of will, give more to him of hopeful direction. After dinner he listened to jazz and read fiction or watched an old movie on television until, without lust or even the need of a sleeping woman beside him, he went to bed: a blessing, but a disturbing one. He had assumed, as a husband and then an adulterous one, that his need for a woman was as carnal as it was spiritual. But now celibacy was easy; when he imagined a woman, she was drinking with him, eating dinner. So his most intense and perhaps his only need for a woman was then; and all the reasons for the end of his marriage became distant, blurred, and he wondered if the only reason he was alone now was a misogyny he had never recognized: that he did not even want a woman except at the day's end, and had borne all the other hours of woman-presence only to have her comfort as the clock's hands moved through their worst angles of the day.

Planning to tell all this to David and Kathi, knowing he would need gin to do it, he was frightened, already shy as if they sat with him now in the living room. A good sign: if he were afraid, then it took courage; if it took courage, then it must be right. He drank more bourbon than he thought he did, and went to bed excited by intimacy and love.

He slept off everything. In the morning he woke so amused at himself that, if he had not been alone, he would have laughed aloud. He imagined telling his children, over egg rolls and martinis and Shirley Temples, about his loneliness and his rituals to combat it. And *that* would be his new fatherhood, smelling of duck sauce and hot mustard and gin. Swallowing aspirins and orange juice, he saw clearly why he and the children were uncomfortable together, especially at Wednesday night dinners: when he lived with them, their talk had usually dealt with the immediate (I don't like playing with Cindy anymore; she's too bossy. I wish it would snow; it's no use being cold if it doesn't snow); they spoke at dinner and breakfast and, during holidays and summer, at lunch; in the car and stores while running errands; on the summer lawn while he prepared charcoal; and in their beds when he went to tell them goodnight; most of the time their talk was deep only because it was affectionate and tribal, sounds made between creatures sharing the same blood. Now their talk was the same, but it did not feel the same. They talked in his car and in places he took them, and the car and each place would not let them forget they were there because of divorce.

So their talk had felt evasive, fragile, contrived, and his drunken answer last night had been more talk: courageous, painful, honest. *My God*, he thought, as in a light snow that morning he ran out of his hangover, into lucidity. *I was going to have a Goddamn therapy session with my own children.* Breathing the smell of new snow and winter air he thought of this fool Peter Jackman, swallowing his bite of pork fried rice, and saying: And what do you feel at school? About the divorce, I mean. Are you ashamed around the other kids? He thought of the useless reopening and sometimes celebrating of wounds he and Norma had done with the marriage counselor, a pleasant and smart woman, but what could she do when all she had to work with was wounds? After each session he and Norma had driven home, usually mute, always in despair. Then, running faster, he imagined a house where he lived and the children came on Friday nights and stayed all weekend, played with their friends during the day, came and left the house as they needed, for food, drink, bathroom, diversion, and at night they relaxed together as a family; saw himself reading as they painted and drew at the kitchen table ...

That night they ate dinner at a seafood restaurant thirty minutes from their town. When he drove them home he stayed outside their house for a while, the three of them sitting in front for warmth; they talked about summer and no school and no heavy clothes and no getting up early when it was still dark outside. He told them it was his favorite season too because of baseball and the sea. Next morning when he got into his car, the inside of his windshield was iced. He used the small plastic scraper from his glove compartment. As he scraped the middle and right side, he realized the grey ice curling and falling from the glass was the frozen breath of his children.

At a bar in the town where his children lived, he met a woman. This was on a Saturday night, after he had taken them home from the Museum of Fine Arts. They had liked Monet and Cézanne, had shown him light and color they thought were pretty. He told them Cézanne's *The Turn in the Road* was his favorite, that every time he came here he stood looking at it and he wanted to be walking up that road, toward the houses. But all afternoon he had known they were restless. They had not sledded that morning. Peter had gone out drinking the night before, with his only married friend who could leave his wife at home without paying even a subtle price, and he had slept through the time for sledding, had apologized when they phoned and woke him, and on the drive to the museum had told them he and Sibley (whom they knew as a friend of their mother too) had been having fun and had lost track of time until the bar closed. So perhaps they wanted to be outdoors. Or perhaps it was the old resonance of place again, the walls and ceiling of the museum, even the paintings telling them: You are here because your father left home.

He went to the bar for a sandwich, and stayed. Years ago he had come here often, on the way home from work, or at night with Norma. It was a neighborhood bar then, where professional fishermen and lobstermen and other men who worked with their hands drank, and sometimes brought their wives. Then someone from Boston bought it, put photographs and drawings of fishing and pleasure boats on the walls, built a kitchen which turned out quiche and crêpes, hired young women to tend the bar, and musicians to play folk and bluegrass. The old customers left. The new ones were couples and people trying to be a couple for at least the night, and that is why Peter stayed after eating his sandwich.

Within an hour she came in and sat at the bar, one empty chair away from him: a woman in her late twenties, dark eyes and light brown hair. Soon they were talking. He liked her because she smiled a lot. He also liked her drink: Jack Daniel's on the rocks. Her name was Mary Ann; her last name kept eluding him. She was a market researcher, and like many people Peter knew, she seemed to dismiss her work, though she was apparently good at it; her vocation was recreation: she skied down and across; backpacked; skated; camped; ran and swam. He began to imagine doing things with her, and he felt more insidious than if he were imagining passion: he saw her leading him and Kathi and David up a mountain trail. He told her he spent much of his life prone or sitting, except for a daily five-mile run, a habit from the Marine Corps (she gave him the sneer and he said: Come on, that was a long time ago, it was peacetime, it was fun), and he ran now for the same reasons everyone else did, or at least everyone he knew who ran: the catharsis, which kept his body feeling good, and his mind more or less sane. He said he had not slept in a tent since the Marines; probably because of the Marines. He said he wished he did as many things as she did, and he told her why. Some time in his bed during the night, she said: 'They probably did like the paintings. At least you're not taking them to all those movies now.'

'We still go about once a week.'

'Did you know Lennie's has free matinees for children? On Sunday afternoons?'

'No.'

'I have a divorced friend; she takes her kids almost every Sunday.'

'Why don't we go tomorrow?'

'With your kids?'

'If you don't mind.'

'Sure. I like kids. I'd like to have one of my own, without a husband.'

As he kissed her belly he imagined her helping him pitch the large tent he would buy, the four of them on a weekend of cold brook and trees on a mountainside, a fire, bacon in the skillet . . .

In the morning he scrambled their eggs, then phoned Norma. He had a general dislike of telephones: talking to his own hand gripping plastic, pacing, looking about the room; the timing of hanging up was tricky. Nearly all these conversations left him feeling as disconnected as the phone itself. But talking with Norma was different: he marvelled at how easy it was. The distance and disembodiment he felt on the phone with others were good here. He and Norma had hurt each other deeply, and their bodies had absorbed the pain: it was the stomach that tightened, the hands that shook, the breast that swelled then shrivelled. Now fleshless they could talk by phone, even with warmth, perhaps alive from the time when their bodies were at ease together. He thought of hav-

ing a huge house where he could live with his family, seeing
Norma only at meals, shared for the children, he and Norma
talking to David and Kathi; their own talk would be on extension phones in their separate wings: they would discuss the
children, and details of running the house. This was of course
the way they had finally lived, without the separate wings,
the phones. And one of their justifications as they talked of
divorce was that the children would be harmed, growing up
in a house with parents who did not love each other, who
rarely touched, and then by accident. There had been
moments near the end when, brushing against each other in
the kitchen, one of them would say: Sorry. Now as Mary Ann
Brighi (he had waked knowing her last name) spread jam on
toast, he phoned.

'I met this woman last night.'

Mary Ann smiled; Norma's voice did.

'It's about time. I was worried about your arm going.'

'What about you?'

'I'm doing all right.'

'Do you bring them home?'

'It's not them, and I get a sitter.'

'But he comes to the house? To take you out?'

'Peter?'

'What.'

'What are we talking about?'

'I was wondering what the kids would think if Mary Ann
came along this afternoon.'

'What they'll think is Mary Ann's coming along this
afternoon.'

'You're sure that's all?'

'Unless you fuck in front of them.'

He turned his face from Mary Ann, but she had already
seen his blush; he looked at her smiling with toast crumbs on
her teeth. He wished he were married and lovemaking were
simple. But after cleaning the kitchen he felt passion again,
though not much; in his mind he was introducing the children
to Mary Ann. He would make sure he talked to them, did not

leave them out while he talked to her. He was making love while he thought this; he hoped they would like her; again he saw them hiking up a trail through pines, stopping for Kathi and David to rest; a sudden bounding deer; the camp beside the stream; he thanked his member for doing its work down there while the rest of him was in the mountains in New Hampshire.

As he walked with David and Kathi he held their hands; they were looking at her face watching them from the car window.

'She's a new friend of mine,' he said. 'Just a friend. She wants to show us this night club where children can go on Sunday afternoons.'

From the back seat they shook hands, peered at her, glanced at Peter, their eyes making him feel that like adults they could sense when people were lovers; he adjusted the rearview mirror, watched their faces, decided he was seeing jumbled and vulnerable curiosity: Who was she? Would she marry their father? Would they like her? Would their mother be sad? And the night club confused them.

'Isn't that where people go drink?' Kathi said.

'It's afternoon too,' David said.

Not for Peter; the sky was grey, the time was grey, dark was coming, and all at once he felt utterly without will; all the strength he had drawn on to be with his children left him like one long spurt of arterial blood: all his time with his children was grey, with night coming; it would always be; nothing would change: like three people cursed in an old myth they would forever be thirty-three and eight and six, in this car on slick or salted roads, going from one place to another. He disapproved of but understood those divorced fathers who fled to live in a different pain far away. Beneath his despair, he saw himself and his children sledding under a lovely blue sky, heard them laughing in movies, watching in awe like love a circling blue shark in the aquarium's tank; but these seemed beyond recapture.

He entered the highway going south, and that quick transition of hands and head and eyes as he moved into fast traffic snapped him out of himself, into the sound of Mary Ann's voice: with none of the rising and falling rhythm of nursery talk, she was telling them, as if speaking to a young man and woman she had just met, about Lennie's. How Lennie believed children should hear good music, not just the stuff on the radio. She talked about jazz. She hummed some phrases of 'Somewhere Over the Rainbow,' then improvised. They would hear Gerry Mulligan today, she said, and as she talked about the different saxophones, Peter looked in the mirror at their listening faces.

'And Lennie has a cook from Tijuana in Mexico,' Mary Ann said. 'She makes the best chili around.'

Walking into Lennie's with a pretty woman and his two healthy and pretty children, he did not feel like a divorced father looking for something to do; always in other places he was certain he looked that way, and often he felt guilty when talking with waitresses. He paid the cover charge for himself and Mary Ann and she said: All right, but I buy the first two rounds, and he led her and the children to a table near the bandstand. He placed the children between him and Mary Ann. Bourbon, Cokes, bowls of chili. The room was filling and Peter saw that at most tables there were children with parents, usually one parent, usually a father. He watched his children listening to Mulligan. His fingers tapped the table with the drummer. He looked warmly at Mary Ann's profile until she turned and smiled at him.

Often Mulligan talked to the children, explained how his saxophone worked; his voice was cheerful, joking, never serious, as he talked about the guitar and bass and piano and drums. He clowned laughter from the children in the dark. Kathi and David turned to each other and Peter to share their laughter. During the music they listened intently. Their hands tapped the table. They grinned at Peter and Mary Ann. At intermission Mulligan said he wanted to meet the children. While his group went to the dressing room he sat on the edge

of the bandstand and waved the children forward. Kathi and
David talked about going. Each would go if the other would.
They took napkins for autographs and, holding hands, walked
between tables and joined the children standing around Mulligan. When it was their turn he talked to them, signed their
napkins, kissed their foreheads. They hurried back to Peter.

'He's *neat*,' Kathi said.

'What did you talk about?'

'He asked our names,' David said.

'And if we liked winter out here.'

'And if we played an instrument.'

'What kind of music we liked.'

'What did you tell him?'

'Jazz like his.'

The second set ended at nearly seven; bourbon-high,
Peter drove carefully, listening to Mary Ann and the children
talking about Mulligan and his music and warmth. Then
David and Kathi were gone, running up the sidewalk to tell
Norma, and show their autographed napkins, and Peter fol-
lowed Mary Ann's directions to her apartment.

'I've been in the same clothes since last night,' she said.

In her apartment, as unkempt as his, they showered
together, hurried damp-haired and chilled to her bed.

'This is the happiest day I've had since the marriage
ended,' he said.

But when he went home and was alone in his bed, he saw
his cowardice again. All the warmth of his day left him, and
he lay in the dark, knowing that he should have been wily
enough to understand that the afternoon's sweetness and
ease meant he had escaped: had put together a family for the
day. That afternoon Kathi had spilled a Coke; before Peter
noticed, Mary Ann was cleaning the table with cocktail napkins, smiling at Kathi, talking to her under the music, lifting a
hand to the waitress.

Next night he took Mary Ann to dinner and, driving to
her apartment, it seemed to him that since the end of his marriage, dinner had become disproportionate: alone at home it

was a task he forced himself to do, with his children it was a fragile rite, and with old friends who alternately fed him and Norma he felt vaguely criminal. Now he must once again face his failures over a plate of food. He and Mary Ann had slept little the past two nights, and at the restaurant she told him she had worked hard all day, yet she looked fresh and strong, while he was too tired to imagine making love after dinner. With his second martini, he said: 'I used you yesterday. With my kids.'

'There's a better word.'

'All right: needed.'

'I knew that.'

'You did?'

'We had fun.'

'I can't do it anymore.'

'Don't be so hard on yourself. You probably spend more time with them now than when you lived together.'

'I do. So does Norma. But that's not it. It's how much I wanted your help, and started hoping for it. Next Sunday. And in summer: the sort of stuff you do, camping and hiking; when we talked about it Saturday night—'

'I knew that too. I thought it was sweet.'

He leaned back in his chair, sipped his drink. Tonight he would break his martini rule, have a third before dinner. He loved women who knew and forgave his motives before he knew and confessed them.

But he would not take her with the children again. He was with her often; she wanted a lover, she said, not love, not what it still did to men and women. He did not tell her he thought they were using each other in a way that might have been cynical, if it were not so frightening. He simply followed her, became one of those who make love with their friends. But she was his only woman friend, and he did not know how many men shared her. When she told him she would not be home this night or that weekend, he held his questions. He held onto his heart too, and forced himself to make her a part of the times when he was alone. He had married young, and life to him was surrounded by the sounds and touches of a family. Now in this foreign land he felt so vulnerably strange that at times it seemed near madness as he gave Mary Ann a function in his time, ranking somewhere among his running and his work.

When the children asked about her, he said they were still friends. Once Kathi asked why she never came to Lennie's anymore, and he said her work kept her pretty busy and she had other friends she did things with, and he liked being alone with them anyway. But then he was afraid the children thought she had not liked them; so, twice a month, he brought Mary Ann to Lennie's.

He and the children went every Sunday. And that was how the cold months passed, beginning with the New Year, because Peter and Norma had waited until after Christmas to end the marriage: the movies and sledding, museums and aquarium, the restaurants; always they were on the road, and whenever he looked at his car he thought of the children. How many conversations while looking through the windshield? How many times had the doors slammed shut and they re-entered or left his life? Winter ended slowly. April was cold and in May Peter and the children still wore sweaters or windbreakers, and on two weekends there was rain, and everything they did together was indoors. But when the month ended, Peter thought it was not the weather but the patterns of winter that had kept them driving from place to place.

Then it was June and they were out of school and Peter took his vacation. Norma worked, and by nine in the morning he and Kathi and David were driving to the sea. They took a large blanket and tucked its corners into the sand so it wouldn't flap in the wind, and they lay oiled in the sun. On the first day they talked of winter, how they could feel the sun warming their ribs, as they had watched it warming the earth during the long thaw. It was a beach with gentle currents and a gradual slope out to sea but Peter told them, as he had every summer, about undertow: that if ever they were caught in one, they must not swim against it; they must let it take them out and then they must swim parallel to the beach until the current shifted and they could swim back in with it. He could not imagine his children being calm enough to do that, for he was afraid of water and only enjoyed body-surfing near the beach, but he told them anyway. Then he said it would not happen because he would always test the current first.

In those first two weeks the three of them ran into the water and body-surfed only a few minutes, for it was too cold still, and they had to leave it until their flesh was warm again. They would not be able to stay in long until July. Peter showed them the different colors of summer, told them why on humid days the sky and ocean were paler blue, and on dry days they were darker, more beautiful, and the trees they passed on the roads to the beach were brighter green. He bought a whiffle ball and bat and kept them in the trunk of his car and they played at the beach. The children dug holes, made castles, Peter watched, slept, and in late morning he ran. From a large thermos they drank lemonade or juice; and they ate lunch all day, the children grazing on fruit and the sandwiches he had made before his breakfast. Then he took them to his apartment for showers, and they helped carry in the ice chest and thermos and blanket and their knapsack of clothes. Kathi and David still took turns showering first, and they stayed in longer, but now in summer the water was still hot when his turn came. Then he drove them home to Norma, his skin red and pleasantly burning; then tan.

When his vacation ended they spent all sunny weekends at the sea, and even grey days that were warm. The children became braver about the cold, and forced him to go in with them and body-surf. But they could stay longer than he could, and he left to lie on the blanket and watch them, to make sure they stayed in shallow water. He made them promise to wait on the beach while he ran. He went in the water to cool his body from the sun, but mostly he lay on the blanket, reading, and watching the children wading out to the breakers and riding them in. Kathi and David did not always stay together. One left to walk the beach alone. Another played with strangers, or children who were there most days too. One built a castle. Another body-surfed. And, often, one would come to the blanket and drink and take a sandwich from the ice chest, would sit eating and drinking beside Peter, offer him a bite, a swallow. And on all those beach days Peter's shyness and apprehension were gone. It's the sea, he said to Mary Ann one night.

And it was: for on that day, a long Saturday at the beach, when he had all day felt peace and father-love and sun and salt water, he had understood why now in summer he and his children were as he had yearned for them to be in winter: they were no longer confined to car or buildings to remind them why they were there. The long beach and the sea were their lawn; the blanket their home; the ice chest and thermos their kitchen. They lived as a family again. While he ran and David dug in the sand until he reached water and Kathi looked for pretty shells for her room, the blanket waited for them. It was the place they wandered back to: for food, for drink, for rest, their talk as casual as between children and father arriving, through separate doors, at the kitchen sink for water, the refrigerator for an orange. Then one left for the surf; another slept in the sun, lips stained with grape juice. He had wanted to tell the children about it, but it was too much to tell, and the beach was no place for such talk anyway, and he also guessed they knew. So that afternoon when they were all lying on the blanket, on their backs, the children flanking him, he simply said: 'Divorced kids go to the beach more than married ones.'

'Why?' Kathi said.

'Because married people do chores and errands on weekends. No kid-days.'

'I love the beach,' David said.

'So do I,' Peter said.

He looked at Kathi.

'You don't like it, huh?'

She took her arm from her eyes and looked at him. His urge was to turn away. She looked at him for a long time; her eyes were too tender, too wise, and he wished she could have learned both later, and differently; in her eyes he saw the car in winter, heard its doors closing and closing, their talk and the sounds of heater and engine and tires on the road, and the places the car took them. Then she held his hand, and closed her eyes.

'I wish it was summer all year round,' she said.

He watched her face, rosy tan now, lightly freckled; her small scar was already lower. Holding her hand, he reached over for David's, and closed his eyes against the sun. His legs touched theirs. After a while he heard them sleeping. Then he slept.

FINDING A GIRL IN AMERICA

Sorrow is one of the vibrations that prove the fact of living.
ANTOINE DE SAINT EXUPÉRY
Wind, Sand and Stars

for Suzanne and Nicole

On AN OCTOBER NIGHT, lying in bed with a nineteen-year-old girl and tequila and grapefruit juice, thirty-five-year-old Hank Allison gets the story. They lie naked, under the sheet and one light blanket, their shoulders propped by pillows so they can drink. Lori's body is long; Hank is not a tall man, and she is perhaps a half inch taller; when she wears high-heeled boots and lowers her face to kiss him, he tells her she is like a swan bending to eat. Knowing he is foolish, he still wishes she were shorter; he has joked with Jack Linhart about this, and once Jack told him: *Hell with it: just stick out that big chest of yours and swagger down the road with that pretty girl.* Hank never wishes he were taller.

Tonight they have gone to Boston for a movie and dinner, and at the Casa Romero, their favorite restaurant, they started with margaritas but as they ate appetizers of Jalapeño and grilled cheese on tortillas, of baked cheese and sausage, they became cheerful about the movie and food and what they would order next, and switched to shots of tequila chased with Superior. They ate a lot and left the restaurant high though not drunk; then Hank bought a six-pack of San Miguel for the forty-five minute drive home, enough for one cassette of Willie Nelson and part of one by Kristofferson, Hank doing most of the talking, while a sober part of himself told him not to, reminded him that he must always control his talking with Lori; for he loves her and he knows that with him, as with everyone else, she feels and thinks much that she cannot say. He guesses her mother has something to do with this, a talk-crackling woman who keeps her husband and three daughters generally quiet, who is good-looking and knows it and works at it, and is a flirt and, Hank believes from the bare evidence Lori so often murmurs in his bed, more than that. But he does not work hard at discovering why it is so difficult for Lori to give the world, even him, her heart in words. He believes some mysterious balance of power exists between lovers, and if he ever fully understands the bonds that tie her tongue, and if he tells her about them, tries to help her cut them, he will no longer be her lover. He settles for the virtues he sees in her, and waits for her to see them herself. Often she talks of her childhood; she cannot remember her father ever kissing or hugging her; she loves him, and she knows he loves her too. He just does not touch.

Until they got back to his apartment and took salty dogs to bed, Hank believed they would make love. He thought of her long body under him. But, his heart ready, his member was dull, numb, its small capacity for drink long passed. So Hank parted her legs and lowered his face: when she came he felt he had too: the best way to share a woman's orgasm, the only way to use all his senses: looking over the mound at her face between breasts, touching with hands and tongue, the lovely taste and smell, and he heard not only her moan-breaths but his tongue on her, and her hands' soft timpani against his face.

Now he lies peacefully against the pillows; the drinks on his desk beside the bed are still half-full, and he hands one to Lori. Sometimes he takes a drag from her cigarette, though he remembers this is the way to undo his quitting nine years ago when he faced how long it took him to write, and how long he would have to live to write the ten novels he had set as his goal. He is nearly finished the second draft of his third. Lori is talking about Monica. Something in her voice alerts him. She and Lori were friends. Perhaps he is going to learn something new; perhaps Monica was unfaithful while she was still here, when she was his student and they were furtive lovers, as he and Lori are now. He catches a small alcoholic slip Lori makes: No, I can't, she says, in the midst of a sentence which seems to need no restraint.

'You can't what?'

'Nothing.'

'Tell me.'

'I promised Monica I wouldn't.'

'When I tell a friend a secret, I know he'll tell his wife or woman. That's the way it is.'

'It'll hurt you.'

'How can anything about Monica hurt me? I haven't seen her in over a year.'

'It will.'

'It can't. Not now.'

'You remember when she came down that weekend? Last October? You cooked dinner for the three of us.'

'Shrimp scampi. We got drunk on hot sake.'

'Before dinner she and I went to the liquor store. She kept talking about this guy she'd met in art class.'

'Tommy.'

'She didn't say it. But I knew she was screwing him then. I could tell she wanted me to know. It was her eyes. The way she'd smile. And I got pissed at her but I didn't say anything. I loved her and I'd never had a friend who had two lovers at once and I thought she was a bitch. I was starting to love you too, and I hated knowing she was going to hurt you, and I couldn't see why she even came to spend the weekend with you.'

'So she was screwing him before she told me it was over. Well, I should have known. She talked about him enough: his drawings anyway.'

'That wasn't it. She was pregnant. She found out after she broke up with you.' He has never heard Lori's voice so plaintive except when she speaks of her parents. 'You know how Monica is. She went hysterical; she phoned me at school every night, she phoned her parents, she went to three doctors. Two in Maine and one in New York. They all placed it at the same time: it was yours. By that time she was two months pregnant. Her father took her in and they had it done.'

An image comes to Hank: he sees his daughter, Sharon, thirteen, breast-points under her sweater: she is standing in his kitchen, hair dark and long; she is chopping celery at the counter for their weekly meal. He pulls Lori's cheek to his chest and strokes her hair.

'I'm all right,' he says. 'I had to know. I know if I didn't know I'd never know I didn't know; but I hate not knowing. I don't want to die not knowing everything about my life. You had to tell me. Who else would? You know I have to know. I'm all right. Shit. Shit that bitch. I could have—it would have been born in spring—I would have had all summer off—I could have taken it. I can raise a kid—I'm no Goddamn—I have to piss—'

He leaves the bed so quickly that he feels, barely, her head drop as his chest jerks from beneath it. He hurries down the hall, stands pissing, then as suddenly and uncontrollably as vomiting he is crying; and as with vomiting he has no self, he is only the helpless and weak host of these sounds and jerks and tears, and he places both palms on the wall in front of him, standing, moaning; the tears stop, his chest heaves, he groans, then tears come again as from some place so deep inside him that it has never been touched, even by pain. Lori stands naked beside him. She is trying to pull his arm from its push against the wall; she is trying to hold him and is crying

too and saying something but he can only hear her comforting tone like wind-sough in trees that grew in a peaceful place
he left long ago. Finally he turns to her, he will let her hold
him and do what she needs to do; yet when he faces her tall
firm body, still in October her summer tan lingering above
and between breasts and loins, he swings his fists, pulling
short each punch, pulling them enough so she does not even
back away, nor lift an arm to protect herself; left right left
right, short hooked blows at her womb and he hears himself
saying No no no—He does not know whether he is yelling or
mumbling. He only knows he is sounds and tears and
death-sorrow and strong quick arms striking the air in front
of Lori's womb.

Then it stops; his arms go to her shoulders, he sags, and
she turns him and walks him back down the hall, her left arm
around his waist, her right hand holding his arm around her
shoulders. He lies in bed and she asks if he wants a drink; he
says he'd better not. She gets into bed, and holds his face to
her breast.

'Seven months,' he says. 'That's all she had to give it. Then
I could have taken it. You think I couldn't do that?'

'I know you could.'

'It would be hard. Sometimes it would be terrible. I wasn't
swinging at you.'

'I know.'

'It was just the womb.'

'Monica's?'

'I don't know.'

That night he dreams: it is summer, the lovely summers when
he does not teach, does not have to hurry his writing and running before classes, and in the afternoons he picks up Sharon
and sometimes a friend or two of hers and they go to Seabrook
beach in New Hampshire; usually Jack and Terry Linhart are
there with their daughter and son, and all of them put their
blankets side by side and talk and doze and go into the sea,

the long cooling afternoons whose passage is marked only by the slow arc of the sun, time's symbol giving timelessness instead. His dream does not begin with those details but with that tone: the blue peaceful days he teaches to earn, wakes in the dark winter mornings to write, then runs in snow and cold wind and over ice. The dream comes to him with an empty beach: he feels other people there but does not see them, only a stretch of sand down to the sea, and he and Sharon are lying on a blanket. They are talking to each other. She is on his right. Then he rolls slightly to his left to look down at the fetus beside him; he is not startled by it; he seems to have known it is there, has been there as long as he and Sharon. The dream tells him it is a girl; he loves her, loves watching her sleep curled on her side: he looks at the disproportionate head, the small arms and legs. But he is troubled. She is bright pink, as if just boiled, and he realizes he should have put lotion on her. She sleeps peacefully and he wonders if she will be all right sleeping there while he and Sharon go into the surf. He knows he will bring her every afternoon to the beach and she will sleep pink and curled beside him and Sharon and, nameless, she will not grow. His love for her becomes so tender that it changes to grief as he looks at her flesh in the sun's heat.

The dream does not wake him. But late next morning, when he does wake, it is there, as vivid as if he is having it again. He sees and feels it before he feels his headache, his hung-over dry mouth, his need to piss; before he smells the cigarette butts on the desk beside him, and the tequila traces in the glasses by the ashtray. Before he is aware of Lori's weight and smell in bed. Quietly he rises and goes to the bathroom then sneaks back into bed, not kindness but because he does not want Lori awake, and he lies with his dream. His heart needs to cry but his body cannot, it is emptied, and again he thinks it is like vomiting: the drunken nights when he suddenly wakes from a dream of nausea and goes quickly to the toilet, kneeling, gripping its seat, hanging on through the last dry heaves, then waking in the morning still sick, red splotches beside his eyes where the violence of his puking has broken vessels, and feeling that next moment he would be at the toilet again, but there is nothing left to disgorge and he simply lies in bed for hours.

But this will not pass. He will have to think. His employers at the college and his editor and publisher believe his vocations have to do with thinking. They are wrong. He rarely thinks. He works on instincts and trying to articulate them. What his instincts tell him now is that he'd better lie quietly and wait: today is Sunday and this afternoon he and Lori are taking Sharon for a walk on Plum Island. He lies there and imagines the three of them on the dunes until he senses Lori waking.

She knows what he likes when he wakes hung over and, without a word, she begins licking and caressing his nipples; his breath quickens, he feels the hung-over lust whose need is so strong it is near-desperate, as though only its climax can return him from the lethargy of his body, the spaces in his brain, and he needs it the way others need hair of the dog. Lori knows as well as he does that his need is insular, mastur-batory; knows that she is ministering to him, her lips and fin-gers and now her mouth medicinal. But she likes it too. Yet this morning even in her soft mouth he remains soft until finally he takes her arms and gently pulls her up, rolls her onto her back, and kneels between her calves. When it is over he is still soft, and his lust is gone too.

'It wasn't tequila,' he says. 'This morning.'

'I know.'

Then he tells her his dream.

The day, when they finally leave his apartment, is crisp enough for sweaters and windbreakers, the air dry, the sky deep blue, and most of the trees still have their leaves dying in bright red and orange and yellow. It has taken them two hours to get out of the apartment: first Hank went to the bathroom, leaving a stench that shamed him, then he lay in bed while Lori went; and because he was trying to focus on anything to keep the dream away, he figured out why his girl friends, even on a crapulent morning like this one, never left a bad smell. Always they waited in bed, let him go first; then they went, bringing their boxes and bottles, and after sitting on the seat he had warmed they showered long and when they were finished, he entered a steamy room that smelled of woman: clean, powdered, whatever else they did in there. Very simple, and thoughtful too: let him go first so he would not have to wait with aching bowels while they went through the process of smell-changing; and they relied on him, going first, not to shower and shave and make them wait. It was sweetly vulpine and endearing and on another morning he would have smiled.

While he showered, Lori dressed and put on bacon. At breakfast he talked about last night's movie, about the day as it looked through the window near the table, about Plum Island's winter erosion, about the omelette, about anything, and Lori watched him with her soft brown eyes, and he knew she knew and was helpless, and he wished she didn't hurt that way, he knew the pain of being helpless with a lover, but there was nothing he could do except wish they both weren't helpless.

Driving the car, he is in love with Sharon, needs to see her, listen to her voice, touch her as they walk on the beach. At the house, Lori waits in the car, for she is shy about going in; she and Edith have talked outside, either because Edith was in the yard when they arrived or she walked with Hank and Sharon to the car and leaned over to talk to Lori at the window. Edith divorced him, and he has told Lori that she feels no jealousy or pain, but still Lori is uncomfortable. Hank understands this. He would feel the same. What he does not understand is why Lori loves him, and he prefers not to try, for he is afraid he will find no reason strong enough for him to rely on.

It is not the age of his body that makes him wonder. In the past three or four years, love handles and a bald spot have appeared, and all his running has no effect on the love handles, and he knows they are here to stay, and the bald spot will spread like a tonsure. But it isn't that. It's the fettered way he is thirty-five. When Monica left him, she flared after a night of silence when her eyes in turn glowered and sulked; she said, as they were finishing their last drinks in the bar near her college in Maine: *I want out. You worry about your writing first, your daughter second, money third, and I'm last.* All evening he had known something was coming. But he had never been broken up with so cleanly, precisely, succinctly. At once he was calm. He simply watched Monica's face. She was taut with fury. He was not. He was not even sad yet. He watched her, and waited for whatever he was going to say. He had no idea what it would be. He was simply repeating her words in his mind. Then he said: *You're right. Why should you put up with that shit?* Her fury was still there. Perhaps she wanted a fight. Yet all he felt was forgiveness for her, and futility because he had loved a woman so young.

Then he felt something else: that his forgiveness and futility were familiar, coming from foreknowledge, as if on that first night he took her to dinner in Boston and they ate soft-shelled crabs and his heart began to warm and rise, he had known it would end; that at the most he would get love's year. It ended with the four sentences in the bar, his two the last, and they drove quietly to her apartment near the campus; at the door he embraced her more tightly than he had intended, because holding her he saw images of death, hers and his years from now, neither knowing of the death of the first, the odds bad that it would be him since he had fifteen years on her and was a man. Then he gave her a gentle closed-lip kiss, and was walking back to his car before she could speak.

He put Waylon Jennings in the deck, and on the two-hour moonlit drive home he longed for a beer and did not cry. When he got to his apartment he drank a six-pack with bourbon and did cry and nearly phoned her; all that kept him from it was his will to keep their last scene together sculpted forever with him, Hank Allison Goddamnit, showing only dignity and strength and tenderness. She had seen him as he was now, on nights when writing or money or guilt and sorrow about Sharon or, often enough, all three punched him around the walls of his apartment, and he counter-punched with one hand holding a beer, the other a bourbon on the rocks. But she had never seen him like this because of her. So each time he went to the kitchen to get another beer or more bourbon and looked at the phone on the wall, he remembered how he was and what he said when she told him in the bar, and how he was at the door, and turned, sometimes lunged, away from the phone.

He drank in his bedroom, at his desk but with his back to it, and he listened to Dylan, the angry songs about women, the volume low because he rented the upstairs of a house whose owners were a retired couple sleeping beneath him, and he started his cure: he focused on every one of her flaws, and with booze and will and Dylan's hurt and angry encouragement, he multiplied them by emotion until they grew so out of proportion that he could no longer see what he had loved about her. He relived her quick temper and screaming rage, so loud and long that some nights he was afraid she was going mad, and always he had to command her to stop, squeeze her arms, tell her she would wake the couple downstairs; and her crying, never vulnerably, never seeming to need comfort, more a variation of her rage and nearly as loud, as she twisted from him and fled from room to room until again he had to hold and command; and the source of these rages and tears never defined so he could try to deal with them, these sources always just a little concrete but mostly abstract so on those nights he felt the impotence of believing she already was mad; and his impotence brought with it a detachment which in turn opened him up to shades of despair: he imagined her ten years from now, when her life would be more complicated and difficult, when it would attack her more often, with more strength. Listening to 'Positively Fourth Street' he sipped the smooth Jack Daniel's and chased it with the foamy bite of beer and thought if she had stayed with him she would have so drained his energy that, after spending his nights as a shrink and a lion-tamer, he would wake peaceless and weary to face his morning's work. He recalled her mischievous face as, in front of his friends, in bars or at the beach, she pinched his love handles or kissed his bald spot. This usually did not bother him because he was in good condition, and she smoked heavily and could not run half a mile, was slender only because she was made that way, and she was young, and she dieted. And he guessed she was doing this for herself rather than to him; testing herself; actually touching his signs of age to see if she really wanted a man fifteen years older, with an ex-wife, a twelve-year-old daughter, and child support.

Beneath the teasing, though, something was in her eyes: something feral, and at times as she smiled and teased he looked into her eyes and felt a stir of fear which had nothing to do with her fingers squeezing his flesh, her lips smacking his crown. It was more like the detached fear he had once, looking at a Russell's viper in a zoo, the snake coiled asleep behind glass, and Hank read the typed card on the cage, about this lethargic snake and how one of its kind finally got Russell and his name.

He went to the kitchen, did not even look at the phone as he passed it. He was thinking of the snake, and one night Jack saying that after the one bit Russell, he wrote down the effects of the poison as it killed him; and Jack said: *You know, maybe he studied those bastards so long that finally he had to go all the way, know it all, and he just reached down and touched it ...* In the dark bedroom which tomorrow would still be a bedroom, a dreary and hung-over place, not a study as it became most mornings, he listened to 'Just Like a Woman' and thought *Maybe that's what I was doing, waiting for that bitch to give me the venom, end it between us, between me and all of them, between me and—*He stopped. It was time to finish the drinks, swallow aspirins and vitamin B and go to bed, for—had he completed the sentence in his mind—it would have concluded with some euphemism for suicide. He went to bed hating Monica; it was a satisfying hatred; it felt like the completion of a long-planned revenge.

He woke with relief, nearly happiness, nearly strength. He knew, for today, that was enough: last night's cure had worked. As it had with every young girl who left him since his divorce. They all left. One night he told Jack: *I think I'll get a fire escape up to my window, so they can just climb out while I'm taking a piss.* When Edith sent him away, he did not have a cure.

Five years ago, when all his pleas and arguments and bargains and accusations lay on the living room floor between them (he actually felt he was stepping on his own words as he paced while she sat watching), and he knew that she really wanted him to leave, he believed it was because he had been unfaithful. So his grief was coupled with injustice, for she had had lovers too; and even as Hank talked that night her newest and, she said, her last lover so long as she was married, was dying early of cancer: Joe Ritchie, an ex-priest who taught philosophy at the college where Hank worked.

When he moved to his apartment he was too sad to be angry at Edith. He tried to be. Alone at night, and while running, and watching movies, he told himself that he and Edith had lived equally. Or almost. True, he had a head start on her, had student girl friends before she caught him because he was with a woman more demanding: a woman not only his own age but rich and from Paris, idling for six months with friends in Boston; a woman who laughed at him when he worried about Edith catching him. Now, at thirty-five, with eight years' distance, he saw how foolish he had been, for she was a woman of no substance: her idea of a good day was to sleep late, buy things at Bonwit Teller or Ann Taylor, and make love with Hank in the afternoon. He was young enough to be excited by her accent, so that he heard its sound more than what it said. He saw her in Boston, on Saturday afternoons, on Tuesdays and Thursdays when he was supposed to be in his office at school, he got careless, and he got caught.

When it happened he realized he had always known that someday it would: that he could not have lived uncaught his entire life, or until he outgrew his crushes that so quickly turned to passion not only for the body, for that lovely first penetration into new yielding flesh, but for the woman's soul too, a passion to know as much of her as he could before they parted (they were students; parting was graduation) and went on with their lives. Sometimes for weeks, even months, he would not notice a particular girl in class. Because while he was teaching he was aware mostly of himself: this was only partly vanity; more, it was his love of teaching, his fear of failing, so that before every class he had stage-fright, had to spend a few minutes in silence in his office or walking about the campus, letting his apprehension and passion grow inside him until, entering the classroom, those were all he felt. When he began to speak about a novel or story, it was as though another man were talking, and Hank listening. He taught three afternoons a week, had many bad days when he became confused, lost the students, and seeing their listless faces, his apprehension overcame his passion and he fearfully waited, still talking, for the fifty minutes to pass. At a week's end, if he had had two good days out of three, he was satisfied. He knew that hardly anyone hit three for three in this work. On his best days he listened to Hank the teacher talking, and he tried to follow the ideas coming from his mouth, ideas he often didn't know he had until he heard them. So, usually, he did not notice a certain girl until she said something in class, something that halted him, made him look at her and think about what she had said. Or, while he was talking, his face sweeping the class, the windows, the ceiling, his hands busy with a pen or keys or coins, his face would suddenly stop, held by a girl whose eyes were fixed on his; sometimes he would stop speaking for a moment, lose the idea he was working on, as he looked at her. Then he would turn away, toss his keys or coin or pen in the air, catch the idea again as he caught the tossed object, and speak. Soon he would be talking to her on the campus.

In his thirties, he understood what those crushes, while he was married, had been. His profession was one of intimacy, but usually it went only from him to the faces sitting in the room. Any student who listened could know as much about him as all his friends, except those two or three truly deep ones. His crushes were rope bridges, built in haste between

him and the girl. It was a need not only to give her more of
what attracted her in the classroom, but to receive from her,
to know her; and with the beginning of that, talking on the
campus sidewalks or in his office, came the passion to know
all of her. The ones he chose (or, he realized in his thirties, the
ones who chose him) were girls who would have been known
as promiscuous when he was in college; or even now in the
seventies if they were salesclerks or cashiers and at night went
to those bars where the young men who had gone to work
instead of college drank and waited. But they were educated,
affluent, and well-travelled; they wore denim to class, but he
knew that what hung in their dormitory closets and in their
closets at home cost at least half of his year's salary. He never
saw those clothes until he was divorced at thirty and started
taking the girls to Boston for the evening; and then he rarely
saw the same dress or skirt and blouse twice; only a favorite
sweater, a warm coat. While married, his lovemaking was in
his car, and what he quiveringly pulled from their thighs was
denim. They all took the pill, they all had what they called a
healthy attitude toward sex, which meant they knew the affair
with Hank, as deep and tender as it might be, so that it certainly felt like love (and, for all Hank knew, it probably was)
would end with the school year in May, would resume (if she
and Hank felt like it) in the fall, and would certainly end on
Commencement Day.

So they made it easy for him. He was a man who planned
most days of his life. In the morning he wrote; then he ran,
then he taught; then he was a husband and father. He tried to
keep them all separated, and most days it worked, and he felt
like three or four different men. When the affairs started, he
made time for them as well. After class or instead of office
hours he drove through town where the girl was walking. She
entered his car as though he had offered her a ride. Even
when they left town and drove north she would sit near her
door until he turned onto the dirt road leading to the woods.
Going back he stayed on the highway, skirted the town,

approached the school from the south, and let her out several blocks away. Then he went home and hugged and kissed Sharon and Edith, and holding their bodies in the warmth of his house, he felt love only for them.

But with Jeanne in Boston he had to lie too much about where he was going and where he had been, and finally when Edith asked him one night: *Are you having an affair with that phony French bitch?* he said: *Yes.* He and Edith had met Jeanne when someone brought her to their Christmas party; Edith had not seen her since, but in April, when she asked him, he did not even wonder how she knew. He was afraid, but he was also relieved. That may have been why he didn't ask how she knew. Because it didn't matter: Edith was dealing with what she believed was an affair with a specific woman. To Hank, his admission of that one was an admission of all of them.

He was surprised that he felt relief. Then he believed he understood it: he had been deluding himself with his scheduled adulteries, as if a girl on his car seat in the woods were time in the classroom or at his desk; the years of lies to himself and Edith had been a detraction from the man he wanted and sometimes saw himself to be. So, once cornered, he held his ground and told her. It broke her heart. He wanted to comfort her, to make fraudulent promises, but he would not. He told her he loved her and wanted to live with no one else. But he would not become like most people he knew. They were afraid; and old, twenty years early. They bought houses, spoke often of mortgages, repairs, children's ailments, and the weight of their bodies. As he talked she wiped from her eyes the dregs of her first heavy weeping. His own eyes were damp because of hers, and more: because of the impotence he felt, the old male-burden of having to be strong for both of them at once, to give her the assurance of his love so she could hear as a friend what he was saying: that he was what he was, that he had to be loved that way, that he could not limit the roads of his life until they narrowed down to one, leading from home to campus. She screamed at him: *You're a writer too! Isn't that enough for one man?* He said: *No. There's never enough. I don't want to have to say no to anything, not ever—*It was the most fearful moment of his marriage until the night over three years later when she told him he had to leave her and Sharon. He felt closer to her than he ever had before, now that all the lies were gone. And he knew he might lose her, right there in that April kitchen; he was sure of her love, but he was sure of her strength too. Yet he would not retreat into lies: he had to win.

He did. She stayed with him. Every night there was talk, and always there was pain. But she stayed. He built a case against monogamy, spoke of it as an abstraction with subtle and insidious roots in the economy: passion leashed so that lovers would need houses and things to put in them. He knew he was using his long apprenticeship to words, not to find truths, but to confuse and win his wife. He spoke of monogamy as unnatural. *The heart is too big for it*, he said. *Yours too.*

In May she started an affair with Jack Linhart, who no longer loved his wife Terry; or believed he no longer loved her. Hank knew: their faces, their voices, and when they were in the same room he could feel the passion and collusion between them as surely as he could smell a baking ham. He controlled his pain and jealousy, his moments of anger at Jack; he remembered the April night in the kitchen. He kept his silence and waited until the summer night Edith told him she was Jack's lover. He was gentle with her. He knew now that, within the marriage he needed and loved, he was free.

That summer he watched her. He had been her only lover till now; he watched the worry about what they were doing to their marriage leave her face, watched her face in its moments of girlish mischief, of vanity, of sensuality that brightened her eyes and shaped her lips, these moments coming unpredictably: as they ate dinner with Sharon, paused at the cheese counter in the supermarket ... Toward the end of the summer he made love twice with Terry, on successive nights, because he liked her, because she was pretty, because she was unhappy, and because he felt he had earned it. That ended everything. Terry told Jack about Hank. Then, desperate and drunk, Jack told Terry about Edith, said he wanted a divorce, and when Terry grieved he could not leave her: all of this in about twelve hours, and within twenty-four Edith and Terry had lunch together, and next afternoon Hank and Jack went running, and that evening, with the help of gin and their long friendship, they all gathered and charcoaled steaks. When the Linharts went home, Hank and Edith stood on the front lawn till the car turned a corner and was gone. Then Edith put her arm around his waist. *We're better off,* she said: *they're still unhappy.* He felt he was being held with all her strength; that strength he had feared last April; he was proud to be loved by her and, with some shame, he was proud of himself, for bringing her this far. That fall they both had new lovers.

When three years later she told him to leave and he tried to believe the injustice of it, he could not. For a long time he did not understand why. Then one night it came to him: he remembered her arm around his waist that summer night, and the pride he had felt, and then he knew why his tallying of her affairs meant nothing. She had not made him leave her life because he was unfaithful; she had made him leave because she was; because he had changed her. So she had made him leave because—and this struck him so hard, standing in his bedroom, he needed suddenly to lie down—he was Hank Allison.

On the morning after Monica jettisoned him, he woke with the images he had brought to bed. He had no memory, as he might have without last night's treatment, of anything about her that was intelligent or kind or witty or tender. Instead of losing a good woman, he had been saved from a bad one. He knew all this was like Novocain while the dentist drilled; but no matter. For what he had to face now was not the loss of Monica; he had to face, once again, what to do about loss itself. He put a banana, wheat germ, a raw egg, and buttermilk in the blender. He brought the drink downstairs and sat on the front steps, in the autumn sunlight. It was a Saturday, and Sharon wanted to see a movie that afternoon. Good: nearly two hours of distraction; he would like the movie, whatever it was. Before picking up Sharon he must plan his night, be sure he did not spend it alone in his apartment. If he called the Linharts and told them about Monica, they would invite him to dinner, stay up drinking with him as long as he wanted. He touched the steps. *It's these steps,* he thought. He looked up and down the street lined with old houses and old trees. *This street. This town. How the fuck can I beat geography?* A small town, and a dead one. The bright women went to other places. The ones he taught with were married. So he was left with either students or the women he knew casually in town, women he had tried talking to in bars—secretaries, waitresses, florists, beauticians—and he had enjoyed their company, but no matter how pretty and good-natured they were, how could he spend much time with a woman who thought Chekhov was something boys did in their beds at night? He remembered a night last summer drinking with Jack at a bar that was usually lined with girls, and he said: *Look at her: she's pretty, she looks sweet, she's nicely dressed, but look at that face: nothing there. Not one thought in her head.* And Jack said: *Sure she's got thoughts: thirty-eight ninety-five ... size nine ... partly cloudy.* Sharon was twelve. He would not move away until she was at least eighteen. He was with her every weekend, and they cooked at his apartment one night during the week. When his second book was published, an old friend offered him a job in Boston: he had thought about the bigger school, more parties with more women, even graduate students, as solemn as they were. But he would not leave Sharon. And when she was eighteen, he would be forty, twice the age of most of his students, and having lived on temporary love for six years, one limping, bloodstained son of a bitch. And if he moved then, who would want what was left of him?

He stood and climbed the stairs to his apartment and phoned the Linharts. Jack answered. When Hank told him, he said to come to dinner; early, as soon as he took Sharon home.

'Maybe I'll invite Lori,' Hank said.

'Why not.'

'I mean, she's just a friend. But maybe she'll keep the night from turning into a wake.'

'Bring her. Just be careful. You fall in love faster than I can fry an egg. What is it with these Goddamn girls anyway? Are they afraid of something permanent? Is that it?'

'Old buddy, I think there's something about me that just scares shit out of them. Something they just can't handle.'

You were all the way across the room, Monica said as soon as he came, before he had even collapsed on her, to nestle his cheek beside hers. So instead he rolled away and marvelled that she knew, that Goddamnit they always knew: his soul *had* been across the room; he had felt it against the wall behind him, opposite the foot of the bed, thinking, watching him and Monica, waiting for them to finish. Because of that, finishing had taken him a long time: erect and eager, his cock seemed attached not to his flesh but to that pondering soul back there; and since it did not seem his flesh, it did not seem to be inside Monica's either: there was a mingling of his hardness and her softness and liquid heat, but it had nothing to do with who he was for those minutes, or for who she was either. He knew it was an occupational hazard. Then, because of why it had just happened on that early Friday evening in winter when she was still his student, had two hours ago been in his class, had then walked to his apartment in cold twilight, he laughed. He had not expected to laugh, he knew it was a mistake, but he could not stop. A warning tried to stop him, to whisper *hush* to the laughter, a warning that knew not only the perils with a woman at a time like this, but the worse peril of being so confident in a woman's love that he could believe she would love his laughter now too, and his reason for it. She got out of bed and went to the bathroom and then the kitchen and when she came back she had a glass of Dry Sack—one glass, not two—and even that sign could not make him serious, for he was caught in the comic precision of what had just happened. She pulled on leotards, slipped into a sweater that she left unbuttoned, and brought a cigarette to bed where she lay beside him, not touching, and the space between them and the sound of her breathing felt to Hank not quite angry yet, not quite subdued either.

'You were right,' he said. He was still smiling. 'I *was* across the room. I can't help it. I was all right until we started; then while we were making love I thought about what I was working on today. I didn't want to. I never want to after I stop for the day. And I wanted to ask you about it but I figured we'd better finish first—'

'Oh good, Hank: oh good.'

'I know, I know. But I was working on a scene about a girl who's only made love once, say a few months ago, and then one night she makes love twice to this guy and again in the morning, and I wanted to know if I was right. In the scene her pussy is sore next day; after the three times. Is that accurate?'

'Yes. You son of a bitch.'

'Now wait a minute. None of this was on purpose. You think I want my Goddamn head to start writing whenever it decides to? It's not like being un*kind*, for Christ's sake. You think surgeons and lawyers and whatever don't go through this too? Shit: you came, didn't you?'

'I could do that alone.'

'Well, what am I supposed to fucking *do?*'

He got out of bed and went for the bottle of sherry and brought it back with another glass; but at the doorway to his room, looking at her leotarded legs, the stretch of belly and chest and the inner swell of breasts exposed by the sweater, at her wide grim mouth concentrating on smoking, and her grey eyes looking at the ceiling, he stopped and stayed at the threshold. He said softly: 'Baby, what am I supposed to do? I don't believe in all this special crap about writers, you know that. We're just like everybody else. *Every*body gets distracted by their work, or whatever.'

He cut himself off: he had been about to say *Housewives too*, but the word was too dangerous and, though he believed that vocation one of the hardest and most distracting of all, believed if he were one he could never relax enough to make unhindered love, he kept quiet. Monica would not be able to hear what he said; she would hear only the word *housewife*, would slip into jargon, think of labels, roles, would not be soothed. She did not look at him. She said: 'You could try harder. You could concentrate more. You could even pretend, so I wouldn't feel like I was getting fucked by a dildo.' She was often profane, but this took him by surprise; he felt slapped. 'And you could shut up about it. And not laugh about it. And you could Goddamn not ask me your fucking questions when you stop laughing. I want a lover, not a Papermate.'

The line pleased him, even cheered him a little, and he almost told her so; but again he heard his own warnings, and stopped.

'Look,' he said, 'let's go to Boston. To Casa Romero and have a hell of a dinner.'

She stayed on his bed long enough to finish the cigarette; she occupied herself with it, held it above her face between drags and studied it as though it were worthy of concentration; watched her exhaled smoke plume and spread toward the ceiling; for all he knew (he still stood naked in the doorway) she was thinking, perhaps even about them. But he doubted it. For a girl so young, she had a lot of poses; when did they start learning them, for Christ's sake? When they still wrote their ages with one digit? She exhaled the last drag with a sigh, put the cigarette out slowly, watching its jabs against the ashtray as if this were her last one before giving them up; then quickly she put on her skirt, buttoned her sweater, pulled on her boots, slung her suede jacket over her shoulder, and walked toward him as if he were a swinging door. He turned sideways; passing, she touched neither him nor the doorjamb. *Awfully slender*, he thought. He followed her down the short hall; stood at the doorway and watched her going down the stairs; he hoped his semen was dripping into the crotch of her leotards, just to remind her that every-thing can't be walked away from. 'Theatrical bitch,' he said to her back, and shut the door.

Which six hours later he opened when she knocked and woke him. She was crying. Her kiss smelled of vermouth. She had been drinking with her roommate. She missed him. She was sorry. She loved him. He took her to bed with fear and sadness which were more distracting than this afternoon's thinking; he pretended passion and tenderness; he urged his cock *Come on come you bastard*, while all the time he felt defeat with this woman, felt it as surely as if it stood embodied behind him, with a raised sword. Some night, some day, the sword would arc swiftly down; all he could do was hang on to the good times with Monica while he waited for the blade.

Monica did, though, give him Lori. They were friends from summers in Maine, where Lori lived, and Monica's parents, from Manhattan, had a summer house. The girls met when Lori was fifteen and Monica sixteen. It was Monica who con-vinced Lori to enroll in the college, and to take Hank's courses. Then Monica transferred to Maine after her freshman year, because she didn't like her art teachers; but Lori came to the college anyway and saw Monica on the weekends when she drove down and stayed with Hank. He liked Lori on those weekends, he liked seeing her in his class, and some week nights they walked to town and drank beer; a few people probably thought they were lovers, but Hank was only afraid of gossip that was true, so he and Lori went to Timmy's, where students drank. And the night after Monica left him, he picked her up at the dormitory, for dinner at the Linharts. They did not become lovers until over a month later and, when they did, Hank realized it was the first time since Edith that he had made love with a woman who was already his good friend. So their transition lacked the fear and euphoria that people called romance. For Hank, it felt comfortable and safe, as though he had loved her for a long and good time.

Finding a Girl in America169

Still, with Lori, he was careful: so careful that at times he thought all the will and control it demanded of him was finally the core of love; that for the first time he knew how to go about it. He watched her shyness, listened to it, loved it, and did not try to cure it. While he did this, he felt his love for her growing deeper, becoming a part of who he was in the world.

She was his fourth young girl since divorce. Each had lasted a year or more; with each he had been monogamous; and they had left him. None but Monica had told him why, in words he could understand. The other two had cried and talked about needing space. When the first left him he was sad, but he was all right. The loss of the second frightened him. That was when he saw his trap. Drinking with Jack, he could smile about it: for what had been spice in his married twenties was now his sustenance. Certainly, he told Jack, when he was married he had fallen in love with his girl friends, or at least had the feeling of being in love, had said the words, had the poignant times when he and the girl held each other and spoke, in the warm spring, of the end that was coming to them on the school calendar. But all those affairs had simply given him emotions which he had believed marriage, by its nature, could not give.

For the first time in his life he felt a disadvantage with women. Too often, as he looked at a young face in his apartment or across a restaurant table, he knew he had nothing to offer this girl with her waiting trust fund, this girl who had seen more of the world than he ever would; he imagined her moving all those clothes and other pelf into his apartment and, as he talked with the girl, he wished for some woman his own age, or at least twenty-five, who was not either married or one of those so badly divorced that their pain was not only infectious but also produced in them anger at all men, making him feel he was a tenuous exception who, at any moment, would not be. They met with women's groups, shrank each other's heads without a professional in the room, and came away with their anger so prodded they were like warriors. He had tried two of those and, bored and weary, had fled. Once with honey-blonde Donna, the last one, he had left a bar to enter a night of freezing rain, ten minutes to chip his windshield clear while she sat in the car; then driving home so slowly and tensely he could feel his heart beating, he said: 'Probably some man froze all this fucking rain too.' Perhaps because she was as frightened as he was, she gently, teasingly, said 'MCP,' and patted his shoulder.

He only argued with Donna once. He believed in most of what women wanted, believed women and men should work together to free themselves, believed *The Wild Palms* had said it first and as well as anyone since. Some trifles about the movement had piqued him: they had appropriated a word he loved, mostly because of its comic root, and he could no longer have the Cold War fun of calling someone a chauvinist. And, on his two marches in Washington during the Vietnam War, he had been angered by the women who took their turn on the speakers' platform and tried to equate dishwashing with being napalmed. The only important feeling he had about these women was he wished they had some joy. The night he argued with Donna he was drunk and, though he kept trying not to see the *Ms.* on her coffee table, it was finally all he could see, and he said abruptly: 'Donna, just as an unknown, average, .260-hitting writer, who sometimes writes a story and tries to publish it, or a piece of a novel, I've got to say one thing: I hate totalitarian magazines whether they're called *Ms.* or *Penthouse.*'

'Totalitarian?'

'That.' He picked up *Ms.* and dropped it on its cover so all he saw was an advertisement encouraging young girls to start working on lung cancer now, older women to keep at it. 'They hate literature. They just want something that supports their position. It's like trying to publish in China, for Christ's sake.' Then, because he was angry at magazines and nothing else, and she was suddenly an angry feminist, they fought.

The fight ended when it was over, so it wasn't serious. But one of the reasons he finally left her, chose loneliness instead, was what she read. She did not read him. This hurt him a little, but not much; mostly, he was baffled. He could not understand why she would make love with him when she was not interested in his work. Because to him, his work was the best of himself. He believed most men who were fortunate enough to have work they loved saw themselves in the same way. Yet Donna's affection was only for what he was at night, when he was relaxing from that day's work, and forgetting tomorrow's, in much the same way he saw most movies that came to town, no matter what they were. And his bantering night-self was so unimportant to him that often, at his desk in the morning, he felt he had not spent last evening with Donna; someone else had talked with her, made love with her; some old, close friend of his.

Typed on a sheet of paper, thumbtacked to the wall over his desk, was this from *Heart of Darkness*: *No, I don't like work. I had rather laze about and think of all the fine things that can be done. I don't like work—no man does—but I like what is in the work—the chance to find yourself. Your own reality—for yourself, not others—what no other man can ever know. They can only see the mere show, and never can tell what it really means.* A woman had to know that: simply know it, that was all. He did not need praise from her, he rarely liked to talk about his work, and he had no delusions about it: he liked most novels he read better than he liked his own. But the work was his, and its final quality did not matter so much as the hours it demanded from him. It made the passage of time concrete, measurable. It gave him confidence, not in the work itself, but in Hank Allison: after a morning at the desk he had earned his day on earth. When he did not work, except by choice, he disliked himself. If these days occurred in succession because of school work, hangovers, lack of will, sickness, he lost touch with himself, felt vague and abstract, felt himself becoming whomever he was with. So he thought Donna knew little more about him than she would if, never having met him, she came across his discarded clothing and wallet on her bedroom floor. At times this made him lonely; it also made him think of Edith, all of her he had not known during their marriage, especially the final three polygamous years; and with no way now to undo, to soothe, to heal, he loved her and grieved for what she had suffered: the loneliness of not being fully known.

One night in Donna's bed, lying tensely beside her peaceful, post-orgasmic flesh, in the dark yet seeing in his mind the bedroom cluttered with antique chairs and dressing table and family pictures on the wall and, resting on the mantel of the sealed fireplace, faces of her grandparents and parents and herself with her two children, a son and daughter, he wondered why he was with her. He knew it was because of loneliness, but why her, with her colliding values, her liberated body which she had shared—offered actually—on their second date, lying here among the testaments of family, marriage, traditions? He suspected that her feminism existed solely because, as her marriage ended, her husband had become mean. He was behind on child support; often he broke dates with the children. Hank believed she was happy now, in these moments this night, because she had just made love, her children slept healthy down the hall, and she was lying amid her antiques and photographs of her life, on a four-poster bed that had been her great-aunt's. When he tired of trying to understand her, he said: 'I don't know why you like me.'

'Why *Hank.*'

Her voice was wrong: she thought he felt unloved, needed comfort. He left the bed to piss, to break the mood. When he returned and covered himself he said: 'You're not interested in my work. That's me. All you see is what's left over. I don't think that's me.'

'I've hurt you, and it was stupid and selfish. Bring them over tomorrow night. I'll read them in order.'

'Wait.' He spoke with gentle seriousness, as he did at times with Sharon, when they were discussing a problem she was having or a difference between them, and he wanted her to hear only calm father-words, and not to listen for or worry about his own emotions beneath them. 'I'm not hurt. I just don't understand how you can feel for me, and know nothing at all about that part of my life. Maybe two-thirds of it; only about an eighth of my day, in hours, but usually two-thirds of it, which is all of it except sleeping; no matter what I'm doing, it's down there inside me, I can feel it at work; whether I'm with Sharon or you or teaching; or anything.' He was about to explain that too, but veered away: some nights with Donna he had the same trouble he would have with Monica much later; but Donna either had not noticed or, more likely, because she had been with more men, she had simply understood; probably she had her own nights like that, as they moved together in that passion which, true as it was, did not totally absorb them, but existed in tandem with them.

'What about my work?' she said.

There was no edge on her voice; not yet; but he could sense the blade against whetstone in her heart. He watched her eyes, kept his voice the same, though with a twinge of impatience he felt he *was* talking to Sharon. Why was he so often comforting women? He wished he could see himself as they saw him: his face, his body, his gestures; wished he could hear the voice they heard. For now he felt like a mean lover, and he did not want to be, but maybe he was and could not do anything about it; or maybe (he hoped) he simply appeared that way. Whatever, he was sad and confused and lonely, felt lost and homeless and womanless, though he lay in bed with a good woman, a good companion; and he needed answers, or even just one, yet now he must give answers, and in a controlled and comforting voice whose demand on him clenched his fists, tightened his arms.

'It's not,' he said. 'You told me it wasn't. We were eating at Ten Center Street, and you said: "It's not work; I wouldn't grace it with the name. It's just a job till I find out what I really want to do."' He was still tense, but her face softened with his voice.

'You're right,' she said.

'I also know about your job. I've listened. I can tell you your typical day. But mostly with me you talk about your children and rearing them alone and shithead Max not coming through with the money and not seeing the children when he's supposed to, because he's become a chic-freak smoking dope all day with young ass and bragging about leaving the engineering rat-race, when the truth is he was laid off with the rest of the poor bastards during the recession, and he talks about opening a bar when he can hardly afford to drink at one because he's drawing unemployment. And you mostly talk about men and women. And how everything's changed since you and Max bought this house and it's got you muddled and sad and pissed-off and you want to do something about it, for yourself and other women too if you could think of a way, but you don't know how yet. I don't mean any of this as an insult. You talk about these things because that's who you are right now, that's your struggle, and it never bores me. Because I care about you and because I'm going through my version of the same thing. Everything's changed for me too. When we were pregnant—'

'We?'

'Of course we. Not just Edith. I didn't vomit and my pants size didn't change and my breasts didn't swell and I didn't feel any pain. But it was we. It always is, unless some prick pretends it isn't.'

'Like Max.'

'I don't know what he felt then. You said he was different then—' He waved an arm at the dark room, was about to say *He liked all this stuff*, but did not.

'What did *you* feel?' she said:

'Guilt. Fear. I'd read *A Farewell to Arms* too recently. Three or four years earlier, but for me that was too recently.' He saw in her face she did not know the book, and he was about to explain, but thought that would be a worse mistake than his mentioning it. 'I was afraid she'd die. Off and on, until it was over. While she was delivering I hated my hard-on that had been so important whatever night it seemed so important and the diaphragm wasn't enough.'

'Men shouldn't feel that way.'

'Should and shouldn't don't have much to do with feelings. Anyway, we got married. We were in graduate school and we didn't know any feminists. We were too busy, and our friends were other young couples who were busting their asses to pay bills and stay in school. It made sense then, graduate school: there were jobs waiting. And I saw Edith as a wife in I suppose the same way my father saw my mother. Which somewhat resembles a nineteenth-century aristocrat, I guess: some asshole out of Balzac or Tolstoy.' (This time, remembering his marriage, he did not even notice that literature had moved into the bed again, like a troublesome cat.) 'Well, not that bad. But bad enough. I don't think I knew it, most of the time. Or maybe I just believed I was right, *it* was right. It's the only way I had ever seen marriage. I'm not excusing myself. It gets down to this: I nearly drowned her in my shit creek till one night she found a paddle and broke it over my head. Then she shoved the handle through me. I still feel the splinters. All of which is to say I'm not just politely nodding my head when you talk about trouble between men and women. You're talking to a comrade in arms, and I lost too.'

Goddamn: he had gotten off the track again, for now she held him with both arms, pulled him against her, and he let her quietly hold him a while, then he shifted, got an arm around her, pulled her head to his shoulder so he was talking to her hair, and said: 'All of which got us away from the original question. You're a lovely woman. You could have as many kinds of men as you're lucky enough to meet—doctor lawyer Indian chief—so what I want to ask is, why me? A man you met at a party, you came up and said "You have foam on your moustache," and I licked it off and you said "I like watching men lick beer from their moustaches." Why in the world me?'

She turned and kissed him long, then raising her face above his, she said: 'Because you're so *alive*.'

As if she had suddenly pulled the blankets from him, a chill went up his back and touched his heart, which felt now dry and withered, late autumn's leaf about to fall slowly through his body. Feeling her bones against him, he thought of her as a skeleton lying amid the antiques in the dark, a skeleton with a voice struggling for life, with words that were the rote of pain and anger from the weekly meetings of women. Then he felt like crying for her. It seemed that, compared to hers, his own life was full and complex and invigorating. He wished he knew a secret, and that he could give it to her: could lay his hand on her forehead and she would sleep and wake tomorrow with the same dreary job as a bank teller, the same mother-duties, and confusion and loneliness and the need to feel her life was something solid she was sculpting, yet with an excited spirit ready to engage the day, to kick it and claw it and gouge its eyes until it gave her the joy she deserved. But he had nothing to tell her, nothing to give. He held her quietly, for a long time. Then he rose and dressed. He never spent the night with her. She did not want the children, who were three and five, to know; nor did Hank; and it was implicit between them that since their affair had begun impetuously soon, it was tenuous, was at very best—or least— a trial affair. There would probably be another man, and another, and her children should not grow up seeing that male succession at breakfast. He leaned over and kissed her, whispered sweetly, then drove home.

The point was, finally, that Donna did not read. He guessed all men did not have to love women who were interested in their work; somehow a veterinarian could leave his work with its odors in the shower before dinner, spend his evening with a beloved woman who did not want a house pet. But he could not. Literature was what he turned to for passion and excitement, where he entered a world of questions he could not answer, so he finished a novel or poem or story feeling blessed with humility, with awe of life, with the knowledge that he knew so little about how one was supposed to live. So, better to have the company of a girl who loved literature and simply had not read much because she was young, far more exciting to listen to a girl's delight at her first reading of *Play It As It Lays* or *Fat City*, than to be with a woman in her thirties who did not read because she had chosen not to, had gone to the magazines and television.

Two nights later they went to dinner and, with coffee and brandy, sipping the courage to hurt her, he spoke about their starting too fast, becoming lovers too soon, before they really knew each other; he said their histories were very different, and being sudden lovers blurred their ability to see whether they were really—he paused, waiting for a series of concrete words besides the one word *compatible*, wanting his speech to at least sound different from the ones other men and women were hearing across the land that night. During his pause she said: 'Compatible.'

Then relief filled her face as quickly as pain does, the pain he had predicted, and for an instant he was hurt. Then he smiled at his fleeting pride. He was happy: she had wanted out too. Then she told him she had been three days late last week and her waiting had made her think about the two of them, she had been frightened, and had wanted to stop the affair. But not their friendship. They ordered second brandies and talked, without shyness, about their children. They split the bill, he drove her home, and they kissed goodnight at her door.

As he leaves Lori in the car in front of Edith's house he kisses her quickly, says he loves her. Edith opens the door: small body, long black hair, her eyes and mouth smiling like an old friend. He supposes that is what she is now and, because they have Sharon, in some way they are still married. Though he cannot define each scent, the house smells feminine to him. Like Donna, Edith does not let lovers stay the night, and for the same reasons. Hank knows this because, in their second year of divorce, when he could ask the question without risking too deep a wound, he did. Now he asks: 'What kind of smell does a man bring into a house?'

'Bad ones.'

'I smell bacon and the Sunday paper. Both neuter. But there's something female. Or non-male.'

'It's your imagination. But there *has* been a drought.'

'I'm sorry. What happened to what's-his-face?'

She shrugs, and for a moment the smile leaves her eyes: not sadness but resignation or perhaps foreknowledge of it, years of it. Then she looks at him more closely.

'What happened?' she says.

'Something shitty.'

'With Lori?'

'No.'

'Good. I think she's the one.'

'Really? Why?'

'I don't know. I hope you can keep her. What is it? Work?'

'No. I'll talk to you tonight. Where's Sharon?'

'Cleaning her room. I'll get her.'

She goes to the foot of the stairs and calls: 'Sharon, Dad's here.'

'I'm sorry about the drought,' he says.

'What the hell. I should have been a teacher so I'd have more livestock to pasture with. It's all right now, did you know that? For women. A friend of mine is having an affair with one of her students. She's thirty-seven and he's nineteen.'

She is not attacking him; those days are long past. He is sorry for her, knows her problem is geographical too, that she would do better in Boston. He is grateful and deeply respects her for staying here so he and Sharon can be near each other, but he can only tell her such things on the phone when he's had some drinks.

Sharon comes down in jeans and a sweater, carrying a wind-breaker. He hugs her and they kiss. Her new breasts make him uncomfortable; he rarely looks at them, and when he embraces her he doesn't know where to put them, what to do about their small insistence against him. They both kiss Edith and walk arm-in-arm to the car. Lori opens the door, and Sharon gets into the back seat.

Sharon and Lori get along well, and sometimes talk like two teen-aged girl friends, as if he's not there. That they are both teenagers, one in her first year of it, the other in her last, gives Hank both a smile and a shiver. He wonders if someday he will have a girl who is Sharon's age. It could happen in five years. And who, he wonders as he drives on a country road winding east, ever started the myth that a young girl gave an older man his youth again? Not that he would want his confused youth again. But they were supposed to make you feel younger. All he knows is that with Lori he feels unattractive, balding, flabby. That she wakes with a hangover looking strong and fresh, and is; while at thirty he lost that resilience and now a bad hangover affects his day like the flu. Remembering how in his twenties he could wake six hours after closing a bar, then eat breakfast and write, he feels old. And when people glance at him and Lori while, in Boston, they walk holding hands, or enter a restaurant, he feels old. The beach is worse: he watches the lithe young men and wonders if Lori watches them too, and his knowing that most of them, probably all except the obsessively vain and those who are simply exempt by nature, will in a few years have enough flesh at their waists to fill a woman's hands, does not help. He feels old. Yet with Donna and the divorcée before her, he had felt young, too young, his spirit quickly wearied by their gravity. So, again, no answers: all he knows is that whoever spread the word about young girls had not been an older man in love with one.

Sharon and Lori are talking about school and their teachers and homework and how they discipline themselves to do it, how they choose which work to do first (Lori works in descending order, beginning with the course she likes most: Sharon does the opposite; they both end with science). Last summer Sharon started and stopped smoking; quit when Edith kissed her just after running, and smelled Sharon's breath and hair; which she might not have, she told Hank on the phone, if her sense of smell hadn't been cleansed of her own cigarettes by an hour's run. Hank liked that: he had a notion that kids got away with smoking now because their parents didn't kiss them much; when he was a boy, he and his friends had chewed gum and rubbed lemon juice on their fingers before going home, because someone always kissed them hello. Edith talked to Sharon, and that night Hank took her to dinner and talked to her, pleaded with her, and she promised him, as she had Edith, that she was not hooked, had smoked maybe two packs, and from now on, she said, she would not give in to peer pressure. That was the night Hank and Edith started worrying about dope, talked on the phone about it, and he wondered how divorced parents who were too hurt and angry to talk to each other dealt with what their children were doing. Now, at least once a month, while he and Sharon cook dinner in his small kitchen, he mentions dope. She tells him not to worry, she's seen enough of the freaks at school, starting with their joints on the bus at seven in the morning.

He is not deeply worried about dope, because he trusts Sharon, knows she is sensible; that she tried cigarettes with her girl friends because at thirteen she wouldn't think of death; but he is as certain as he can be that, seeing the stoned and fruitless days of the young people around her, she will take care of herself.

What really worries him about Sharon has to do with him and Lori, and with him and Monica, and with the two girls before Monica. It also has to do with Edith: although her lovers have not spent the night, have probably not even used the house, by now Sharon must know Edith has had them. But he doesn't worry much about Edith, because he feels so confused, guilty, embarrassed, honest and dishonest about himself and his lovers and Sharon, that he has little energy left to worry about Edith's responsibilities. Also, he understands very little about mothers and daughters, the currents that run between them. But about Sharon he knows this: with each of his young girl friends—she did not meet Donna or the divorcée before her—she has been shy, has wanted to be their friend, more to them than her father's daughter. He has also sensed jealousy, which has disturbed him, and he doesn't know whether Sharon feels the girl is taking her mother's place, or her own, in his life. Always he has talked with her about his girl friends, and pretended they were not lovers. Yet he knows that she knows. So he is hung on his own petard: he does not want her to have lovers early, before she has grown enough to protect herself from pain. He wants to warn her that, until some vague age, a young boy will stick it in anything and say anything that will let him stick it. He doesn't know when he will tell her this. He does not want her girlhood and young womanhood to become a series of lovers, he does not want her to become cynical and casual about making love. He does not, in fact, want her to be like his girl friends. Yet, by having four whom she's known in five years, and two whom she hasn't, that is exactly the way he is showing her how to live.

Lori makes things better. When he became her friend, she had had one quick and brutal affair with a co-worker in a restaurant in Maine where they both waited tables the summer before she came to college. He hurt her physically, confused her about what she was doing with him, and after two weeks she stopped. So she was more the sort of girl he wanted Sharon to be. And Lori—shy, secretive not by choice, brooding (though it didn't appear on her smooth face; he had to look at her drooping lip-corners)—was warm and talkative with Sharon, enjoyed being with her, and Hank thought they were good for each other: Sharon, with her new breasts and menses, her sophistication that came from enduring divorce and having parents who were not always honest with her yet tried to be as often as they could, for the two purposes of helping her with divorce and preparing her to face the implacable and repetitive pains in a world that, when they were much younger, neither of them had foreseen. On the other hand Lori: with her quiet, tender father, his voice seldom heard, his presence seeming to ask permission for itself, and her loud mother whose dominance was always under a banner of concern for her daughter and, beneath that (Hank guessed), Lori's belief that her father was, had been, and would be a cuckold, and not only that but one without vengeance, neither rage nor demand nor even the retaliatory relief of some side-pussy of his own. So as Hank listens he thinks Sharon needs warm recognition from Lori, and that Lori needs to be able to talk, giggle, be silly, say whatever she wants, and from Sharon (and yes: him at the wheel beside her) she draws the peace to be able to talk without feeling that someone is standing behind her, about to clamp a hand on her shoulder and tell her she's wrong.

Wondering about Sharon and Lori gives him some respite but it is not complete. For all during the drive there is the cool hollow of sadness around his heart, and something is wrong with his body. Gravity is more intense: his head and shoulders and torso are pulled downward to the car seat. He crosses the bridge to the island, turns right into the game preserve, driving past the booth which is unmanned now that summer is over. To their right is the salt marsh, to their left dunes so high they cannot see the ocean. He parks facing a dune, and walking between Lori and Sharon, holding their hands, he starts climbing the grass-tufted slope of sand; his body is still heavy.

At the dune's top the sea breeze strikes them cool but not cold, coming over water that is deep blue, for the air is dry, and they stop. They stand deeply inhaling the air from the sea. On the crest of the dune, his eyes watering from the breeze, holding Lori's and Sharon's hands, breathing the ocean-smell he loves, Hank suddenly does not know what he will do about last year's dead fetus, last night's dream of her on the summer beach with him and Sharon; he cannot imagine the rest of his life. He sees himself growing older, writing and running and teaching, but that is all, and his tears now are not from the breeze.

'Let's go,' he says, and they walk southward, releasing each other's hands so they can file between the low shrubs on the dune's top. He turns back to the girls and points at Canadian geese far out in the marsh, even their distant silhouettes looking fat, and he thinks of one roasting, the woman—who? his mother? he sees no face—bending over to open the oven door, peering in, basting. They walk quietly. He can feel them all, free of house-wood and car-metal that surround most of their time, feeling the hard sand underfoot, the crisp brown shrubs scratching their pants, their eyes looking ahead and down the slopes of the dune, out at the marsh with its grass and, in places, shimmer of standing water, and its life of tiny creatures they can feel but not see; and at the ocean, choppy and white-capped, and he imagines a giant squid and killer whale struggling in a dance miles deep among mountains and valleys. For an instant he hopes Lori is at least a bit sad, then knows that is asking too much.

They walk nearly two miles, where the dune ends, and beneath them the island ends too at the river which flows through the marsh, into the sea. The river is narrow and, where it meets the sea, the water is lake-gentle. It is shallow and, in low tide, Hank and Sharon have waded out to a long sandbar opposite the river's mouth. Hank goes down a steep, winding path, and they move slowly. At the bottom they cross the short distance of sand and watch the end of the river, and look southeast where the coast below them curves sharply out to sea. They turn and walk up the beach, the sand cool and soft. He is walking slightly ahead of them, holding back just enough to be with them and still alone; for he feels something else behind him too, so strongly that his impulse is to turn and confront it before it leaps on him. He wants to run until his body feels light again. They move closer to the beach and walk beside washed-up kelp and green seaweed. He stops and turns to Lori and Sharon. Their faces are wind-pink, their hair blows across cheeks and eyes.

'I don't know where the car is,' he says. 'But I know a restaurant it can get us to.'

Sharon points at the dune.

'On the other side,' she says.

'Oh. I thought I parked it in the surf.'

'It's *right* over there.'

'No.'

He looks at the dune.

'You want to bet?'

'Not with you. You'd bet a dinner at the Copley against a hamburger at Wendy's.'

'Okay. What's the Copley?'

'A place I'm not taking you. Lori and I go Dutch.'

'That expensive, huh?'

'We go everywhere Dutch. You can't tell me that part of the dune looks different.'

'See the lifeguard tower?'

He looks north behind him, perhaps a half-mile away. Sharon talks to his back.

'When we climbed the dune I looked that way and saw it.'

He looks at her. 'If you're right, I'll buy you a meal.'

'You already said you'd do that.'

'Right. Let's climb, ladies.'

He leads them up and, at the top, they see the car to the south.

'I was a bit off,' Sharon says.

'No more than a hundred yards.'

The restaurant is nearby, on the mainland road that curves away from the island; and it is there, seated and facing Sharon and Lori, that whatever pursued him on the beach strikes him: lands howling on his back. He can do nothing about it but look at Sharon's cheerful face while he feels, in the empty chair beside him, the daughter salined or vacuumed from Monica a year ago. The waitress is large and smiling, a New England country woman with big, strong-looking hands, and she asks if they'd like something to drink. Sharon wants a Shirley Temple, Lori wants a margarita, and Hank wants to be drunk. But he is wary. When his spirit is low, when he can barely feel it at all, just something damp and flat lying over his guts, when even speaking and eating demand effort, and he wants to lie down and let the world spin while he yearns for days of unconsciousness, he does not drink. The only cure then is a long run. It does not destroy what is attacking him, but it restores his spirit, and he can move into the world again, look at people, touch them, talk. Only once in his life it has not worked: the day after Edith told him to leave. He would like to run now. Whatever leaped on his back has settled there, more like a deadly snake than a mad dog. He must be still and quiet. He remembers one of his favorite scenes in literature, in Kipling: 'Rikki-Tikki-Tavi,' when Nagaina the mother cobra comes to the veranda where the family is eating, coiled and raised to strike the small boy, the three of them—father, mother, son—statues at their breakfast table.

'A mongoose,' he says.

'He'll ask me how to make that one.'

'It comes with a cobra egg in its mouth.' She is looking down at him, her eyes amused yet holding on to caution too, perhaps anger, waiting to see if this is harassment or friendly joking. It's the last egg in the nest. He's killed the others. He comes up behind the cobra and she turns on him just long enough for the father to reach over the table and grab his son and pull him away.'

'Sounds like a good one,' she says. 'Must start with rum and keep building.'

She is smiling now, and he is ashamed, for he sees in her quickly tender eyes that she knows something is wrong.

'I'm sorry,' he says.

'For what? I like a good story. If we had cobras around here I swear to God I'd go live up ten flights of stairs in Boston and never see grass or stars again. You going to drink that?'

'I'll have a Coke with a wedge of lime.'

'So that's a mongoose. I think I'll call it that, see what he comes up with. Now I like Jackson. But he's his own man behind the bar. Any time—*every* time—somebody orders a sombrero, he says, What do you think this is, a dairy bar? Doesn't matter who they are. He makes them, but he always says that. Won't make a frozen daiquiri. Nobody orders them anyway. Maybe five-six a year. He just looks at them and says, Too much trouble; I'll quit my job first. Young guy came in the other night and ordered a flintlock. Ever hear of that one?'

'No.'

'Neither did Jackson. He said, Go home and watch Daniel Boone, and he went to the other end of the bar till finally the guy goes down there and asks can he have a beer. Jackson looks at him a while then opens up the bottle and says, You want a glass with that or a powder horn?'

Hank keeps smiling, thinking that on another day he would stay here for hours, drinking long after his meal, so he could banter with this woman with the crinkles at her eyes and the large hands he guesses have held many a happy man. He could get into his country-western mood and find the songs on the jukebox and ask about her children and wonder how many heartbreaks she had given and received.

'Better just tell him Coke then,' he says. 'You order a mongoose and he'll send me the snake.'

'He's a bit of one himself. Coke with a wedge,' and she is gone. He looks at Lori. She understands, and he glances away from her, down at the red paper placemat. When the waitress brings their drinks, they order food, taking a long time because Sharon cannot decide and the waitress, who is not busy this early in the afternoon, enjoys helping her, calls her Honey, tells her the veal cutlet is really pork tenderloin but it's good anyway, the fisherman's platter is too big but if she doesn't stuff on the fries she might eat most of the fish, with maybe some help from the mongoose-drinker. Sharon orders a sirloin, and Hank is glad: he wants to watch her eating meat.

When it comes he does watch, eating his haddock without pleasure or attention: Sharon is hungry and she forks and cuts fast, and he watches the brown and pink bite go into her mouth, watches her lips close on it and her jaws working and the delight on her face. He remembers the smell of the sea, the feel of her hand in his, the sound of her breath beside him. *Life*, he thinks, and imagines the taste of steak in her mouth, the meat becoming part of her, and as his heart celebrates these pleasures it grieves, for he can see only the flesh now, Sharon's, and the flesh of the world: its terrain and its seasons of golden and red, then white, then mud and rain and green, and the blue and green months with their sun burning then tanning her skin. All trials of the spirit seem nothing compared to this: his grave and shameful talk with Monica and her parents, Monica's tears and seven more months of gestation, his taking the girl home, blanket-wrapped on his lap on the plane: cries in the night and diapers, formula and his impatience and frustration and anger as he powdered the pink peach of her girlhood, staying home with her at night

and finding babysitters so he could teach—all this goes
through his mind like blown ashes, for he can only feel the
flesh: Sharon's and his and the daughter in the chair beside
him: she is a small child now, has lived long enough to love
the sun on her face and the taste of steak. And for the first
time in his life he understands that grief is not of the mind but
the body. He can dull his mind, knock it out with booze and
sleeping pills. But he can do nothing about his pierced body
as he watches Sharon eat, can do nothing about its pieces sitting beside him in the body of a daughter, nor about the part
of it that was torn from him last October, that seems still to
live wherever they dumped it in the hospital in New York. He
offers Sharon dessert. The waitress says the apple pie is hot
and homemade, just out of the oven. Sharon orders it with
vanilla ice cream, and Hank watches her mouth open wide for
the cold-hot bites, and hears the sea waves again, and sees the
long rubbery brown kelp washed up on the sand.

He does not phone Edith that night because Lori stays with
him. She ought to go back to the dormitory: Friday night she
walked to his house with clothes and books in a knapsack,
and if she goes back now she can say she spent the weekend
in Boston. If anyone asks. No one does, because her friends
know where she is. Tomorrow she will have to wake at six
while the students are still sleeping and no one is at work
except the kitchen staff and one security guard who might
see her walking from the direction of Hank's apartment, not
the bus stop. The security guard and kitchen staff are not
interested; even if they were, their gossip doesn't travel
upward to the administration; student, secretarial, and faculty gossip does. Lori and Hank have been doing this for
nearly a year, with a near-celibate respite last summer when,
except for her one day off a week, they saw each other in
Maine, after she had finished waitressing for the night. The
drive from his apartment was only an hour, but he decided,
grinning at himself, that it meant he truly loved her, that he

had not just turned to her during the school year because he was lonely. He had not done anything so adolescent since he had been one: at ten he met her in the restaurant, they went to a bar for a couple of hours, then to her house for coffee in the kitchen, talking quietly while her parents slept; they kissed goodnight for a long time, then he drove home. He did not even consider making love in the car, told her if he did that, hair would grow on his bald spot, his love handles would disappear, and he'd probably get pimples. Some nights her family, or part of it, was at the restaurant, and they all went out together: father, mother, and one or both of her sisters home for a weekend. Hank liked her father, though he was hard to talk with, for he rarely spoke; Lori's mother did most of that, and the two sisters did most of the rest. Everyone pretended Hank and Lori were friends, not lovers, and although Hank wanted it that way, it made him uncomfortable, increased his guilt around Lori's father, and kept him fairly quiet. Often he wanted to take Mr. Meadows aside and tell him he and Lori were lovers and that he loved her and was not using her. He felt none of this with Mrs. Meadows, perhaps because as father of a daughter he imagined Mr. Meadows's concern. Hank danced with all the women in the family and the mother was foxier on the floor than her daughters. She told Hank how pretty she was by joking about how old she was, about her lost figure (the body he held was as firm as Lori's); she asked if he wanted to go to the parking lot for some fresh air, smiling in a way that made him believe and disbelieve the invitation; she did not ask what he was doing with Lori, but when she talked about Lori she looked at him, as they danced, with various expressions: interrogation, dislike, and, most disconcerting of all, jealousy and lasciviousness. On Lori's day off each week she drove down to Hank's, telling her mother the beach was better there, sand instead of rocks; she needed to get out of town for a day; Hank did all that driving back and forth and she owed him one day of visiting him; told her mother all sorts of surface truths her

mother did not believe, and on that day they made love and
after dinner she drove home again.

Hank does not call Edith Sunday night because he does
not know whether or not his turning to her will hurt Lori, and
he does not have the energy to ask her. When he realizes that
is the only reason, he then wonders if he has the energy to
love. He does not remember the woman he was with, or the
specific causes, or even the season or calendar year, but he
remembers feeling like this before, and he is frightened by its
familiarity, its reminder that so much of his life demands
energy. He imagines poverty, hunger, oppression, exile, im-
prisonment: all those lives out there whose suffering is so
much worse than his, their endurance so superior, that his
own battles could earn only their scorn. He knows all this is
true, but it doesn't help, and he makes a salty dog for Lori and,
after hesitating, one for himself. Halfway through his drink,
as they lie propped on the bed—he has no chairs except the
one at his desk—watching *All in the Family*, he decides not to
have a second drink. He has become mute, as if the day-long
downward-pulling heaviness of his body is trying to paralyze
him. So he holds Lori's hand. At nine they undress and get
under the covers and watch *The New Centurions*. When
George C. Scott kills himself, they wipe their eyes; when Sta-
cey Keach dies, they wipe them again, and Lori says: 'Shit.'
Hank wishes he had armed enemies and a .38 and a riot gun.
He thinks he would rather fight that way than by watching
television and staying sober and trying to speak. He goes
through the apartment turning out lights, then gets into bed
and tightly holds Lori.

'I still can't,' he says.

'I know.'

He wants to tell her—and in fact does in his mind—how
much he loves her, how grateful he is that she was with him all
day, quietly knowing his pain, and that as bad as it was, the day
would have been worse without her; that she might even have
given him and Sharon the day, for without her he might not

have been able to get out of bed this morning. But silence has him and the only way he can break it is with tears as deep and wrenching as last night's, and he will not go through that again, does not know if he can bear that emptying again and afterward have something left over for whatever it is he has to do.

Some time in the night he dreams of him and Sharon lying on the blanket at the beach, the fetus curled pink and sweetly beside him, and asleep he knows as if awake that he is dreaming, that in the morning he will wake with it.

Monday night he eats a sandwich, standing in the kitchen by the telephone, and calls Jack and asks him to go out for a drink after dinner. Then he phones Edith. When she asks what happened he starts to tell her but can only repeat I three times and say *Monica*; then he is crying and cursing his tears and slapping the wall with his hand. Edith tells him to take his time (they *are* forever married, he thinks) and finally with her comforting he stops crying and tells the whole story in one long sentence, and Edith says: 'That little bitch. She didn't even let you *know? I* could have taken it. I would have taken your baby.'

'*I* would have.'

'You would?'

'You're Goddamned right. I didn't even get a fucking shot at it. That's why she didn't let me know. She knew I'd have fought it.'

'You keep surprising me. That's what happens in marriage, right? People keep changing.'

'Who says I changed?'

'I just didn't know you felt that way.'

'I never had to before.'

'I'm sorry, baby. I never did like that girl. Too much mischief in those eyes.'

'It was worse than that.'

'Too many lies deciding which would come out first.'

'That's her.'

'I really would have taken it. If things had gotten bad for
you.'

'I know.'

'Is there anything I can do?'

'Forgive me.'

'For what?'

'Everything.'

'You are. Sharon was very happy when she came home
yesterday.'

Hank's drinks are bourbon, beer, gin, and tequila, and he
knows where each will take him. Bourbon will keep him in
the same mood he's in when he starts to drink; beer does the
same. Either of them, if he drinks enough, will sharpen his
focus on his mood, but will not change it, nor take it too far.
So they are reliable drinks when he is feeling either good or
bad. He has never had a depressed or mean tequila drunk; it
always brings him up, and he likes to use it most when he is
relaxed and happy after a good day's work. He can also trust it
when he is sad. He likes gin rickeys, and his favorite drink is a
martini, but he does not trust gin, and drinks it very carefully:
it is unpredictable, can take him any place, can suddenly—
when he happily began an evening—tap some anger or sorrow
he did not even know he had. Since meeting Lori, who loves
tequila, he has been replacing the juniper with the cactus.

Tonight, with Jack, he drank gin rickeys, and it is not
until he is lying in bed and remembering the fight he has just
won that he can actually see it. Timmy's is a neighborhood
bar, long and narrow, with only a restroom for men. Beyond
its wall is the restaurant, with booths on both sides and one
line of tables in the middle; the waitresses in there get drinks
through a half door behind the bartender; when customers
are in the dining room, the door is kept closed on the noise
from the bar. Students rarely drink on the bar side; they stay
in the dining room.

Tonight the bar was lined with regulars, working men whose ages are in every decade between twenty and seventy. Two strangers, men in their mid-twenties, stood beside Hank. Their hands were tough, dirty-fingernailed, and their faces confident. Hank noticed this because he was trying to guess what they did for a living. Some of the young men who drank at Timmy's were out of work and drawing unemployment and it showed in their eyes. After the second drink Jack said: 'It's either woman-trouble or work-trouble. Which one?'

'Neither.'

'It's got to be. It's always one or the other, with a man. Or money.'

'Nope.'

'Jesus. Are we here to talk about it?'

'No, just to shoot the shit.'

Johnny McCarthy brought their drinks: in his mid-twenties, he is working his way through law school; yet always behind the bar, even when he is taking exams, he is merry; he boxed for Notre Dame five or six years ago and looks and moves as though he still could. Hank paid for the round, heard 'nigger' beside him, missed the rest of the young man's sentence, and asked Jack if he ran today.

'No, I got fucked into a meeting. Did you?'

'Just a short one by the campus. Let's run Kenoza tomorrow.'

'Good.'

'I'll pick you up.'

The talk to his right was louder, and he tried not to hear it as he and Jack talked about teaching, punctuated once by the man bumping his right side, an accident probably but no apology for it; then more talk until he heard 'Lee' and, still listening to Jack and talking to him, he also listened to blond big-shouldered cocky asshole on his right cursing Hank's favorite man on the Red Sox, that smooth pitcher, that competitor. In his bed he cannot count the gin rickeys or the time that passed before he heard 'Lee,' then turned and no longer saw the broad shoulders. Drunk, he felt big and strong and fast and, most of all, an anger that had to be released, an anger so intense that it felt like hatred too. As a grown man he had come close to fighting several times, in bars, but he never had because always, just short of saying the final words that would do it, he had images of the consequences: it was not fear of being hurt; he had played football in high school and was not unduly afraid of pain; it was the image of the fight's end: the bartender, usually a friend, sober and disgusted as he ejected Hank; or, worse, cops, sober and solemn and ready for a little action themselves, and he could not get past those images of dignity-loss, of shame, of being pulled up from the floor where he rolled and fought like a dog. So always he had stopped, had felt like a coward till next morning when he was glad he had stopped. But this time he turned to the man and said: 'You don't know what the fuck you're talking about.'

The man stepped back to give himself room.

'What's that?'

'Lee's the best clutch pitcher on the staff.'

'Fucking loudmouth spaceman is what he is.'

'Oh that's it. I thought I heard nigger a while back. You don't like what he *says*, is that it?' He could feel rather than hear the silence in the bar, could hear Johnny across the bar talking to him, urging, his voice soft and friendly. 'It's bussing, is that it? You don't like Lee because he's for bussing? Pissed you off when he didn't like the war?'

'Fuck *him*. I was *in* Nam, motherfucker, and I don't want to fucking hear you again: you drink with that other cunt you're with.'

'I'm glad you didn't get killed over there,' Hank said, his voice low, surprising him, and he turned away, nodded at Johnny, then he reached for his glass, confused, too many images now—and in his bed smiling he can understand it: dead children and women and scared soldiers and dead soldiers; and in Washington he and Jack quietly crying as they watched the veterans march, old eyes and mouths on their young bodies or what was left of some of them: the legless black with his right arm raised as a friend pushed his wheelchair, the empty sleeves, empty trouser-legs on that cold Inauguration Day; in his bed he can understand it: the man had given him a glimpse of what might have been his long suffering in Vietnam, for a moment he had become a man instead of an asshole with a voice. Then Hank surprised himself again: his rage came back, and into his drink he said: 'Fuck you anyway.'

They were standing side by side, nearly touching: they turned together, Hank's left fist already swinging, and his right followed it, coming up from below and behind his waist; then he seemed to be watching himself from the noise and grasping hands around him, felt the hands slipping from him as he kept swinging, and the self he was watching was calm and existed in a circle of silence, as if he were a hurricane watching its own eye. The man was off-balance from Hank's first two punches, so he could not get his feet and body set, and all his blows on Hank's arms, ribs, side of the head, came while going backward and trying to plant his feet and get his weight forward; and Hank drove inside and with short punches went for the blood at the nose and mouth. Then the man was against the wall, and Hank felt lifted and thrown though his feet did not leave the floor; the small of his back was pressed against the bar's edge, his arms spread and held to the bar by each wrist in Johnny's tight hands. Then it was Jack holding his wrists, talking to him, and over Jack's shoulder he watched Johnny push aside the two regulars holding the man against the wall. The man's friend was there, yelling, cursing. Johnny turned to him, one hand on the blond's chest, and said: 'I'm sick of this shit. Open your mouth again and you'll look like your friend there.' Then he turned to Jack: 'Will you get Hank the fuck *out* of here.'

Then he was outside, arm-in-arm with Jack, and he was laughing.

'Are you all right?'

He could feel Jack trembling; he was trembling too.

'I feel *great*,' he said.

'You tore his ass. You crazy bastard, I didn't know you could fight.'

'I can't,' Hank said, sagging from Jack's arm as he laughed. 'I just did, that's all.'

He is awake a long time but it is excitement and when finally he sleeps he is still happy. The dream is familiar now: it comes earlier than usual, or Hank feels that it does, and next morning at ten he wakes to that and much more. He is grateful the sun is coming in; it doesn't help, but a grey sky would be worse: he lies thinking of Johnny's anger last night, and he wonders who the man is, and hopes that somewhere he is lying with a gentle woman who last night washed his cuts. Then he is sad. It has been this way all his life, as long as he can remember, even with bullies in grade school, and he has never understood it: he can hate a man, want to hurt him or see him hurt; but if he imagines the man going home to a woman (as the bullies went to their mothers) he is sad. He imagines the man last night entering his apartment, the woman hurrying to his face, the man vulnerable with her as he is with no one else, as he can be with no one else, loving her as she washes each cut— *Does that hurt? Yes*—the man becoming a boy again as she gently cleans him, knowing this is the deepest part of himself beneath all the layers of growing up and being a man among men and soldiering: this—and he can show it only to her, and she is the only one in his life who can love it.

'I hope he finds me and beats shit out of me,' Hank says aloud. Then he can smile: he does not want the shit beat out of him. He drives to Jack's house. In the car, when Hank tells him how he feels now, Jack says: 'Fuck that guy; he wanted a fight all night. And after school we'll go see Johnny. He'll start laughing as soon as he sees you.' Immediately Hank knows this is true. He wonders what men without friends do on the day after they've been drunken assholes.

At Lake Kenoza he parks at the city tennis courts and locks his wallet and their windbreakers in the car. They start slowly, running on a dirt road, in the open still, the sun warm on Hank's face: he looks at the large pond to his left. The purple loose-strife is gone now; in summer it grows bright purple among the reeds near the pond. The road curves around the pond, which is separated from the lake by a finger of tree-grown earth. As they leave the pond they enter the woods, the road sun-dappled now, deeply rutted, so he has to keep glancing down at it as he also watches the lake to his left; the road is close to it, just up the slope from its bank lapped by waves in the breeze; to his right the earth rises, thick with trees. He and Jack talk while they run.

He wishes Lori ran. He has never had a woman who did. Edith started after their marriage ended. Running is the most intimate part of his friendship with Jack. Hank does not understand precisely why this is true. Perhaps it has something to do with the rhythm of their feet and breath. But there is more: it is, Hank thinks, setting free the flesh: as they approach the bend marking the second mile, the road staying by the lake and moving deeper into the woods which rise farther and farther to their right, he is no longer distracted by anything: he sees the lake and road and woods and Jack's swinging arms and reaching legs as he could never see them if he were simply walking, or standing still. It is this: even in lovemaking the body can become a voyeur of its own pleasure. But in the willful exertion of running, nothing can distract the flesh from itself.

Which is why he waits for the long hill that comes at the middle of their nearly six-mile run. They are close to it now, and are both afraid of it, and know this about each other. The road climbs away from the lake and they go up it, then leave it, onto a dirt trail dropping to the lake again. Here the lake's bank is sheer, there are rocks at its base, pebbles on the sand; to the right is the slope of the hill, steep, covered brown with pine needles, nearly all its trees are pines, and looking up there Hank cannot see the top of the hill or even the sky; always here he thinks of *For Whom the Bell Tolls*, sees Robert Jordan and Anselmo in the opening pages, lying up there among the pines. The trail often rises and falls, and then it goes down and to the right and up and they are on it: the long curving deceptive hill. It took Hank nearly a year to stop believing the next crest was the last one: short of breath, legs hurting, he looks up the road which is so steep and long that he cannot see beyond the next crest; he has never counted them, or the curves between them; he does not want to know. He prefers to run knowing only that it will get worse; and by doing this he always has that weary beat of joy when he sees that finally, a quarter of a mile or so ahead, is the top.

'Monet again,' Jack says.

Hank looks past him, down the hill; between the pines he can see sweat-blurred flashes of the lake; but it is the sun on the trees he's looking at. Jack is right; the sun touches the trees like Monet. Now they run harder, to reach the top, end the pain, and slowly the road levels and they shorten their strides: fast dry breaths, and Jack shakes his hand; they are at the center of the top of the hill, and suddenly, shaking Jack's hand and running beside him, Hank sees the dream again; the hill has not worked, he has run out of cures, and he releases Jack's hand and shouts through his own gasping: 'I can't get cafucking*tharsis*—'

Going downhill now, watching the road so he won't turn an ankle in a rut, he tells Jack about Monica; and the dream, which is with him now as he talks past trees and lake, talks all the way out of the woods into the sunlight where finally he stops talking for their last sprint to the tennis courts, the car, the water fountain.

'Marry Lori,' Jack says, as he bends toward the fountain; he walks away gargling, then spits out the water and returns. 'The fucking country's gone crazy,' he says. 'Marry her.'

Lori worries too much. Sometimes she thinks if she could stop worrying about so many parts of her life, and focus on her few real problems, there would be an end to those times, which are coming at least weekly now so she is afraid of an ulcer, when she is eating and it seems her food drops onto tense muscles and lies there undigested and after the meal it is still there and she is nauseated; and she could stop smoking so much; and she could stop staring at her school work at night instead of doing it; and she could ask questions in class, and could say what she was thinking when the teacher tried to start a discussion, instead of sitting there with her stomach tightening and feeling sorry for him because no one else is talking either. She could talk to her friends at school, girls and boys; she talks to them now, but usually only about what they are saying; she doesn't think they even realize this, but she knows it is why they like her and think of her as sweet and kind, their faces warm when she joins them at a table in the dining room or snack bar; but they don't know any of her secrets, and they are good friends who would listen, so it is her fault. She has been able to talk to Hank, so he knows more about her than anyone, but still she has not talked to him enough. She suspects though—and this makes her feel safely loved— that he understands more about her than she has told him.

Yet on the one night, two weeks ago, when she tried to separate her smaller problems from her essential ones, made parallel lists on a legal pad, she found that they were all connected, so the vertical lists, beginning with *my stomach* in the left column and *career* in the right column, became a letter to herself.

As she wrote it she was both excited and frightened: excited because she was beginning to see herself, and lovingly, on the paper on her desk; and frightened because she did not know where the writing was taking her; and because it might take her no place at all, might end on the very next page, in mid-sentence—Her first line was: *My name is Lori Meadows.* She wrote that she was nineteen years old, would be twenty in January, was a sophomore in college and was screwed up. But as soon as those two words appeared on the yellow page, she did not believe them. She was a C student. That was in her file in the registrar's office: 2.4 next to her name. Her mother said she would never get to graduate school like that. Lori always nodded, always said *I know I know I'll bring it up.* She never asked her mother what she was supposed to study in graduate school. She was all right, she wrote, except when she thought about the future. She liked going to her classes and sometimes she even came out excited; but then at night she could not study. Hank told her it was easy: she only had to spend two or three hours on school nights going over the notes from that day's classes and reading the assignments, she would be free by nine every night, and when exams came there would be no cramming, no all-nighters, all she would have to do was go over the notes again and the passages she had marked in the books. She loved the books. She loved owning them, and the way they looked on the shelves in her small room. But at night she didn't want to open them. Hank said he studied that way all through college and was on the dean's list every semester. But he was smarter than she was, and she worried about that too. But maybe that wasn't it. He was writing then; before he got out of college he wrote a novel and burned it. She would have to ask him if he studied like that so he'd have time to write, or if that was just the way he did things.

She didn't have any reason to study like that except to make grades and she didn't know what to make grades for except so she wouldn't feel like a dumb shit, and so her mother wouldn't start in on her. So at night she talked with people or went to Hank's. At least she didn't smoke dope. She didn't smoke it at all, but she was thinking of those who just went to their rooms and turned on the stereo and smoked themselves to sleep. Often in February, or even before Christmas, they packed their things and went home. In the morning she woke in panic because she hadn't done her work. Last year she got a D in biology because she couldn't memorize, but she liked the classes. But she could memorize. She just didn't. She got Bs last year in Hank's literature courses because she had a crush on him and she liked the stories and novels he assigned and she could write about them on tests. And she'd probably get a B or A in his Chekhov course this fall. Maybe it was love last year, not a crush. They were drinking friends then, in September, and often she went drinking with him and Monica and sometimes just she and Hank walked down to Timmy's and sat in a booth in the dining room. She could talk to him then too. But she fell in love with him when he started taking her out after Monica, and when he made love with her so gently the first time and she came for the first time with a man, but if she hadn't had the crush she wouldn't have fallen in love holding hands on Boylston Street and stopping in the bookstore and making love that night, so maybe it was called a crush when you were in love without touching.

She didn't understand about school. She was not lazy. She worked hard learning to ride and won three cups for jumping before she was fifteen and then she stopped riding except for fun. Some girls stayed with horses, at a certain age, and they didn't change after that; they didn't go for boys. At least the girls she had known. She worked hard at the restaurant last summer and the summer before. She knew everything about those two summers, the work and what she had read and the beach and her friends, loving her quiet father and loving her mother too, wishing she and her father could talk and touch, watching him, wondering what he thought, what pictures were in his mind when she entered a room and he looked up at her, and his face loved her; and wishing she could talk to her mother instead of just listen to the words that seemed to come as long as her mother was awake, like a radio left on; but this radio was dangerous, sometimes it was witty, sometimes cheerful, sometimes just small talk, but each day there were always other things, nearly always subtle, sometimes even with a smile: warnings, reprimands, disapprovals, threats, most of them general, having to do with things as vague as growth, the future, love, being a woman. None of these was vague but they were when her mother talked about them: cryptic, her voice implying more than the words; her mother never spoke as if, in the world, there was a plan. And when Lori listened closely enough to this she heard or felt she heard the real cause: some brittle disappointment in her mother's voice, and she wanted to say *Are you unhappy Mother? What is it you want? What is it you want for me?*

For they had never had any real trouble. Lori had avoided

dope because the first time she smoked it she didn't like it, she only got very sleepy and very hungry at once and was suddenly asleep at the party; and she was afraid to swallow anything, did not want something down in her stomach where she could not throw it away. She was obedient, and had always been. She was pretty, as her sisters were. She had a notion, which she didn't want, that if she were not pretty, her mother would not forgive her for that. They had never really quarrelled. She had watched her mother flirt with boys who came for her or her sisters, and with men, in front of her father; had watched her father's face, not quite grim, mostly calm. She knew her mother needed to flirt, see her effect on the boys who blushed and the men who did not. Her mother flirted with Hank too, but when he wasn't there she frowned when Lori spoke of him. *He's too old for you*, she said. *We're just friends. What kind of friends? I get lonely at school; he's good to talk to. This is summer. He's still my friend.* Wishing she could say *I'm in love* and *What does too old mean? That he'll die first? I could drown tomorrow.* She had told Hank. He said *It's not age. It's money. If I were a doctor or a Republican senator she'd bring us coffee in bed.*

She did not know if her mother did more than flirt. But all through the years there were times when her mother would go away, tell husband and daughters she needed a vacation, and she would go to Mexico, or the Caribbean, and return a week or two later with a tan and presents for everyone; and when Lori was fifteen she realized that for at least two years she had been trying not to wonder what a flirtatious, pretty and slender woman did alone at Puerto Vallarta, Martinique ... Now the words on the legal pad told her exactly what her mother did and she understood why her father was even gentler than usual as he cooked for the three daughters while his wife screwed men she had met hours before. Why did her mother need that? It frightened her, as though it were an illness that ran in the women in the family, and she was ashamed that there were men walking the earth who had screwed her mother, who might crazily someday even meet her, realize she was the daughter of that six-day woman winters ago, and how could her mother do that to her—to them?

She did not know why she made love to Blake summer before last; could remember, as she wrote, moments in the restaurant when they smiled at each other as they hurried with trays, and then drank at the bar when the kitchen closed and they were done for the night. It was simply, she knew now, the camaraderie of people working together, an assurance that they were not really carriers of trays, smiling servants, charming targets of well-mannered abuse. He could have been a woman. Then at the night's end, after their drinks, Lori and the woman would have separated, as they would at the summer's end; by the time the leaves fell they would fondly think of each other, in their separate schools, as summer friends, waitress friends. But because he was a man, that affinity of coworkers, especially those with menial jobs, grew to passion and all its tributaries of humor and tenderness and wanting to know and be known; and she was eighteen, the last virgin among her friends and in her home; the last virgin on the block, her sisters teased.

It was August, she had been working all summer, school was coming. Blake was going back to Illinois, it seemed time: time to complete or begin or both, and there was tequila and cheer, the very sound of her laugh seeming different to her, something of freedom in it; there was the dirt path near the cliff's edge over the sea and rocky beach, and tenderly she walked with him and tenderly she kissed him and went to the earth with him and was not afraid, was ready, here on the cliff she had walked as a child, so much better than in a dormitory, waves slapping rocks as if they knew she was up there between them and the moving clouds and moon and stars. Then she was afraid: the slow tenderness of the walk was gone with her clothes he removed too quickly; she lay waiting, her eyes shut, listening to his clothes sliding from his skin, then too soon he was in her, big and she was tight, and everything was fast and painful and she cried, not only that night but every night after work, not because it always hurt, but because she couldn't tell him how to make it better and finally after two weeks when the summer was ending and he came, then rolled away and sat naked looking at the sea while beside him she lay softly crying, he said: *You're screwed up.* She said nothing. She got up fast and dressed and was on the path before he called to her to wait. She did not. She walked faster. But she knew he would catch up with her, so she crouched behind a pine tree, heard him coming, watched him trot past. Then she left the tree and sat near the cliff's edge and watched the ocean, listening. When she was certain she heard only wind and waves, she rose and walked down the path.

She did not want to walk the four miles home. She went to a bar where she knew her girl friends would be. She found their table; they waved and beckoned as she went to them. Monica was there. They had pitchers of beer and were laughing and on the bandstand a group was singing like Crosby Stills Nash and Young: the same songs, the same style. Her friends were talking to her: she was smiling, talking, accepting a mug. But she was angry. She did not know why and it made her feel unpredictable and moody like her mother, and guilty because her friends had not hurt her, it was Blake, yet he was only a shard of pain inside her anger. Yet writing about it over a year later she understood, and was delighted at the understanding till she paused and put her pen in her mouth and sucked on it and wondered if tonight she could have understood this without Hank. Had he taught her to see? She felt diminished. Her long-time voice with its long-time epithet whispered at her spine: *You're a dumb shit.* Then she was angry. At herself. It was Chekhov, that wonderful man dead too young; his story, when the old doctor said: *Why do you hate freedom so?* Chekhov who wrote about the perils, even the evil, of mediocrity. Hank merely assigned the stories and talked about them. And wasn't that really why she was in school? She stopped writing. Made a dash, indented. Wrote about the bar again, her friends, her anger, or else she would forget and she must get that down quickly because she had started to discover something else and if she didn't get back to the bar now she might never.

It was the people singing, and her friends' clapping praise. While she sat with the pains of Blake's attacks: the one with his cock, the one with his tongue, the one with his heart. And her friends were listening to four boys in their early twenties who were content to imitate someone else. While her betrayal on the cliff called for poetry or an act of revenge. Up *there*. On *that* cliff, where in the brightest daylight of sun on ocean she had lain beside her sisters; where she and her friends had gone with sandwiches and apples in the days of dirty hands and knees, up *there* she had tried for love and felt nothing but that cruel cock—And she walked down alone, with some brav-ery against pain, with some pride in her bravery, and re-en-tered a lowland of laughter and mediocrity, where she could never explain what had happened up there above the sea. The guitars and voices taunted her: the safe musicians who prac-ticed to albums. Her friends' laughter drained her.

But what was that before? The anger, the *You dumb shit* voice—Yes: Hank. It was Chekhov. And first of all, she had no way of knowing whether tonight's understanding of her anger in that bar over a year ago came from reading Chekhov. But it didn't matter. What if she had learned from reading, even from hearing Hank talk about Chekhov? That didn't mean she was too dumb to understand her own life without some-one else's help. It meant she was getting smarter. Now she wrote with joy, with love for herself in the world. Wasn't that what she was in school for? To enter classrooms and to hear? And if that made her understand her life better, wasn't that enough and wasn't that why she could not study for the grades for the graduate school which would give her a job she could not even imagine and therefore could not imagine the graduate school either? Wasn't she in fact an intelligent young woman trying to learn how to live, and if no profession pulled at her, if she could not see herself with a desk and office and clothes and manners to match them, that only meant she was like most people. This fall Hank talking in class about 'The Kiss' and what people had to endure when they had jobs instead of vocations; Ryabovich, with his dull career, existing more in the daydreams he constructed from the accidental kiss than he did in the saddle of his horse.

She wanted to phone Hank and tell him but she did not want to stop writing, and now it was time to write about Hank anyway. Already she was with her second lover and she had tried not to think about the future but it kept talking to her anyway at times when she was alone, but she would not talk back, would not give words to her fear, but now her pen moved fast because her monologue with her future had been there for some time and she knew every word of it though she had refused, by going to sleep or going to talk to someone, ever to listen to it. Already two lovers and she wished she could cancel the first and, if she and Hank broke up, there would be a third and she would be going the way of her sisters who had recovered, she thought, too many times from too many lovers, were growing tougher through repeated pain; were growing, she thought, cynical; and when they visited home, they talked about love but never permanent love any-more, and all the time she *knew* but wouldn't say because they still talked to her like a baby sister and because she didn't want to loosen what she saw as a fragile hold on their lives, she knew what they needed was marriage. Two lovers were enough. Three seemed deadly. If she could not stay with the third, it seemed the next numbers were all the same, whether four or fifteen: some path of failure, some sequence of repeti-tions that would change her, take her further and further from the Lori she was beginning to love tonight.

And now here was Hank on a sunny October Saturday, having for the first time since she had known him cancelled his day with Sharon, walking beside her, on his back a nylon knap-sack he said held wine and their lunch, a blanket folded over his left arm, his right arm loosely around her waist as they walked on his running road she had never seen except in her mind when he talked about it. And he was happy, his boyish happiness that she loved, for the first time since last Saturday night when she told him about Monica because she could not hide from him any longer something she knew he would want to know. Tuesday night she had gone to his apartment and he told her of his fight Monday and that he and Jack had just been to Timmy's where he had apologized to Johnny and bought the bar a round, and he said Jack had been right. Johnny had grinned and said: *The middleweight champ of Timmy's* as soon as he walked in; and he told her about running with Jack and how it hadn't worked. She slept with him that night and Wednesday and Thursday and Friday, and he held her and talked. He did not tell her he still couldn't make love. He did not even mention it. During those four nights she felt he was talking to spirits, different ones who kept appearing above them where he gazed, felt that he was struggling with some, agreeing with others, and lying beside him she was watching a strange play.

He said Jack was right. The country had gone fucking crazy. He said I'll bet ninety percent of abortions are because somebody's making love with somebody they shouldn't. So were too many people. So had he, for too long. But no more. Things were screwed up and the women had lost again. A sexual revolution and a liberation movement and look what it got them. Guys didn't carry rubbers anymore. Women were expected to be on the pill or have an IUD and expected also to have their hearts as ready as their wombs. And women were even less free than before, except for the round-heels, and there were more of them around now but he didn't know any men who took them any more seriously than the roundheels from the old days of rubbers in the wallet and slow courting. Goddamn. The others (*Like you*, he said to Lori) are trapped. Used to be a young woman when they were called girls could date different guys and nobody had a hold on her, could date three guys in one weekend; by the end of a year in college she might have dated six, ten, any number, gone places, had fun,

been herself. Now girls are supposed to fuck. Most students
don't even date: just go to the dormitory room and drink and
smoke dope and get laid. Guy doesn't even have to work for it.
But then he's got the girl. Unless she's a roundheel, and
nobody gives a shit about them. But the good ones. Like you.
What they do is go through some little marriages. First one
breaks up, then there's another guy. Same thing. Three days
or three room-visits or whatever later, and they're lovers.
Somebody else meets her, wants to take her to Boston to hear
some music, see a play, she can't. Boy friend says no. Can't
blame him; she'd say no if he wanted to take somebody to
hear some music. Girl gets out of college and what she's had
is two or three monogamous affairs, even shared the same
room. Call that freedom? Men win again. Girls have to make
sure they don't get pregnant, they have to make love, have to
stay faithful. Some revolution. Some liberation. And everybody's so fucking happy, you noticed that? Jack is right, Goddamnit; Jack is right. He's glad now they stuck it out. He and
Terry. He said I've got a good friend who's also my wife and
I've got two good children, and the three of them make the
house a good nest, and I sit and look out the window at the
parade going by: some of my students are marching and some
of my buddies, men and women, and the drum majorette is
Aphrodite and she's pissed off and she's leading that parade to
some bad place. I don't think it's the Styx either. It's some
place where their cocks will stay hard and their pussies wet,
some big open field with brown grass and not one tree, and
nobody's going to say anything funny there. Nobody'll laugh.
All you'll hear is pants and grunts. Maybe Aphrodite will
laugh, I don't know. But I don't think she's that mean. Just a
trifle pissed-off at all this trifling around.

'It's beautiful,' Lori says, as they enter the woods and she can
see the lake.
    'This is the first time I've walked it,' Hank says.
    'It is? You've never brought a woman here?'

'No. Not even Sharon.'

'Why?'

'Never thought about it. When I think of this place I think of running. I've never even been here after it snows. Too slippery.'

'Not for walking. With boots.'

'No.'

'Can we come here in winter?'

'Sure.'

He moves his arm from her waist and takes her hand. They walk slowly. An hour passes before they start up the long hill; he looks down the slope at sun on the pines, and their needles on the earth, at boulders, and the lake between branches. At the top he says: 'Blackberries grow here.'

'Do you and Jack ever pick them?'

'We say we will. But when we get to the top we just sort of look at them as we gasp on by.'

He turns left into the woods, and they climb again, a short slope above the road; then they are out of the trees, standing on a wide green hill, looking down and beyond at the Merrimack Valley, the distant winding river, and farms and cleared earth; surrounding all the houses and fields, and bordering the river, are the red and yellow autumn trees. He unfolds the blanket and she helps him spread it on the grass. He takes off the pack and brings out a bottle of claret, devilled eggs wrapped in foil, a half-gallon jug of apple cider, two apples, a pound of Jarlsberg cheese, Syrian bread, and a summer sausage. She is smiling.

'Cider?'

She nods and takes the jug from him and he watches the muscle in her forearm as she holds it up and drinks, watching her throat moving, her small mouth. When she hands him the jug he drinks, then opens the wine with a corkscrew from the pack.

'I didn't bother with glasses.' They pass the bottle. She lightly kisses him and says: 'You went to a lot of trouble. I thought you'd just buy a couple of subs.'

They eat quietly, looking at the valley. Then Hank lies on his back while Lori sits smoking. When she puts out the cigarette she returns it to her pack.

'That does it,' he says.

'What?'

'Anybody who'd take a stinking butt home instead of leaving it here ought to be loved forever.'

She lies beside him, rests her head on his right shoulder, and he says: 'I think when we started making love I wasn't in love with you. I felt like you were one of my best friends, and I needed someone to keep me going. I figured you'd be like the other young ones, give me a year, maybe a little more, then move on. But I chose that over staring at my walls at night. I wasn't thinking much about you. Then after a few months I didn't have to think about you anyway, because I was in love, so I knew I wasn't going to hurt you. I figured you'd leave me, and I'd just take a day at a time till you did. Like I did with Monica. I should never have made love with Monica. I haven't had the dream since Monday after the fight—'

'—She shouldn't have made love with you.'

'Same thing. I can't do that again. Ever. With anyone. Unless both of us are ready for whatever happens. No more playing with semen and womb if getting pregnant means solitude and death instead of living. And that's all I mean: living. Nobody's got to do a merry dance, have the faulty rubber bronzed. But living. Worry; hope the rabbit doesn't die; keep the Tampax ready; get drunk when the rabbit dies; but laugh too. So I can't make love with you. I'm going to court you. And if someday you say you'll marry me, then it'll be all right, and—'

'—It's all right now.'

She kisses him, the small mouth, the slow tongue that always feels to him shy and trusting. Then she pulls him so his breast covers hers and she holds his face up and says: 'I want to finish college.' She smiles. 'For the fun of it. But we're engaged.'

'That's almost three years. What if we get pregnant?'

'Then we'll get married and I'll go to school till the baby comes and I'll finish later, when I can.'

'You've thought about it before?'

'Yes.'

'For how long?'

'I don't know. But longer than you.'

'Are you going to tell your folks?'

'Sure.'

'They won't like it.'

'She won't. My father won't mind.'

'We might as well do it in the old scared-shitless way: drive up there together and tell them.'

'I'd like that.'

'Do you want a ring?'

'No. Something else.'

'What?'

'I don't know. We'll find something.'

'I like this. So next Saturday we go to Boston and find something. And we don't know what it is. But it'll mean we're getting married.'

'Yes.'

'And that night we go to your folks' for dinner and we say we have a little announcement to make.'

'Yes.'

'And your mother will hate it but she'll try not to show it. And your father will blush and grin and shake my hand.'

'Maybe he'll even hug me.'

'And for three years your mother will hope some rich guy steals you from me, and your father will just go on about his business.'

'That's it.' Then she presses both palms against his jaw and says: 'And we're never going to get a divorce. And we're not going to have American children. We're going to bring them up the way you and Edith were.'

'Look what that got us.'

'A good daughter.'

'You really think she's all right?'

'Man, that chick's got her shit together,' she says, then she is laughing and he tries to kiss her as she turns away with her laughter and when it stops she says: 'Clean tongues and clean lungs and no Monicas and Blakes. That's how we'll bring them up. Let's make love.'

'The Trojan warriors are at home.'

'You really *did* think you'd have to court me. Then let's go home.'

He kisses her once, then kneels, uncorks the wine bottle, holds it to her lips while she raises her head to swallow; then he drinks and returns the cork and puts the bottle in the pack. As he stands and slips his arms through the straps, Lori shakes out the blanket, and they fold it.

'Can I keep this in my room at school?'

'Sure.'

She rests it over her arm and takes his hand and looks down at the valley. Then she turns to the woods, and quietly they leave the hill and go down through the trees to the road above the lake.

'It took us a long time to get here,' she says. 'Did you say this is the halfway point?'

'Right about where we're standing.'

'We didn't walk very fast. It'll be quicker, going back.'

'It always is,' he says, and starts walking.

THE TIMES ARE NEVER SO BAD

to Philip and Michel Spitzer

. . . the man in the violent situation reveals those qualities least dispensable in his personality, those qualities which are all he will have to take into eternity with him. . .
    FLANNERY O'CONNOR
    "On Her Own Work"

The times are never so bad but that a good man can live in them.
    SAINT THOMAS MORE

THE PRETTY GIRL

*But because thou art lukewarm, and neither cold nor hot,
I am about to vomit thee out of my mouth....*
SAINT JOHN
The Apocalypse

*for Roger Rath
out among the stars*

I DON'T KNOW how I feel till I hold that steel. That was always true: I might have a cold, or one of those days when everything is hard to do because you're tired for no reason at all except that you're alive, and I'd work out, and by the time I got in the shower I couldn't remember how I felt before I lifted; it was like that part of the day was yesterday, and now I was starting a new one. Or a hangover: some of my friends and my brother too are hair-of-the-dog people, but I've never done that and I never will, because a drink in the morning shuts down the whole day, and anyway I can't stand the smell of it in the morning and my stomach tells me it would like a Coke or a milkshake, but it is not about to stand for a prank like a shot of vodka or even a beer.

It was drunk out last night, Alex says. And I always say: *A severe drunk front moved in around midnight.* We've been saying that since I was seventeen and he was twenty-one. On a morning after one of those, when I can read the words in the *Boston Globe* but I can't remember them long enough to understand the story, I work out. If it's my off day from weights, I run or go to the Y and swim. Then the hangover is gone. Even the sick ones: some days I've thought I'd either blow my lunch on the bench or get myself squared away and, for the first few sets, as I pushed the bar up from my chest, the booze tried to come up too, with whatever I'd eaten during the night, and I'd swallow and push the iron all the way up and bring it down again, and some of my sweat was cool. Then I'd do it again and again, and add some weights, and do it again till I got a pump, and the blood rushed through my muscles and flushed out the lactic acid, and sweat soaked my shorts and tank shirt, the bench under my back was slick, and all the poison was gone from my body. From my head too, and for the rest of the day, unless something really bothered me, like having to file my tax return, or car trouble, I was as peaceful as I can ever be. Because I get along with people, and they don't treat me the way they treat some; in this world it helps to be big. That's not why I work out, but it's not a bad reason, and one that little guys should think about. The weather doesn't harass me either. New Englanders are always bitching about one thing or another. Once Alex said: *I think they just like to bitch, because when you get down to it, the truth is the Celtics and Patriots and Red Sox and Bruins are all good to watch, and we're lucky they're here, and we've got the ocean and pretty country to hunt and fish and ski in, and you don't have to be rich to get there.* He's right. But I don't bitch about the weather: I like rain and snow and heat and cold, and the only effect they have on me is what I wear to go out in them. The weather up here is female, and goes from one mood to another, and I love her for that.

So as long as I'm working out, I have good days, except for those things that happen to you like dead batteries and forms to fill out. If I skip my workouts I start feeling confused and distracted, then I get tense, and drinking and talking aren't good, they just make it worse, then I don't want to get out of bed in the morning. I've had days like that, when I might not have got up at all if finally I didn't have to piss. An hour with the iron and everything is back in place again, and I don't know what was troubling me or why in the first place I went those eight or twelve or however many days without lifting. But it doesn't matter. Because it's over, and I can write my name on a check or say it out loud again without feeling like a liar. This is Raymond Yarborough, I say into the phone, and I feel my words, my name, go out over the wire, and he says the car is ready and it'll be seventy-eight dollars and sixty-five cents. I tell him I'll come get it now, and I walk out into the world I'd left for a while and it feels like mine again. I like stepping on it and breathing it. I walk to the bank first and cash a check because the garage won't take one unless you have a major credit card, which I don't because I don't believe in buying something, even gas, that I don't have the money for. I always have enough money because I don't buy anything I can't eat or drink. Or almost anything. At the bank window I write a check to Cash and sign both sides and talk to the girl. I tell her she's looking good and I like her sweater and the new way she's got her hair done. I'm not making a move; I feel good and I want to see her smiling.

 · But for a week or two now, up here at Alex's place in New Hampshire, the iron hasn't worked for me. While I'm pump-ing I forget Polly, or at least I feel like I have, but in the shower she's back again. I got to her once, back in June: she was scared like a wild animal, a small one without any natural weapons, like a wounded rabbit, the way they quiver in your hand and look at you when you pick them up to knock their heads against trees or rocks. But I think she started to like it anyways, and if I had wanted to, I could have made her come. But that's Polly. I've known her about twelve years, since I was fourteen, and I think I knew her better when we were kids than I ever did after high school when we started going together and then got married. In school I knew she was smart and pretty and tried to look sexy before she was. I still

don't know much more. That's not true: I can write down a
lot that I know about her, and I did that one cold night early
last spring, about fifty pages on a legal pad, but all of it was
what she said to me and what she thought I said to her and
what she did. I still didn't understand why she was that way,
why we couldn't just be at peace with one another, in the evenings drink some beer or booze, talking about this and that,
then eat some dinner, and be easy about things, which is what
I thought we got married for.

   We were camping at a lake and not catching any trout
when we decided to get married. We talked about it on the
second night, lying in our sleeping bags in the tent. In the
morning I woke up feeling like the ground was blessed, a
sacred place of Indians. I was twenty-two years old, and I
thought about dying; it still seemed many years away, but I
felt closer to it, like I could see the rest of my life in that tent
while Polly slept, and it didn't matter that at the end of it I'd
die. I was very happy, and I thought of my oldest brother,
Kingsley, dead in the war we lost, and I talked to him for a
while, told him I wished he was here so he could see how
good I felt, and could be the best man. Then I talked to Alex
and told him he'd be the best man. Then I was asleep again,
and when I woke up Polly was handing me a cup of coffee and
I could hear the campfire crackling. Late that afternoon we
left the ground but I kept the tent; I didn't bring it back to the
rental place. I had a tent of my own, a two-man, but I rented a
big one so Polly could walk around in it, and arrange the food
and cooler and gear, the way women turn places into houses,
even motel rooms. There are some that don't, but they're not
the kind you want to be with for the whole nine yards; when a
woman is a slob, she's even worse than a man. They had my
deposit, but they phoned me. I told them we had an accident
and the tent was at the bottom of Lake Willoughby up in Ver-
mont, up in what they call the Northern Kingdom. He asked
me what it was doing in the lake. I said I had no way of knowing because that lake was formed by a glacier and is so deep in
places that nobody could know even how far down it was,

much less what it was doing. He said *on* the lake, what was it doing *on* the lake? Did my boat capsize? I said, What boat? He had been growling, but this time he barked: then how did the tent get in the fucking lake? I pitched it there, I said. That's the accident I'm talking about. Then he howled: the deposit didn't cover the cost of the boat. I told him to start getting more deposit, and hung up. That tent is out here at Alex's, folded up and resting on the rafters in the garage. This place was Kingsley's, and when his wife married again she wanted to give it to me and Alex, but Alex said that wasn't right, he knew Kingsley would want her to do that, and at the same time he knew Kingsley would expect us to turn it down and give her some money; their marriage was good, and she has his kid, my niece Olivia who's nearly ten now. I was still in school, so Alex bought it.

What I thought we had—I know we had it—in the tent that morning didn't last, and even though I don't understand why everything changed as fast as our weather does, I blame her because I tried so hard and was the way I always was before, when she loved me; I changed toward her and cursed her and slapped her around when every day was bad and the nights worse. There are things you can do in the daytime that make you feel like your marriage isn't a cage with rattlesnakes on the floor, that you can handle it: not just working out, but driving around for a whole afternoon just getting eggs and light bulbs and dry cleaning and a watchband and some socks. You listen to music in the car and look at people in their cars (I've noticed often you'll see a young girl driving alone, smiling to herself; maybe it's the disc jockey, maybe it's what she's thinking), and you talk to people in their stores (I always try to go to small stores, even for food), and your life seems better than it was when you walked out of the house with the car key. But at night there's nothing to distract you; and besides at night is when you really feel married, and need to; and there you are in the living room with all those snakes on the floor. I was tending bar five nights a week then, so two nights were terrible and sad, and on the others I came home tired and crept into the house and bed, feeling like I was doing something wrong, something I didn't want her to wake up and see. Then near the end Vinnie DeLuca was in that bed on the nights I worked, and I found out and that was the end.

I treated her well. I shared the housework, like my brothers and I did growing up. I've never known a woman who couldn't cook better than I do, but still I can put a meal on the table, and I did that, either fried or barbecued; I cooked on the grill outside all year round; I like cooking out while snow is falling. I washed the dishes when she cooked, and sometimes remembered to vacuum, and I did a lot of the errands, because she hated that, probably because she went to supermarkets and never talked to anybody, while I just didn't quite enjoy it.

Never marry a woman who doesn't know what she wants, and knows she doesn't. Mom never knew what she wanted either, but I don't think she knew she didn't, and that's why she's stayed steady through the years. She still brings her Luckies to the table. When I was little I believed Mom was what a wife should look like. I never thought much about what a wife should be like. She was very pretty then and she still is, though you have to look at her for a while to see it. Or I guess other people do, who are looking for pretty women to be young, or the other way around, and when they see a woman in her fifties they don't really look at her until they have to, until they're sitting down talking to her, and seeing her eyes and the way she smiles. But I don't need that closer look. She's outdoors a lot and has good lines in her face, the kind of lines that make me trust someone.

Mom wants Lucky Strikes and coffee, iced in summer after the hot cups in the morning, and bourbon when the sun is low. When she has those she's all right, let it rain where we're camping or the black flies find us fishing. During the blizzard of 1978 Mom ran out of Luckies and Jim Beam, and the coffee beans were low; the old man laughs about it, he says she was showing a lot of courage, but he thought he better do something fast or be snowed in with a crazy woman, so he went on cross-country skis into town and came back with a carton and a bottle and a can of coffee in his parka pockets. I tried to stop you, she says when they joke about it. Not as hard as you've tried to stop me going other places, the old man says. The truth is, it was not dangerous, only three miles into town from their house, and I know the old man was happy for an excuse to get out into the storm and work up a sweat. Younger, he wouldn't have needed an excuse, but I think his age makes him believe when there's a blizzard he should stay indoors. He's buried a few friends. At the store he got to in the snow they only had regular coffee, not the beans that Mom buys at two or three stores you have to drive to. He says when he came home she grabbed the carton first and had one lit before he was out of his ski mask, and she had two drinks poured while he was taking off his boots; then she held up the can of coffee and said: Who drinks this? You have a girl friend you were thinking about? He took the drink from her and said I don't have time for a girl friend. And she said I know you don't. They didn't tell us any more of that story; I know there'd be a fire going, and I like to think he was down to his long underwear by then, and he took that off and they lay in front of the fireplace. But probably they just had bourbon and teased one another and the old man took a shower and they went upstairs to sleep.

I hope the doctors never tell Mom she has to give up her Luckies and coffee and bourbon. You may call that an addiction. So what is my pumping iron? What is Polly?

She would say I raped her in June and so would her cop father and the rest of her family, if she told them, which she probably did because she moved back in with them. But maybe she didn't tell them. She didn't press charges; Alex keeps in touch with what's going on down there, and he lets me know. But I've stayed up here anyway. It's hard to explain: the night I did it I naturally crossed the state line and came up here to the boondocks; I knew when they didn't find me at home or at work, Polly would tell them to try here, but it was a good place to wait for a night and a day, a good place to make plans. In the morning I called Alex and he spoke to a friend on the force and called me back and said, Nothing yet. Late that afternoon he called again, said, Nothing yet. So I stayed here the second night, and next morning and afternoon he called me again, so I stayed a third night and a fourth and fifth, because every day he called and said there was nothing yet. By then I had missed two nights of a job I liked, tending bar at Newburyport, where I got good tips and could have girls if I wanted them. I knew that a girl would help, maybe do more than that, maybe fix everything for me. But having a girl was just an idea, like thinking about a part of the country where you might want to live if you ever stopped loving the place where you were.

So I wanted to want a girl, but I didn't, not even when these two pretty ones came in almost every night I worked and sat at the bar and talked to me when I had the time, and gave me signs with their eyes and the way they joked with me and laughed at each other. I could have had either one, and I don't know how the other one would have taken it. Sometimes I thought about taking both of them back to my place, which is maybe what they had in mind anyway, but that wouldn't be the same as having a girl I wanted to want, and I couldn't get interested enough to go through the trouble. Once, before Polly, I went to a wedding where everyone got drunk on champagne. I noticed then something I hadn't noticed before: girls get horny at weddings. I ended up with two friends of the bride; I had known them before, but not much. They were dressed up and looking very good, and when the party broke up we went to a bar, a crowded bar with a lot of light, one of those places where the management figures it draws a crowd with all kinds in it, so one way to keep down fights and especially guys pulling knives is have the place lit up like a library. I sat between them at the bar and rubbed their thighs, and after we drank some more I had a hand up each of them; it was late spring and their legs were moist, squeezing my hands; then they opened a little, enough; I don't remember if they did this at the same time or one was first. Then I got my hands in their pants. The bar was crowded and people were standing behind us, drinking in groups and pairs, buying drinks over the girls' shoulders, and I was stroking clitoris. When I told Alex this he said, How did you drink and smoke? I said I don't know. But I do know that I kept talking and pretending to each girl that I was only touching her. I got the drinking done too. Maybe they came at the bar, but pretty soon I couldn't take it anymore, and I got them out of there. But in the car I suddenly knew how drunk and tired I was; I was afraid I couldn't make it with both of them, so I took the plump one to her apartment and we told her good night like a couple of innocent people going home drunk from a wedding. Then I brought the other one to my place, and we had a good night, but every time I thought of the bar I was sorry I took the plump one home. Probably the girl with me was sorry too, because in the morning I took a shower and when I got out, the bed was made and she was gone. She left a nice note, but it was strange anyway, and made the whole night feel like a bad mistake, and I thought since it didn't really matter who I got in bed with, it should have been the one that was plump. She was good-looking and I'm sure was not lonesome or hard up for a man, but still for the rest of the day and that night I felt sorry when I remembered her leaving the car and walking up the walk to her apartment building, because you know how women are, and she was bound to feel then that her friend was slender and she wasn't and that was the only reason she was going home alone drunk, with juicy underpants. She was right, and that's why I felt so bad. Next day I decided to stop thinking about her. I do that a lot: you do some things you wish you hadn't, and thinking about them afterward doesn't do any good for anybody, and finally you just feel like your heart has the flu. None of this is why I didn't take the two girls this summer back to my place.

What is hard to explain is why, when I knew Polly wasn't going to press charges, I stayed here instead of giving my boss some almost true story. I thought of some he would believe, or at least accept because he likes me and I do good work, something just a few feet short of saying Hey, lookit, I was running from a rape charge. But I didn't go back, except one night to my apartment for my fishing gear and guns and clothes and groceries. Nothing else in there belonged to me.

When I came up here that night I did it, I went to my place first and loaded the jeep with my weights and bench and power stands. So when I knew nobody was after me, all I did was work out, lifting on three days and running and swimming in the lake on the others. That was first thing in the morning, which was noon for everybody else. Every day was sunny, and in the afternoons I sat on a deck chair on the wharf, with a cooler of beer. Near sundown I rowed out in the boat and fished for bass and pickerel. If I caught one big enough for dinner, I stopped fishing and let the boat drift till dark, then rowed back and ate my fish. So all day and most of the night I was thinking, and most of that was about why I wasn't going back. All I finally knew was something had changed. I had liked my life till that night in June, except for what Polly was doing to it, but you've got to be able to separate those things, and I still believe I did, or at least tried to hard enough so that sometimes I did, often enough to know my life wasn't a bad one and I was luckier than most. Then I went to her house that night and I felt her throat under the Kabar, then her belly under it. I don't just mean I could feel the blade touching her, the way you can cut cheese with your eyes closed; it wasn't like that, the blade moving through air, then stopping because something—her throat, her belly—was in the way. No: I felt her skin touching the steel, like the blade was a finger of mine.

They would call it rape and assault with a deadly weapon, but those words don't apply to me and Polly. I was taking back my wife for a while; and taking back, for a while anyway, some of what she took from me. That is what it felt like: I went to her place torn and came out mended. Then she was torn, so I was back in her life for a while. All night I was happy and I kept getting hard, driving north and up here at Alex's, just remembering. All I could come up with in the days and nights after that, thinking about why I didn't go back to my apartment and working the bar, was that time in my life seemed flat and stale now, like an old glass of beer.

But I have to leave again, go back there for a while. Every-thing this summer is breaking down to for a while, which it seems is as long as I can keep peaceful. Now after my workout I get in the hot shower feeling strong and fresh, and rub the bar of soap over my biceps and pecs, they're hard and still pumped up; then I start to lose what the workout was really for, because nobody works out for just the body, I don't care what they may say, and it could be that those who don't lift or run or swim or something don't need to because they've got most of the time what the rest of us go for on the bench or road or in the pool, though I'm not talking about the ones who just drink and do drugs. Then again, I've known a lot of women who didn't need booze or drugs or a workout, while I've never known a man who didn't need one or the other, if not both. It would be inter-esting to meet one someday. So I flex into the spray, make the muscles feel closer to the hot water, but I've lost it: that feeling you get after a workout, that yesterday is gone and last night too, that today is right here in the shower, inside your body; there is nothing out there past the curtain that can bring you down, and you can take all the time you want to turn the water hotter and circle and flex and stretch under it, because the time is yours like the water is; when you're pumped like that you can't even think about death, at least not your own; or about any of the other petty crap you have to deal with just to have a good day; you end up with two or three minutes of cold water, and by the time you're drying off, the pump is easing down into a relaxed state that almost feels like muscle fatigue but it isn't: it's what you lifted all that iron for, and it'll take you like a stream does a trout, cool and easy the rest of the day.

I've lost that now: in the shower I see Polly walking around town smiling at people, talking to them on this warm dry August day. I don't let myself think anymore about her under or on top of or whatever and however with Vinnie DeLuca. I went through that place already, and I'm not going back there again. I can forget the past. Mom still grieves for Kingsley, but I don't. Instead of remembering him the way he was all those years, I think of him now, like he's forever twenty years old out there in the pines around the lake, out there on the water, and in it; Alex and I took all his stuff out of here and gave it to his wife and Mom. What I can't forget is right now. I can't forget that Polly's walking around happy, breathing today into her body. And not thinking about me. Or, if she does, she's still happy, she's still got her day, and she's draining mine like the water running out of the tub. So lately after my workout I stand in the shower and change the pictures; then I take a sandwich and the beer cooler out to the wharf and look at the pictures some more; I do this into the night, and I've stopped fishing or whatever I was doing in the boat. Instead of looking at pictures of Polly happy, I've been looking at Polly scared shitless, Polly fucked up, Polly paying. It's time to do some more terrorizing.

So today when the sun is going down I phone Alex. The lake is in a good-sized woods, and the trees are old and tall; the sun is behind them long before the sky loses its light and color, and turns the lake black. The house faces west and, from that shore, shadows are coming out onto the water. But the rest of it is blue, and so is the sky above the trees. I drink a beer at the phone and look out the screen window at the lake.

'Is she still living with Steve?' I say to Alex. A month ago he came out here for a few beers and told me he heard she'd moved out of her folks' house, into Steve Buckland's place.

'Far as I know,' Alex says.

'So when's he heading north?'

Steve is the biggest man I know, and he has never worked out; he's also the strongest man I know, and it's lucky for a lot of people he is also the most laid back and cheerful man I know, even when he's managed to put away enough booze to get drunk, which is a lot for a man his size. I've never seen him in a fight, and if he ever was in one, I know I would've heard about it, because guys would talk about that for a long time; but I've seen him break up a few when he's tending bar down to Timmy's, and I've seen him come out from the bar at closing time when a lot of the guys are cocked and don't want to leave, and he herds them right out the door like sheep. He has a huge belly that doesn't fool anybody into throwing a punch at him, and he moves fast. Also, we're not good friends, I only know him from the bar, but I like him, he's a good man, and I do not want to fuck over his life with my problem; besides, the word is that Polly is just staying with him till he goes north, but they're not fucking, then she'll sublet his place (he lives on a lake too; Alex is right about New England) while he stays in a cabin he and some guys have in New Hampshire, and after hunting season he'll ski, and he won't come back till late spring. Alex says he's leaving after Labor Day weekend. I have nothing against Steve, but Vinnie DeLuca is another matter. So I ask Alex about that gentleman's schedule.

'He's a bouncer at Old Colony. I think they call him a doorman.'

'I'll bounce his ass.'

'He might be carrying something, you know. With that job.'

'Shit. You think anybody'd let that asshole carry a gun?'

'Sure they would, but I was thinking blackjack. Want me to come along?'

'No, I'm all set.'

'If you change your mind, I'll be here.'

I know he will. He always has been, and I'm lucky to have a brother who's a friend too; I'm so lucky, I even had two of them; or unlucky because now I only have the one, depending on how I feel about things at the time I'm thinking of my brothers. I bring a beer out and sit on the wharf and watch the trees on the east side of the lake go from green to black as the sun sets beyond the tall woods. Then the sky is dark and I get another beer and listen to the lake sloshing against the bank, like someone is walking on it out there in the middle, his steps pushing the water around, and I think about Kingsley in the war. At first I don't want to, then I give in to it, and I picture him crawling in the jungle. He bought it from a mine; they didn't tell us if he was in a rice paddy or open field or jungle, but I always think of him in jungle because he loved to hunt in the woods and was so quiet in there. After a while I

swallow and tighten my chest and let out some air. Polly said
I was afraid to cry because it wasn't macho. That's not true.
I sure the fuck cried when Mom and the old man told me and
Alex about Kingsley, there in the kitchen, and I would've
cried no matter who was there to watch. I fight crying because
it empties you so you can't do anything about what's making
you cry. So I stop thinking about Kingsley, that big good-looking wonderful son of a bitch with that look he had on his face
when he was hunting, like he could see through the trees, as
he stepped on a mine or tripped a wire. By the time I stop
thinking about him, I know what else I'll do tonight, after I
deal with Mr. DeLuca A.K.A. the doorman of Old Colony.

It is a rowdy bar at the north end of town, with a band
and a lot of girls, and it draws people from out of town instead
of just regulars, so it gets rough in there. I sit in my jeep in the
parking lot fifteen minutes before closing. The band is gone,
but the parking lot is still full. At one o'clock they start coming out, loud in bunches and couples. Some leave right away,
but a lot of them stand around, some drinking what they
sneaked out of the bar. The place takes about twenty minutes
to empty; I know that's done when I see Vinnie come into the
doorway, following the last people to leave. He stands there
smoking a cigarette. He's short and wide like I am, and he is
wearing a leisure suit with his shirt collar out over the lapels.
He's got a chain around his neck. The cruiser turns into the
parking lot, as I figured it would; the cops drive very slowly
through the crowd, stopping here and there for a word; they
pass in front of me and go to the end of the lot and hang a slow
U and come back; people are in their cars now and driving off.
I feel like slouching down but will not do this for a cop, even
to get DeLuca. The truth is I'm probably the only one in the
parking lot planning a felony. They pass me, looking at the
cars leaving and the people still getting into cars, then they
follow everybody out of the lot and up the road. Vinnie will
either come right out or stay inside and drink while the waitresses and one bartender clean the place and the other bartender counts the money and puts it in the safe. It's amazing

how many places there are to rob at night, when you think about it; if that's what you like. I hate a fucking thief. Polly used to shoplift in high school, and when she told me about it, years later, telling it like it was something cute she and her pals did, I didn't think it was funny, though I was supposed to. There are five cars spread around the lot. I don't know what he's driving, so I just sit watching the door, but he stays inside, the fucker getting his free drinks and sitting on a barstool watching the sweeping and table-wiping and the dirty ashtrays stacking up on the bar and the bartender washing them. Maybe he's making it with one of the waitresses, which I hope he isn't. I do not want to kick his ass with a woman there. If he comes out with a bartender or even both of them, it's a problem I can handle: either they'll jump me or try to get between us, or run for the phone; but I'll get him. With a woman, you never know. Some of them like to watch. But she might start screaming or crying or get a tire iron and knock the back of my head out my nose.

He comes out with three women. The women are smoking, so I figure they just finished their work and haven't been sitting around with a drink, they're tired and want to go home. A lot of people don't know what a long, hard job that is. I'm right: they all stand on the little porch, but he's not touching any of them, or even standing close; then they come down the steps and one woman heads for a car down on the left near the road, and the other two go to my right, toward the car at the high end of the lot, and he comes for the one straight ahead of him, off to my left maybe a couple of hundred feet. The TransAm: I should have known. I'm out the door and we're both walking at right angles to his car. He looks at me once, then looks straight ahead. Headlights are on his blue suit, and the two women drive down and pass behind him; the other one is just getting to her car, and she waves and they toot the horn, and turn onto the road. I get to the car first and plant myself in front of it and watch his chain. It's gold and something hangs from it, a disc of some kind.

'Ray,' he says, and stops. 'How's it going, Ray?' His voice is smooth and deep in his throat, but I can see his eyes now. They look sad, the way scared eyes do. His skin is dark and he is hairy and his shirt is unbuttoned enough to show this, and the swell of his pecs. I think of Alex, and look at Vinnie's hands down by his jacket pockets; I'm looking at his face too, and I keep seeing the gold chain, a short one around his neck so the disc shows high on his chest. My legs are shaky and cool and I need a deep breath, but I don't take it; I swing a left above the chain, see it hit his jaw, then my right is there in his face, and I'm in the eye of the storm, I don't hear us, I don't feel my fists hitting him, but I see them; when my head rocks he's hit me; I hit him fast and his face has a trapped look, then he's inside my arms, grabbing them, his head down, and I turn with him and push him onto the car, his back on the hood. There is a light on his face, and blood; I hold him down with my left hand on his throat and pound him with the right. There is a lot of blood on his mouth and nose and some on his forehead and under an eye. He is limp under my hand, and when I let him go he slides down the hood and his back swings forward like he's sitting up, and he drops between me and the grill. He lies on his side. My foot cocks to kick him but I stop it, looking at his face. The face is enough. The sky feels small, like I could breathe it all in. Then I look into the light. It's the headlights of the waitress's car, the one alone; it's stopped about twenty feet away with the engine running and the lights aimed at me. She's standing beside the car, yelling. I look around. Nobody else is in the lot; it feels small too. I look down at DeLuca, then at her. She's cursing me. I wave at her and walk to my jeep. She is calling me a motherfucking, cocksucking string of other things. I like this girl. With the lights off, I back the jeep up away from the club and make a wide half-circle around her to the road, so she can't read my plates. I pull out and turn on the lights.

I take a beer from the cooler on the floor and light a ciga-rette. My hands are shaky, but it's the good kind. Kingsley taught me about adrenaline, long before he used it over there, when I started first grade, which for boys means start learning to fight too. He said when you start to tremble, that's not fear, it just feels like it; it's to help you, so put it to use. That is why I didn't say to DeLuca the things I thought of saying. When I know I have to fight I never talk. Adrenaline makes guys start talking at each other, and you can use it up; I hold it in till I've got to either yell or have action.

The street is wide and quiet, most of the houses dark. I pass a cemetery and a school. I don't know why it is, but I know of four schools in this town either next to or across the street from a cemetery. I'm talking elementary schools too. Maybe it's an old custom, but it's weird looking at little girls and boys on a playground, and next door or across the street are all those tombstones over the dead. King is buried in one with trees and no school or anything else around but woods and the Merrimack River. The sky is lit up with stars and moon, the kind of night you could drive in with your lights off if you were the only one on the road, just follow the grey pavement and look at the dark trees and the sky and listen to the air rushing at the window. I turn on the radio and get onto 495 north. My knuckles are sore but the fingers work fine. I suck down the beer and get another from under the ice, and it feels good on my hand. I'm getting WOKQ from Dover, New Hampshire. Every redneck from southern Maine to Boston listens to that station. New Hampshire is also a redneck state, though the natives don't know it because they get snow every winter. When King was at Camp LeJeune he wrote to the family and said they could move New Hampshire down there and everybody would be happy except for the heat, which he wasn't happy with either. The heat got to him in Nam too; he wrote and said the insects and heat and being wet so much of the time were the worst part. I think about that a lot; was he just saying that so we wouldn't worry, or did he mean it? Most of the time I think he meant it, which taught me something I already knew but didn't always know that I knew: it gets down to what's happening to you right now, and if you're hot and wet and itching, that's what you deal with. You'll end up tripping a mine anyways, so you might as well fight the bugs and stay cool and dry till then.

Mostly there's woods on the sides of the highway. People are driving it fast tonight. I pull into the right lane, Crystal Gayle is singing sad, and take the exit. I hope Waylon comes on; I'm in a Waylon mood. I cross the highway on the overpass, cars going under me without a sound I can hear over Crystal, and go on a two-lane into the town square of Merrimac, where they leave off the *k*. I don't know why. The square has a rotary and some lights and is empty. I turn right onto 110, two-lane and hilly with curves, and I have to piss. It's not just beer, it's nerve-piss, and I shiver holding it in. Nobody's on the road, and when I turn left toward the lake I cut the lights and can see clearly: the road is narrow with trees on its sides, and up ahead where the road turns left, there are trees too, a thin line of them at the side of the lake. I shift down and turn and back up and turn, and park it facing 110. I take the gasoline can from behind my seat, then piss on the grass, looking up at the stars and smelling the pines among the trees. I carry the gasoline can in my left hand, the side away from the road, and walk on grass, close to the trees. I have on my newest jeans, the darkest I've got, and a dark blue shirt with long sleeves. My fingers try to stiffen, holding the can. That's from DeLuca, maybe the first one, that came up from behind my ass and got his jaw; he saw it but only in time to turn his face from it a little, so all he did was stretch his jaw out for me to hit. He should have dropped his chin, caught it on the head. I hear the lake, then see it through the trees. It's bigger than ours but there are more houses too, all around it, and in summer they're filled. We only have a few houses, on the east and north sides, because it's way out in the boondocks and the west and south sides belong to some nature outfit that a rich guy gave his land to, and all you can do there is hike and look at trees and birds. The road turns left, between the woods and the backs of houses, and I follow it near the trees. A dog barks and some others pick it up. But it's just the bitchy barking of pets, there's not a serious one in there, and I keep walking, and nobody talks to the dogs or comes out for a look, and they stop.

All the houses are so close together I won't see Steve's until I'm at it. I know it's on this road and it's brown. King wrote to me and Alex once from there; he didn't want the folks to read it; he wrote about patrols and ambushes. He said *Don't get me wrong, I wish right now I was back there with you guys and a case of Bud in the cooler out on a boat pulling in mackerel. They must be in, about now. But I'll say this: I'll never feel the adrenaline like this again, not even with bluefish or deer or kicking ass. I understand now what makes bankers and such go skydiving on Saturdays.* Then I see Polly's red Subaru and Steve's van, and I freeze, then lower the can to the ground and kneel beside it. I wonder if this is close to what King felt. When I think of the arsenal Steve's got inside, I believe maybe it is. I kneel listening. There's a breeze and the water lapping in front of the house. I listen some more, then unscrew the cap and get up to a crouch and cross the road. I stand behind his van and look up and down the road and in the yards next door. Every yard is small, every house is small, no rich man's lake here, but people that work. Her car and the van are side by side in a short dirt driveway; on the right, by the corner of the house, there's a woodpile. I look at the dark windows, then go for the wood. I'm right under a window, and all I can hear is the breeze and the water. I move up the side of the house, under windows, toward the lake. At the front yard I stop, breathing through my mouth but slow and quiet as I can. There's a tree that looks like an oak in the yard, then the wharf. He's got a cement patio with some chairs and a hammock and a barbecue grill and table with empty beer bottles on it. I run to the lake side of the tree and press my back against it; he has a short wharf with an outboard and a canoe. I look around the tree at the front of the house. Then I step toward the lake, move out far enough so I'm past the branches—it's an oak— and I start pouring: walking backward parallel to the house that I'm watching all the time, and when I clear it, I turn and back toward the road, watching Steve's and the house on my left too. The gasoline is loud, back and forth in the can, and pouring onto the grass.

I back up past their cars and my back is stiff, I'm breathing short and quiet and need more of it but won't; I make a wide circle around their cars, and take the can cap from my pocket and drop it there, and go around the house again, the corner with the woodpile, and I back toward the lake, checking the other house on my left now, my head going back and forth but mostly forth, waiting for Steve to stick a Goddamn .30-06 or 12-gauge out one of the windows, then I'm past the house and feeling the lake behind me and I keep going to the tree and around it, and all I can smell is gasoline. I empty the can near where I started so the lines will meet. Then I straighten up and step down off a low concrete wall to the beach. I go up the beach past three houses, then out between them to the road, and I cross it and lay the can in the woods. Then I cross again and stand at the road with her car and his van between me and the house. I look down till I see the gas cap. Then I take one match from a book and strike it and hold it to the others; they catch with a hiss, and I toss them at the cap: the gasoline flares with a whoosh and runs left and right and dances around the corners into the breeze, curving every which way, and I run back into the road where I can look past the house in time to see the flames coming at each other around the house, doing some front-yard patterns like ice skaters where I emptied the can. Then they meet and I am running on the grass beside the road, down the road and around the corner, on the grass in the dark by the woods, to my jeep up there. The key is in my hand.

In the upstairs bedroom she wakes to firelight and flickering shadows on the walls that do not yet feel like her own, and she is so startled out of sleep that she is for a moment displaced, long enough for this summer's fear—that no walls and roof will ever feel like her own—to rise in her heart before it is dissipated by this new fear she has waked to; then she is throwing back the sheet and crossing the floor. Out the front window she looks at sinuous flames surrounding the yard between her and the lake; calling Steve, she goes to the side window and looks down at fire, then into the back room where Steve's mattress on the floor is empty, still made since morning. She steps on and over it, to the rear window overlooking the yard and car and van and the ring of fire. She switches on the stair light and descends, calling; by the bottom step she knows she is not trapped and her voice softens, becomes quizzical. Downstairs is a kitchen, darkened save for the wavering light on the walls, and a living room where he sleeps sitting on the couch, his feet on the coffee table, the room smelling of beer and cigarette smoke.

'Steve?' He stirs, shakes his head, drops his feet to the floor. She points out the wide front window. 'Look.'

He is up, out the front door, turning on the faucet and pulling the coiled hose across the patio. In places the fire has spread toward the house, but it is waning and burns close to the ground.

'It's all around,' she says, as, facing the lake, he moves the hose in an arc; neighbor men shout and she trots to either side of the house and sees them: the men next door with their hoses and wives and children. Steve belches loudly; she turns and sees him pissing on the fire, using his left hand, while his right moves the hose. He yells thanks over each shoulder; the men call back. The fire is out, and Steve soaks the front lawn, then both sides, joining his stream with the others. He asks her to turn it off, and he coils the hose and she follows him to the backyard. The two men come, and their wives take the children inside.

'Jeesum Crow,' one says. 'What do you figure that was about?'

'Tooth fairy,' Steve says, and offers them a beer. They accept, their voices mischievous as they excuse themselves for drinking at this hour after being wakened. They blame the fire. Polly has come to understand this about men: they need mischief and will even pretend a twelve-ounce can of beer is wicked if that will make them feel collusive while drinking it. Steve brings out four bottles, surprises her by handing her one he had not offered; she is pleased and touches his hand and thanks him as she takes it. She sits on the back stoop and watches the men standing, listens to their strange talk: about who would want to do such a thing, and what did a guy want to get out of doing it, and if they could figure out what he was trying to get done, then maybe they could get an idea of who it might be. But their tone will not stay serious, moves from inquisitive to jestful, without pattern or even harmony: while one supposes aloud that teenaged vandals chose the house at random and another agrees and says it's time for the selectmen to talk strict curfew and for the Goddamn cops to do some enforcing, the first one cackles and wheezes about a teenaged girl he watched water skiing this afternoon, how she could come to his house any night and light some fire. They clap hands on shoulders, grab an arm and pull and push. Steve takes in the empties and brings out four more.

Polly goes upstairs for cigarettes and stands at the back window, looking down at them. Steve has slept in here since she moved in; some nights, some days, one of them has stood in the short hall between their rooms and tapped on the door, with a frequency and need like that of a couple who have lived long together: not often, and not from passion, but often enough for release from carnal solitude. She does not want to join the men in the yard and does not want to be alone in the house; she goes downstairs and sits on the stoop, smoking, and staring at the woods beyond them. She imagines Ray lying under the trees, watching, his knife in his hand. One of the men stoops and rises with something he shows the others. A cap from a gasoline can, they say. Sitting between the house and the men, she still feels exposed, has the urge to look behind her, and she smokes deeply and presses her fingers against her temples, rubs her eyes to push away her images of him softly paddling a canoe on the lake, standing on the front lawn, creeping into hiding in the living room, up the stairs to her bedroom; in the closet there. The men are leaving. They tell her good night, and she stands and thanks them. Steve comes to her, three bottles in his large hand. He places the other on her shoulder.

'Looks like your ex is back,' he says.

'Yes.'

'Dumb asshole.'

'Yes.'

Vinnie is a bruise on the pillow, and from a suspended bottle of something clear, a tube goes to his left arm and ends under tape. He is asleep. She stands in the doorway, wanting to leave; then quietly she goes in, to the right side of the bed. His flesh is black and purple under both eyes, on the bridge of his nose, and his right jaw; cotton is stuffed in his nostrils; his breath hisses between swollen lips, the upper one stitched. Polly has not written a card for the zinnias she cut from her mother's garden but, even so, she can let him wake to them and phone later, come back later, do whatever later. When she puts them on the bedside table, his eyes open.

'I brought you some flowers,' she says. She looks over her shoulder at the door, then takes from her purse a brown-bagged pint of vodka. Smiling, she pulls out the bottle so he can see the label, then drops it into the bag. He only watches her. She cannot tell whether his eyes show more than pain. She pushes the vodka under his pillows.

'Do you hurt?'

'Drugs,' he says, through his teeth, only his lips moving, spreading in a grimace.

'Oh Jesus. Your jaw's broken?'

He nods.

'Will you hurt if I sit here?'

'No.'

She sits on the side of the bed and takes his right hand lying on the sheet, softly rubs his bare forearm, watching the rise and fall of his dark hair, its ends sun-bleached gold. His arm is wide and hard with muscle, her own looks delicate, and as she imagines Ray's chest and neck swelling with rage, a cool shiver rises from her legs to her chest. She reaches for her purse on the bedside table.

'Can I smoke in here?'

'I guess.'

He sounds angry; she knows it is because his jaw is wired, but still she feels he is angry at her and ought to be. She finds an ashtray in the drawer of the bedside table, cocks her head at the hanging bottle of fluid, and says: 'Is that your food?'

'Saline. Eat with a straw.'

'Can you smoke?'

'Don't know.'

She holds her cigarette between his lips, on the right side, away from the stitches. She cannot feel him drawing on it; he nods, she removes it, and he exhales a thin stream.

'Are you hurt anywhere else? Your body?'

'No. How did you know?'

'My father called me.' She offers the cigarette, he nods, and as he draws on it, she says: 'He said you're not pressing charges.'

His face rolls away from the cigarette, he blows smoke toward the tube rising from his arm, then looks at her, and she knows what she first saw in his eyes and mistook for pain.

'I don't blame you,' she says. 'I wouldn't either. In June he came into my apartment with a fucking knife and raped me. I was afraid to do anything, and I kept thinking he was gone. *Really* gone, like California or someplace. Because Dad checked at where he worked and his apartment, and he never went back after that night. Even if I knew he hadn't gone, I wouldn't have. Because he's fucking *crazy.*'

She stands and takes her cigarettes and disposable lighter from her purse and puts them on the table.

'I'll leave you these. I have to go. I'll be back.'

Her eyes are filling. Besides Steve, Vinnie is the only person outside her family she has told about the rape, but his eyes did not change when she said it; could not change, she knows, for the sorrow in them is so deep. She has known him in passion and mirth, and kissing his forehead, his unbruised left cheek, his chin, she feels as dangerous as Ray, more dangerous with her slender body and pretty face.

'I guess it wasn't worth it,' she says.

'Nothing is. I'm all broken.'

Sometimes, on her days off that summer, she put on a dress and went to Timmy's in early afternoon to drink. It was never crowded then, and always the table by the window was empty, and she sat there and watched the Main Street traffic and the people walking outside in the heat; or, in the rain, cars with lights and windshield wipers on, the faces of drivers and passengers blurred by rain and dripping windows.

She slept late. She was twenty-six and, for as long as she could remember, she had hated waking early; now that she worked at night, she not only was able to sleep late, but had to; she lived at home and no longer felt, as she had when she was younger and woke to the family voices, that she had wasted daylight sleeping while everyone else had lived half a day. There had been many voices then, but now two brothers and a sister had grown and moved away, and only Margaret was at home. She was seventeen and drank a glass of wine at some family dinners, had never, she said, had a cigarette in her mouth, had not said but was certainly a virgin, and early in the morning jogged for miles on the country roads near their home; during blizzards, hard rain, and days when ice on the roads slowed her pace, she ran around the indoor basketball court at the YMCA. She received Communion every Sunday and, in the Lenten season, every day. She was dark and pretty, but Polly thought all that virtue had left its mark on her face, and it would never be the sort that makes men change their lives.

Polly liked her sister, and was more amused than annoyed by the way she lived. She could not understand what pleasures Margaret drew from running and not drinking or smoking dope or even cigarettes, and from virginity. She did understand

Margaret's religion, and sometimes she wished that being a
Catholic were as easy for her as it was for Margaret. Then she
envied Margaret, but when envy became scorn she fought it
by imagining Margaret on a date; certainly she felt passion, so
maybe her sacramental life was not at all easy. Maybe waking
up and jogging weren't either; and she would remember her
own high school years when, if you wanted friends and did
not want to do what the friends did, you had to be very strong.
So those times when she envied, then scorned Margaret
ended with her wondering if perhaps all of Margaret's life
was good because she willed it.

Polly went to Mass every Sunday, but did not receive
communion because she had not been in the state of grace for
a long time, and she did not confess because she knew that
she could not be absolved of fornication and adultery while
wearing an intrauterine device whose presence belied her
firm intention of not sinning again. She was not certain that
her lovemaking since the end of her marriage was a sin, or
one serious enough to forbid her receiving, for she did not
feel bad about it, except when she wished during and afterward that she had not gone to bed with someone, and that had
to do with making a bad choice. She had never confessed her
adultery while she was married to Raymond Yarborough,
though she knew she had been wrong, had felt wicked as well
as frightened; but, remembering now (she had filed for
divorce and changed her name back to Comeau), her short
affair with Vinnie when the marriage was in its final months
was diminished by her sharper memory of Raymond yelling
at her that she was a spoiled, fucked-up cunt not worth a shit
to anybody, Raymond slapping her, and, on the last night, hitting her with his fist and leaving her unconscious on the bedroom floor, where she woke hearing Jerry Jeff Walker on the
record player in the living room and a beer bottle landing on
others in the wastebasket. Her car key was in there with him,
so she climbed out the window and ran until she was nauseated and her legs were weak and trembling; then she walked,
and in two hours she was home. She had to wake them to get

in, and her mother put ice on her jaw, Margaret held her hand
and stroked her hair, and her father took his gun and nightstick and drove to the apartment, but Raymond was gone in his
jeep, taking with him his weights and bench and power stands,
fishing rods and tackle box, two shotguns and a .22 rifle, the
hunting knife he bought in memory of his brother, his knap-
sack and toilet articles and some clothes. When she moved
from that apartment two weeks later, she filled a garbage bag
with his clothes and Vietnam books, most of them hardcover,
and left it on the curb; as she drove away, she looked in the
rear view mirror at the green bulk and said aloud: 'Adiós,
motherfucker.'

She also did not go to confession because, as well as not
feeling bad about her sexual adventures, and knowing that
she would not give them up anyway, she did believe that in
some way her life was not a good one, but in a way the Church
had not defined. Neither could she: even on those rare and
mysterious nights when drinking saddened her and she went
to bed drunk and disliking herself and woke hung over and
regretful, she did not and could not know what about herself
she disliked and regretted. So she could not confess, but she
went to Mass with her family every Sunday and had gone
when she lived alone, because it was one religious act she
could perform, and she was afraid that neglecting it would
finally lead her to a fearful loneliness she could not bear.

Dressing for Mass was different from dressing for any
other place, and she liked having her morning coffee and cigarette while, without anticipating drinks or dinner or a man
or work or anything at all, she put on makeup and a dress and
heels; and she liked entering the church where the large
doors closed behind her and she walked down the aisle under
the high, curved white ceiling, and between stained-glass
windows in the white walls whose lower halves were dark
brown wood, as the altar was and the large cross with a
bronze Christ hanging from the wall behind it. When she was
with her family, her father chose a pew and stood at it while
Margaret went in, then Polly, then her parents; alone, she

looked for a pew near the middle with an aisle seat. She kneeled on the padded kneeler, her arms on the smooth old wood of the pew in front of her, and looked at the altar and crucifix and the stained-glass window behind them; then sat and looked at people sitting in front of her on both sides of the aisle. There was a scent of perfume and sometimes leather from purses and coats, tingeing that smell she only breathed here: a blending of cool, dry basement air with sunlight and melting candle wax. As the priest entered wearing green vestments, she rose and sang with the others, listened to her voice among theirs, read the Confiteor aloud with them, felt forgiven as she read *in what I have done and in what I have failed to do*, those simple and general words as precise as she could be about the life, a week older each Sunday, that followed her like a bridal train into church where, for forty minutes or so, her mind was suspended, much as it was when she lay near sleep at the beach. She did not pray with concentration, but she did not think either, and her mind wandered from the Mass to the faces of people around her. At the offertory she sang with them and, later, stood and read the Lord's Prayer aloud; then the priest said *Let us now offer each other a sign of peace* and, smiling, she shook the hands of people in front of her and behind her, saying *Peace be with you.*

She liked to watch them receive communion: children and teenagers and women and men going slowly in two lines up the center aisle and in single lines up both side aisles, to the four waiting priests. Coming back, they chewed or dissolved the host in their mouths. Sometimes a small boy looked about and smiled. But she only saw children when they crossed her vision; she watched the others: the old, whose faces had lost any sign of beauty or even pleasure, and were gentle now, peacefully dazed, with God on their tongues; the pretty and handsome young, and the young who were plain or homely; and, in their thirties and forties and fifties, women and men who had lost the singularity of youth, their bodies unattractive, most of them too heavy, and no face was pretty or plain, handsome or homely, and all of these returned to their pews with clasped hands and bowed heads, their faces both serious and calm. She tenderly watched them. Now that she was going to Mass with her family, she watched them too, the three dark faces with downcast eyes: slender Margaret with her finely concave cheeks, and no makeup, her lips and brow bearing no trace of the sullen prudery she sometimes turned on Polly, sometimes on everyone; her plump mother, the shortest in the family now, grey lacing her black hair, and her frownlike face one of weariness in repose, looking as it would later in the day when, reading the paper, she would fall asleep on the couch; her father, tall and broad, his shirt and coat tight across his chest, his hair thick and black, and on his face the look of peaceful concentration she saw when he was fishing; and she felt merciful toward them, and toward herself, not only for her guilt or shame because she could not receive (they did not speak to her about it, or about anything else she did, not even—except Margaret—with their eyes), but for her sense and, often at Mass, her conviction that she was a bad woman. She rose and sang as the priest and altar boys walked up the aisle and out the front of the church; then people filled the aisle and she moved with them into the day.

She had always liked boys and was very pretty, so she had never had a close girl friend. In high school she had the friends you need, to keep from being alone, and to go with to places where boys were. Those friendships felt deep because at their heart were shared guilt and the fond trust that comes from it. They existed in, and because of, those years of sexual abeyance when boys shunned their company and went together to playing fields and woods and lakes and the sea. The girls went to houses. Waiting to be old enough to drive, waiting for those two or three years in their lives when a car's function would not be conveyance but privacy, they gathered at the homes of girls whose mothers had jobs. They sat on the bed and floor and smoked cigarettes.

Sometimes they smoked marijuana too, and at slumber

parties, when the parents had gone to bed, they drank beer or wine bought for them by an older friend or brother or sister. But cigarettes were their first and favorite wickedness, and they delightfully entered their addiction, not because they wanted to draw tobacco smoke into their lungs, but because they wanted to be girls who smoked. Within two or three years, cigarette packs in their purses would be as ordinary as wallets and combs; but at fourteen and fifteen, simply looking at the alluring colored pack among their cosmetics excited them with the knowledge that a time of their lives had ended, and a new and promising time was coming. The smooth cellophane covering the pack, the cigarette between their fingers and lips, the taste and feel of smoke, and blowing it into the air, struck in them a sensual chord they had not known they had. They watched one another. They always did that: looked at breasts, knew who had gained or lost weight, had a pimple, had washed her hair or had it done in a beauty parlor, and, if shown the contents of a friend's closet, would know her name. They watched as a girl nodded toward a colored disposable lighter, smiled if smoke watered her eyes, watched the fingers holding the cigarette, the shape of her lips around the tip, the angle of her wrist.

So they were friends in that secret life they had to have; then they were older and in cars, and what they had been waiting for happened. They shared that too, and knew who was late, who was taking the pill, who was trusting luck. Their language was normally profane, but when talking about what they did with boys, they said *had sex, slept with, oral sex, penis.* Then they graduated and spread outward from the high school and the houses where they had gathered, to nearby colleges and jobs within the county. Only one, who married a soldier, moved out of the state. The others lived close enough to keep seeing each other, and in the first year out of high school some of them did; but they all had different lives, and loved men who did not know each other, and soon they only met by chance, and talked on sidewalks or at coffee counters.

Since then Polly had met women she liked, but she felt

they did not like her. When she thought about them, she knew she could be wrong, could be feeling only her own discomfort. With her girlhood friends she had developed a style that pleased men. But talking with a woman was scrutiny, and always she was conscious of her makeup, her pretty face, her long black hair, and the way her hands moved with a cigarette, a glass, patting her hair in place at the brow, pushing it back from a cheek. She studied the other woman too, seeing her as a man would; comparing her, as a man would, with herself; and this mutual disassembly made them wary and finally mistrustful. At times Polly envied the friendships of men, who seemed to compete with each other in everything from wit to strength, but never in attractiveness or over women; or girls like Margaret, who did nothing at all with her beauty, so that, seeing her in a group of girls, you would have to look closely to know she was the prettiest. But she knew there was more, knew that when she was in love she did not have the energy and time to become a woman's friend, to go beyond the critical eye, the cautious heart. Even men she did not love, but liked and wanted, distracted her too much for that. She went to Timmy's alone.

But not lonely: she went on days when, waking late, and eating a sandwich or eggs alone in the kitchen, she waited, her mind like a blank movie screen, to know what she wanted to do with her day. She saw herself lying on a towel at the beach; shopping at the mall or in Boston; going to Steve's house to swim in the lake or, if he wanted to run the boat, water-ski; wearing one of her new dresses and drinking at Timmy's. That was it, on this hot day in July: she wanted to be the woman in a summer dress, sitting at the table by the window. She chose the salmon one with shoulder straps, cut to the top of her breasts and nearly to the small of her back. Then she took the pistol from the drawer of her bedside table and put it in her purse. By one o'clock she was at the table, sipping her first vodka and tonic, opening a pack of cigarettes, amused at herself as she tasted lime and smelled tobacco, because she still loved smoking and drinking as she had ten years ago when they were secret pleasures, still at times (and today was one) felt in the lifted glass and fondled pack a glimmer of promise from out there beyond the window and the town, as if the pack and glass were conduits between the mysterious sensuous rhythms of the world and her own.

She looked out the window at people in cars and walking in the hot sunlight. Al was the afternoon bartender, a man in his fifties, who let her sit quietly, only talking to her when she went to the bar for another drink. Men came in out of the heat, alone or in pairs, and drank a beer and left. She drank slowly, glanced at the men as they came and went, kept her back to the bar, listened to them talking with Al. For the first two hours, while she had three drinks, her mood was the one that had come to her at the kitchen table. Had someone approached and spoken, she would have blinked at the face while she waited for the person's name to emerge from wherever her mind had been. She sat peacefully looking out the window, and at times, when she realized that she was having precisely the afternoon she had wanted, and how rare it was now and had been for years to have the feeling you had wanted and planned for, her heart beat faster with a sense of freedom, of generosity; and in those moments she nearly bought the bar a round, but did not, knowing then someone would talk to her, and what she had now would be lost, dissipated into an afternoon of babble and laughter. But the fourth drink shifted something under her mood, as though it rested on a foundation that vodka had begun to dissolve.

Now when she noticed her purse beside her hand, she did not think of money but of the pistol. Looking out at people passing on foot or in cars, she no longer saw each of them as someone who loved and hoped under that brilliant, hot sky; they became parts again, as the cars did, and the Chevrolet building across the street where behind the glass front girls spoke into telephones and salesmen talked to couples, and as the sky itself did: parts of this town, the boundaries of her life.

She saw her life as, at best, a small circle: one year as a commuting student, driving her mother's car twenty minutes to Merrimack College, a Catholic school with secular faculty, leaving home in the morning and returning after classes as she had since kindergarten, discovering in that year—or forcing her parents to discover what she had known since ninth grade—that she was not a student, simply because she was not interested. She could learn anything they taught, and do the work, and get the grades, but in college she was free to do none of this, and she chose to do only enough to accumulate eight Cs and convince her parents that she was, not unlike themselves, a person whose strengths were not meant to be educated in schools.

She did not know why she was not interested. In June, when her first and last year of college was a month behind her, she remembered it with neither fondness nor regret, as she might have recalled movies she had seen with boys she did not love. She had written grammatical compositions she did not feel or believe, choosing topics that seemed both approachable and pleasing to the teacher. She discovered a pattern: all topics were approachable if she simply rendered them, with an opening statement, proper paragraphs, and a conclusion; and every topic was difficult if she began to immerse in it; but always she withdrew. In one course she saw herself: in sociology, with amusement, anger, resignation, and a suspended curiosity that lasted for weeks, she learned of the hunters, the gatherers, the farmers, saw herself and her parents defined by survival; and industrialization bringing about the clock that, on her bedside table, she regarded as a thing which was not inanimate but a conscience run on electricity, and she was delighted, knowing that people had once lived in accord with the sun and weather, and that punctuality and times for work and food and not-work and sleep were later imposed upon them, as she felt now they were imposed upon her.

In her other classes she listened, often with excitement, to a million dead at Borodino, Bismarck's uniting Germany, Chamberlain at Munich, Hitler invading Russia on the twenty-second of June because Napoleon did, all of these people and their actions equally in her past, kaleidoscopic, having no causal sequence whose end was her own birth and first eighteen years. She could say 'On honeydew he hath fed / And drunk the milk of paradise' and '... the women come and go / Talking of Michelangelo,' but they, and Captain Vere hanging Billy Budd, and Huck choosing Nigger Jim and hell, joined Socrates and his hemlock and Bonhoeffer's making an evil act good by performing it for a friend, and conifers and deciduous trees, pistils and stamens, and the generals and presidents and emperors and kings, all like dust motes in the sunlight of that early summer, when she went to work so she could move to an apartment an hour's walk from the house she had lived in for nineteen years, and which she forced herself to call *my parents' house* instead of home until that became habitual.

She was a clerk in a department store in town. The store was old and had not changed its customs: it had no cash registers. She worked in the linen department, and placed bills and coins into a cylinder and put that in a tube which, by vacuum, took the money to a small room upstairs where women she never met sent change down. She worked six days a week and spent the money on rent and heat and a used Ford she bought for nine hundred and eighty-five dollars; she kept food for breakfasts and lunches in her refrigerator, and ate dinners with her parents or dates or bought pieces of fish, chicken, or meat on the way home from work. On Sundays she went to the beach.

A maternal uncle was a jeweler and owned a store, and in fall she went to work for him, learned enough about cameras and watches to help customers narrow their choices to two or three; then her uncle came from his desk, and compared watches or cameras with a fervor that made their purchase seem as fraught with possibilities of happiness and sorrow as choosing a lover. She liked the absolute cleanliness of the store, with its vacuumed carpets and polished glass, its lack of any distinctive odors, and liked to believe what she did smell was sparkle from the showcases. Her grey-haired uncle always wore a white shirt and bow tie; he told her neckties got in the

way of his work, the parts of watches he bent over with loupe
and tweezers and screwdriver and hand remover. She said
nothing about a tie clasp, but thought of them, even glanced
at their shelf. She liked them, and all the other small things in
their boxes on the shelves: cuff links and rings and pins and
earrings. She liked touching them with customers.

She worked on Saturdays, but on Wednesday afternoons
her uncle closed the store. It was an old custom in the town,
and most doctors and lawyers and dentists and many owners
of small stores kept it still. She had grown up with those
Wednesday afternoons when she could not get money at the
bank or see a doctor or buy a blouse, but now they were holidays for her. She had been in school so much of her life that
she did not think of a year as January to January, but September to June and, outside of measured time, the respite of summer. Now her roads to and from work wound between trees
that were orange and scarlet and yellow, then standing naked
among pines whose branches a month later held snow, and
for the first time in her memory autumn's colors did not mean
a school desk and homework, and snow the beginning of the
end of half a year and Christmas holidays. One evening in
December, as she crossed her lawn, she stopped and looked
down at the snow nearly as high as her boots; in one arm she
cradled a bag of groceries; and looking at the snow, she knew,
as if for the first time, though she had believed she had known
and wanted it for years, that spring's trickle of this very snow
would not mean now or ever again the beginning of the end of
the final half-year, the harbinger of those three months when
she lived the way they did before factory whistles and clocks.

The bag seemed heavier, and she shifted its weight and
held it more tightly. Then she went inside and up two flights
of stairs and into her apartment. She put the groceries on the
kitchen table and sat looking from the bag to her wet boots
with snow rimming the soles and melting on the instep. She
took off her gloves and unbuttoned her coat and put her damp
beret on the table. For a long time she had not been afraid of
people or the chances of a day, for she believed she could bear

the normal pain of being alive: her heart had been broken by girls and boys, and she had borne that, and she had broken hearts and borne that too, and embarrassment and shame and humiliation and failure, and she was not one of those who, once or more wounded, waited fearfully for the next mistake or cruelty or portion of bad luck. But she was afraid of what she was going through now: having more than one feeling at once, so that feeling proud and strong and despairing and resigned, she sat suspended in fear: *So this is the real world they always talked about.* She said it aloud: 'the real world,' testing its sound in the silence; for always, when they said it, their tone was one of warning, and worse, something not only bitter and defeated but vindictive as well, the same tone they had when they said *I told you so.* She groped into the bag, slowly tore open a beer carton as she looked at the kitchen walls and potted plants in the window, drew out a bottle, twisted off the cap, but did not drink. Her hand went into her purse, came out with cigarettes and lighter, placed them beside the beer. She hooked a toe under the other chair, pulled it closer, and rested both feet on it. *I don't believe it. And if you don't believe it, it's not true, except dying.*

What she did believe through that winter and spring was that she had entered the real world of her town, its time and work and leisure, and she looked back on her years of growing up as something that had happened to her outside of the life she now lived, as though childhood and her teens (she would soon be twenty) were, like those thirteen summers from kindergarten until the year of college, a time so free of what time meant to her now that it was not time but a sanctuary from it. Now, having had those years to become herself so she could enter the very heart of the town, the business street built along the Merrimack, where she joined the rhythmic exchange of things and energy and time for money, she knew she had to move through the town, and out of it. But, wanting that motion, she could not define it, for it had nothing to do with place or even people, but something within herself: a catapult, waiting for both release and direction, that would send her away from these old streets, some still of brick, and old brick leather factories, most of them closed but all of them so bleak, so dimly lit beyond their dirty windows that, driving or even walking past one, you could not tell whether anyone worked inside.

On a Wednesday afternoon in May, at a bar in Newburyport, where the Merrimack flowed through marshes to the sea, she sat alone on the second-floor sun deck, among couples in their twenties drinking at picnic tables. She sat on a bench along the railing, her back to the late-afternoon sun, and watched the drinkers, and anchored sailboats and fishing boats, and boats coming in. A small fishing boat followed by screaming gulls tied up at the wharf beside the bar, and she stood so she could look down at it. She had not fished with her father since she started working; she would call him tonight—no, she would finish this drink and go there for dinner and ask him if he'd like to go Sunday after Mass. Then Raymond Yarborough came around the cabin, at the bow, swinging a plastic bag of fish over his left shoulder. One of the men—there were six—gave him a beer. Her hand was up in a wave, her mouth open to call, but she stopped and watched. He had a beard now, brown and thick; he was shirtless and sunburned. She wore a white Mexican dress and knew how pretty she looked standing up there with the sun on her face and the sky behind her, and she waited. He lifted the bag of fish to the wharf and joined the others scrubbing the cleaning boards and deck. Then he went into the cabin and came out wearing a denim work shirt and looked up and laughed.

'Polly Comeau, what are you doing up there?'

She wondered about that, six years later, on the July afternoon at Timmy's; and wondered why, from that evening on, she not only believed her life had changed but knew that indeed it had (though she was never comfortable with, never sure of, the distinction between believing something about your life and that something also being true). But something did happen: when Ray became not the boy she had known in high school but her lover, then husband, she felt both released and received, no longer in the town, a piece of its streets and time, but of the town, having broken free of its gravity, so that standing behind the jewelry counter she did not feel rooted or even stationary; and driving to and from work, or pushing a cart between grocery shelves, were a new sort of motion whose end was not the jewelry store, the apartment, the supermarket cash register, but herself, the woman she saw in Raymond's face.

In her sleep she knew she was dreaming: she was waitressing at the Harbor Schooner, but inside it looked like the gymnasium in high school with tables for prom night, and the party of four she was serving changed to a crowd, some were familiar, and she strained to know them; then her father was frying squid in the kitchen and she was there with a tray, and he said *Give them all the squid they want*; then a hand was on her mouth and she woke with her right hand pushing his wrist and her left prying his fingers, and in that instant before opening her eyes, when her dream dissolved into darkness, she knew it was Ray. She was on her back and he was straddling her legs. She kneed him but he moved forward and she struck bone. He sat on her thighs and his right hand went to his back and she heard the snap, and the blade leaving its sheath; then he was holding it close to her face, his dark-bladed knife; in the moonlight she saw the silver line of its edge. Then its point touched her throat, and his hand left her mouth.

'Turn over,' he said.

He rose to his knees, and she turned on her stomach, her back and throat waiting for the knife, but then his knees were between her legs, his hand under her stomach, lifting: she kneeled with her face in the pillow, heard his buckle and snap and zipper and pants slipping down his legs; he pushed her nightgown up her back, the knife's edge touched her stomach, and he was in, rocking her back and forth. She gripped the pillow and tensed her legs, trying to remain motionless, but his thrusts drove her forward, and her legs like springs forced her to recoil, so she was moving with him, and always on her tightened stomach the knife flickered, his breathing faster and louder then Ah Ah Ah, a tremor of his flesh against hers, the knife scraping toward her ribs and breasts, then gone, and he was too; above his breathing and her own she heard the ascent of pants, the zipper and snap and buckle, but no sheathing of the blade, so the knife itself had, in the air above her as she collapsed forward, its own sound of blood and night: but please God oh Jesus please not her gripping the pillow, her chin pressed down covering her throat, not her in the white Mexican dress with her new sunburn standing at the rail, seeing now Christ looking down through her on the sun deck that May afternoon to her crouched beneath the knife—

'Good, Polly. You got a little juiced after a while. Good.'

His weight shifted, then he was on the floor. She heard him cut the telephone cord.

'See you later, Polly.'

His steps on the floor were soft: he shut the door and in the corridor he was quiet as night. Her grip on the pillow loosened; her hands opened; still she waited. Then slowly and quietly she rolled over and got out of bed and tiptoed to the door and locked it again. She lit a cigarette, sat on the toilet in the dark, wiped and flushed and went to the window beside the bed, where she stood behind the open curtain and looked down at the empty street. She listened for his jeep starting, heard only slow and occasional cars moving blocks away, in town, and the distant voices and laughter of an outdoor party, and country music from a nearby window. She dressed and went down the hall and three flights of stairs and outside, pausing on the front steps to look at the street and parked cars and, on the apartment's lawn and lawns on both sides of it and across the street, the shadowed trunks of trees. She could not hear the sounds of the party or the music from the record player. Then he was dripping out of her and she went up the stairs and sat on the toilet while he pattered into the water, then scrubbed her hands, went out again, down the walk, and turned left, walking quickly in the middle of the sidewalk between tree trunks and parked cars, and looked at each of them and over her shoulders and between the cars for two and a half blocks to the closed drugstore, lighted in the rear where the counter was. In the phone booth she stood facing the street; the light came on when she closed the door, so she opened it and called her father.

She knew his steps in the hall and opened the door before he knocked. He was not in uniform, but he wore his cartridge belt and holstered .38. She hugged his deep, hard chest, and his arms were around her, one hand patting her back, and when he asked what Ray had done to her, she looked up at his wide sunburned face, his black hair and green eyes like her own, then rested her face on his chest and soft old chamois shirt, and said: 'He had his knife. He touched me with it. My throat. My stomach. He cut the phone wire—' His patting hand stopped. 'The door was locked and I was asleep, he doesn't even *have* a credit card, I don't know what he used, I woke up with his hand on my mouth then he had that big knife, that M*arine* knife.'

His mouth touched her hair, her scalp, and he said: 'He raped you?'

She nodded against his chest; he squeezed her, then his hands were holding her waist and he lifted her and his shoulders swung the left and he put her down, as though moving her out of his path so he could walk to the bed, the wall, through it into the third-story night. But he did not move. He inhaled with a hiss and held it, then blew it out and did it again, and struck his left palm with his right fist, the open hand gripping the fist, and he stood breathing fast, the hand and fist pushing against each other. He was looking at the bed, and she wished she had made it.

'You better come home.'

'I want to.'

'Then I'm going look for him.'

'Yes.'

'You have anything to drink?'

'Wine and beer.'

When he turned the corner into the kitchen, she straightened the sheets; he came back while she was pulling the spread over the pillows.

'I'll call Mom,' he said. He stood by the bed, his hands on the phone. 'Then we'll go to the hospital.'

'I'm all right.'

He held the cord, looking at its severed end.

'They take care of you, in case you're pregnant.'

'I'm all right.'

He swallowed from the bottle, his eyes still on the cord. Then he looked at her.

'Just take something for tonight. We can come back tomorrow.'

She packed an overnight bag and he took it from her; in the corridor he put his arm around her shoulders, held her going slowly down the stairs and outside to his pickup; with a hand on her elbow he helped her up to the seat. While he drove he opened a beer she had not seen him take from the apartment. She smoked and watched the town through the windshield and open window: Main Street descending past the city hall and courthouse, between the library and a park, to the river; she looked across the river at the street climbing again and, above the streetlights, trees and two church steeples. On the bridge she saw herself on her knees, her face on the pillow, Ray plunging, Ray lying naked and dead on her apartment floor, her father standing above him. She looked at the broad river, then they were off the bridge and climbing again, past Wendy's and McDonald's and Timmy's, all closed. She wanted to speak, or be able to; she wanted to turn and look at her father, but she had to be cleansed first, a shower, six showers, twelve; and time; but it was not only that.

It was her life itself; that was the sin she wanted hidden from her father and the houses and sleeping people they passed; and she wanted to forgive herself but could not because there was no single act or even pattern she could isolate and redeem. There was something about her heart, so that now glimpsing herself waiting on tables, sleeping, eating, walking in town on a spring afternoon, buying a summer blouse, she felt that her every action and simplest moments were soiled by an evil she could not name.

Next day after lunch he brought her to a small studio; displayed behind its front window and on its walls were photographs, most in color, of families, brides and grooms, and what she assumed were pictures to commemorate graduation from high school: girls in dresses, boys in jackets and ties. The studio smelled of accumulated cigarette smoke and filled ashtrays, and the woman coughed while she seated Polly on a stool in the dim room at the rear. The woman seemed to be in her fifties; her skin had a yellow hue, and Polly did not want to touch anything, as if the walls and stool, like the handkerchief of a person with a cold, bore traces of the woman's tenuous mortality. She looked at the camera and prepared her face by thinking about its beauty until she felt it. They were Polaroid pictures; as she stood beside her father at the front desk, glancing at portraits to find someone she knew, so she could defy with knowledge what she defied now with instinct, could say to herself: *I know him, her, them; they're not like that at all; are fucked up too*, and, her breath recoiling from the odor of the woman's lungs that permeated the walls and pictures, she looked down at the desk, at her face as it had been only minutes ago in the back room. With scissors, the woman trimmed it. She watched the blade cutting through her breasts. The black-and-white face was not angry or hating or fearful or guilty; she did not know what it was but very serious and not pretty.

At City Hall they went to the detectives' office at the rear of the police station. Two detectives sat at desks, one writing, one drinking coffee. They greeted her father, and she stood in the doorway while he went to the desk of the coffee-drinker, a short man wearing a silver revolver behind his hip. Then her father leaned over him, hiding all but his hand on the coffee cup, and she watched her father's uniformed back, listened to his low voice without words. The other detective frowned as he wrote. Her father turned and beckoned: 'Okay, Polly.'

The detective rose to meet her, and she shook his hand and did not hear his name. His voice was gentle, as if soothing her while dressing a wound; he led her across the room and explained what he was doing as he rolled her right forefinger on ink, then on the license. There was a sink and he told her to use the soap and water, the paper towels, then brought her to his desk where her father waited, and held a chair for her. It had a cushioned seat, but a straight wooden back and no arms, so she sat erect, feeling like a supplicant, as she checked answers on a form he gave her (she was not a convicted felon, a drunk, an addict) and answered questions he asked her as he typed on her license: *one twenty-six, black* (he looked at her eyes and said: 'Pretty eyes, Polly'), *green*. He gave her the card and signed the front and looked at the back where he had typed *Dark* under Complexion, *Waitress* under Occupation, and, under Reason for Issuing License: *Protection*. He said the chief would sign the license, then it would go to Boston and return laminated in two weeks; he offered them coffee, they said no, and he walked them to the office door, his hand reaching up to rest on her father's shoulder. The other detective was still writing. In the truck, she said: 'He was nice.'

The gun, her father said, looked like a scaled-down Colt .45: a .380 automatic which they bought because it was used and cost a hundred and fifteen dollars (though he would have paid three hundred, in cash and gladly, for the .38 snubnose she looked at and held first; they were in the store within twenty hours of his bringing her home, then driving to Newburyport, to Ray's empty apartment, where he had kicked open the locked door and looked around enough to see in the floor dust the two bars of clean wood where the weight-lifting bench had been, and the clean circles of varying sizes left by the steel plates and power stands); and because of the way it felt in her hand, light enough so it seemed an extension of her wrist, a part of her palm, its steel and its wooden grips like her skinned bone, and heavy enough so she felt both safe and powerful, and the power seemed not the gun's but her own; and because of its size, which she measured as one and a half Marlboro boxes long, and its shape, flat, so she could carry it concealed in the front pocket of her jeans, when she left home without a purse.

They bought it in Kittery, Maine, less than an hour's drive up New Hampshire's short coast, at the Kittery Trading Post, where as a virgin, then not one but still young enough to keep that as secret as the cigarettes in her purse, she had gone with her father to buy surf rods and spinning rods, parkas, chamois and flannel shirts. It was also the store where Ray, while shopping for a pocketknife, had seen and bought (*I had to*, he told her) a replica of the World War II Marine knife, with the globe and anchor emblem on its sheath. It came in a box, on whose top was a reproduction of the knife's original blueprint from 1942. When he came home, he held the box toward her, said *Look what I found*, his voice alerting her; in his face she saw the same nuance of shy tenderness, so until she looked down at the box she believed he had brought her a gift. *I don't need it*, he said, as she drew it from the sheath, felt its edge, stroked its blood gutter. *But, see, we gave all his stuff away.* That was when she understood he had been talking about Kingsley, and she had again that experience peculiar to marriage, of entering a conversation that had been active for hours in her husband's mind. Now she brought her father to the showcase of knives and showed him, and he said: 'Unless he's good with it at thirty feet, he might as well not have it at all. Not now, anyways.'

Next day, in the sunlit evening of daylight savings time, at an old gravel pit grown with weeds and enclosed by woods on three sides, with a dirt road at one end and a bluff at the other, her father propped a silhouette of a man's torso and head against the bluff, walked twenty paces from it, and gave her the pistol. He had bought it in his name, because she was waiting for the license, and he could not receive the gun in Maine, so a clerk from the Trading Post, who lived in Massachusetts where he was also a gun dealer, brought it home to Amesbury, and her father got it during his lunch hour.

'It loads just like the .22,' he said.

A squirrel chattered in the trees on the bluff. She pushed seven bullets into the magazine, slid it into the handle, and, pointing the gun at the bluff, pulled the slide to the rear and let it snap forward; the hammer was cocked, and she pushed up the safety. Then he told her to take out the magazine and eject the chambered shell: it flipped to the ground, and he wiped it on his pants and gave it to her and told her to load it again; he kept her loading and unloading for ten minutes or so, saying he was damned if he'd get her shot making a mistake with a gun that was supposed to protect her.

'Shoot it like you did the .22 and aim for his middle.'

He had taught her to shoot his Colt .22, and she had shot with him on weekends in spring and summer and fall until her midteens, when her pleasures changed and she went with him just often enough to keep him from being hurt because she had outgrown shooting cans and being with him for two hours of a good afternoon; or often enough to keep her from believing he was hurt. She stood profiled to the target, aimed with one extended hand, thumbed the safety off, and, looking over the cocked hammer and barrel at the shape of a man, could not fire.

'The Miller can,' she said, and, shifting her feet, aimed at the can at the base of the bluff, held her breath, and squeezed to an explosion that shocked her ears and pushed her arm up and back as dust flew a yard short of the can.

'Jesus *Christ*.'

'Reminds me of what I forgot,' he said and, standing behind her, he pulled back her hair and gently pushed cotton into her ears. 'Better go for the target. They didn't make that gun to hit something little.'

'It's the head. If we could fold it back.'

He patted her shoulder.

'Just aim for the middle, and shoot that piece of cardboard.'

Cardboard, she told herself as she lined up the sights on the torso's black middle and fired six times, but *shoulder* she thought when she saw the first hole, *missed, stomach, chest, shoulder, stomach*, and she felt clandestine and solemn, as though performing a strange ritual that would forever change her. She was suddenly tired. As she loaded the magazine, images of the past two nights and two days assaulted her, filled her memory so she could not recall doing anything during that time except kneeling between a knife and Ray's cock, riding in her father's truck—home, to the studio, to City Hall, to Kittery, home, to this woods—and being photographed and fingerprinted and questioned and pointing guns at the walls and ceiling of the store, and tomorrow night she had to wait tables, always wiping them, emptying ashtrays, bantering, smiling, soberly watching them get drunk, their voices louder than the jukebox playing music she would like in any other place. She fired, not trying to think *cardboard*, yielding to the target's shape and going further, seeing it not as any man but Ray, so that now as holes appeared and her arm recoiled from the shots muted by cotton and she breathed the smell of gunpowder, and reloaded and fired seven more times and seven more, she saw him attacking her and falling, attacking her and falling, and she faced the target and aimed with both hands at head and throat and chest, and once heard herself exhale: '*Yes*.'

Two weeks later her father brought her license home, but he had told her not to wait for it, no judge would send her to jail, knowing she had applied, and knowing why. So from that afternoon's shooting on, she carried it everywhere: in her purse, jeans, shorts, beach bag, in her skirt pocket at work and on the car seat beside her as, at two in the morning, she drove home, where she put it in the drawer of her bedside table and left her windows open to the summer air. At Timmy's on that sunlit afternoon in July she rested her hand on it, rubbed its handle under the soft leather of her purse. She knew she was probably drunk by police or medical standards, but not by her own. Her skin seemed thickened, so she could feel more sharply the leather and the pistol handle beneath it than her fingers themselves when she rubbed them together. For a good while she had been unaware of having legs and feet; her cheeks and lips were numb; sometimes she felt an elbow on the table, or the base of her spine, or her thighs when they pressed on the chair's edge, then she shifted her weight. But she was not drunk because she knew she was: she knew her reflexes were too slow for driving, and she would have to concentrate to walk without weaving to the ladies' room. She also knew that the monologue coming to her was true; they always were. She listened to what her mind told her when it was free of the flesh: sometimes after making love, or waking in the morning, or lying on the beach for those minutes before the sun warmed her to sleep, or when she had drunk enough, either alone or with someone who would listen with her; but for a long time there had been no one like that.

Only three men were at the bar now. She brought her glass and ashtray to it, told Al to fill one and empty the other, and took two cocktail napkins. She paid and tipped, then sat at the table and wiped it dry with the napkins, and waited for Steve. At ten to five he came in, wearing a short-sleeved plaid shirt, his stomach not hanging but protruding over his jeans. Halfway to the bar he saw her watching him and smiled, his hand lifting. She waved him to her and looked at his narrow hips as he came.

'Steve? Can I talk to you a minute?'

He glanced over her at the bar, said he was early, and sat. Even now in July, his arms and face looked newly sunburned, his hair and beard, which grew below his open collar, more golden.

'You're one of those guys who look good everywhere,' she said. 'Doing sports outside, drinking in a bar—you know what I mean? Like some guys look right for a bar, but you see them on a boat or something, and they look like somebody on vacation.'

'Some girls too.'

She focused on his lips and teeth.

'You're always smiling, Steve. Don't you ever get down? I've never seen you down.'

'No time for it.'

'No time for it. What did you do today, with all your time?'

'Went out for cod this morning—'

'Did you catch any?'

'Six. Came back to the lake, charcoaled a couple of fillets, and crapped out in the hammock. What's wrong—you down?'

'Me? No, I'm buzzed. But let me tell you: I've been think-ing. I'm going to ask you a favor, and if it's *any* kind of *hass*le, you say no, all right? But I think it might be good for both of us. Okay? But if it's not—'

'What is it?'

'No, but wait. I'm sitting here, right? and looking out the window and thinking, and I've got to leave home. See'—she leaned forward, placed her hands on his wrists, and lowered her voice—'I'm living with my folks because I had a nice apartment and I liked being there, but last month, last month Ray broke in one night while I was sleeping and he held a knife on me and raped me.' She did not know what she had expected from his face, but it surprised her: he looked hurt and sad, and he nodded, then slowly shook his head. 'So I moved in with my folks. I was scared. I mean, it's not as bad as some girls get it, from some stranger, like that poor fifteen-year-old last year hitchhiking and he had a knife and made her *blow* him; it was just Ray, you know, but still—I've got a gun too, a permit, the whole thing.' He nodded. 'It's right here, in my purse.'

'That's the way it is now.'

'What is?'

'Whatever. Women need things; you're built too small to be safe anymore.'

'Steve, I got to move. But I'm still scared of having my own place. I was thinking, see, if I could move in with you, then I could do it gradually, you know? And when you leave in the fall I could sublet, I'd pay the whole rent for you till you get back, and by then—when do you come back?'

'Around April.'

'I'd be ready. Maybe I'd move to Amesbury or Newburyport. Maybe even Boston. I don't know why I said Boston. Isn't it funny it's right there and nobody ever goes to live there?'

'Not me. Spend your life walking on concrete? Sure: move in whenever you want.'

'Really? I won't be a problem. I can cook too—'

'So can I. Here.' He reached into his pocket, brought out a key ring and gave her a key. 'Anytime. Call me before, and I'll help you move.'

'No. No, I won't bring much: just, you know, clothes and cassette player and stuff. My folks won't like this.'

'Why not?'

'They'll think we're shacking up.'

'What are you, twenty-five?'

'Six.'

'So?'

'I know. It'll be all right. It's just I keep giving them such a bad time.'

'Hey: *you*'re the one having the bad time.'

'Okay. Can I move in tonight? No, I'm too buzzed. Tomorrow?'

'Tonight, tomorrow. Better bring sheets and a pillow.'

'I can't believe it.' He looked at the bar, then smiled at her and stood. 'All worked out, just like that. Jesus, you're saving my life, Steve. I'll start paying half the rent right away, and look: I'll stay out of the way, right? If you bring a girl home, I won't *be* there. I'll be shut up in my room, quiet as a mouse. I'll go to my folks' for the night, if you want.'

'No problem. Don't you even want to know how much the rent is?'

'I don't even *care*,' and she stood and put her arm around his back, her fingers just reaching his other side, and walked with him to the bar.

Polly's father comes down the slope of the lawn toward the wharf and I'm scared even while I look past him at the pickup I heard on the road, then down the driveway, and I look at his jeans and shirt; then I'm not scared anymore. For a second there, I thought Polly or maybe Vinnie had pressed some charges, but it all comes together at once: he's not in a cruiser and he's got no New Hampshire cops with him and he's wearing civvies, if you can call it that when he's wearing his gun and his nightstick too. I decide to stay in the deck chair. He steps onto the wharf and keeps coming and I decide to take a swallow of beer too. The can's almost empty and I tilt my head back; the sun is behind me, getting near the treetops across the lake. I'm wearing gym shorts and nothing else. I open the cooler and drop in the empty and take another; I know what my body looks like, with a sweat glisten and muscles moving while I shift in the chair to pull a beer out of the ice, while I open it, while I hold it up to him as he stops spread-legged in front of me.

'Want a beer, John?'

I don't know what pisses him off most, the beer or *John*; his chest starts working with his breath, then he slaps the can and it rolls foaming on the wharf, stops at the space between two boards.

'You don't like Miller,' I say. 'I think I got a Bud in there.'

He unsnaps his nightstick, moves it from his left hand to

his right, then lowers it, holding it down at arm's length, gripping it hard and resting its end in his left hand. This time I
don't shift: I watch his eyes and pull the cooler to me and
reach down through the ice and water. I open the beer and
take a long swallow.

'*Ass*hole,' he says. 'You want to *rape* somebody, *ass*hole?
You want to set fucking *fires?*'

I watch his eyes. At the bottom of my vision I see the stick
moving up and down, tapping his left hand. I lower the beer
to the wharf and his eyes go with it, just a glance, his head
twitching left and down; I grab the stick with my left hand
and let the beer drop and get my right on it too. He holds on
and I pull myself out of the chair, looking up at his eyes and
pushing the stick down. My chest is close to his; we stand
there holding the stick.

'What's the gun for, John?' I've got an overhand grip; I
work my wrists up and down, turning the stick, and his face
gets red as he holds on. I don't stop. 'You want to waste me,
John? Huh? Go for it.'

I'm pumping: I can raise and lower the stick and his arms
and shoulders till the sun goes down, and now he knows it
and he knows I know it; he is sweating and his teeth are
clenched and his face is very red with the sun on it. All at once
I know I will not hurt him; this comes as fast as laughing, is
like laughing.

'Go for the gun, John. And they'll cut it out of your ass.' I
walk him backward a few steps, just to watch him keep his
balance. 'They can take Polly's nose out too.'

'Fucker,' he says through his teeth.

'Yes I did, John. Lots of times. On the first date too. Did
she tell you that?' He tries to shove me back and lift the stick;
all he does is strain. 'It wasn't a date, even. I came in from
fishing, and there she was, drinking at Michael's. We went to
her place and fucked, and know what she said? After? She
said, Once you get the clothes off, the rest is easy. Now what
the fuck does *that* mean, John? What does that *mean?*'

I'm ahead of him again. Before he gets to the gun my left

hand is on it; I swing the stick up above my head, his left hand still on it; I unsnap the holster and start lifting the gun up against his hand pressing down; it comes slowly but it never stops, and his elbow bends as his hand goes up his ribs. When the gun clears the holster he shifts his grip, grabs it at the cylinder, but his fingers slip off and claw air as I throw it backward over my shoulder and grab his wrist before the gun splashes. I lift the stick as high as I can. He still has some reach, so I jerk it down and free, and throw it with a backhand sidearm into the lake. He is panting. I am too, but I shut my mouth on it.

'Go home, John.'

'You leave her alone.'

He is breathing so hard and is so red that I get a picture of him on his back on the wharf and I'm breathing into his mouth.

'Go get some dinner, John.'

'You—' Then he has to cough; it nearly doubles him over, and he turns to the railing and holds it, leans over it, and hacks up a lunger. I turn away and pick up the beer I dropped. There's still some in it; I drink that and take one from the ice, then look at him again. He's standing straight, away from the rail.

'You leave her alone,' he says. 'Fire last night. What are you, crazy? DeLuca.'

'DeLuca who?'

He lifts a hand, waves it from side to side, shakes his head.

'I don't care shit about DeLuca,' he says. 'Let it go, Ray. You do anything to her, I'll bring help.'

'Good. Bring your buddies. What are friends for, that's what I say.'

'I mean it.'

'I know you do. Now go on home before that club floats in and we have to start all over.'

He looks at me. That's all he does for a while, then he turns and goes up the wharf, wiping his face on his bare arm. He walks like he's limping, but he's not. I get another beer and follow him up the lawn to his pickup. By the time he climbs in and starts it, I'm at his window. I toss the beer past him, onto the seat. He doesn't look at me. He backs and turns and I wait for gravel to fly, but he goes slowly up the driveway like the truck is tired too. At the road he stops and looks both ways. Then the beer comes out the window onto the lawn, and he's out on the blacktop, turning right, then he's gone beyond a corner of woods.

Last night waiting tables she was tired, and the muscles in her back and legs hurt. She blamed that afternoon's water skiing, and worked the dining room until the kitchen closed, then went upstairs to the bar and worked there, watching the clock, wiping her brow, sometimes shuddering as a chill spread up her back. She took orders at tables, repeated them to the bartender, garnished the drinks, subtracted in her mind, made change, and thanked for tips, but all that was ever in her mind was the bed at Steve's and herself in it. At one o'clock the Harbor Schooner closed, and when the last drinkers had gone down the stairs, the bartender said: 'What'll it be tonight?' and she went to the bar with the other two waitresses, scanned the bottles, shaking her head, wanting to want a drink because always she had one after work, but the bottles, even vodka, even tequila, could have been cruets of vinegar. She lit a cigarette and asked for a Coke.

'You feeling all right?' he said.

'I think I'm sick,' and she left the cigarette and carried the Coke, finishing it with long swallows and getting another, as she helped clean the tables, empty the ashtrays, and stack them on the bar.

She wakes at two o'clock in the heat of Labor Day weekend's Sunday afternoon, remembers waking several times, once or more when the room was not so brightly lit, so hot; and remembers she could not keep her eyes open long enough to escape the depth of her sleep. Her eyes close and she drifts downward again, beneath her pain, into darkness; then she opens her eyes, the lids seeming to snap upward against pressing weight. She grasps the edge of the mattress and pulls while she sits and swings her legs off the bed, and a chill grips her body and shakes it. Her teeth chatter as she walks with hunched shoulders to the bathroom; the toilet seat is cold, her skin is alive, crawling away from its touch, crawling up her back and down her arms, and she lowers her head and mutters: 'Oh Jesus.'

She does not brush her teeth or hair, or look in the mirror. She goes downstairs. There are no railings, and she slides a palm down the wall. She drinks a glass of orange juice, finds a tin with three aspirins behind the rice in the cupboard, swallows them with juice, and phones the Harbor Schooner. Sarah the head waitress answers.

'Is Charlie there?'

'No.'

'Who's tending bar?'

'Sonny.'

'Let me talk to him.'

She ought to tell Sarah, but she does not like to call in sick to women; they always sound like they don't believe her.

'I'm sick,' she says to Sonny. 'I think the flu.'

He tells her to go to bed and take care of herself, and asks if she needs anything.

'No. Maybe I'll come in tomorrow.'

'Get well first.'

'I'll call.'

She takes the glass and pitcher upstairs, breathing quickly as she climbs. The sun angles through her bedroom windows, onto the lower half of the bed. There are shades, but she does not want to darken the room. She puts the pitcher and glass on the bedside table, lies on the damp sheet, pulls up the top sheet and cotton spread, and curls, shivering, on her side. Her two front windows face the lake; she hears voices from there, and motors, and remembers that she has been hearing them since she woke, and before that too, from the sleep she cannot fight. It is taking her now; she wants juice, but every move chills her and she will not reach for it. She stares at the empty glass and wonders why she did not fill it again, drinking would be so much easier, so wonderfully better, if she did not have to sit up and lift the pitcher and pour, so next time she drinks she will refill the glass because then it won't be so hard next time, and if she had a hospital straw, one of bent glass. Vinnie was last week with the tube in his arm and the bandages, but in memory he is farther away than a week, a summer; last night is a week away, going from table to table to table to bar to table to table and driving home, hours of tables and driving. Her memory of making love with Vinnie is clear but her body's aching lethargy rejects it, denies ever making love with anyone, ever wanting to, so that Vinnie last spring, early when the rivers began to swell with melting snow, is in focus as he should be: not loving him then she made love because, it seems to her now, he was something to do, one of a small assortment of choices for a week night; and she remembers him now without tenderness or recalled passion.

When she wakes again she is on her left side, facing the front windows, and the room's light has faded. The chills are gone, and she is hungry. There is ham downstairs, and eggs and cheese and bread, and leftover spaghetti, but her stomach refuses them all. She imagines soup, and wants that. But it is down the stairs and she would have to stand as she opened and heated it, then poured it into a cup so she could climb again and drink it here; she turns onto her right side and waits, braced against chills, but they don't come. Evening sunlight beams through the side window, opposite the foot of her bed, which is now in the dark spreading across the floor and dimming the blue walls. As though she can hear it, she senses the darkness in all the downstairs rooms, and more of it flowing in from the woods and lake. There are no motors on the water. Voices rise and waft from lawns touching the beach. She switches on the bedside lamp, pushes herself back and up till she sits against the pillows, and pours a glass of orange juice. She drinks it in three swallows, refills the glass, then lies on her back, closes her hot eyes, thinks of Ray, of danger she cannot feel, and lets the lamp burn so she will not wake in the dark.

For a while she sleeps, but she is aware that she must not, there is something she must do, and finally she wakes, her head tossing on the pillow, legs and arms tense. She reaches for the drawer beside her, takes the gun, holds it above her with both hands; she pulls the slide to the rear and eases it forward, watching the bullet enter the chamber. She lowers the hammer to half-cock and pushes up the safety. She turns on her side, slips the gun under the pillow, and goes to sleep holding the checkered wood of its handle.

She wakes from a dream that is lost when she opens her eyes to light, though she knows it was pleasant and she was not in it, but watched it. The three windows are black. Steve is looking down at her, his smell of beer and cigarettes, his red face and arms making her feel that health, that life even, are chance gifts to the lucky, kept by the strong, and she was not to have them again.

'Sorry,' he says. 'You want to go back to sleep?'

'No.' Her throat is dry, and she hears a plea in her voice. 'I'm sick.'

'I figured that. Can I do anything?'

'I think I want to smoke.'

He takes cigarette papers from his shirt pocket, a cellophane pouch from his jeans.

'No, a cigarette. In my purse.'

He lights it and hands it to her.

'Could I have some soup?'

'Anything else?'

'Toast?'

'Coming up.'

He goes downstairs, and she smokes, looking at the windows; she cannot see beyond the screens. Neither can her mind: her life is this room, where her body's heat and pain have released her from everyone but Steve, who brings her a bowl of soup on a plate with two pieces of toast. He pushes up the pillows behind her, then pulls a chair near the bed.

'I'm leaving in the morning.'

'What time is it?'

'Almost one.'

 She shakes her head.

'That way I beat the traffic.'

'Good idea.'

'I can leave Tuesday, though. Or Wednesday.'

'You're meeting your friends there.'

'They'll keep.'

'No. Go tomorrow, like you planned.'

'You sure?'

'It's just the flu.'

'No fun having it alone.'

'All I do is sleep.'

'Still. You know.'

'I'll be all right.'

'What'll you do about the ex?'

'Maybe he won't come back.'

'Don't bet on it.'

'My father went to see him.'

'Yeah? What did he say?'

'Who, Ray? I don't know.'

'No, your dad.'

'He told him if he harassed me again, he'd take some people out there and break bones.'

'Thing about Ray is he doesn't give a shit.'

'He doesn't?'

'Think about it.'

'He gives a shit about a lot of things.'

'Not broken bones. That little gun you got: if he comes, fire a couple over his head.'

'Why?'

'Because I don't think you could use it on him, and you might just leave it in the drawer. Then there's nothing you can do. So think about scaring him off.'

'I'd use it. You don't know what it's like, a man—what's the *matter* with him?'

He shrugs and takes the bowl and plate.

'Think two shots across the bow,' he says and stands; then, leaning over her, he is huge, blocking the ceiling and walls, his chest and beard lowering, his face and breath close to hers; he kisses her forehead and right cheek and smooths the hair at her brow. She watches him cross the room; at the door he turns and says: 'I'll leave this open; mine too. If you need something, give a shout.'

'You've got a nice ass,' she says, and smiles as his eyes brighten and his beard and cheeks move with his grin. She listens to his steps going down, and the running water as he washes her dishes. When he starts upstairs she turns out the lamp. In his room his boots drop to the floor, there is a rustle of clothes, and he is in bed. He shifts twice, then is quiet. She sits against the pillows in the dark; and wakes there, Steve standing beside her, the room sunlit and cool. The lake is quiet.

'You're going?'

'It's time.'

'Have fun.'

'Sure. You want breakfast?'

'No.'

She takes his hand, and says: 'I'll see you in April, I guess. Good hunting and all. Skiing.'

'If you don't find a place, or you want to stay on in spring, that's fine.'

'I know.'

'Well—' His thumb rubs the back of her hand.

'Thanks for everything,' she says.

'You too.'

'The room. Good talks. Whatever.'

'Whatever,' he says, smiling. Then he kisses her lips and is gone.

In early afternoon she phones the Harbor Schooner and tells Charlie, the manager, that she is still sick and can't make it that night but will try tomorrow. She eats a sandwich of ham and cheese, makes a pitcher of orange juice, and brings it upstairs. She reaches the bed weak and short of breath. Through the long hot afternoon she lies uncovered on the bed, asleep, awake, asleep, waking always to the sound of motor-boats, the voices of many children, and talk and shouts and laughter of men and women. When the sun has moved to the foot of the bed and the room is darkening, she smells charcoal smoke. She turns on the lamp and lies awake listening to the beginning of silence: the boats are out of the water, most of them on trailers by now; she hears cars leaving, and on the stretch of beach below her windows, families gather, their voices rising with the smells of burning charcoal and cooking meat. Tomorrow she will wake to quiet that will last until May.

She closes her eyes and imagines the frozen lake, ever-greens, the silent snow. After school and on weekends boys will clean the ice with snow shovels and play hockey; she will hear only burning logs in the fireplace, will watch them from the living room, darting without sound into and around one another. She will have a Christmas tree, will eat dinner at her parents', but on Christmas Eve she could have them and Margaret here for dinner before midnight Mass. She will live here—she counts by raising thumb and fingers from a closed fist—eight months. Or seven, so she can be out before Steve comes back. Out where? She shuts her eyes tighter, frowning, but no street, no town appears. In the Merrimack Valley she likes Newburyport but not as much since she started working there, and less since Ray moved there. Amesbury and Merri-mac are too small, Lawrence is mills and factories, and too many grocery stores and restaurants with Spanish names, and Haverhill: Jesus, Haverhill: some people knew how to live there, her parents did, Haverhill for her father was the police department and their house in the city limits but in the coun-try as well, with the garden her mother and father planted each spring: tomatoes, beans, squash, radishes, beets; and woods beyond the garden, not forest or anything, but enough to walk in for a while before you came to farmland; and her father ice-fished, and fished streams and lakes in spring, the ocean in summer. Everyone joked about living in Haverhill, or almost everyone: the skyline of McDonald's arch and old factories and the one new building on the corner of Main Street and the river, an old folks' home and office building that looked like a gigantic cinder block. But it wasn't that. The Back Bay of Boston was pretty, and the North End was interesting with all those narrow streets and cluttered apartments of Italians, but Jesus, Boston was dirtier than Haverhill and on a grey winter day no city looked good. It was that nothing happened in Haverhill, and she had never lived outside its limits till now, and to go back in spring was going downhill backward. A place would come. She would spend the fall and winter here, and by then she would know where to go.

She looks at the walls, the chest with her purse and cassette player on its top, the closed door of the closet; she will keep this room so she'll have the lake (and it occurs to her that this must have been Steve's, and he gave it up), and she'll hang curtains. She will leave his room, or the back room, alone; will store in it whatever she doesn't want downstairs, that chair with the flowered cover he always sat in, and its hassock, the coffee table with cigarette burns like Timmy's bar; she will paint the peeling cream walls in the kitchen. For the first time since moving in, she begins to feel that more than this one room is hers; not only hers but her: her sense of this seems to spread downward, like sentient love leaving her body to move about the three rooms downstairs, touching, looking, making plans. Her body is of no use to her but to move weakly to the bathroom, to sleep and drink and, when it will, to eat. Lying here, though, is good; it is like the beach or sleeping late, better than those because she will not do anything else, cannot do anything else, and so is free. Even at the beach you have to—what? Go into the water. Collect your things and drive home. Wash salt from suit, shower, wash hair, dry hair. Cook. Eat. But this, with no chills now, no pain unless she moves, which she won't, this doesn't have to end until it ends on its own, and she can lie here and decorate the house, move furniture from one room to another, one floor to another, bring all her clothes from her parents' house, her dresser and mirror, while outside voices lower as the smell of meat fades until all she smells is smoke. Tomorrow she will smell trees and the lake.

She hears a car going away, and would like to stand at the window and look at the darkened houses, but imagines them instead, one by one the lights going out behind windows until the house becomes the shape of one, locked for the winter. She is standing at the chest, getting her cigarettes, when she hears the people next door leaving. *Do it*, she tells herself. She turns out the bedside lamp, crouches at a front window, her arms crossed on its sill, and looks past trees in the front lawn at the dark lake. She looks up at stars. To her right, trees enclose the lake; she cannot see the houses among them. Water laps at the beach and wharf pilings. She can see most of the wharf before it is shielded by the oak; below her, Steve's boat, covered with tarpaulin, rests on sawhorses. Her legs tire, and she weakens and gets into bed, covers with the sheet and spread, and lights a cigarette, the flame bright and large in the dark. She reaches for the lamp switch, touches it, but withdraws her hand. She smokes and sees the bathroom painted mauve.

For a long while she lies awake, filling the ashtray, living the lovely fall and winter: in a sweater she will walk in the woods on brown leaves, under yellow and red, and pines and the blue sky of Indian summer. She will find her ice skates in her parents' basement; she remembers the ponds when she was a child, and wonders how or why she outgrew skating, and blames her fever for making her think this way, but is uncertain whether the fever has made her lucid or foolish. She is considering a snow blower for the driveway, has decided to buy one and learn to use it, when he comes in the crash of breaking glass and a loud voice: he has said something to the door, and now he calls her name. She moves the ashtray from her stomach to the floor, turns on her side to get the gun from under the pillow, then lies on her back.

'Polly?' He is at the foot of the stairs. 'It's me. I'm coming up.'

He has the voice of a returning drunk, boldly apologetic, and she cocks the hammer and points the gun at the door as he climbs, his boots loud, without rhythm, pausing for balance, then quick steps, a pause, a slow step, evenly down the few strides of hall, and his width above his hips fills the door; he is dark against the grey light above him.

'You in here?'

'I've got a gun.'

'No shit? Let me see it.'

She moves her finger from the trigger, and pushes the safety down with her thumb.

'It's pointed at you.'

'Yeah? Where's the light in here?'

'You liked the dark before.'

'I did? That's true. That little apartment we had?'

'I mean June, with that fucking knife.'

'Oh. No knife tonight. I went to the Harbor Schooner—'

'Shit: what *for*.'

'—So I goes Hey: where's Polly? Don't she work here? Sick, they said. To see you, that's all. So I did some shots of tequila and I'm driving up to New Hampshire, and I say what the fuck? So here I am. You going to tell me where the light is?'

His shoulders lurch as he steps forward; she fires at the ceiling above him, and he ducks, his hands covering his head.

'Pol*ly*.' He lowers his hands, raises his head. 'Hey, Polly. Hey: put that away. I just want to talk. That's all. That was an asshole thing I did, that other time. See—'

'Go away.'

Her hand trembles, her ears ring, and she sits up in the gunpowder smell, swings her feet to the floor, and places her left hand under her right, holding the gun with both.

'I just want to ask you what's the difference, that's all. I mean, how was it out here with Steve? You happy, and everything?'

'It was *great*. And it's going to be better.'

'Better. Better without Steve?'

'Yes.'

'Why's that? You got somebody moving in?'

'No.'

'But it was good with Steve here. Great with Steve. So what's the difference, that's what I think about. Maybe the lake. The house? I mean, what if it was with me? Same thing, right? Sleep up here over the lake. Do some fucking. Wake up. Eat. Swim. Work. How come it was so good with Steve?'

'We weren't *married*.'

'Oh. Okay. That's cool. Why couldn't it be us then, out here? What did I ever do anyways?'

'Jesus, what is this?'

'No, come on: what did I do?'

'Nothing.'

'Nothing? I must've done something.'

'You didn't do anything.'

'Then why weren't you happy, like with Steve? I mean, I thought about it a lot. It wasn't that asshole DeLuca.'

'You almost killed him.'

'Bullshit.'

'You could have.'

'You see him?'

'I brought him flowers, is all.'

'See: it wasn't him. And I don't think it was me either. If it was him, you'd be with him, and if it was me, well, you got rid of me, so then you'd be happy.'

'I *am* happy.'

'I don't know, Polly.'

She can see the shape and muted color of his face, but his eyes are shadows, his beard and hair darker; his shoulders and arms move, his hands are at his chest, going down, then he opens his shirt, twists from one side to the other pulling off the sleeves.

'Don't, Ray.'

Flesh glimmers above his dark pants, and she pushes the gun toward it.

'Let's just try it, Polly. Turn on the light, you'll see.' He unbuckles his belt, then stops, raises a foot, holds it with both hands, hops backward and hits the doorjamb, pulls off the boot, and drops it. Leaning there, he takes off the other one, unzips his pants, and they fall to his ankles. He steps out of them, stoops, pushing his shorts down. 'See. No knife. No clothes.' He looks down. 'No hard-on. If you'd turn on a light and put away that hogleg—'

He moves into the light of the door, into the room, and she shakes her head, says No, but it only shapes her lips, does not leave her throat. She closes her eyes and becomes the shots jolting her hands as she pulls and pulls, hears him fall, and still pulls and explodes until the trigger is quiet and she opens her eyes and moves, leaping over him, to the hall and stairs.

In the middle of the night I sit out here in the skiff and I try to think of something else but I can't, because over and over I keep hearing him tell me that time: *Alex, she's the best fuck I've ever had in my life.* I don't want to think about that. But I look back at the house that was Kingsley's and I wish I had put on the lights before I got in the boat, but it wasn't dark yet and I didn't think I'd drift around half the night and have to look back at it with no lights on so it looks like a tomb, with his weights and fishing gear in there. I'll have to get them out. It looks like we're always taking somebody's things out of that house, and maybe it's time to sell it to somebody who's not so unlucky.

He bled to death, so even then she could have done something. I want to hate her for that. I will, too. After he knew he loved her, he didn't talk about her like that anymore, but it was still there between us, what he told me, and he knew I remembered, and sometimes when we were out drinking, me and somebody and him and Polly, and then we'd call it a night and go home, he'd grin at me. What I don't know is how you can be like that with a guy, then shoot him and leave him to bleed to death while you sit outside waiting for your old man and everybody. This morning we put him next to Kingsley and I was hugging Mom from one side and the old man hugging her from the other, and it seemed to me I had two brothers down there for no reason. Kingsley wouldn't agree, and he wouldn't like it that I don't vote anymore, or read the newspapers, or even watch the news. All Ray did was fall in love and not get over it when she got weird the way women do sometimes.

So I sit out here in the skiff and it's like they're both out here with me. I can feel them, and I wish I'd see them come walking across the lake. And I'd say, Why didn't you guys do something else? Why didn't you wait to be drafted, or go to Canada? Why didn't you find another girl? I'd tell them I'm going to sell this—and oh shit it starts now, the crying, the big first one, and I let it come and I shout against it over the water: 'I'm going to *sell* this fucking *house*, you *guys*. And the one in *town*, and I'm moving in with *Mom* and the *old man*; I'm going to get them to sell *theirs* too and get the fuck *out* of here, take them down to *Flor*ida and live in a *condo*. We'll go fishing. We'll buy a boat, and fish.'

BLESS ME, FATHER

At Easter vacation Jackie discovered that her father was committing adultery, and four days later—after thinking of little else—she wrote him a letter. She was a dark, attractive girl whose brown eyes were large and very bright. She would soon be nineteen, she had almost completed her freshman year at the University of Iowa, and she knew, rather proudly, that her eyes had lost some of their innocence. This had happened in the best possible way: she hadn't actually done anything new, but she had been exposed to new people, like Fran, her roommate, who was a practicing nonvirgin. Fran's boy friend was a drama student and sometimes Jackie double-dated with them, and they went to parties where people went outside and smoked marijuana. Jackie had also drunk bourbon and ginger at football games and got herself pinned to Gary Nolan. Being pinned to Gary did not interfere with her staying in the state of grace; every Sunday she went to the Folk Mass at the chapel, and she usually received Communion, approaching the altar rail to the sound of guitars. It had been a good year for growing up: seven months ago she had been so naive that she never would have caught her father, much less written him a letter.

Before writing the letter, she talked to Fran, then Gary. The night she got back from vacation she told Fran; they talked until two in the morning, filling the room with smoke, pursing their lips, waving their hands. As sophisticated as Fran was, she agreed with Jackie that her father was wrong, that her parents' marriage was in danger, and that her mother must be delivered from this threat of terrible and gratuitous pain. Again and again they sighed, and said in gloomy, disillusioned, yet enduring voices that something had to be done. The next night she talked to Gary. There was a movie he wanted to see, but she asked him if they couldn't go drink beer. I have to talk to you, she said.

They sat facing each other in a booth at the rear, where it was dark, and using fake identification cards they drank beer, and she watched his eyes reflecting the sorrow and distraction in her own. Her story lasted for three beers; then, as she ended by saying she would write her father a letter, her tone changed. Now she was purposeful, competent, striking back. This shift caught Gary off guard, nearly spoiling his evening. He had liked it much better when she had so obviously needed his comfort. So he nodded his head, agreeing that a letter was probably the thing to do, but he looked at her with compassion, letting her know how well he understood her, that she was not as cool as she pretended to be, and that a letter to her father would never ease the pain in her heart. Then he took her out to his car, drove to the stadium and parked in its shadow, and soothed her so much that, on the following Saturday, she went to confession and told the priest she had indulged in heavy petting one time.

By then, she had written and mailed the letter. It was seven pages long, using both sides of the stationery, and she had read the first draft to Fran, then written another. Five days later she had heard nothing. When she mailed the letter, she had thought there were only two possible results: either her father would break off with the woman and renew his fidelity to her mother, or he would ignore the letter (although she didn't see how he could possibly do that; the letter was there at his office; her knowledge of him was there; and—this was it—his knowledge of himself was there too: he could not ignore these things). But after a week she was afraid: she saw other alternatives, even more evil than the affair itself. Feeling trapped, he might confront her mother with the truth, push a divorce on her. Or he might bolt: resign his position at the bank and flee with the other woman to California or Mexico, leaving her mother to live her life, shamed and hurt, in Chicago. She thought of the awful boomerangs of life, how the letter—written to save the family—could very well leave her a scandaled half-orphan; as the last unmarried child, she saw herself bravely seeking peace for her mother, taking her on trips away from their lovely house that was now hollow, echoing, ghost-ridden.

Then, at seven o'clock on a Wednesday morning, exactly one week after she had mailed the letter, her father phoned. He woke her up. By the time she was alert enough to say no, she had already said yes. Then she lit a cigarette and got back in bed. From the other bed, Fran asked who was that on the phone.

'My father. He's driving down to lunch.'

'Oh Lord.'

When he arrived at the dormitory she was waiting on the front steps, for it was a warm, bright day. He was wearing sunglasses, and he smiled easily as he came up the walk, as though—trouble or not—he was glad to see her. He was a short man who at first seemed fat until you noticed he was simply rounded, his chest and hips separated by a very short waist; he kept himself in good condition, swimming every day in their indoor pool at home, and he could still do more laps than she could. Jackie rose and went down the steps. When he leaned forward to kiss her, she turned her cheek, receiving his lips a couple of inches from hers.

He followed her to the Lincoln, opened the door for her, and she directed him to the bar and grill where she and Gary had talked, then led him to the same booth, where it was dark even in the afternoon and people couldn't distinguish your face unless they walked past you. He wanted a drink before lunch, and Jackie ordered iced tea.

'Nothing stronger?' he said.

'They won't serve me.'

She thought now he would wait until his Scotch came.

'You said you saw her at the train station,' he said.

She nodded and put her purse on the table and offered him a cigarette; he said no, they were filtered, and she lit one and looked past his shoulder.

'When I was getting off I saw you nod your head to somebody, and I looked that way and saw her getting into a taxi.'

Then she tried to look into his eyes, but the best she could do was his mouth.

'She's a blonde,' she said.

'A lot of blondes nowdays. When I was a kid—before TV, you know—the blondes in movies were always bad. If a woman was blonde and smoked, you knew right away she was bad.'

The drinks came and she told the waiter she'd have a hamburger with everything but onions; her father ordered a salad, then winked and patted his belly, and she thought of him naked with that blonde, whom she would see forever in a black coat stepping into a taxi.

'Then you heard me on the phone. On Holy Saturday, you said.'

She nodded and sipped her tea. She was smoking fast, deeply, knowing she would need another as soon as she finished this one, while he sat calmly, drinking without a cigarette, and it struck her that perhaps he was a corrupt, remorseless man. She tried to remember the last time he had received Communion. Of course at Easter he had stayed in the pew while she and her mother went to the altar rail; returning to the pew, she had kept her head bowed, hoping he was watching her. She didn't know about Christmas because, while she was on a date, her parents had gone to midnight Mass. She couldn't remember the Sunday of Thanksgiving vacation, but she knew he had received last summer, kneeling beside her. So apparently he still had the faith, but he sat calmly, enclosing a mortal heart, one year away from fifty: the decade of sudden death when a man had to be careful not only about his body but his soul as well. Now she was shaking another cigarette from her pack.

'How much do you smoke?' he said.

'A pack.' It was a lie, but one she also told herself.

'I should have paid you not to, the way some parents do.'

'Or set an example,' she said quickly, but then she flushed and lowered her eyes. She wasn't ready to fight him and, looking into her glass of tea, she thought if her own husband was ever unfaithful, she didn't want to know about it.

'I suppose that's best,' he said. 'What if you made a mistake?'

'Did I?'

'No, I just wanted to see if you'd be disappointed.'

'That's sick,' she said. 'It really is.'

'Suppose your mother had seen that letter.'

'I sent it to the bank.'

'Letters get seen. Suppose I was sick or something, and they'd sent it home?'

'People get heard talking on the phone too.'

'That's right, they do. And I sounded like a—wait a second.'

He took her letter and a pair of glasses from his inside coat pocket, put on his glasses, and scanned the pages.

'Here it is: "That voice on the phone was not yours. I might as well be honest and say it was the voice of a silly old man. I was so ashamed that I couldn't move"—'

'Daddy—'

'Wait: "I would think at least your respect for Mother would keep you from making a phone call to your mistress right in our home".'

'Well it's true.'

'True? What's true?'

He took off the glasses and put them and the letter in his coat pocket.

'What you just read.'

'You think I don't respect your mother?'

'I'd think if you did you wouldn't be doing what you're doing.'

His smile seemed bitter, perhaps scornful, but his eyes had that look she had seen for years: loving her because she was a child.

'So you want me to stop seeing this woman before your mother gets hurt.'

'Yes.'

'And go to confession.'

'I hope you will.'

'Just like that.'

'Don't you still believe in it?'

'Sure. Do you?'

'Of course I do.'

'Are you a virgin?'

'Me!' She leaned toward him, keeping her voice low. 'Oh, that's petty. That's so petty and mean and perverted. *Yes,* I am.'

'What, then? Semivirgin? Never mind: I didn't come for that. Anyway, I went to confession.'

'You did?'

Now the waiter was at their booth, and she was thankful for that, because she felt she ought to be happy now, but she wasn't, and she didn't know what to say next. She watched her hamburger descending, then looked over her father's shoulder, blinking as though looking up from a book: a group of boys and girls came in and sat at a long table in the front. When the waiter left, she said: 'That's wonderful.'

'Is it?'

'Well, of course it is.'

'*I* don't feel so good about it.'

'I won't listen to that. I'm not interested in how *hard* it is to break up with some—'

'Wait—I didn't feel good while it was going on, either. You think I *like* being involved with this woman?'

'But you're *not* involved, Daddy. Not if you've been to confession.'

'You sound like the priest. I told him the first mistake was sleeping with her. He bought that, all right. But he wouldn't buy it when I told him I felt just as sinful about leaving her. She's alone, you know. She didn't cry when I broke it off, she's too old for that, but I know she hurts now. It's not love, it's—'

'I should hope not.'

'It's a lie. Don't you know that?'

'What is?'

'Adultery. A sweet lie, sometimes a happy lie, but a lie. You know what happens? We'd see each other for an hour or two, and that's not real. What's real is with your mother. The other's just a game, like you and that boy in a car someplace.'

'Would you *please* get over this compulsion of yours? Accusing me of what *you're* doing?'

'Compulsion—that's a good word. Now I'm compulsive, old, and silly. Is that right?'

'Well, you have to be old, but you don't have to be silly.'

'That's absolutely right. And you don't have to be selfish.'

'Selfish?'

'Sure. Why did you write a letter like that and hurt your father?'

'I didn't want to hurt you.'

'Come on.'

'I was worried about Mother.'

'Come on.'

'I *was.*'

He finished his salad and pushed the bowl away; then, smoking, he watched her eating, and now the hamburger was dry and heavy, something to hurry and be done with.

'You did it for yourself,' he said.

'That's not true.'

'Sure it is. It's okay for Richard Burton but not your father.'

'It's not okay for him either. I think they're disgusting.'

'Not glamorous and wicked? Not silly, anyway. Or old. You think your mother doesn't know about it?'

'*Does* she?'

'Probably. The point is, we've been married twenty-five years and you can never know what we're like, mostly because it's none of your business. You know what she said two nights ago? After dinner? She said: You must have broken up with your girl friend; you're not being so sweet to me anymore. Joking, you see. Smiling. So I smiled back and said: Sure, you know how it is. That's all we said. Last night I took her out for beer and pizza and a cowboy show—'

In her confusion Jackie thought she might suddenly cry, for she knew the story was sentimental, even corny, but it touched her anyway. She looked at her watch: she had missed gym.

'I'll tell you this too, so you'll know it,' he said. 'I don't know one man who's faithful. Not in here anyway.' He tapped his forehead. 'Or whatever it is.' His dropping hand gestured toward his chest. 'Some don't get many chances. Or they're afraid to see a chance.'

'That letter didn't do a bit of good, did it? Come on, I've already missed one class.'

'I told you, I broke it off. And you know why? For you and me.'

'Sorry,' she said. 'I'm not one of those daughters.'

'Jesus—don't they teach anything but psychology around here? Listen, Jackie: we'll have a good summer, and I don't want suspicious looks every time I walk out of the house.'

'I don't believe you anymore. I don't think you even broke it off.'

'That's right: I drove two hundred and fifty miles to lie to an eighteen-year-old kid.'

'All right. You broke up with her.'

'But I'm not saying it right. I should be happy, I should be thanking you and blowing my nose. Right, Peter Pan?'

'What?'

'You used to read Peter Pan, over and over. That's what you were playing: Peter Pan, make everybody happy, save Wendy and Tiger Lily. Or maybe you were Tinker Bell. Remember?

She flew ahead because she was jealous and she wanted the boys to shoot Wendy.'

'Oh *stop* it.'

'Okay. That was mean.'

He reached across the table and touched her face, then trailed his fingers down her cheek.

'It just happens that I don't like to tell people goodbye, especially if it's a woman I've slept with. It reminds me of dying.'

'I have to get back,' she said. 'I have a class.'

He signalled the waiter, paid, and left a two dollar tip on the table. She slipped out of the booth and walked out, feeling him behind her as though she were being stalked; on the sidewalk she stopped, blinking in the sun. Then his hand was on her arm and he led her to the car. As they rode to the dormitory she watched students on the sidewalks, hoping to see Gary, for she could not be alone now and she could not go to math, which was the same as being alone, only worse. They passed the classroom buildings and, looking ahead now, she saw Fran climbing the dormitory steps; when her father stopped, she opened the door.

'Wait,' he said. 'Sit a minute and cool off.'

He shifted on the seat, hitching his right leg up, and faced her. At first she thought she would look straight ahead through the windshield but she didn't really know what she wanted to do, so—sitting straight—she turned her face to him.

'When you come home you'll have to carry your load, the same as Mother.'

'Meaning what?'

'Meaning don't look at me that way anymore. Mother doesn't.'

'She must be terribly hurt.'

'The difference between you and your mother is she knows me and you don't. Here: take this.'

Now the letter was out of his pocket, crossing the space between them, into her lap.

'Read it over tonight and see who you wrote it for.'

'For *her*,' she said, looking down at her own handwriting of a week ago.

'Think it over. And take this.'

Raising himself, he got his wallet; she was shaking her head as, barely looking at them, he pulled out some bills and pressed them into her hand. She left her fingers open.

'Get a dress or take your boy friend to dinner. Go on, take it.'

The top one was a five, and it was a thick stack; she folded it and dropped it in her purse.

'I'm not buying you, either. It's just a present.'

'All right.'

She was looking down, her warm cheek profiled to him, knowing it was a humble posture, but she could not lift her eyes.

'I want you to be straightened out by June.'

'Maybe I shouldn't come home.'

'Yes you will. And you'll be all right too. Now give me a kiss.'

She leaned toward him and kissed his mouth, then she was hugging him and, closing her eyes, she rubbed them quickly on his coat. He got out and came around her side, held the door open, and walked with her up the sidewalk and dormitory steps.

'Be careful driving back,' she said.

'Always.' Then he was grinning, shrugging his shoulders. 'What the hell, I've been to confession.'

She smiled, and held it while he got into the car, put on his sunglasses, waved, and drove off. Then she went inside and took the elevator to her floor. Fran was lying on her bed, wearing a slip.

'What happened?'

Jackie shook her head, went to the window, and looked down at the girls walking to class.

'What did he say?'

'He broke up with her.'

'Great! So it's okay now.'

Jackie left the window and lay on her bed.

'I'm going to cut this afternoon,' she said. 'Do you think we can find Dick and Gary?'

'Sure.'

'Let's go someplace. Maybe to a movie, then out for dinner. It's on me.'

'How much did he give you?'

'I don't know, but it's enough.'

'Okay,' Fran said. 'We won't tell the boys how you got it, though.'

'No,' Jackie said, 'we won't.'

She closed her eyes. When Fran was dressed, she got up and they went down the elevator and out into the sunlight to find the boys.

GOODBYE

ON A SUNDAY MORNING in June, Paul and Judith finished cleaning their apartment, left the key in the mailbox, and drove across town to the house Paul had left on a grey and windy day last March. It was the first house his father had ever bought: a small yellow one with a green door, a picture window, a car port. His father had bought it four years ago, when they moved from Lafayette to Lake Charles; it was a new house, built for selling in a residential section where at first there were half a dozen houses and wide, uncut fields where cottontails and meadowlarks lived. There were few trees. *My prairie*, Paul's mother called it. Now the fields were lawns and everywhere you looked there was a house, but still she said to friends: *Come out to the prairie and see us.* She said this in front of Paul's father too, her tone joking on the surface, yet no one could fail to hear the caverns of shame and bitterness beneath it. *Come to my little yellow house on the prairie*, she said.

Now, with hangered dresses lying on the back seat, and his new Marine uniform with the new gold bars hanging in a plastic bag from the hook above the window, he came in sight of the house, rectangular and yellow against the pale blue of the hot afternoon, and he felt a sense of dread, as though he were a child who had done something foolish and disobedient, and now must go home and pay the price. But he was also

293

in luck (though he couldn't actually call it that, for he had planned it, and left enough cleaning and packing for after Mass so they wouldn't arrive in time to have lunch with his father): his mother's Chevrolet stood alone in the car port, his father's company car was gone, and glancing at his watch, Paul imagined him about now within sight of the oaks, the fairways, the limp red flags. He reached across the overnight bag and took Judith's hand, this nineteen-year-old blond girl who he knew had saved him from something as intangible as love and fear. He held her hand until he had to release it to turn left at what he still thought of as his street, then right into the driveway where, as though in echo of his incompetent boyhood, he depressed the clutch too late, and the Ford stopped with a shudder.

When he had unloaded what they needed for the night, he went to the kitchen. In the refrigerator were two six-packs of Busch-Bavarian beer. There were also cantaloupes, which he and Judith could not afford, and for a moment he allowed himself to believe his last day and night at home would be a series of simple, tangible exchanges of love: his father, who rarely drank beer, had bought some for him; he would drink it, as he would eat the roast tonight and the cantaloupes tomorrow. But when he took a beer into the living room, where his mother and Judith sat with demitasses poised steady and graceful above their pastel laps, his mother said: 'Oh, you found your beer.' Then to Judith: 'His Daddy brought two six-packs home yesterday and I said those children will never drink all that, but all he said was Paul likes his beer. And I got some cantaloupes, for your breakfast tomorrow.'

'Good,' he said, and sat in his father's easy chair.

After a while his mother went to her room for a nap. Judith got a magazine from the rack and sat on the couch, under a large water-color of magnolias, painted long ago by a friend of his parents. Paul was looking at *Sports Illustrated* when his mother called him to the bedroom. She stood at the foot of her bed, wearing a slip and summer robe.

'Would you get my pen from under the bed?' she said

loudly, motioning with her head toward the living room and Judith. 'Your young body can bend better than mine.'

'Your pen?' He even started to bend over, to look; he would have crawled under the bed if she hadn't stopped him with a hand on his arm, a finger to her lips.

'I went to see Monsignor,' she whispered. 'To see if you and Judith were bad. I—'

'You did *what?*'

Her hand quickly tightened on his arm, her fingers rose to her lips; he whispered: 'You did *what?*'

'I had to know, Paul, and it's good I went, he was very nice, he said you were both very good young people, that the bad ones don't get into trouble—'

'You mean pregnant?'

Nodding quickly, her finger to her lips again: '—that only the innocent ones did because they didn't plan things.'

'Mother—Mother, why did you have to ask him that? Why didn't you *know* that?'

'Well because—'

'What's *wrong* with you?'

But he did not want to know, not ever—turning from her, leaving the room, down the hall past the photographs of him and his sisters, Amy and Barbara; he had only this afternoon and tonight to be at home, and he did not want to know anything more. Judith was looking at him.

'I think I'll go run,' he said.

'In this heat? After drinking a beer?'

'Yes.'

'But your things are packed. And they're clean.'

'I'll unpack them and you can throw them in the washer when I finish.'

Under the early afternoon sun he ran two miles on hot blacktop; for a while he ran in anger, then it left him when he was too hot to think of anything but being hot. When he got back his mother was sleeping. He took a beer into the shower and stayed a long time.

At six-thirty his mother began watching the clock, her eyes quick and trapped. She was in the pale green kitchen, moving through the smell of roast; Paul and Judith sat at the table, drinking beer.

'Don't y'all want to go to the living room instead of this hot old kitchen? You don't have to stay in here with me.'

Paul told her no, he didn't like the smell of air-conditioned rooms, he wanted to smell cooking. He was watching the clock too. Certainly she must remember the meals after Amy and Barbara had gone: if she didn't talk, the three of them ate to the sounds of silverware on china. There was nothing else her memory could give her, unless she had dreamed this night of goodbyes out of some memory of her own childhood, with the five brothers and four sisters, the loud meals at that long table where he too had sat as a child and watched black hands lowering bowls and platters, and had daydreamed beneath the voices, the laughter of the Kelleys, who had once had money and perhaps dignity and now believed they had lost both because they had lost the first. The lawyer father had died in debt, with his insurance lapsed, and the sons had sold their house, whose grounds were so big that, when Paul played there, he had not needed to imagine size: it seemed as large as Sherwood Forest. Jews bought the house, tore the vines from its brick walls, and painted the first story pink. Maybe they had got around to painting the top story; he didn't know. He hadn't been to New Iberia in years, and when his mother went she refused to pass the house.

He watched her at the stove. If his father missed the cocktail hour, Paul would be spared while she suffered; and more: he knew by now, after those nights—one or two a month—that when his father came home late for dinner, drunk (she called it tight), gentle, and guilty, Paul sided with him; and in the face of his mother's pique they played a winking, grinning game of two men who by their natures were bound to keep the sober women waiting at their stoves. He even drew pleasure from it, though as a boy he had loved his mother more than anyone on earth, he loved her still, he had always been able to talk with her, although now he had things to say that she didn't want to hear: hardly reason enough to make her the sheep he offered for a few warm and easy (not really: faked, strained) moments with his father. But he would probably do it again. Since waking from her nap, she had not tried to speak to him alone; she had kept them with Judith; and her voice and eyes asked his forgiveness.

By seven-thirty, when the roast was done, they had moved with their drinks to the living room: Paul in his father's chair, his head resting on the doily, on the same spot (from Vaseline hair tonic, two drops a day, and Paul used it too) faintly soiled by his father's head. His mother, sitting with Judith on the couch, was not wearing a watch; but at exactly seven-thirty, she asked Paul the time.

'All right, he'd rather drink out there with his friends than with his own family. All right: I'm used to that. I've lived with it. But not the dinner. He can't do this to the dinner. Call him, Paul. I'm sorry, Judith: families should be quiet about these things. Paul, call your father.'

'Not me.' He shook his head. 'No: not me.'

When he was a boy in Lafayette she had sometimes told him to call the golf course and ask his father how long before he'd be home. He did it, feeling he was an ally against his father, whose irritation—*All right: tell her I'm coming*—was not, he knew, directed at him; was even in collusion with him; but that knowledge didn't help. Also, at thirteen and fourteen and then fifteen his voice hadn't changed yet, so he was doubly humiliated: when he asked for his father the clerk always said: *Yes ma'am, just a second*—

'Then I'll call,' his mother said. 'Should I call him, Judith, or should we just go ahead and eat without him?'

'Maybe we could wait another few minutes.'

'All right. Fifteen. I'll wait until quarter to eight. Paul, fix your mother a drink. I might as well get tight, then. That's what they say: join your husband in his vices.'

'Drinking isn't Daddy's vice.'

'No, who said it was? It's that *golf* that's his vice. I might as well have married a sea captain, Judith, at least then I wouldn't be out here on my prairie—'

'You could live by the sea,' Judith said, 'and have a widow's walk.'

Paul took his mother's glass and pushed through the swinging kitchen door, out of the sound and smell of air-conditioning, into the heat, and the fragrance of roast.

At twenty before ten, they sat down to dinner. His mother set Paul's plate at the head of the table, but Paul said no, Daddy might come home while we're eating. He sat opposite Judith. His mother said they should have eaten at eight-fifteen. It took fifteen minutes to drive home from the club, and at eight o'clock she had gone to her room, and slid the door shut in a futile attempt at privacy in a house too small to contain what it had to. They heard her voice: hurt, bitter, whining. And at once—though his mother was right, his father wrong by something as simple as an hour and a half—he was against her. Maybe if she didn't whine, if she had served dinner at seven-thirty and said the hell with him, the old bastard can eat it cold when he gets home, maybe then he would have joined her. But he knew that wasn't true either, that it wasn't her style he resented so much as her vision—or lack of it— which allowed her to have that style and feel it was her due. When perhaps all the time his father, by staying away, was telling her: *You shouldn't have planned this, you are not helping us all but failing us all, and I choose not to bear the pain of it.* But if that were true, then his father's method was cowardly, and his cowardice added to or even created the problem he couldn't face.

For nearly three hours after the call his mother went on with the recitation of betrayal which was her attack. It was not continuous. Often enough, with the voice of someone waiting for a phone call that will change her life, she was able to talk of other things: guesses about what their new life would be like, what sort of people they would meet at Quan-

tico (all educated, I'm sure; a lot of Northerners too; I hope
y'all get along); and it was a blessing there wasn't a war, Paul
was lucky, too young for Korea and now it looked like there
would be peace for a long time unless those Russians did
something crazy; she said his father had been saved from war
too, he had grown up between them, so Paul was the first
Clement to be in the service; there had been three Kelleys,
her nephews, in World War II, they had all fought and all
come home; but no one in the family had ever been a Marine
lieutenant. And she spoke to Judith of food prices and ways to
save; she offered recipes; and once she mentioned the child:
she said she hoped Judith would be able to go back to college
after the baby came. Always, though, she returned to the
incredible and unpredictable violation of her evening; again
and again she told them, with anger posing as amazement,
how his father had said they were playing gin and time had
slipped up on him, had taken him by surprise, had passed him
by. And he had said he was coming. Thirty minutes ago, and
the way he drives it only takes ten minutes. An hour ago. With
all that drinking from—from four, four-thirty on, that's when
they finish—maybe he was in an accident.

'Paul, you'd better call and see if he's left, maybe he's—'

Around a mouthful of mayonnaised pineapple, Paul
said no.

'Well, all right, youth is callous, you know he was in an
accident before, he was lucky it was so clearly the other man's
fault, because he had been drinking, he had played golf that
day, and then we went out to eat with the Bertrands. He's a
wonderful driver, Judith. But how could—oh, that *mis*erable
man, we'll have to go get him. He won't be able to drive.'

Paul thought they wouldn't have to, that surely his father
would weave in, blinking, flirting with Judith in his deep,
mellow drinking voice, averting his eyes from the woman
whose face showed years of waiting not only for him but for
all that she wanted—money, prominence, perhaps even love:
or perhaps only that, and was it impossible, and if so, who had
made it impossible?—and dealing her a series of bourbon-

thickened apologies, renunciations, promises. But it didn't happen. At ten-forty the dishwasher was doing its work, the women had wiped and swept every crumb from the table and floor, sponged every spot of grease from the stove, and drunk second cups of coffee. Then his mother said: 'Oh that *man*. I'm going to bed, I've had a lovely evening with you two anyway; Paul, give me a kiss, and you and your wife go get him.'

'Why don't we just leave him alone?'

'He's been drinking for seven *hours*, he's got to come *home*.'

'He can handle it.'

'All right, I won't go to bed, I'll go alone, and we'll leave his car at the club all night for everyone to see in the morning, if he doesn't have any pride, why should I care, his friends would think it's funny, oh look there's old Paul's car; I wish that damn company had never got him into the club, I don't know if Paul told you this, Judith, but his company pays the dues, we don't have that kind of money; when they transferred him from Lafayette he said he wouldn't come unless they got him into the club and paid his dues, because there's no golf course here, and they did it, it's all they've ever done for him all these years, and I wish they'd never done that—'

Paul was about to say *But think how unhappy he'd be*, when he realized that was precisely what she meant, and perhaps not only for vengeance but also to cut off all his avenues of escape and force him to find happiness for her and with her, or find none at all.

'—well, I'm used to it, I don't care, I'm past caring now—'

'Mother.'

'—in Lafayette he left me and married the golf course, and now he's married to his old country club, he might as well bring a bed—'

'Mother, we'll go.'

'No, you don't have to, I can—'

'Go to bed, if you want. We'll go.'

The shells of the parking lot were white in the moonlight. Paul stopped beside his father's car in the shadow of palmettos and told Judith she might as well wait outside, because his father would be in the locker room. She said she'd wait at the wharf, and he touched her hand, then slid out of the car and went slowly to the front door, where he paused and looked out at the lake; on that wharf he had first kissed Judith. Then he went in, past loud men with their wives at tables in the bar, into the locker room. The four men sat at a card table between rows of tall green wall lockers; his father's back was turned. Mr. Clay looked up and said: 'Young man you know, Paul.'

His father turned, the reddening of his already sun-red face starting up at once, with his grin; then as he beckoned to a chair he began to cough, that deep, liquid body-wrenching cough that Paul had heard for years, a cough from about four hundred thousand cigarettes and two or three lies his father told himself: *a holder helps, filters make a difference, sometimes switching brands.* Now he came out of it, patted his chest and swallowed while his eyes watered; his voice was weak: 'Hi, Son. Have a seat and we'll get you a drink.'

'Judith's waiting outside.'

'Oh? Did your momma come out too? We could buy 'em a drink, couple of good-looking women, we could handle that—'

'She's home.'

'Oh.' He looked at the cards on the table, took a drink from his bourbon and water. 'Did you drink all that beer?'

'Just about.'

'You all packed and ready?'

'Yep.'

'This boy would like to be called Lieutenant by you old bastards. Second lieutenant, United States Marine Corps. He'll do my *fight*in' for me.'

'He can do something else for you too, you old hoss.'

'When do you leave, son?' Mr. Clay said.

'Tomorrow.'

'Tomorrow?' He looked at Paul's father. Then he stood up. 'Well, I'm going home and boil me an egg.'

'Me too,' another said. 'Before y'all win my house and bird dog too.'

His father rose, grinning, lighting a cigarette, and Paul tensed for the cough, but it didn't come; it was down there, waiting.

They walked through the bar, his father weaving some, his shoulders forward in a subtle effort to balance his velocity and weight.

'Judith's down at the wharf.'

'Oh?' Then the cough came. Paul stood watching him; he thought of his father collapsing: he would catch him before his face struck the shells, carry him to the car. His father brought up something from deep in his body and spit. 'Okay, good. We'll go see Judith at the wharf.'

They crunched over shells, then walked quietly on damp earth sloping to the wharf, then onto it, walking the length of it, their footsteps loud, over the lapping of waves on the pilings and the shore. Ahead of them, at the wharf's end, Judith's moonlit hair was silver.

'Hi, darling,' his father said, and put his arm around her; Paul moved to the other side, and the three of them stood arm in arm, looking out at the black water shimmering under the moon.

'I wanted to see it before we left,' Judith said.

'Is this where y'all did it?'

He felt Judith stiffen then relax, and then he felt her hugging his father.

'No,' he said. 'No, it's where we first kissed.'

They started back, still arm in arm; holding Judith, Paul was guiding his father. Judith said: 'Will you be all right?'

'That car responds to me, darling. You can come with me, though, for company; one of y'all.'

They left the wharf and started up the gentle slope. When they reached the shells Judith said: 'Okay.' Paul was looking straight ahead, at the palmettos before the shadowed colonial front of the club. He felt his father looking at Judith.

'How come my bride doesn't know I got to get drunk to tell my boy goodbye? We had our first kiss on a porch swing, his momma and me. That's where we courted in those days. Maybe that's why nothing happened.'

'What *did* happen?' Paul said.

They crossed the deep shells. He thought his father had not heard, or, hearing, hadn't understood. But when they reached the company car, his father said: 'God knows, Son.' Then he opened the door and got in.

Judith waited, looking up at Paul. His father started the engine. Then Paul turned quickly away, toward his own car, Judith got in with his father, and he followed them home, watching their heads moving as they talked. The house was quiet, and they crept in and went to bed.

In the morning they were together for about an hour. The talk was of the details of departure, and their four voices called from room to room, from house to car, and filled the kitchen as they ate cantaloupes and bacon and eggs. No one mentioned last night; it showed on no one's face. At the door he kissed and embraced his quietly weeping mother. 'There goes our last one,' she said. 'We should have had more.' He looked through tears into his father's damp eyes, and they hugged fiercely, without a word. He did not look at them again until he had backed out of the driveway: they stood in their summer robes, his father's hand resting on his mother's shoulder. They waved. His father coughed, his lifted arm faltering, dropping; then he recovered, and waved again. Paul waved back, and drove down the road.

LESLIE IN CALIFORNIA

WHEN THE ALARM RINGS the room is black and grey; I smell Kevin's breath and my eye hurts and won't open. He gets out of bed, and still I smell beer in the cold air. He is naked and dressing fast. I get up shivering in my nightgown and put on my robe and go by flashlight to the kitchen, where there is some light from the sky. Birds are singing, or whatever it is they do. I light the gas lantern and set it near the stove, and remember New England mornings with the lights on and a warm kitchen and catching the school bus. I won't have to look at my eye till the sun comes up in the bathroom. Dad was happy about us going to California; he talked about sourdough bread and fresh fruit and vegetables all year. I put water on the stove and get bacon and eggs and milk from the ice chest. A can of beer is floating, tilting, in the ice and water; the rest are bent in the paper bag for garbage. I could count them, know how many it takes. I put on the bacon and smoke a cigarette, and when I hear him coming I stand at the stove so my back is to the door.

'Today's the day,' he says.

They are going out for sharks. They will be gone five days, maybe more, and if he comes back with money we can have electricity again. For the first three months out here he could not get on a boat, then yesterday he found one that was short a man, so last night he celebrated.

'Hey, hon.'

I turn the bacon. He comes to me and hugs me from behind, rubbing my hips through the robe, his breath sour beer with mint.

'Let me see your eye.'

I turn around and look up at him, and he steps back. His blond beard is damp, his eyes are bloodshot, and his mouth opens as he looks.

'Oh, hon.'

He reaches to touch it, but I jerk my face away and turn back to the skillet.

'I'll never do that again,' he says.

The bacon is curling brown. Through the window above the stove I can see the hills now, dark humps against the sky. Dad liked the Pacific, but we are miles inland and animals are out there with the birds; one morning last week a rattlesnake was on the driveway. Yesterday some men went hunting a bobcat in the hills. They say it killed a horse, and they are afraid it will kill somebody's child, but they didn't find it. How can a bobcat kill a horse? My little sister took riding lessons in New England; I watched her compete, and I was afraid, she was so small on that big animal jumping. Dad told me I tried to pet some bobcats when I was three and we lived at Camp Pendleton. He was the deer camp duty officer one Sunday, and Mom and I brought him lunch. Two bobcats were at the edge of the camp; they wanted the deer hides by the scales, and I went to them saying here, kitty, here, kitty. They just watched me, and Dad called me back.

'It wasn't you,' Kevin says. 'You know it wasn't you.'

'Who was it?'

My first words of the day, and my voice sounds like dry crying. I clear my throat and grip the robe closer around it.

'I was drunk,' he says. 'You know. You know how rough it's been.'

He harpoons fish. We came across country in an old Ford he worked on till it ran like it was young again. We took turns driving and sleeping and only had to spend motel money twice. That was in October, after we got married on a fishing boat, on a clear blue Sunday on the Atlantic. We had twenty-five friends and the two families and open-faced sandwiches and deviled eggs, and beer and wine. On the way out to sea we got married, then we fished for cod and drank, and in late afternoon we went to Dad's for a fish fry with a fiddle band. Dad has a new wife, and Mom was up from Florida with her boy friend. Out here Kevin couldn't get on a boat, and I couldn't even waitress. He did some under-the-table work: carpenter, mechanic, body work, a few days here, a few there. Now it's February, a short month.

'Hon,' he says behind me.

'It's three times.'

'Here. Let me do something for that eye.'

I hear him going to the ice chest, the ice moving in there to his big hands. I lay the bacon on the paper towel and open the door to pour out some of the grease; I look at the steps before I go out. The grease sizzles and pops on the wet grass, and there's light at the tops of the hills.

'Here,' he says, and I shut the door. I'm holding the skillet with a pot holder, and I see he's wearing his knife, and I think of all the weapons in a house: knives, cooking forks, ice picks, hammers, skillets, cleavers, wine bottles, and I wonder if I'll be one of those women. I think of this without fear, like I'm reading in the paper about somebody else dead in her kitchen. He touches my eye with ice wrapped in a dish towel.

'I have to do the eggs.'

I break them into the skillet and he stands behind me, holding the ice on my eye. His arm is over mine, and I bump it as I work the spatula.

'Not now,' I say.

I lower my face from the ice; for awhile he stands behind me, and I watch the eggs and listen to the grease and his breathing and the birds, then he goes to the chest and I hear the towel and ice drop in.

'After, okay?' he says. 'Maybe the swelling will go down. Jesus, Les. I wish I wasn't going.'

'The coffee's dripped.'

He pours two cups, takes his to the table, and sits with a cigarette. I know his mouth and throat are dry, and probably he has a headache. I turn the eggs and count to four, then put them on a plate with bacon. I haven't had a hangover since I was sixteen. He likes carbohydrates when he's hung over; I walk past him, putting the plate on the table, seeing his leg and arm and shoulder, but not his face, and get a can of pork and beans from the cupboard. From there I look at the back of his head. He has a bald spot the size of a quarter. Then I go to the stove and heat the beans on a high flame, watching them, drinking coffee and smoking.

'We'll get something,' he says between bites. 'They're out there.'

Once, before I met him, he was in the water with a sword-fish. He had harpooned it and they were bringing it alongside, it was thrashing around in the water, and he tripped on some line and fell in with it.

'We'll get the lights back on,' he says. 'Go out on the town, buy you something nice. A sweater, a blouse, okay? But I wish I wasn't going today.'

'I wish you didn't hit me last night.' The juice in the beans is bubbling. 'And the two before that.'

'I'll tell you one thing, hon. I'll never get that drunk again. It's not even me anymore. I get drunk like that, and somebody crazy takes over.'

I go to his plate and scoop all the beans on his egg yellow. The coffee makes me pee, and I leave the flashlight and walk through the living room that smells of beer and ashtrays and is grey now, so I can see a beer can on the arm of a chair. I sit in the bathroom where it is darkest, and the seat is cold. I hear a car coming up the road, shifting down and turning into the driveway, then the horn. I wash my hands without looking in the mirror; in the gas light of the kitchen, and the first light from the sky, he's standing with his bag and harpoon.

'Oh, hon,' he says, and holds me tight. I put my arms around him, but just touching his back. 'Say it's okay.'

I nod, my forehead touching his chest, coming up, touching, coming up.

'That's my girl.'

He kisses me and puts his tongue in, then he's out the door, and I stand on the top step and watch him to the car. He waves and grins and gets in. I hold my hand up at the car as they back into the road, then are gone downhill past the house. The sun is showing red over the hills, and there's purple at their tops, and only a little green. They are always dry, but at night everything is wet.

I go through the living room and think about cleaning it, and open the front door and look out through the screen. The house has a shadow now, on the grass and dew. There are other houses up here, but I can't see any of them. The road goes winding up into the hills where the men hunted yesterday. I think of dressing and filling the canteen and walking, maybe all morning, I could make a sandwich and bring it in my jacket, and an orange. I open the screen and look up the road as far as I can see, before it curves around a hill in the sun. Blue is spreading across the sky. Soon the road will warm, and I think of rattlesnakes sleeping on it, and I shut the screen and look around the lawn where nothing moves.

THE NEW BOY

A SATURDAY NIGHT in summer: his mother and two sisters had dates, and he did not want to greet the boys and the man, so he sat by the swimming pool, with his back to the house, and gazed at the lake and the woods beyond it. The house was on the crest of a ridge and, past the pool, the lawn was a long slope down to the lake. The sun was low over the trees, and their shadows spread toward him on the water. When he heard the last car, most of the lake was dark and the sun was nearly gone beyond the trees. The cars would return in the same order: Stephanie by twelve, Julie by two now that she was eighteen, then his mother; he would wake as each one turned into the driveway, and sleep after the front door closed and light footsteps had gone from kitchen to bathroom to bedroom. Stephanie was sixteen and stayed longest at the front door and in the kitchen; his mother was quickest at the door and did not stop at the kitchen unless a man came in for a drink; then Walter slept and woke again when the car started in the driveway, and he listened to his mother climbing the stairs and going to her room. Now she called him, and he looked over his shoulder at her standing behind the screen door.

'I'm going now.'

'Have a good time.'

When the car was gone, he rose and walked around the

pool, then downhill to the lake, darker now than the sky. The
sun showed through the woods as burning leaves. Then it
was gone, leaving him in the black and grey solitude that
touched him, and gave him the peaceful joy of sorrow that
was his alone, that singled him out from all others. A sound
intruded: above the frogs' croaking and the flutter and soft
plash of stirring geese, so familiar that they were, to him,
audible silence, he heard now the rhythmic splashes and lapping of a swimmer. He looked to his right, near the shore,
where purple loose-strife stood, deflowered by night, like
charcoal strokes three feet tall. Beyond their tops he saw a
head and arms and the small white roil of water at the feet.
The swimmer angled toward him. Above and behind him, he
felt the presence of his house: that place where, nearly always,
he could go when he did not want something to happen. He
stared at the head and arms coming to him. They rose: slender chest and waist of a boy walking through the dark water,
then light bathing suit and legs, and the boy stepped onto the
bank and shook his head, sprinkling Walter's face, then he
pushed his hair back from his forehead. He was neither taller
nor broader than Walter, who glanced at the boy's biceps and
did not see in them, either, the source of his fear.

'It's against the law to swim in there,' he said. 'That's a
reservoir.'

'I pissed in it too. Let's swim in your pool.'

'How do you know I have one?'

'You live here?'

'Yes.'

'Everybody on this road's got one. I can see all the backyards from the sun deck.'

'Don't you have one?'

'It's empty.' He started walking up the slope. 'Which
house?'

'Straight ahead.'

Walter followed him up to the lighted house and stood at
the shallow end while the boy went to the deep end and dived
in and swam back, then stood.

'I have to go put on my suit.'

'Turn on the underwater lights.'

He turned them on with the switch near the door and went upstairs; his room looked over the pool, and in the dark he stood at the window and undressed, watching the boy splashing silver as he moved fast through the water that was greener now in the light from the bottom of the pool. Naked, he looked beyond at the slope and lake and, on its far side, the trees like a tufted black wall. He put on his damp trunks and went down the carpeted hall and stairs and out through the kitchen, then ran across flagstones to the side of the pool, glimpsing the boy to his left, in the deep end, and dived, opening his eyes to bubbles and the pale bottom coming up at him. He touched it with his fingers. Under the night sky the water felt heavy, deeper. He arched his back and started to rise; the boy was up there, breaststroking, then bending into a dive, coming down at Walter, under his lifted arms: a shoulder struck his chest, an arm went around it, then the boy was behind him, the arm moved and was around his neck, tightening and pulling, and he went backward toward the bottom, and with both hands jerked at the wrist and forearm, cool and slick under his prying fingers. His jaws were clamped tight on the pressure rising from his chest. He released some, and bubbles rose toward the dark air. He rolled toward the bottom, touched it for balance with a hand, swung his feet down to it, and thrust upward with straightening legs; he had exhaled again; he released the boy's arm and stroked upward and kicked and kept his mouth closed against the throbbing emptiness in his chest, then breathed water and rose to the air choking, inhaling, coughing. The boy's arm had left his throat. He did not look behind him. Slowly he swam away, head out of the water, coughing; he climbed out of the pool and, bent over, coughed and spat on the flagstones. He heard the feet behind him.

'You're crazy,' he said, then straightened and turned and looked at the boy's eyes. He had seen them before, on school playgrounds: amused, playful, and with a shimmer of affection, they had looked at him as knowingly as his family and his closest friends did. Boys with those eyes never fought in fury; they rarely fought at all. They threw your books in the mud, pushed you against walls, pulled your hair, punched your arm or stomach, shamed and goaded you, while watching boys and girls urged you to fight. Two years ago, when he was twelve, he had leaped into those voices, onto the bully, and they rolled grappling in the dust, then he was on his back, shoulders pinned by knees, fists striking his face before some- one pulled the boy away. For the rest of the school year he was free; and for the rest of his boyhood, for he knew that the months of peace were worth the fear and pain of the first quick fight, so he was ready for that, and so was left alone. This boy's eyes were brown; Walter swung his right fist at them and struck the nose. The boy raised a hand to it, and looked at blood on the fingers. He wiped them on his trunks; blood had reached his lip now.

'I didn't know you were scared,' the boy said.

'Scared my ass.'

'I mean underwater.'

'I couldn't breathe.'

The boy folded his arms.

'I could.'

'Let's go inside and fix your nose.'

'Let's go inside and eat.'

The boy turned and dived. Swimming underwater, he pinched and rubbed his nose, and blood wafted from his fin- gers, became the green-tinted pale blue of the pool. He swam to the other side; Walter walked around the pool and they went into the kitchen. The boy stood at the bar. Looking into the refrigerator, Walter said: 'Peaches, grapes, liverwurst, cheese—four kinds of cheese—' He turned and looked at the boy; his eyes had not changed.

In the still heat of Sunday morning he slept long and woke, clammy, to the voices of his sisters and mother rising from the terrace. Every day in summer his sisters slept late, and his mother did on weekends, and he loved those mornings, going downstairs, quiet and alone, to eat cereal and read the baseball news, feeling in the kitchen silence their sleeping behind the three closed doors above him. They woke loudly, talking in the hall and from one bathroom door to another, and through bedroom doors as they altered their hair and faces; their voices came down the stairs and into the kitchen, then they entered, red-lipped and tan and scented; talking, they turned on the radio and made coffee and lit cigarettes. It seemed that always at least one of them was smoking, at least one was talking, and all three of them were now, on the terrace beneath his window; he had not waked when they came home in the night, so his own night of sleep seemed long; and, having no place to go, he still felt that he was late. He looked down at them sitting at the glass table; their hair, chestnut in three seasons, was lighter; they wore two-piece bathing suits, and his mother and Julie drank Bloody Marys; Stephanie had a glass of wine. His mother let her drink wine at dinner and at Sunday brunch, and only Walter knew that when she drank at brunch she got drunk, for they stayed at the table longer than at any dinner except Thanksgiving and Christmas, and neither Julie nor his mother was sober enough to notice her rose cheeks and shining eyes. He put on his trunks and made his bed and moved past their rooms, glancing at their beds that would not be made until old Nora from Ireland came to work Monday afternoon, down the stairs into the undulant sound of their voices. He stepped into the sunlight and Stephanie said: 'Well *finally*.'

They smiled at him; they wished him a good morning and he returned it; Julie said why couldn't she meet someone as good-looking as her brother; his mother puckered her lips for a kiss and he gave her one. Their hair and bathing suits were dry. He stood above them in the warmth of the sun and their love, and his for them; their eyes flushed his cheeks, and he left: went to the deep end and dived in and swam fast laps of the pool until he was winded, then returned to them. Someone had poured him a glass of orange juice. His mother blew smoke and said: 'Spinach crepes, kid. Can you handle it?'

'Sure.'

Stephanie looked down at herself and said: 'I shouldn't handle anything.'

'You're not fat,' he said.

'I need to lose seven pounds.'

'Bull.'

'She does,' his mother said. 'But not today.'

'Do it gradually,' Julie said. 'Give yourself three weeks.'

'That's August. I'd like to get into my bathing suit before August.'

He looked through the glass table at her black pants like a wide belt around her hips.

'You're in it,' he said.

'And look what shows,' and she pinched flesh above the pants.

'You have to be really skinny to wear those things,' he said, then grinned, looking through glass at his mother's and Julie's flat skin above the maroon and blue swaths, and Julie said: 'Okay, everybody stare at Walter's pelvis.'

He stood and, profiled to them, he drew in his stomach muscles, expanded his chest, flexed his left arm, and looked down at them over the rising and falling curve of his bicep as he rotated his wrist.

'Our macho man,' Julie said, and his father was there: not a memory of the broad, hairy chest, and hair curling over the gold watchband as he read the Sunday paper before swimming his laps, but his father in Philadelphia, in that apartment of leaves: plants growing downward from suspended pots and upward from pots on tables and floor, his father like a man reading in a jungle clearing; he sat and drank juice and his mother said: 'Were you up late last night?'

'No.'

'What did you do?'

'Nothing.'

He picked up a green cigarette pack, let it fall, pushed it toward Stephanie. He looked beyond Julie at Canadian geese on the lake; his mother and the girls were talking again, and he leaned back in the canvas deck chair and looked up at the blue sky, then closed his eyes and turned his face to the sun, and breathed deeply into the chill of his lie until it was gone, and his mother went to the kitchen, and he opened his eyes and watched the girls talking. They rarely said anything he wanted to know, but he liked hearing their voices and watching their faces and hands: they spoke of clothes, and he looked with tender amusement at their passionate eyes, their lips closing on cigarettes with sensuous pouts he knew they had practiced; hair fell onto their cheeks, and their hands rose to it and lightly swept it back, as if stroking a spider web. From the house behind him, his mother came with a broad tray: a bottle of white wine in an ice bucket, a bowl of fruit, four plates with crepes, a glass of milk, and ringed napkins. He believed Julie—but maybe Stephanie—had asked one Sunday: *What did you do with Dad's napkin ring?* But since he could not remember the answer, he was not sure anyone had ever asked; perhaps he had dreamed it, or had imagined someone asking, and had waited for that; he slipped linen from silver, and his mother asked him to pour the wine. For over a year of Sundays and dinners he had poured the wine, but always he waited for his mother to ask him: he disliked doing what his father had done, felt artificial and very young and disloyal too, as if he were helping to close the space his father had left behind; and he disliked her never saying that she wanted him to pour because his father was gone. While his sisters nibbled and moaned and sipped, he ate fast, head down, waiting for his mother to strike back, knowing she was watching yet would not tell him the truth: that she wanted him to eat with slow appreciation of her work. She would tell him that eating fast was bad for—Then he heard the squeak-skid of brakes and tires and turned to see him at the edge of the terrace, straddling his bicycle, bare-chested, wearing cut-off jeans and sneakers without socks. Walter nodded to him, ate the last of the crepe, and stood, looking at his mother as he swallowed and wiped his mouth.

'I'm going bike riding.'

'Who's that?'

'Mark Evans.' Walking away, he looked back over his shoulder and said: 'They moved in yesterday.'

In the woods near the road he and Mark lay face down in the shadow of trees and looked through branches and brown needles of a larger fallen branch of pine; Mark had dragged it from deeper in the woods, where their bicycles were chained to a tree. Moist dead leaves were cool against Walter's flesh. Out in the sunlight the white handkerchief hung: folded over a length of fishing line tied to trees on either side of the narrow road, it was suspended three feet above the blacktop, motionless in the still air.

'It's like waiting in ambush,' Walter said.

'It's better at night. It looks like a ghost at night.'

'It looks like one now.'

The first car that came around the curve down the road to their left was green and foreign; Walter pressed his palms and bare toes against the earth and saw a second shape behind the windshield, a woman, and then two more figures in the back, and now the driver's face: a man beyond the hood, wearing sunglasses, right hand at the top of the wheel, peering now, shifting down, slowing and slowing, the woman's hands in front of her, pushing toward the windshield, then her head out of the window saying 'What is it?' and the children leaning forward, arms and hands out of the windows, and the man stopped and got out, he was tall and wore a suit, and Walter pressed against the leaves and watched him holding the line and looking down both of its ends; then breaking it, and watching the handkerchief fall, and standing with fists on his hips, turning his head from one side of the road to the other as he spoke: 'I want you boys to think about something while you're in there laughing and having your fun. You could kill somebody. You could make somebody swerve into another car. I've got two kids in mine. You could have caused some-

thing you'd regret for the rest of your lives.' Then he went
back to his car. Before he got in, his wife said: 'Don't just leave
it in the road.'

   'I don't want to *touch* it.'

   She opened the door but he said 'Let's go' and got in and
shifted and drove slowly by, his wife hunting the woods, her
eyes sweeping the fallen pine branch. Then the car was hidden by trees, and he listened to it going faster up the road, and
laughing, he stood and squeezed Mark's shoulders and
hopped and skipped in a circle, pulling Mark with him, forcing the sound of his laughter faster when it slowed and louder
when it lulled; he stopped dancing and laughing, but still
quivering with jubilance, he squeezed Mark's shoulder and
shouted: 'I don't want to touch it.'

When he rode his bicycle up the driveway, the sun was low
above the trees across the lake, and his mother and sisters
were still at the glass table; then, coming out of the garage, he
saw that it was not still but again: his mother and Julie wore
dresses and Stephanie wore shorts; beyond them, downwind,
smoke rose from charcoal in the wheeled grill.

   'I'll be right down,' he said.

   'I'm coming up,' his mother said.

   He went into the pale light of the house, up the stairs,
hearing the screen door open and shut, and the clack of her
steps on the kitchen floor then muted by carpets as she followed him up. His room was sunlit. He looked down at Julie
and Stephanie, then turned to face the door a moment before
she entered it. Her dress was white and, between its straps, a
pearl necklace lay on her tan skin. She had a cigarette in one
hand and a drink in the other: a tall, clear one with a piece of
lime among the bubbles and ice.

   'Did you have a good day?'

   'Yes.'

   'Where did you go?'

'Bike riding.'

She put her drink on the chest of drawers and flicked ashes into her hand.

'That's quite a workout.'

'We went to the woods too.'

'You were right across the lake?'

'The big woods. By the highway.'

'Oh. You said—Mark?—moved here yesterday? When did you meet him?'

'Last night.'

'Where?'

'Here. He was looking around.'

'Well, I don't want to'—she glanced at her drink, drew on her cigarette, flicked ashes in her hand—'I don't want to make a big thing out of it, but why didn't you tell me?'

'I don't know.'

'You really don't? That's so—I don't know, it's so—*strange.*' With forefinger and thumb of her ash-hand she picked up her drink. 'Well. Will you do something for me? Ask him to come over sometime when I'm home. We'll have dinner. Will you do that?'

'I'll ask him.'

He looked at the cigarette burning close to her fingers.

'Good. I like meeting your friends. You have time to shower before dinner, pal.'

'I was about to.'

She smiled and left, and he followed her to the door and said to her back as she moved down the hall, gingerly holding the drink and cigarette: 'Will I have time to swim? After my shower?'

'Plenty of time,' she called over her shoulder. 'It's pork.'

The apartment in Philadelphia smelled of the city, not only exhaust but something else that came through the open windows: a staleness, as though Philadelphia itself were enclosed by ceiling and walls, and today's breeze carried to his lungs yesterday's cement and stirred dust; when the windows were closed, the apartment's motionless air had no smell, and that too, for Walter, was Philadelphia. With his father in the apartment she had filled with plants was blond Jenny, who, that first morning when he visited them for a weekend, knocked on his door, and he woke remembering where he was and said *Yes*, and she came in with a tray holding hot chocolate and bread she had baked last night, wrapped in hot foil—*that child*, his mother had said, *that child. With those clothes from Nashville by way of Hollywood. What is she? There aren't any more hippies. I'm sorry, children, he's your father but I cannot can not live quietly through this mad time. She was born the year we were married and I've spent twenty-two years giving my life to my husband and my home and now it feels like I was just taking care of him while she did nothing but get taller and busty so he could leave with her*—Jenny sat on the bed and talked to him while he drank the chocolate and ate the bread and liked her, and understood his father loving her, and so shared his father's guilt. He was the first to visit; in two weeks Stephanie would come, and then Julie, because there was only the one guest room, his father said, and his mother said: *He's protecting that girl from handling all of you at once.* Jenny said: *You probably don't like breakfast in bed*, and he said: *No, not even when I'm sick*, and she blushed, smiling at herself, and said: *I don't either. I'll stop trying so hard. Are you all right?* At first he thought she meant the bed, the room, his hunger, then looking at her he knew she didn't, and he said: *Yes. And Stephanie and Julie? They'll be all right. They're not now? They'll get better. Is your Mom? No. That's why they're not. It's awful. I wish*—He wanted to hear the wish: perhaps behind her worried blue eyes she wished his father had no wife, no children, that he and his mother and Julie and Stephanie were dead or had never lived; now sadly he saw them, the woman and girls he had left at home: they were in the living room, talking, then they vanished; for moments their voices lingered in the room and then faded with them into space. *There's too much to wish*, she said; *there's nothing to wish.*

I just have to hope. For what? That nobody's hurt too badly for too long. Sunday night he boarded an airplane for the second time in three days and in his life; he had spent most of the flight Friday afternoon imagining the weekend, making himself shy and awkwardly intrusive in his father's new home and life before he saw either. He had met Jenny, had eaten dinner in restaurants with her and his father and sisters; but that was all. Sunday in the plane he liked being alone with the small light over his head and the black sky at his cool window; a man sat beside him, but he was alone: no one knew him, and when the stewardess spoke to him as though he were either boy or man, he felt that his age as well as his name had remained on the earth. Philadelphia was done; Philadelphia was good; he could go back, and now he was going home.

His mother and sisters ate dinner in Boston, then met him at the airport, and he sat in the back seat with Stephanie; the night was cool, and in the closed car he remembered what he had forgotten to remember until now: Jenny and his father smelled of soap and cloth and flesh, and no smoke drifted toward his face through the still air of their rooms. He started to say this, nearly said: *At least she doesn't smoke*; then he knew he must not.

'So how was it,' Stephanie said, and watching his mother in part-profile, hair and upper cheek, her hand on the wheel, smoke pluming from her mouth he could not see, he told of the weekend without once saying *Jenny*. For the next few nights, when at dinner they questioned him or he remembered something about the weekend that he wanted to make alive again with words so it would be more than just a memory, he glanced from his sisters to his mother's face, her eyes quick and lips severely set, and said *Dad* and *we* and all but twice was able to avoid saying even *they*, until finally he could no longer bear the shame of loving two women and betraying them both, and he kept his memories in silence. Then Stephanie went to Philadelphia and came back, and he watched his mother's face at the dinners and said nothing or little and began to rid himself of shame, and in the week after Julie's visit he knew he had never had reason for shame, that he had not been afraid to tell his mother he loved Jenny too, that it was not him but she who needed the lie; and, loving her, he felt detached and older, and at times he was lonely.

The extended family, she calls us. I hope we can be like sisters someday; she actually said that. What did you say? I wanted to say Right, airhead: incest. She gives him three eggs a week. She doesn't know what to call him. When she talks about him to us. She said that. She feels funny when she says Walter and funny when she says Your father. So what does she do? She takes turns. And if she's talking to him she says Hon. Or Darling. No: nobody says darling except in books. She watches his salt too. And every day before dinner they go to this health club and swim. How cute. She's the one who needs it, old thunder thighs. She had a pimple. She looks out of those big blue eyes and talks about how much he cares about us, and I wanted to tell her if he cares so much why is he here with you, and she's got a pimple on her chin—

.He watched them: their faces over plates of food glowed with malice, the timbre of their voices was sensually wicked, their throaty laughter mischievous. They were eerie and fascinating; he had never seen them like this. He knew his silence was not disloyal to his father and Jenny; sometimes he gave his mother's eyes what they had to see: he smiled, even laughed.

At night the handkerchief was a pale shape in the air, then lit by headlights, and he knew that to the driver it had suddenly appeared without locomotion or support, and the cars stopped faster, and the voices from them were more frightened and then more angry. One night they rode past the woods to the bridge over the highway and leaned on the steel fence and watched the four lanes of cars coming to them and passing below. They pressed against the vertical railings and pissed arcs dropping into headlights.

'I've got to shit,' he said, and started for the woods.

'Wait. We can use that.'

He stopped and looked at Mark, then down at the cars.

'You think I'm going to squat on that little fence and shit over the highway?'

Near the bridge the woods ended at a small clearing before the slope going steeply down to the highway. Among beer bottles and cans Mark found a paper bag.

'It won't do anything,' Walter said. 'When it hits the car. *If* it hits it.'

'You have any matches?'

'No.'

'We'll get some. Go on.'

He started to go into the woods, but Mark turned and walked back to the bridge, so he squatted in the clearing and looked at bottles and tire tracks in the grass that was high enough to tickle his shins, and wondered when the teenagers parked here; he had seen them: once there were three or four cars and boys and girls sitting on fenders or standing, but the other times it was only one car nestled in the shadows of the woods, dully and for an instant reflecting his mother's head-lights as she drove off the bridge. Always he had seen them from his mother's car, when they had been to a movie or dinner and were coming home late. Carrying the bag away from his body, he went onto the bridge, his face turned to the breeze.

'If we wait, we can get some parkers,' he said.

'Get our asses whipped too.'

'We could sneak through the woods. Let the air out of the back tires, then throw this in the front window.'

'What do you think he'll be doing while all that hissing is going on?'

'Getting out and beating our asses. We could get close enough to listen, though. Maybe even look in.'

'Now you're talking. Maybe we can think up a trap. Some-thing he'd drive into and couldn't get out of. Let's go find a front porch to burn your dinner on.'

With headlights on, they rode fast over the winding road past the woods and then open country where the lighted houses were separated by low ridges and shallow draws and trees planted in lines and orchards, and up Walter's driveway, onto the terrace, where he placed the bag beside his kick-stand. In the kitchen they looked on counters and in drawers and behind the bar.

'They use lighters.'

He went upstairs with Mark following, into his mother's room, and switched on the ceiling light, standing a moment looking at her wide bed covered with light blue, and felt behind him Mark breathing the air of the room while his eyes probed it. He moved to the dresser, and when Mark pulled open a drawer of the chest at another wall, he raised his face and looked at himself in the mirror. Then he looked down, and between a hairbrush and an ashtray saw a glossy black matchbook bearing a name in gold script.

'Let's go,' he said, and crossed the room and closed the drawer as Mark's hand, dropping a stack of silk pants, withdrew.

He did not know any of the neighbors well enough to choose a target, so with lights off they rode to the last house before the woods and walked their bicycles up the long drive-way between tall trees, and lay them on the ground where the pavement curved and rose through open lawn to the garage beside the house. Upstairs one room was lighted, and light came through the two high windows on either side of the small front porch with a low narrow roof and two columns. At the base of a tree they lay on their bellies and watched the windows, and Mark whispered: 'Don't ever think your shit doesn't stink,' and they pressed hands against their mouths and laughed through their noses. Then, crouching, they ran to the front porch and listened and heard nothing. Walter set the bag near the screen door and unfolded its top and listened again, then struck the match and held the flame to one corner of the opening and then another, and stood, and when fire was moving down the sides, Mark pressed the doorbell and held it chiming inside the house, then they ran to the tree, and Walter dived beside it and rolled behind it next to Mark. The door swung inward, a short, wide man stepped into its frame, then said something fast and low, and pushed open the screen and with one foot stomped the flames smaller and smaller to embers and smoke, then he cursed, and Mark was running and Walter was too, hearing cursing and heavy running steps coming as he ran beside his bicycle down the driveway and jumped onto the seat, passing Mark before the road, where he turned and pumped for the woods.

Across the glass table Mark's wet hair was sleek in the sunlight. He sat beside Julie; the sun, nearing the trees across the lake, was behind and just above him, so that Walter squinted at him. Walter's mother had thawed chicken, then when she came home early from the boutique she had bought after going to court with his father, she said she had decided on hamburgers because some people were clumsy about eating barbecued chicken with a knife and fork and she didn't want to make it hard on him. Walter had said Mark could eat chicken with his hands, and she said she knew he could and Walter would like to, and that's what she meant about making it hard on Mark.

She could clean the bones of a chicken with knife and fork as daintily as if she were eating lima beans, so he liked watching her with a hamburger: it was thick and it dripped catsup and juice from the meat and tomatoes and pickles; she leaned over the plate and opened her mouth wide enough to close on both buns, yet with that width of jaws she took only a small bite from the edge and lowered the hamburger, then sat straight to chew with her lips closed. Julie's and Stephanie's bites were larger but still small, and neither had to use a napkin. He and Mark had stayed in the pool until now, so his mother was asking questions between eating: Where he was from and what his father did and did his mother work, how many brothers and sisters and where had he gone to school. Some of this was new to Walter; the rest of it he had learned in the woods, during the heat of afternoons as they lay on cool shadowed grass and spoke to avoid silence. His mother's questions ended before her hamburger did; she held her wineglass toward Walter and he filled it, then she said: 'And your sisters,' and he reached to their places and poured, then held the bottle over Mark's glass of milk, and Mark said: 'Go ahead.'

'Just two more years,' his mother said, and she leaned toward him and tousled his wet hair. 'This boy of mine,' she said to Mark, and dried her hand with her napkin.

'He'll be doing more than wine in two more years,' Julie said.

'A lot more,' Stephanie said, and smiled at Mark.

'Like what?' Walter said.

'You'll have a girl,' Julie said.

'Maybe not.'

'You will. Some girl will take care of that.'

'Wow,' he said to Mark. 'I'll have a *date.*'

'In the *car,*' Mark said.

'With a *girl.*'

'And you'll love it,' his mother said. 'You two guys will beg for the car and start looking in the mirror. We have blueberry pie and ice cream.'

'Tell me you didn't,' Stephanie said. 'Not *blue*berry. I'm going to be very fat tonight.'

'You might get an older man,' his mother said. 'Dessert is for these boys who swim and ride bikes all day.'

'I swam this morning,' Stephanie said, and stood, and then Julie and his mother did, and when he pushed back his chair she said: 'Stay with your guest. We'll do it,' and they were all in motion, clearing and wiping the table and setting it again with ashtrays and cigarette packs and plates and three demitasses and a silver coffeepot, and pie and ice cream for everyone, though he and Mark had the biggest slices and scoops. When his mother reached for her cigarettes, he stood and said: 'Let's go down to the lake.'

He rolled his napkin and pushed it into the ring, and when Mark started to, he told him to leave it, the guest napkin gets washed.

Near the bank of the lake he found a small flat rock and skimmed it hitting once on the sunlit surface and three times in the shadows before it sank. He paced up and down, looking for another rock, and Mark lay on the grass in the sun, and said: 'They're pretty.'

He sat beside Mark and looked at the flowers of purple loose-strife and then at a crow rising from the trees.

'Sometimes I wish I lived with my father.'

'Can you?'

'They never asked me to.'

He did not like the sound of his voice; in its softening he heard tears coming, and for a long time he had not cried about anything. He sat up and plucked a blade of grass and chewed it. Julie did not like the monthly visits to his father because she missed her boy friend, and Stephanie did not like them because she could not smoke there and she missed her boy friend, and neither one of them had forgiven his father. He would like to spend the school year with his father and Jenny and the summer here, and he knew now that for a long time he had made himself believe his father had never asked or even hinted because the apartment was too small.

'Do they fuck?' Mark said.

'Who?'

He pointed a thumb over his shoulder, and Walter turned and looked up the hill; sunlight splashed bronze on their hair.

'How would *I* know?' he said, and looked at his bare toes in the grass.

'Lots of ways, if you wanted to.'

'I never thought about it.'

'You're weird.'

'Sometimes I think about it. When they go out.'

He was awake when they came home, starting with Stephanie at eighteen minutes past midnight on his luminous digital clock and ending with his mother at three twenty-nine, and if he slept at all he did not know it, for even if he did, he still saw in his mind what he saw awake. *Too much*, Mark had said as Walter's hand rose from Stephanie's drawer with the third plastic case like a clam shell, and he snapped it open and it was empty too. *Everybody's fucking but you. I'll have to jerk off tonight.* But not him: he lay on the warm sheet in the cooling night air and listened for them, and then to them: the downstairs footsteps when the sound of the car was gone—a sound that chilled him with yearning hatred, as though he were bound to the bed by someone he could not hit—then steps climbing the stairs and into their bedrooms that he felt part of now (and was both ashamed and vengeful because Mark was part of them too) and, in there, slower and lighter steps so that for moments he did not hear them and then did again, at another part of the room. He tried to think but could not: tried to focus on each of them, force the other two from his mind, and reasonably say to himself: *Dad has Jenny and she ought to have someone too* or *Julie's eighteen and people when they're eighteen* but he could get no further and did not even try with Stephanie, for as soon as he focused on one, the other two were back in his room, among its shadows and furniture, and they all merged: naked, their legs embracing the cruelly plunging bodies of the two boys and one man he knew, and he saw their three open-mouthed wild-haired faces, and heard sounds he had not known he knew: fast, heavy breath and soft cries and grunts and, between their legs, sloshing thuds; heard these as he waited and as they climbed the stairs and turned on faucets and flushed toilets—Did it drip out of them and drop spreading and slowly sinking like thick sour milk, droplets left on that hair he had never seen, and did they— *wipe* it then with paper, the motion of arm and hand, the expressions on their faces as common as if nothing were there and in the water below their—again: naked—flesh but piss? Or did it stay in the diaphragm that Mark said was shaped like half an orange peel with the fruit gone? He tightened his legs and arms, shook his head on the pillow, shut his eyes to a darker dark; between his legs he felt nothing. When did they take it out? And how did their faces look when they took it out? He saw them frowning, nauseated, wickedly pleased. Once he had a large boil on his leg and the doctor froze it and lanced it, and for weeks he had to fight his memory when he ate. He could not imagine them now in clothes, nor in bathing suits, nor simply eating on the terrace or at the kitchen or dining room table; he tried to remember them in winter, fur-covered, leaving the house and walking with short, careful steps over the icy sidewalk, moving into the vapor of their breath as it wafted about their heads. But he could not, as though all he had known of them clothed was a mask that tonight he had pulled from their faces. When at last his mother's steps ended, he imagined them all settled between sheets, their legs closed now, at rest, and he thought: *They must stink.*

He woke to a bird's shriek and sunlight, and went barefooted down the hall, looking at each door closed on the darkened blind-drawn cool of the room and bed and soft breathing of sleep, and out of the house and onto his bicycle. He rode toward the woods. He was hungry and thirsty and had not brushed his teeth, so the taste of night was still in his mouth, and he opened it to the breeze. Then he was there: the fragrance of pines sharper among the other smells of green life and earth and the old dappled leaves moist and soft under his feet as he walked his bicycle without trail or pattern between and under tall trees and around brush, the sweat from his ride drying now, cooling him in the shade as he moved farther into the woods that had waked while he slept: above him squirrels rustled leaves as they moved higher and birds fluttered from perches, and twice he heard the sudden flight of a rabbit. In a glade lit by the sun he stood up his bicycle and lay on his back with hands clasped behind his head and closed his eyes. The sun warmed his face, and beneath his eyelids he felt the heat and saw specks of red and orange in the darkness, and he tried to see them as he had known them, but he could not dress them, could not cover their nakedness, and could not keep them naked alone: behind his eyes they slowly revolved, coupling with the two boys and the man, and he tried to see nothing at all but the speckled dark, and then tried to see the food his stomach wanted, the juice for his dry throat, and then tried to concentrate his rage only on the two boys and the man whose faces had the glazed look of a dog's above the bitch's back, but he could not do that either, and the sounds from the six writhing bodies were louder than the woods.

He stood and moved out of the sunlight, into the shade of a maple, and unzipped and pissed, then stroked, shutting his eyes against the softness his hand encircled, seeing an infected and oozing orange peel, the softness even receding as though trying to withdraw from his abrasive fingers. He opened his eyes. Then he lay on his belly in the sunlight and pressed his cheek against the earth and held its grass with both hands.

We had to leave before you came home. We went shopping in Boston and will be back before dinner. Mark was looking for you and said he'd be back after lunch. Love, Mom, and a smiling line for a mouth drawn inside a circle with two eyes and a nose. He left the note on the table in front of him while he ate cereal and a peanut butter sandwich, then he took the small garbage basket from under the sink and went upstairs. He went to Stephanie's room first. It was still darkened, and he opened the blinds and looked at the tossed-back top sheet and bedspread and stuffed brown bear and blue rabbit near a pillow; actors and singers watched him from the walls; he opened the drawer and took out the case and opened it with a click that tensed his arms. *It's more like a hollowed-out mushroom;* then he realized he was holding his breath, and he let it out, and breathing fast and shallow he turned the case over and watched the diaphragm drop softly among banana peels and milk carton and tuna fish can. As he put the case under silk in the drawer, he knew why he had gone to her room first: the youngest, only a few years removed from the time when pranks on each other were as much part of their days as laughter.

The basket was wicker and lined with a plastic bag. He brought it to Julie's room and opened her blinds and was crossing the floor when his name rose from outside, into the room; he stool still, gripping the basket, while Mark called again, then rang the back doorbell and called and then was quiet, but Walter could feel him down there, and he stood looking at the soft yellow wall, listening to the slow breeze and a car coming and passing by, then crept to the window and looked down at the empty terrace. Quickly he took the case from the drawer and emptied it in the basket.

In his mother's room he did not open the blinds; he walked softly as though she were sleeping there; he glanced at the sheets and pillows, and quietly slid open the drawer where last night Mark had found it, the first one they had found, while Walter was opening leather boxes of jewelry at her dresser and telling Mark to start in another room so they could work faster. He put the basket on the floor and held the open case in both hands. He lifted it closer to his eyes. He looked at it until his breathing slowed; and when he stopped hearing his breathing, he was suddenly tired, and as he lowered one hand and turned the other and watched the brief white descent, he wanted to sleep.

Their voices woke him, and when they started up the stairs, he turned quietly onto his side, his back to the door, and heard the girls with soft-crackling shopping bags going into their rooms and his mother coming to his; she stopped at the doorway and he breathed as though asleep until she turned and went to her room. He opened his eyes to the lake and trees and the low sun. He waited until he heard showers in all three bathrooms. Then he ran on tiptoes down the hall and stairs, and at the terrace he sprinted: past the pool and down toward the widening lake, and fell forward and struck with knees and palms, and rolled and stood and ran again, weight on his heels now, leaping when his balance shifted forward: running and leaping to the bottom of the hill where he could not stop: with short flat-footed steps he went across the narrow mud bank and into the water deep as his knees and then was sitting in it.

He stood and looked up at the house, and higher and beyond it at the sky. Then he eased backward into the water and floated. Behind him the geese stirred and he listened to their wings as they rose and settled again. He backstroked toward the middle, then floated. Now the trees were on his left and he looked at their green crowns and the sky and waited for his mother's voice calling from the terrace.

THE CAPTAIN

for Gunnery Sergeant Jim Beer

His son wore a moustache. Over and between tan faces and the backs of heads with hair cut high and short, and green-uniformed shoulders and chests and backs, Harry saw him standing with two other second lieutenants at the bar. His black moustache was thick. Only one woman was at happy hour, a blond captain: she had a watchful, attractive face that was pretty when she laughed. Harry stepped forward one pace, then another, and stood with his back to the door, breathing the fragrance of liquor and cigarette smoke, as pleasing to him as the smell of cooking is to some, and feeling through his body the loud talk and laughter and shouts, as though he watched a parade whose music coursed through him. In his own uniform with captain's bars and ribbons, he wanted to stand here and have one Scotch. He did not feel that he stood to the side of the gathered men, but at their head, looking down the axis of their gaiety. A tall man, he did look down at most of them, and he wanted to watch his son from this distance. But there were no waitresses, so he went to the bar and spoke over Phil's shoulder: 'There's one nice thing about a moustache.'

The eyes in the turning face were dark and happy. Then Harry was hugging him, and Phil's arms were around his waist, tighter and tighter, and Phil leaned back and lifted him from the floor, the metal buttons of their blouses clicking together, then scraping as Phil lowered him, and introduced him to the two lieutenants as *my father, Captain LeDuc, retired.* Harry shook hands, not hearing their names, focusing instead on their faces and tightly tailored blouses and the silver shooting badges on their breasts: both wore the crossed rifles and crossed pistols of experts, and above those, like Phil, they wore only the one red and gold ribbon that showed they were in the service during a war they had not seen. He saw them scanning his four rows of ribbons, pretended he had not, and turned to Phil, letting his friends look comfortably at the colored rectangles of two wars and a wound and one act that had earned him a Silver Star. Beside Phil's crossed rifles was the Maltese cross of a sharpshooter. The bartender emptied the ashtray, and Phil ordered another round and a Scotch and water, and Harry said: 'What happened with the .45?'

'I choked up. What bothers me is knowing I'm better and having to wear this till next year. *Then* I'll—' He smiled and his eyes lowered and rose. 'Jesus.'

'Good,' Harry said. 'If we couldn't forget, we'd never enjoy anything after the age of ten. Or five.'

Phil turned to his friends standing at his left and said he had just told his father he didn't like having to wear the sharpshooter badge until he qualified again next year, and the three of them laughed and joked about rice paddies and Monday and jungle and Charlie, and Harry saw the bartender coming with their drinks and paid him, thinking of how often memory lies, of how so often the lies are good ones. When he was twenty-four years old, he had learned on Guadalcanal that the body could endure nearly anything, and after that he had acted as though he believed it could endure everything: could work without sleep or rest or enough food and water, heedless of cold and heat and illness; could survive penetration and dismemberment, so that death in combat was a matter of bad luck, a man with five bullets in him surviving another pierced by only one. He was so awed by the body's strength

and vulnerability that he did nothing at all about prolonging
its life. This refusal was rooted neither in confidence nor an
acceptance of fate. His belief in mystery and chance was too
strong to allow faith in exercising and in controlling what he
ate and drank and when he smoked. Phil had forgotten who
he was and where he was going; was that how the mind survived? The body pushed beyond pain, and the mind side-
stepped. How else could he stand here, comfortable, proud of
his son, when his own mind held images this room of cheerful
peace could not contain? He raised a knee and drew his pack
of cigarettes from his sock, and Phil gave him a light with a
Zippo bearing a Marine emblem, and said: 'What's the one
nice thing about a moustache?'

'If I have to tell you, you're fucking up on more than
the .45.'

'They don't give out badges for that.'

'One girl?'

'No.'

'Good. It's too rough on them.'

'They'll *all* miss me, Pop.'

'I'd rather be in the middle of it. I didn't have a girl, when
I was in the Pacific. But, Jesus, I was never warm in the Reservoir, not for one minute, there was always *some*thing cold—'

'Frozen Chosin,' one of the lieutenants said, and drank
and eyed Harry's ribbons over the glass.

'—Right: *I* was frozen. *Every*body: we'd come on dead
Chi*nese* frozen. And tell you the truth, I didn't think we'd get
out, more fucking Chinese than snow, but I'd rather have
been freezing my ass off and trying to keep it from getting
between a Chinaman's bullet and thin air than back home like
your mother. How do you keep waking up every day and
doing what there is to do when you know your man is getting
shot at? Ha.' He looked from Phil to the two lieutenants
watching him, respectfully embarrassed, then back at Phil,
whose dark saddened eyes had never looked at him this way
before, almost as a father gazing at a son, and in a rush of age

he saw himself as father of a man grown enough to give him pity. 'I guess I'm fucking well about to find out.'

'Fucking-A,' Phil said, and clapped his shoulder and turned to his drink.

At three in the morning, a half-hour before the alarm, his heart woke him, its anticipatory beat freeing him as normally caffeine did from that depth of sleep whose paradox he could not forgive: needing each night that respite so badly that finally nothing could prevent his having it, then each morning having to rise from it with coffee and tobacco so that he could resume with hope those volitive hours that would end with his grateful return to the oblivion of dreams. He coughed and swallowed, and coughed again and swallowed that too. Phil was in a sleeping bag on an air mattress in the middle of the small room. Last night after dinner at the officers' club, where they had talked of hunting and today's terrain, they had spread out on Phil's desk a map he got from the sportsmen's club when he drew their hunting area from a campaign hat three nights earlier, and Harry looked, nodded, and listened while Phil, using a pencil as a pointer, told him about the squares of contoured earth on the map that Harry could not only read more quickly, and more accurately, but also felt he knew anyway because, having spent most of his peacetime career at Camp Pendleton, he felt all its reaches were his ground. But he remained amused, and nearly agreed when Phil showed him two long ridges flanking a valley, and said this was the place to get a deer and spend the whole Saturday without seeing one of the other eight hunters who had drawn the same boundaries.

'It'll take us too long to walk in,' Harry said.

'I got the CO's jeep. I told him you were coming to hunt.'

At three-fifteen by the luminous dial of his Marine-issued wristwatch that he felt he had not stolen but retired with him, he quietly left the bed and stood looking down at Phil. He lay on his back, a pillow under his head, all but his throat and face hidden and shapeless in the bulk of the sleeping bag. His face was paled by sleep and the dark, eyeless save for brows and curves, and his delicate breathing whispered into the faint hum, the constant tone of night's quiet. Harry had not watched him sleeping since he was a boy, and now he was pierced as with a remembrance of fatherhood, but of something else too, as old as the earth's dust: in the darkened bedrooms of Phil and the two daughters he had felt this tender dread; and also looking at the face of a woman asleep, even some he did not love when he woke in the night: his children and the women devoid of anger and passion and humor and pain, so that he yearned during their fragile rest to protect them from and for whatever shaped their faces in daylight.

'Lieutenant,' he said, his deep voice, almost harsh, snapping both him and Phil into the day's hunt: 'The good thing about a moustache is you can smell her all night while you sleep, and when you wake up you can lick it again.'

The eyes opened and stared from a face still in repose; the mouth was slower to leave sleep, then it smiled and Phil said: 'You ex-enlisted men talk dirty.'

They dressed and went quickly down the corridor, rifles slung on their shoulders, Phil carrying in one hand a pack with their breakfast and lunch; they wore pistol belts with canteens and hunting knives, and jeans, and sweat shirts over their shirts, and wind-breakers; Harry wore a wide-brimmed straw hat. Still, the act of arming himself to go into the hills made him feel he was in uniform, and as Phil drove the open jeep through fog, Harry shivered and pushed his hat tighter on his head and watched both flanks, an instinct so old and now useless that it amused him. He had learned to use his senses as an animal does, and probably as his ancestors in Canada and New Hampshire had, though not his father, whose avocation was beer and cards and friends in his kitchen or theirs, the men's talk with the first beers and hands of penny ante poker in French and English, then later only in the French that had crossed the ocean centuries before the invention of things, so in the flow of words that Harry never learned he now and then heard engine and car and airplane and electric fan. So in 1936, never having touched a rifle or pistol, he went into the Marine Corps with a taste for beer and a knowledge of poker acquired in his eighteenth year and last at home, when his father said he was old enough to join the table, and he trained with young men who had killed game since boyhood, and would learn cards in the barracks and drinking in bars. Four years later he returned home; in the summer evening he walked from the bus station over climbing and dropping streets of the village to the little house where his father sat on the front steps with a bottle of beer; he had not bathed yet for the dinner that Harry could smell cooking; he had taken off his shirt, and his undershirt was wet and soiled; sweat streaked the dirt on his throat and arms, and he hugged Harry and called to the family, took a long swallow of beer, handed the bottle to Harry, and said: 'I got you a job at the foundry.' Two days later, Harry took a bus to the recruiting office and reenlisted.

The jeep descended into colder air; fog hid the low earth, so that Harry could not judge the distance from the road to the dark bulk of hills on both sides. He stopped looking, and at once felt exposed and alert; he smiled and shook his head and leaned toward the dashboard to light a cigarette. He could see no stars; the wet moon was pallid, distant. He watched the road, grey fog paled and swathed yellow by the headlights, and said: 'There was a battalion cut off, when the Chinese came in.'

'*What?*'

He turned to Phil and spoke away from the rushing air, loudly over the vibrating moan of the jeep: the Chosin Reservoir, the whole Goddamned division was surrounded and a battalion cut off, and they had to go through Chinese to get there and break the battalion out and bring it to the main body. So they could retreat through all those Chinese to the sea. The battalion was pinned down about five miles away, so they started on foot, with a company on each flank playing leapfrog over the hills: two battalions, one of them Royal

Marines, and their colonel was in command. A feisty little bastard. 'I've never *liked* Limeys, but the Royal Ma*rines* are *good.*' He guessed he liked Limey troops, it was just the country that pissed him off. The reason Marines had such good liberty in Australia in World War II was the Aussies were off in Africa fighting for England. Even the chaplain probably got laid. 'They loved Ma*rines* and still *do,* and if you ever get a chance to go to Aust*ral*ia, *take* it.' Their boys were fighting the Goddamn Germans, so it was the Marines keeping Australia safe, and they'd go there for R and R and get all the thanks too. The Limeys were good at that, getting other people to go off and fight in somebody else's yard. 'Do you read *his*tory?'

'Not since college.'

'You've *got* to.' He shivered and caught his hat before it blew off, and the jeep climbed into lighter fog. 'If you're going to be a ca*reer* man, you've got to start *stud*ying this stuff *now.* Not just *tac*tics and *strat*egy; but how these wars get *start*ed, and *why,* and who *starts* them.'

'I *will.* What about that bat*tal*ion?'

The flank companies kept making contact in the hills, and the troops in the road would assault and clear that hill, then start moving again; but they were moving too slowly, it was one firefight after another, so the colonel called back for trucks and brought the people down from the hills, and they all mounted up in the trucks and hauled ass down the road till they got hit; then they'd pile out and attack, and when they'd knocked out whatever it was or it had run off to some other hill, they'd hi-diddle-diddle up the road again—

'Holy *shit.*'

'I never felt so *much* like a moving *tar*get.' He rode shotgun in a six-by; the driver was a corporal and he pissed all over himself; he was good, though; he just kept cussing and shifting gears; probably he was praying too; maybe it was all praying: Jesus Christ God*damn*—pissssss—shit *Je*sus—From the front of the six-by he watched the hills, but what good was it to watch where it's going to come from, when you're moving so fast that you know you can't see anything till you draw fire? He felt like he was searching the air for a bullet. He told the corporal he wished he were up there and the Chinese were down here. Probably that was a prayer too—Harry grabbed his hat as the brim slapped the crown; he put it in his lap, and the air was cool on his bald spot. '*De*-fense is *best*, you know. Or don't they *tell* you *that*.' 'Course they don't, Marines always attack; but with helicopters you can go behind them and cut off their line of supply and defend that. 'Read Lid*del* Hart. And learn *Span*ish. That's where it's *go*ing to *be*.'

'*Where*?'

'*Mex*ico to Ti*err*a del *Fue*go. We got the bat*tal*ion out.'

He twisted and reached behind his left hip for his canteen.

'So the *col*onel was *right*.'

'*Sure* he was.' He gargled, then swallowed, and drank again and offered the canteen to Phil, who shook his head. 'We *lost* people we might *not* have, if we'd *done* it the *right* way. But we had to *do* it the *fast* way.'

The jeep climbed, and above him the fog was thinning; to his right he could see a ridge outlined clearly against the sky.

'Have you *seen* your *mother* yet?'

'*Last* night. She and the *girls*. We had *din*ner. *Cath*erine's screwed up.'

'*Not dope*?'

'*No*. She doesn't *think* I should *go*. At the same *time* she—' He shrugged, glanced at Harry, then watched the road.

'*Loves* her *brother*,' Harry said.

'Yes.'

'Just the *wom*en? No *boy* friends?'

'I *don't* think they *like* Ma*rines*.'

'*Fuck* 'em.'

'I'll leave *that* to *Cath*erine and *Joyce*.'

'*Ea*sy now. My *daugh*ters are *vir*gins.'

'*Right*.'

'I wish your *skipper* had left the *top* on the *jeep*.'

'—*soon*.'

'*What?*'

'To*day* will be *hot.*'

Harry nodded and put on his hat, pressing it down, and watched the suspended motion of fog above the road.

The deer camp duty officer's table was near the fire. He wore hunting clothes and was rankless, as all the hunters were, but was in charge of the camp, logging hunters in and out, and recording their kills, because he had drawn the duty from a hat. A hissing gas lantern was on the table near his log book, and above him shadows cast by the fire danced in trees. Harry and Phil gave him their names and hunting area; he was in his midthirties, looked to Harry like a gunnery sergeant or major; they spoke to him about fog and the cold drive, and he wished them luck as they moved away, to the fire where two men squatted with skillets of eggs and others stood drinking coffee from canteen cups. The fire was in a hole; a large coffeepot rested on two stones at the edge of the flames. Harry poured for both of them, shook the pot, and a lance corporal emerged from the darkness; he wore faded green utilities and was eating a doughnut. He took the pot from Harry and shook it, then placed it beside the hole and returned to the darkness. The two men cooking eggs rose and brought the crackling skillets to the edge of the fire's light, where three men sat drinking coffee. The lance corporal came back with a kettle and put it on the stones, then sat cross-legged and smoked. His boots shone in the fire's light. From above, Harry watched him: he liked his build, lean and supple, and the cocky press of his lips, and his wearing his cap visor so low over his eyes that he had to jut out his chin to see in front of him. Phil crouched and held a skillet of bacon over the fire, and Harry stepped closer to the lance corporal; he wanted to ask him why he was in special services, in charge of a hobby shop or gym or swimming pool, drawing duty as a fire-builder and coffee-maker. Looking down at his starched cap and polished boots and large, strong-looking hands, he wished he could train him, teach him and care for him, and his wish became a yearning: looking at Phil wrapping a handkerchief around the skillet handle, he wished he could train him too. He circled the lance corporal and sat heavily on the earth beside Phil.

'I *used* to be graceful.'

'Civilians are entitled to a beer gut. We forgot a spatula.'

'Civilian my ass. Here.'

He drew his hunting knife and handed it to Phil; behind him, and beyond the line of trees, a car left the road and stopped. Bacon curled over the knife blade; Phil lifted strips free of the skillet, lowered the pale sides into the grease, and said: 'The eggs will break.'

'I'll cook them.'

'Fried?'

'Lieutenant, I've spent more time in chow lines than you've spent in the Marine Corps.'

Three hunters came out of the trees and stood at the table to his left. The lance corporal flipped his cigarette into the flames and crossed his arms on his knees and watched the kettle.

'They use spatulas,' Phil said.

'True enough. But I will turn the eggs. How they come out is in the hands of the Lord.'

'Bless us o Lord in this thy omelet.'

'Over easy. Do you go to Mass?'

'Sometimes. Do you?'

'On Sundays.'

Across the fire the three men rubbed their hands in the heat. A car left the road, then another, and doors opened and slammed, and voices and rustling, cracking footsteps came through the trees. The lance corporal rose without using his hands and took the coffeepot into the darkness.

'Where does he go?' Harry said.

'He's like an Indian.'

'He's like an Oriental.'

Then he heard the water boiling and, as he looked, steam came from the spout. From the pack he took bread, eggs, and paper plates. Phil spread bacon on a plate, then Harry dug a small hole with the knife and poured in some of the bacon grease and covered it. Kneeling, he fried four slices of bread, then broke six eggs, one-handed, into the skillet and was watching the bubbling whites and browning edges when he heard cars on the road; he glanced up at the dimmed stars and lemon moon; the fog was thinner, and smoke rose darkly through its eddying grey. In the skillet the eggs joined, and he was poised to separate them with his knife, then said: 'Look what we have.'

'Your basic sunnyside pie.'

'It's beautiful.'

He slanted the skillet till grease moved to one side, and with the blade he slapped it over the eggs. He held the skillet higher and watched the yellows, and the milky white circling them; he slid his knife under the right edge, gently moved it toward the center, and stopped under the first yolk. Phil held a paper plate, and Harry tilted the skillet over it, working the knife upward as connected eggs slid over the blade and rim, onto the plate.

'I hate to break it,' Phil said. 'Should we freeze it?'

'In our minds.'

Phil took their cups to the coffeepot; Harry watched him pouring, and waited for him to sit at the plate resting on loose dirt. They did not separate the eggs. On the road, cars approached like a convoy that had lost its intervals, and Harry and Phil ate quietly, slowly, watching the disc become oval, then oblong, then a yellow smear for the last of their bread. Men circled them and the fire. Phil reached for the skillet, and Harry said: 'I'll do it.'

He tossed dirt into it and rubbed the hot metal, then wiped it with a paper towel; he stabbed the knife into the earth and worked it back and forth and deeper, and wiped it clean on his trousers. He held his cigarettes toward Phil, but he was shaking one from his own pack. They sat facing the fire, smoking with their coffee. The lance corporal put on a fresh log, and Harry watched flames licking around its bottom and up its sides; above and around him the voices were incoherent, peaceful as the creaking of windblown trees.

Under a near-fogless sky, a half-hour before dawn, he reached the northern and highest peak of the narrow ridge, and walked with light steps, back and forth and in small circles, until his breathing slowed and his legs stopped quivering. Then he sat facing the bare spine of dirt and rock that dipped and rose and finally descended southward, through diaphanous fog, to the jeep. He heard nothing in the sky or on the earth save his own breathing. He rested his rifle on his thighs and watched both sides of the ridge: flat ground to the east until a mass of iron-grey hills; the valley, broken by a dark stand of trees, was to the west; beyond that was the ridge where Phil hunted.

The air and earth were the grey of twilight; then, as he looked down the western slope, at shapes of rocks and low thickets, the valley and Phil's ridge became colors, muted under vanishing mist: pale green patches of grass and brown earth and a beige stream bed. The trees were pines, growing inside an eastward bend of the stream. Brown and green brush spread up the russet slope of Phil's ridge, and beyond it was the light blue of the sea. Harry stood, was on his feet before he remembered to be quiet and still, and watched the blue spreading farther as fog rose from it like steam. He turned to the scarlet slice of sun crowning a hill. From the strip of rose and golden sky, the horizon rolled toward him: peaks and ridges, gorges and low country, and scattered green of trees among the arid yellow and brown. He faced the ocean, saw whitecaps now, and took off his hat and waved it. On the peak of Phil's ridge he could see only rocks. The sea and sky were pale still; he stood watching as fog dissolved into their deepening blue, the sky brightened, and he could see the horizon. He sat facing it.

At eight o'clock he started walking down the ridge: one soft step, then waiting, looking down both slopes; another step; after three he saw Phil: a flash of light, a movement on the skyline. Then Phil became a tiny figure, and Harry stayed abreast of him. Soon the breeze shifted, came from the sea, and he could smell it. Near midmorning he flushed a doe: froze at the sudden crack of brush, as her bounding rump and darting body angled down the side of the ridge; in the valley she ran south, and was gone.

He sat and smoked and watched a ship gliding past Phil, its stacks at his shoulders. Then he stood and took off his jacket and sweat shirt and hung them from his belt. He caught up with Phil, and stalked again. When the sun was high and sparkling the sea, the ridge dropped more sharply, and he unloaded his rifle and slung it from his shoulder, and went down to the jeep. Phil sat on the hood. Behind him was open country and a distant range of tall hills. Harry sat on the hood and drank from his canteen.

'Saved ammo,' Phil said.

'I almost stepped on a doe.'

'How close?'

'Three steps and a good spit.'

'I've never been that close.'

'Neither have I.'

'Pretty quiet, Pop.'

'She startled me. If she'd been a buck, I would have missed.'

They ate sandwiches, then lay on their backs in the shade of the jeep. Harry rested his hat on his forehead so the brim covered his eyes.

'Are you staying for dinner?' Phil said.

'No. I don't like driving tired.'

'We can go back now, if you want.'

'Let's hunt. What will you do tomorrow?'

'Make sure my toothbrush is packed.'

'No girl?'

'There isn't one. I mean no *one*. So why choose now, right? I'll go out with the guys and get drunk.'

'Only way to go. What time Monday?'

'I don't even want to say.'

'They love getting guys up in the dark.'

His boots were warm. He looked out from under the hat: sunlight was on his ankles now; he looked over his feet at the low end of Phil's ridge.

'Orientals can hide on a parade field. Chinese would crawl all night from their lines to ours. A few feet and wait. All night lying out there, no sound, nothing moving, and just before dawn they'd be on top of us. And *Jap*anese: they were like leaves.'

'Except that tank.'

'What tank?'

'Your Silver Star.'

'That was a pillbox.'

'It was?'

'Sure. Did you think I'd go after a tank?'

'Not much difference. Why didn't I know that?'

'Too many war stories, too many Marines; probably a neighbor told *his* kid about a tank.'

'I told *them*. Was it on Tarawa?'

'Yes.'

'At least I got that right.'

'It's not important. It's just something that happened. We were pinned down on the beach. The boxes had interlocking fire. I remember my mouth in the sand, then an explosion to my right front. It was a satchel charge, and a kid named Winslow Brimmer was the one who got it there.'

'Winslow Brimmer?'

'He was a mean little fart from Baltimore. Nobody harassed him about his name. He took whatever was left of his squad to that box, and all but two of them bought it. Then I was running with a flamethrower on my back. If you can call that running.'

'Where did you get the flamethrower?'

'The guy with it was next to me, and he was dead. So I put it on and moved out.'

'Jesus.'

'It was easier than Brimmer's because he had knocked out the one on their left. I had more fresh air than he did.'

'Not much.'

'I can remember doing it, but it's like somebody told me I did it, and that's why I remember. The way it can be after a bad drunk. I don't remember what I felt just before, or what I thought. I remember getting the flamethrower off him and onto me, and that should have taken a while, but it doesn't seem like it. I remember running, but I don't remember hearing anything, not with all those weapons firing, and I don't remember getting there. I was there, and then I burned them. They must have made sounds, but I only remember the smell.'

'Was that when you were wounded?'

'No. That was the next day.'

'I wish I had been there.'

'No you don't. The Navy dropped us in deep water—'

'I know.'

'Dead troops bobbing in it and lying on the reef and the beach. Fuck Tarawa.'

He opened his eyes to the sun, and squinted away from it at the sky. A hawk glided toward the earth, veered away, and climbed west over the ridge.

'You reflected the sun this morning,' he said. 'That's how I saw you.'

'My watch.'

He looked at the chrome band on Phil's wrist.

'Goddamn it, leave that civilian shit at home and get one from supply.'

'It's in my room.'

'Sorry.'

'Okay, Captain.'

He closed his eyes, listening to Phil's breathing. The sun on his face woke him, and he stiffened and pressed his palms against the ground, then knew where he was. Phil was gone. He stood, wiping sweat from his eyes; Phil leaned against the back of the jeep, eating a plum.

'Have some fruit.'

Harry took a peach from the pack and stood beside him.

'Do you want to swap ridges?' Phil said.

'Not unless you do.'

'No, I'm fine.'

'Mine's like home now.'

'We'll probably get back here around six. Thirty minutes to the camp to sign out. Then about forty.'

'Plenty of time. I make it in under three hours. 'Course, there's always the Jesus factor.'

'Like getting a deer.'

'If we do, I'll help you clean it.'

'And take it home with you.'

'Right.'

'All set?'

'Need my hogleg.'

He took the rifle from the back seat and slung it from his shoulder.

'How do you like the .308?' Phil said.

'It's good.'

'Have you zeroed it in?'

'Not this year.'

They walked into the valley and up the hard, cracked earth of the stream bed to the pine trees, and stood in their shade.

'I like the smell of pine,' Harry said. 'Up there I can smell the ocean. Did you see it this morning, when the sun came up?'

'Beautiful.'

'Now we get the sunset. Ready?'

'I'm off.'

'Take care, then.'

'You too.'

They turned from each other and Harry walked out of the trees, into the sunlight, then he lengthened his stride toward the ridge.

SORROWFUL MYSTERIES

W HEN GERRY FONTENOT is five, six, and seven years old, he likes to ride in the car with his parents. It is a grey 1938 Chevrolet and it has a ration stamp on the windshield. Since the war started when Gerry was five, his father has gone to work on a bicycle, and rarely drives the car except to Sunday Mass, and to go hunting and fishing. Gerry fishes with him, from the bank of the bayou. They fish with bamboo poles, corks, sinkers, and worms, and catch perch and catfish. His father wears a .22 revolver at his side, for cottonmouths. In the fall Gerry goes hunting with him, crouches beside him in ditches bordering fields, and when the doves fly, his father stands and fires the twelve-gauge pump, and Gerry marks where the birds fall, then runs out into the field where they lie, and gathers them. They are soft and warm as he runs with them, back to his father. This is in southern Louisiana, and twice he and his father see an open truck filled with German prisoners, going to work in the sugar cane fields.

He goes on errands with his mother. He goes to grocery stores, dime stores, drugstores, and shopping for school clothes in the fall, and Easter clothes in the spring, and to the beauty parlor, where he likes to sit and watch the women. Twice a week he goes with her to the colored section, where they leave and pick up the week's washing and ironing. His mother washes at home too: the bedclothes, socks, underwear, towels, and whatever else does not have to be ironed. She washes these in a wringer washing machine; he likes watching her feed the clothes into the wringer, and the way they come out flattened and drop into the basket. She hangs them on the clothesline in the backyard, and Gerry stands at the basket and hands them to her so she will not have to stoop. On rainy days she dries them inside on racks, which in winter she places in front of space heaters. She listens to the weather forecasts on the radio, and most of the time is able to wash on clear days.

The Negro woman washes the clothes that must be ironed, or starched and ironed. In front of the woman's unpainted wooden house, Gerry's mother presses the horn, and the large woman comes out and takes the basket from the back seat. Next day, at the sound of the horn, she brings out the basket. It is filled with ironed, folded skirts and blouses, and across its top lie dresses and shirts on hangers. Gerry opens the window his mother has told him to close as they approached the colored section with its dusty roads. He smells the clean, ironed clothes, pastels and prints, and his father's white and pale blue, and he looks at the rutted dirt road, the unpainted wood and rusted screens of the houses, old cars in front of them and tire swings hanging from trees over the worn and packed dirt yards, dozens of barefoot, dusty children stopping their play to watch him and his mother in the car, and the old slippers and dress the Negro woman wears, and he breathes her smell of sweat, looks at her black and brown hand crossing him to take the dollar from his mother's fingers.

On Fridays in spring and summer, Leonard comes to mow the lawn. He is a Negro, and has eight children, and Gerry sees him only once between fall and spring, when he comes on Christmas Eve, and Gerry's father and mother give him toys and clothes that Gerry and his three older sisters have outgrown, a bottle of bourbon, one of the fruit cakes Gerry's mother makes at Christmas, and five dollars. Leonard receives these at the back door, where on Fridays, in spring and summer, he is paid and fed. The Fontenots eat dinner at noon, and Gerry's mother serves Leonard a plate and a glass of iced tea with leaves from the mint she grows under the faucet behind the house. She calls him from the back steps, and he comes, wiping his brow with a bandanna, and takes his dinner to the shade of a sycamore tree. From his place at the dining room table, Gerry watches him sit on the grass and take off his straw hat; he eats, then rolls a cigarette. When he has smoked, he brings his plate and glass to the back door, knocks, and hands them to whoever answers. His glass is a jelly glass, his plate blue china, and his knife and fork stainless steel. From Friday to Friday the knife and fork lie at one side of a drawer, beside the compartments that hold silver; the glass is nearly out of reach, at the back of the second shelf in the cupboard for glasses; the plate rests under serving bowls in the china cupboard. Gerry's mother has told him and his sisters not to use them, they are Leonard's, and from Friday to Friday, they sit, and from fall to spring, and finally forever when one year Gerry is strong enough to push the lawn mower for his allowance, and Leonard comes only when Gerry's father calls him every Christmas Eve.

Before that, when he is eight, Gerry has stopped going on errands with his mother. On Saturday afternoons he walks or, on rainy days, rides the bus to town with neighborhood boys, to the movie theater where they watch westerns and the weekly chapter of a serial. He stands in line on the sidewalk, holding his quarter that will buy a ticket, a bag of popcorn, and, on the way home, an ice-cream soda. Opposite his line, to the right of the theater as you face it, are the Negro boys. Gerry does not look at them. Or not directly: he glances, he listens, as a few years later he will do with girls when he goes to movies that draw them. The Negroes enter through the door marked *Colored*, where he supposes a Negro woman sells tickets, then climb the stairs to the balcony, and Gerry wonders whether someone sells them popcorn and candy and drinks up there, or imagines them smelling all the bags of popcorn in the dark beneath them. Then he watches the cartoon and previews of next Saturday's movie, and he likes

them but is waiting for the chapter of the serial whose characters he and his friends have played in their yards all week;
they have worked out several escapes for the trapped hero
and, as always, they are wrong. He has eaten his popcorn
when the credits for the movie appear, then a tall man rides a
beautiful black or white or palomino horse across the screen.
The movie is black and white, but a palomino looks as golden
and lovely as the ones he has seen in parades. Sitting in the
dark, he is aware of his friends on both sides of him only as
feelings coincident with his own: the excitement of becoming
the Cisco Kid, Durango Kid, Red Ryder, the strongest and
best-looking, the most courageous and good, the fastest with
horse and fists and gun. Then it is over, the lights are on, he
turns to his friends, flesh again, stands to leave, then remembers the Negroes. He blinks up at them standing at the balcony wall, looking down at the white boys pressed together in
the aisle, moving slowly out of the theater. Sometimes his
eyes meet those of a Negro boy, and Gerry smiles; only one
ever smiles back.

In summer he and his friends go to town on weekday
afternoons to see war movies, or to buy toy guns or baseballs,
and when he meets Negroes on the sidewalk, he averts his
eyes; but he watches them in department stores, bending over
water fountains marked *Colored*, and when they enter the city
buses and walk past him to the rear, he watches them, and
during the ride he glances, and listens to their talk and laughter. One hot afternoon when he is twelve, he goes with a friend
to deliver the local newspaper in the colored section. He has
not been there since riding with his mother, who has not gone
for years either; now the city buses stop near his neighborhood, and a Negro woman comes on it and irons the family's
clothes in their kitchen. He goes that afternoon because his
friend has challenged him. They have argued: they both have
paper routes, and when his friend complained about his,
Gerry said it was easy work. Sure, his friend said, you don't
have to hold your breath. You mean when you collect? No, man,
when I just ride through. So Gerry finishes his route, then

goes with his friend: a bicycle ride of several miles ending, or beginning, at a neighborhood of poor whites, their houses painted but peeling, their screened front porches facing lawns so narrow that only small children can play catch in them; the older boys and girls play tapeball on the blacktop street. Gerry and his friends play that, making a ball of tape around a sock, and hitting with a baseball bat, but they have lawns big enough to contain them. Gerry's father teaches history at the public high school, and in summer is a recreation director for children in the city park, and some nights in his bed Gerry hears his father and mother worry about money; their voices are weary, and frighten him. But riding down this street, he feels shamefully rich, wants the boys and girls pausing in their game to know he only has a new Schwinn because he saved his money to buy it.

He and his friend jolt over the railroad tracks, and the blacktop ends. Dust is deep in the road. They ride past fields of tall grass and decaying things: broken furniture, space heaters, stoves, cars. Negro children are in the fields. Then they come to the streets of houses, turn onto the first one, a rutted and dusty road, and breathe the smell. It is as tangible as the dust a car raises to Gerry's face as it bounces past him, its unmuffled exhaust pipe sounding like gunfire, and Gerry feels that he enters the smell, as you enter a cloud of dust; and a hard summer rain, with lightning and thunder, would settle it, and the air would smell of grass and trees. Its base is sour, as though in the heat of summer someone has half-filled a garbage can with milk, then dropped in citrus fruit and cooked rice and vegetables and meat and fish, mattress ticking and a pillow, covered it, and left it for a week in the July sun. In this smell children play in the street and on the lawns that are dirt too, dust, save for strips of crisp-looking yellowish grass in the narrow spaces between houses, and scattered patches near the porches. He remembers the roads and houses and yards from riding with his mother, but not the smell, for even in summer they had rolled up the windows. Or maybe her perfume and cigarettes had fortified the car against the moment the laundry woman would open the back door, or reach through the window for her dollar; but he wonders now if his mother wanted the windows closed only to keep out dust. Women and men sit on the front porches, as Gerry and his friend slowly ride up the road, and his friend throws triangular-folded papers onto the yards, where they skip in rising dust.

It is late afternoon, and he can smell cooking too: hot grease and meat, turnip or mustard greens, and he hears talk and laughter from the shaded porches. Everything seems to be dying: cars and houses and tar paper roofs in the weather, grass in the sun; sparse oaks and pines and weeping willows draw children and women with babies to their shade; beneath the hanging tent of a willow, an old man sits with two crawling children wearing diapers, and Gerry remembers Leonard eating in the shade of the sycamore. Gerry's father still phones Leonard on Christmas Eve, and last year he went home with the electric train Gerry has outgrown, along with toy soldiers and cap pistols and Saturday serials and westerns, a growth that sometimes troubles him: when he was nine and ten and saw that other neighborhood boys stopped going to the Saturday movies when they were twelve or thirteen, he could not understand why something so exciting was suddenly not, and he promised himself that he would always go on Saturdays, although he knew he would not, for the only teenaged boy who did was odd and frightening: he was about eighteen, and in his voice and eyes was the desperation of a boy lying to a teacher, and he tried to sit between Gerry and his friends, and once he did before they could close the gap, and all through the movie he tried to rub Gerry's thigh, and Gerry whispered *Stop it*, and pushed at the wrist, the fingers. So he knew a time would come when he would no longer love his heroes and their horses, and it saddened him to know that such love could not survive mere time. It did not, and that is what troubles him, when he wonders if his love of baseball and football and hunting and fishing and bicycles will die too, and wonders what he will love then.

He looks for Leonard as he rides down the road, where

some yards are bordered with colored and clear bottles, half-buried with bottoms up to the sun. In others a small rectangle of flowers grows near the porch, and the smell seems to come from the flowers too, and the trees. He wants to enter one of those houses kept darkened with shades drawn against the heat, wants to trace and define that smell, press his nose to beds and sofas and floor and walls, the bosom of a woman, the chest of a man, the hair of a child. Breathing through his mouth, swallowing his nausea, he looks at his friend and sees what he knows is on his face as well: an expression of sustained and pallid horror.

On summer mornings the neighborhood boys play baseball. One of the fathers owns a field behind his house; he has mowed it with a tractor, and built a backstop of two-by-fours and screen, laid out an infield with a pitcher's mound, and put up foul poles at the edge of the tall weeds that surround the outfield. The boys play every rainless morning except Sunday, when all but the two Protestants go to Mass. They pitch slowly so they can hit the ball, and so the catcher, with only a mask, will not get hurt. But they pitch from a windup, and try to throw curves and knuckleballs, and sometimes they play other neighborhood teams who loan their catcher shin guards and chest protector, then the pitchers throw hard.

One morning a Negro boy rides his bicycle past the field, on the dirt road behind the backstop; he holds a fishing pole across the handlebars, and is going toward the woods beyond left field, and the bayou that runs wide and muddy through the trees. A few long innings later, he comes back without fish, and stops to watch the game. Standing, holding his bicycle, he watches two innings. Then, as Gerry's team is trotting in to bat, someone calls to the boy: Do you want to play? In the infield and outfield, and near home plate, voices stop. The boy looks at the pause, the silence, then nods, lowers his kickstand, and slowly walks onto the field.

'You're with us,' someone says. 'What do you play?'

'I like first.'

That summer, with eight dollars of his paper route money, Gerry has bought a first-baseman's glove: a Rawlings Trapper, because he liked the way it looked, and felt on his hand, but he is not a good first baseman: he turns his head away from throws that hit the dirt in front of his reaching glove and bounce toward his body, his face. He hands the glove to the boy.

'Use this. I ought to play second anyway.'

The boy puts his hand in the Trapper, thumps its pocket, turns his wrist back and forth, looking at the leather that is still a new reddish brown. Boys speak their names to him. His is Clay. They give him a place in the batting order, point to the boy he follows.

He is tall, and at the plate he takes a high stride and a long, hard swing. After his first hit, the outfield plays him deeply, at the edge of the weeds that are the boys' fence, and the infielders back up. At first base he is often clumsy, kneeling for ground balls, stretching before an infielder has thrown so that some balls nearly go past or above him; he is fearless, though, and none of the bouncing throws from third and deep short go past his body. He does not talk to any one boy, but from first he calls to the pitcher: *Come babe, come boy*; calls to infielders bent for ground balls: *Plenty time, plenty time, we got him*; and, to hitters when Gerry's team is at bat: *Good eye, good eye*. The game ends when the twelve o'clock whistle blows.

'That it?' Clay says as the fielders run in while he is swinging two bats on deck.

'We have to go eat,' the catcher says, taking off his mask, and with a dirt-smeared forearm wiping sweat from his brow.

'Me too,' he says, and drops the bats, picks up the Trapper, and hands it to Gerry. Gerry looks at it, lying across Clay's palm, looks at Clay's thumb on the leather.

'I'm a crappy first baseman,' he says. 'Keep it.'

'You kidding?'

'No. Go on.'

'What you going to play with?'

'My fielder's glove.'

Some of the boys are watching now; others are mounting bicycles on the road, riding away with gloves hanging from the handlebars, bats held across them.

'You don't want to play first no more?'

'No. Really.'

'Man, that's some *glove*. What's your name again?'

'Gerry,' he says, and extends his right hand. Clay takes it, and Gerry squeezes the big, limp hand; releases it.

'Gerry,' Clay says, looking down at his face as though to memorize it, or discern its features from among the twenty white faces of his morning.

'Good man,' he says, and turning, and calling goodbyes, he goes to his bicycle, places his fishing pole across the handlebars, hangs the Trapper from one, and rides quickly up the dirt road. Where the road turns to blacktop, boys are bicycling in a cluster, and Gerry watches Clay pass them with a wave. Then he is in the distance, among white houses with lawns and trees; is gone, leaving Gerry with the respectful voices of his friends, and peace and pride in his heart. He has attended a Catholic school since the first grade, so knows he must despise those feelings. He jokes about his play at first base, and goes with his Marty Marion glove and Ted Williams Louisville Slugger to his bicycle. But riding home, he nestles with his proud peace. At dinner he says nothing of Clay. The Christian Brothers have taught him that an act of charity can be canceled by the telling of it. Also, he suspects his family would think he is a fool.

A year later, a Negro man in a neighboring town is convicted of raping a young white woman, and is sentenced to die in the electric chair. His story is the front-page headline of the paper Gerry delivers, but at home, because the crime was rape, his mother tells the family she does not want any talk about it. Gerry's father mutters enough, from time to time, for Gerry to know he is angry and sad because if the woman had been a

Negro, and the man white, there would have been neither execution nor conviction. But on his friends' lawns, while he plays catch or pepper or sits on the grass, whittling branches down to sticks, he listens to voluptuous voices from the porches, where men and women drink bourbon and talk of niggers and rape and the electric chair. The Negro's name is Sonny Broussard, and every night Gerry prays for his soul.

On the March night Sonny Broussard will die, Gerry lies in bed and says a rosary. It is a Thursday, a day for the Joyful Mysteries, but looking out past the mimosa, at the corner streetlight, he prays with the Sorrowful Mysteries, remembers the newspaper photographs of Sonny Broussard, tries to imagine his terror as midnight draws near—why midnight? and how could he live that day in his cell?—and sees Sonny Broussard on his knees in the Garden of Olives; he wears khakis, his arms rest on a large stone, and his face is lifted to the sky. Tied to a pillar and shirtless, he is silent under the whip; thorns pierce his head, and the fathers of Gerry's friends strike his face, their wives watch as he climbs the long hill, cross on his shoulder, then he is lying on it, the men with hammers are carpenters in khakis, squatting above him, sweat running down their faces to drip on cigarettes between their lips, heads cocked away from smoke; they swing the hammers in unison, and drive nails through wrists and crossed feet. Then Calvary fades and Gerry sees instead a narrow corridor between cells with a door at the end; two guards are leading Sonny Broussard to it, and Gerry watches them from the rear. They open the door to a room filled with people, save for a space in the center of their circle, where the electric chair waits. They have been talking when the guard opens the door, and they do not stop. They are smoking and drinking and knitting; they watch Sonny Broussard between the guards, look from him to each other, and back to him, talking, clapping a hand on a neighbor's shoulder, a thigh. The guards buckle Sonny Broussard into the chair. Gerry shuts his eyes, and tries to feel the chair, the straps, Sonny Broussard's fear; to feel so hated that the people who surround him wait for the very throes and stench of his death. Then he feels it, he is in the electric chair, and he opens his eyes and holds his breath against the scream in his throat.

Gerry attends the state college in town, and lives at home. He majors in history, and is in the Naval ROTC, and is grateful that he will spend three years in the Navy after college. He does not want to do anything with history but learn it, and he believes the Navy will give him time to know what he will do for the rest of his life. He also wants to go to sea. He thinks more about the sea than history; by Christmas he is in love, and thinks more about the girl than either of them. Near the end of the year, the college president calls an assembly and tells the students that, in the fall, colored boys and girls will be coming to the school. The president is a politician, and will later be lieutenant-governor. There will be no trouble at this college, he says. I do not want troops or federal marshals on my campus. If any one of you starts trouble, or even joins in on it if one of them starts it, I will have you in my office, and you'd best bring your luggage with you.

The day after his last examinations, Gerry starts working with a construction crew. In the long heat he carries hundred-pound bags of cement, shovels gravel and sand, pushes wheel-barrows of wet concrete, digs trenches for foundations, holes for septic tanks, has more money than he has ever owned, spends most of it on his girl in restaurants and movies and night clubs and bars, and by late August has gained fifteen pounds, most of it above his waist, though beneath that is enough for his girl to pinch, and call his Budweiser belt. Then he hears of Emmett Till. He is a Negro boy, and in the night two white men have taken him from his great-uncle's house in Mississippi. Gerry and his girl wait. Three days later, while Gerry sits in the living room with his family before supper, the news comes over the radio: a search party has found Emmett Till at the bottom of the Tallahatchie River; a seventy-pound cotton gin fan was tied to his neck with barbed wire; he was beaten and shot in the head, and was decomposing. Gerry's father lowers his magazine, removes his glasses, rubs his eyes, and says: 'Oh my Lord, it's happening again.'

He goes to the kitchen and Gerry hears him mixing another bourbon and water, then the back screen door opens and shuts. His mother and the one sister still at home are talking about Mississippi and rednecks, and the poor boy, and what were they thinking of, what kind of men *are* they? He wants to follow his father, to ask what memory or hearsay he had meant, but he does not believe he is old enough, man enough, to move into his father's silence in the backyard.

He phones his girl, and after supper asks his father for the car, and drives to her house. She is waiting on the front porch, and walks quickly to the car. She is a petite, dark-skinned Cajun girl, with fast and accented speech, deep laughter, and a temper that is fierce when it reaches the end of its long tolerance. Through generations the Fontenots' speech has slowed and softened, so that Gerry sounds more southern than French; she teases him about it, and often, when he is with her, he finds that he is talking with her rhythms and inflections. She likes dancing, rhythm and blues, jazz, gin, beer, Pall Malls, peppery food, and passionate kissing, with no fondling. She receives Communion every morning, wears a gold Sacred Heart medal on a gold chain around her neck, and wants to teach history in college. Her name is Camille Theriot.

They go to a bar, where people are dancing to the jukebox. The couples in booths and boys at the bar are local students, some still in high school, for in this town parents and bartenders ignore the law about drinking, and bartenders only use it at clubs that do not want young people. Gerry has been drinking at this bar since he got his driver's license when he was sixteen. He leads Camille to a booth, and they drink gin and tonics, and repeat what they heard at college, in the classroom where they met: that it was economic, and all the hatred started with slavery, the Civil War leaving the poor white no one about whom he could say: *At least I ain't a slave like him*, leaving him only: *At least I ain't a nigger*. And after the war the Negro had to be contained to provide cheap labor in the fields. Camille says it might explain segregation, so long as you don't wonder about rich whites who don't have to create somebody to look down on, since they can do it from birth anyway.

'So it doesn't apply,' she says.

'They never seem to, do they?'

'What?'

'Theories. Do you think those sonsabitches—do you think they tied that fan on before or after they shot him? Why barbed wire if he was already dead? Why not baling wire, or—'

The waitress is there, and he watches her lower the drinks, put their empty glasses on her tray; he pays her, and looks at Camille. Her face is lowered, her eyes closed.

Around midnight, when the crowd thins, they move to the bar. Three couples dance slowly to Sinatra; another kisses in a booth. Gerry knows they are in high school when the boy lights a cigarette and they share it: the girl draws on it, they kiss, and she exhales into his mouth; then the boy does it. Camille says: 'Maybe we should go north to college, and just stay there.'

'I hear the people are cold as the snow.'

'Me too. And they eat boiled food with some kind of white sauce.'

'You want some oysters?'

'Can we get there before they close?'

'Let's try it,' he says. 'Did you French-smoke in high school?'

'Sure.'

A boy stands beside Gerry and loudly orders a beer. He is drunk, and when he sees Gerry looking at him, he says: 'Woo. They *did* it to him, didn't they? 'Course now, a little nigger boy like that, you can't tell'—as Gerry stands so he can reach into his pocket—'could be he'd go swimming with seventy pounds hanging on his neck, and a bullet in his head'—and Gerry opens the knife he keeps sharp for fish and game, looks at the blade, then turns toward the voice: 'Emmett *Till* rhymes with *kill.* Hoo. Hot *damn.* Kill *Till—*'

Gerry's hand bunches the boy's collar, turns him, and pushes his back against the bar. He touches the boy's throat with the point of the knife, and his voice comes yelling out of him; he seems to rise from the floor with it, can feel nothing of his flesh beneath it: 'You like *death? Feel* it!'

He presses the knife until skin dimples around its point. The boy is still, his mouth open, his eyes rolled to his left, where the knife is. Camille is screaming, and Gerry hears *Cut his tongue out! Cut his* heart *out!* Then she is standing in front of the boy, her arms waving, and Gerry hears *Bastard bastard bastard,* as he watches the boy's eyes and open mouth, then hears the bartender speaking softly: 'Take it easy now. You're Gerry, right?' He glances at the voice; the bartender is leaning over the bar. 'Easy, Gerry. You stick him there, he's gone. Why don't you go on home now, okay?'

Camille is quiet. Watching the point, Gerry pushes the knife, hardly a motion at all, for he is holding back too; the dimple, for an instant, deepens and he feels the boy's chest breathless and rigid beneath his left fist.

'Okay,' he says, and releases the boy's shirt, folds the knife, and takes Camille's arm. Boys at the bar and couples on the dance floor stand watching. There is music he cannot hear clearly enough to name. He and Camille walk between the couples to the door.

Two men, Roy Bryant and John William Milan, are arrested, and through hot September classes Gerry and Camille wait for the trial. Negroes sit together in classes, walk together in the corridors and across the campus, and surround juxtaposed tables in the student union, where they talk quietly, and do not play the jukebox. Gerry and Camille drink coffee and furtively watch them; in the classrooms and corridors, and on the grounds, they smile at Negroes, tell them hello, and get smiles and greetings. The Negro boys wear slacks and sport shirts, some of them with coats, some even with ties; the girls wear skirts or dresses; all of them wear polished shoes. There is no trouble. Gerry and Camille read the newspapers and listen to the radio, and at night after studying together they go to the bar and drink beer; the bartender is polite, even friendly, and does not mention the night of the knife. As they drink, then drive to Camille's house, they talk about Emmett Till, his story they have read and heard.

He was from Chicago, where he lived with his mother; his father died in France, in the Second World War. Emmett was visiting his great-uncle in Money, Mississippi. His mother said she told him to be respectful down there, because he didn't know about the South. One day he went to town and bought two cents' worth of bubble gum in Roy Bryant's store. Bryant's wife Carolyn, who is young and pretty, was working at the cash register. She said that when Emmett left the store and was on the sidewalk, he turned back to her and whistled. It was the wolf whistle, and that night Roy Bryant and his half-brother, John William Milan, went to the great-uncle's house with flashlights and a pistol, said *Where's that Chicago boy*, and took him.

The trial is in early fall. The defense lawyer's case is that the decomposed body was not Emmett Till; that the NAACP had put his father's ring on the finger of that body; and that the fathers of the jurors would turn in their graves if these twelve Anglo-Saxon men returned with a guilty verdict, which, after an hour and seven minutes of deliberation, they do not. That night, with Camille sitting so close that their bodies touch, Gerry drives on highways through farming country and cleared land with oil derricks and gas fires, and on bridges spanning dark bayous, on narrow blacktop roads twisting through lush woods, and gravel and dirt roads through rice fields whose canals shimmer in the moonlight. The windows are open to humid air whose rush cools his face.

When they want beer, he stops at a small country store; woods are behind it, and it is flanked by lighted houses separated by woods and fields. Oyster shells cover the parking area in front of the store. Camille will not leave the car. He crosses the wooden porch where bugs swarm at a yellow light, and enters: the store is lit by one ceiling light that casts shadows between shelves. A man and a woman stand at the counter, talking to a stout woman behind it. Gerry gets three six-packs and goes to the counter. They are only talking about people they know, and a barbecue where there was a whole steer on a spit, and he will tell this to Camille.

But in the dark outside the store, crunching on oyster shells, he forgets: he sees her face in the light from the porch, and wants to kiss her. In the car he does, kisses they hold long while their hands move on each others' backs. Then he is driving again. Twice he is lost, once on a blacktop road in woods that are mostly the conical silhouettes and lovely smell of pine, then on a gravel road through a swamp whose feral odor makes him pull the map too quickly from her hands. He stops once for gas, at an all-night station on a highway. Sweat soaks through his shirt, and it sticks to the seat, and he is warm and damp where his leg and Camille's sweat together. By twilight they are silent. She lights their cigarettes and opens their cans of beer; as the sun rises he is driving on asphalt between woods, the dark of their leaves fading to green, and through the insect-splattered windshield he gazes with burning eyes at the entrance to his town.

ANNA

HER NAME WAS ANNA GRIFFIN. She was twenty. Her blond hair had been turning darker over the past few years, and she believed it would be brown when she was twenty-five. Sometimes she thought of dying it blond, but living with Wayne was still new enough to her so that she was hesitant about spending money on anything that could not be shared. She also wanted to see what her hair would finally look like. She was pretty, though parts of her face seemed not to know it: the light of her eyes, the lines of her lips, seemed bent on denial, so that even the rise of her high cheekbones seemed ungraceful, simply covered bone. Her two front teeth had a gap between them, and they protruded, the right more than the left.

She worked at the cash register of a Sunnycorner store, located in what people called a square: two blocks of small stores, with a Chevrolet dealer and two branch banks, one of them next to the Sunnycorner. The tellers from that one—women not much older than Anna—came in for takeout coffees, cigarettes, and diet drinks. She liked watching them come in: soft sweaters, wool dresses, polyester blouses that in stores she liked rubbing between thumb and forefinger. She liked looking at their hair too: beauty parlor hair that seemed groomed to match the colors and cut and texture of their clothing, so it was more like hair on a model or a movie actress, no longer an independent growth to be washed and brushed and combed and cut, but part of the ensemble, as the boots were. They all wore pretty watches, and bracelets and necklaces, and more than one ring. She liked the way the girls moved: they looked purposeful but not harried: one enters the store and stops at the magazine rack against the wall opposite Anna and the counter, and picks up a magazine and thumbs the pages, appearing even then to be in motion still, a woman leaving the job for a few minutes, but not in a hurry; then she replaces the magazine and crosses the floor and waits in line while Anna rings up and bags the cans and bottles and boxes cradled in arms, dangling from hands. They talk to each other, Anna and the teller she knows only by face, as she fills and caps Styrofoam cups of coffee. The weather. Hi. How are you. Bye now. The teller leaves. Often behind the counter, with other customers, Anna liked what she was doing; liked knowing where the pimientos were; liked her deftness with the register and bagging; was proud of her cheerfulness, felt in charge of customers and what they bought. But when the tellers were at the counter, she was shy, and if one of them made her laugh, she covered her mouth.

She took new magazines from the rack: one at a time, keeping it under the counter near her tall three-legged stool, until she finished it; then she put it back and took another. So by the time the girls from the bank glanced through the magazine, she knew what they were seeing. For they always chose the ones she did: *People, Vogue, Glamour*. She looked at *Playgirl*, and in *Penthouse* she looked at the women and read the letters, this when she worked at night, not because there were fewer customers then but because it was night, not day. At first she had looked at them during the day, and felt strange raising her eyes from the pictures to blink at the parking lot, whose presence of cars and people and space she always felt because the storefront was glass, her counter stopping just short of it. The tellers never picked up those magazines, but Anna was certain they had them at home. She imagined that too: where they lived after work; before work. She gave them large, pretty apartments with thick walls so they only heard

themselves; stereos and color television, and soft carpets and
soft furniture and large brass beds; sometimes she imagined
them living with men who made a lot of money, and she saw a
swimming pool, a Jacuzzi.

Near the end of her workday, in its seventh and eighth
hours, her fatigue was the sort that comes from confining the
body while giving neither it nor the mind anything to do. She
was restless, impatient, and distracted, and while talking
politely to customers and warmly to the regular ones, she
wanted to be home. The apartment was in an old building she
could nearly see from behind the counter; she could see the
grey house with red shutters next to it. As soon as she left the
store, she felt as if she had not been tired at all; only her feet
still were. Sometimes she felt something else too, as she
stepped outside and crossed that line between fatigue and
energy: a touch of dread and defeat. She walked past the bank,
the last place in the long building of bank Sunnycorner drugstore department store and pizza house, cleared the corner of
the building, passed the dumpster on whose lee side teenagers on summer nights smoked dope and drank beer, down the
sloping parking lot and across the street to the old near-yard-
less green wooden apartment house; up three flights of voices
and television voices and the smell that reminded her of the
weariness she had just left. It was not a bad smell. It bothered
her because it was a daily smell, even when old Mrs. Battistini
on the first floor cooked with garlic: a smell of all the days of
this wood: up to the third floor, the top of the building, and
into the apartment whose smells she noticed only because
they were not the scent of contained age she had breathed as
she climbed. Then she went to the kitchen table or the bed or
shower or couch, either talking to Wayne or waiting for him
to come home from Wendy's, where he cooked hamburgers.

At those times she liked her home. She rarely liked it
when she woke in it: a northwest apartment, so she opened
her eyes to a twilit room and, as she moved about, she saw the
place clearly, with its few pieces of furniture, cluttered only
with leavings: tossed clothes, beer bottles, potato chip bags,

as if her night's sleep had tricked her so she would see only what last night she had not. And sometimes later, during the day or night, while she was simply crossing a room, she would suddenly see herself juxtaposed with the old maroon couch which had been left, along with everything else, by whoever lived there before she and Wayne: the yellow wooden table and two chairs in the kitchen, the blue easy chair in the living room, and in the bedroom the chest of drawers, the straight wooden chair, and the mattress on the floor, and she felt older than she knew she ought to.

The wrong car: a 1964 Mercury Comet that Wayne had bought for one hundred and sixty dollars two years ago, before she knew him, when the car was already eleven years old, and now it vibrated at sixty miles an hour, and had holes in the floorboard; and the wrong weapon: a Buck hunting knife under Wayne's leather jacket, unsheathed and held against his body by his left arm. She had not thought of the car and knife until he put the knife under his jacket and left her in the car, smoking so fast that between drags she kept the cigarette near her face and chewed the thumb of the hand holding it; looking through the wiper-swept windshield and the snow blowing between her and the closed bakery next to the lighted drugstore, at tall Wayne walking slowly with his face turned and lowered away from the snow. She softly kept her foot on the accelerator so the engine would not stall. The headlights were off. She could not see into the drugstore. When she drove slowly past it, there were two customers, one at the cash register and counter at the rear, one looking at display shelves at a side wall. She had parked and turned off the lights. One customer left, a man bareheaded in the snow. He did not look at their car. Then the other one left, a man in a watch cap. He did not look either, and when he had driven out of the parking lot to the highway it joined, Wayne said Okay, and went in.

She looked in the rearview mirror, but snow had covered the window; she looked to both sides. To her right, at the far end of the shopping center, the doughnut shop was open, and in front of it three cars were topped with snow. All the other stores were closed. She would be able to see headlights through the snow on the rear window, and if a cruiser came she was to go into the store, and if Wayne had not already started, she would buy cigarettes, then go out again, and if the cruiser was gone she would wait in the car; if the cruiser had stopped, she would go back into the store for matches and they would both leave. Now in the dark and heater-warmth she believed all of their plan was no longer risky, but doomed, as if by leaving the car and walking across the short space through soft angling snow, Wayne had become puny, his knife a toy. So it was the wrong girl too, and the wrong man. She could not imagine him coming out with money, and she could not imagine tomorrow or later tonight or even the next minute. Stripped of history and dreams, she knew only her breathing and smoking and heartbeat and the falling snow. She stared at the long window of the drugstore, and she was startled when he came out: he was running, he was alone, he was inside, closing the door. He said *Jesus Christ* three times as she crossed the parking lot. She turned on the headlights and slowed as she neared the highway. She did not have to stop. She moved into the right lane, and cars in the middle and left passed her.

'A *lot*,' he said.

She reached to him, and he pressed bills against her palm, folded her fingers around them.

'Can you see out back?' she said.

'No. Nobody's coming. Just go slow: no skidding, no wrecks. Jesus.'

She heard the knife blade sliding into the sheath, watched yellowed snow in the headlights and glanced at passing cars on her left; she held the wheel with two hands. He said when he went in he was about to walk around like he was looking for something because he was so scared, but then he decided to do it right away or else he might have just walked around the store till the druggist asked what he wanted and he'd end up buying toothpaste or something, so he went down along the side wall to the back of the store—he lit a cigarette and she said *Me too*; she watched the road and taillights of a distant car in her lane as he placed it between her fingers—and he went around the counter and took out the knife and held it at the druggist's stomach: a little man with grey hair watching the knife and punching open the register.

She left the highway and drove on a two-lane road through woods and small towns.

'Tequila,' he said.

In their town all but one package store closed at ten-thirty; she drove to the one that stayed open until eleven, a corner store on a street of tenement houses where Puerto Ricans lived; on warm nights they were on the stoops and sidewalks and corners. She did not like going there, even on winter nights when no one was out. She stopped in front of it, looked at the windows, and said: 'I think it's closed.'

'It's quarter to.'

He went out and tried the door, then peered in, then knocked and called and tried the door again. He came back and struck the dashboard.

'I can't fucking be*lieve* it. I got so much money in my pockets I got no room for my hands, and we got one *beer* at home. Can you believe it?'

'He must've closed early—'

'No shit.'

'—because of the *snow*.'

She turned a corner around a used car lot and got onto the main street going downhill through town to the river.

'I could use some tequila,' she said.

'Stop at Timmy's.'

The traffic lights were blinking yellow so people would not have to stop on the hill in the snow; she shifted down and coasted with her foot touching the brake pedal, drove over the bridge, and parked two blocks from it at Timmy's. When she got out of the car, her legs were weak and eager for motion, and she realized they had been taut all the way home; and, standing at the corner of the bar, watching Johnny McCarthy pour two shots beside the drafts, she knew she was going to get drunk. She licked salt from her hand and drank the shot, then a long swallow of beer that met the tequila's burn as it rose, and held the shot glass toward grinning McCarthy and asked how law school was going; he poured tequila and said *Long but good*, and she drank that and finished her beer, and he poured two more shots and brought them drafts. She looped her arm around Wayne's and nuzzled the soft leather and hard bicep, then tongue-kissed him, and looked down the bar at the regulars, most of them men talking in pairs, standing at the bar that had no stools; two girls stood shoulder to shoulder and talked to men on their flanks. The room was long and narrow, separated from the dining room by a wall with a half-door behind the bar. Anna waved at people who looked at her, and they raised a glass or waved and some called her name, and old Lou, who was drinking beer alone at the other end of the bar, motioned to McCarthy and sent her and Wayne a round. Wayne's hand came out of his jacket and she looked at the bill in it: a twenty.

'Set up Lou,' he said to McCarthy. '*Lou. Can I buy you a shot?*'

Lou nodded and smiled, and she watched McCarthy pour the Fleischmann's and bring it and a draft to Lou, and she wondered if she could tend bar, could remember all the drinks. It was a wonderful place to be, this bar, with her back to the door so she got some of the chill, not all stuffy air and smoke, and able to look down the length of the bar, and at the young men crowded into four tables at the end of the room, watching a television set on a shelf on the wall: a hockey game. It was the only place outside of her home where she always felt the comfort of affection. Shivering with a gulp of tequila, she watched Wayne arm-wrestling with Curt: knuckles white and hand and face red, veins showing at his temple and throat. She had never seen either win, but Wayne had told her that till a year ago he had always won.

'*Pull,*' she said.

His strength and effort seemed to move into the air around her, making her restless; she slapped his back, lit a cigarette, wanted to dance. She called McCarthy and pointed to the draft glasses, then Curt's highball glass, and when he came with the drinks, told him Wayne would pay after he beat Curt. She was humming to herself, and she liked the sound of her voice. She wondered if she could tend bar. People didn't fight here. People were good to her. They wouldn't—A color television. They shouldn't buy it too soon; but when? Who would care? Nobody watched what they bought. She wanted to count the money, but did not want to leave until closing. Wayne and Curt were panting and grunting; their arms were nearly straight up again; they had been going slowly back and forth. She slipped a hand into Wayne's jacket pocket, squeezed the folded wad. She had just finished a cigarette but now she was holding another and wondering if she wanted it, then she lit it and did. There was only a men's room in the bar. 'Draw?' Curt said; 'Draw,' Wayne said, and she hugged his waist and rubbed his right bicep and said: 'I ordered us and Curt a round. I didn't pay. I'm going piss.'

He smiled down at her. The light in his eyes made her want to stay holding him. She walked toward the end of the bar, past the backs of leaning drinkers; some noticed her and spoke; she patted backs, said *Hi How you doing Hey what's happening*; big curly-haired Mitch stopped her: Yes, she was still at Sunnycorner; where had he been? Working in New Hampshire. He told her what he did, and she heard, but seconds later she could not remember; she was smiling at him. He called to Wayne and waved. She said I'll see you in a minute, and moved on. At the bar's end was Lou. He reached for her, raised the other arm at McCarthy. He held her shoulder and pulled her to him.

'Let me buy you a drink.'

'I have to go to the ladies'.'

'Well, go to the ladies' and come back.'

'Okay.'

She did not go. Her shot and their drafts were there and

she was talking to Lou. She did not know what he did either. She used to know. He looked sixty. He came every night. His grey hair was short and he laughed often and she liked his wrinkles.

'I wish I could tend bar here.'

'You'd be good at it.'

'I don't think I could remember all the drinks.'

'It's a shot and beer place.'

His arm was around her, her fingers pressing his ribs. She drank. The tequila was smooth now. She finished the beer, said she'd be back, next round was hers; she kissed his cheek: his skin was cool and tough, and his whiskers scraped her chin. She moved past the tables crowded with the hockey watchers; Henry coming out of the men's room moved around her, walking carefully. She went through the door under the television set, into a short hall, glanced down it into the door-less, silent kitchen, and stepped left into the rear of the dining room: empty and darkened. Some nights she and Wayne brought their drinks in here after the kitchen closed and sat in a booth in the dark. The ladies' room was empty. 'Ah.' Wayne was right: when you really had to piss, it was better than sex. She listened to the voices from the bar, wanted to hurry back to them. She jerked the paper, tore it.

Lou was gone. She stood where he had been, but his beer glass was gone, the ashtray emptied. He was like that. He came and went quietly. You'd look around and see him for the first time and he already had a beer; sometime later you'd look around and he was gone. Behind Wayne the front door opened and a blue cap and jacket and badge came in: it was Ryan from the beat. She made herself think in sentences and tried to focus on them, as if she were reading: *He's coming in to get warm. He's just cold.* She waved at him. He did not see her. She could not remember the sentences. She could not be afraid either. She knew that she ought to be afraid so she would not make any mistakes but she was not, and when she tried to feel afraid or even serious she felt drunker. Ryan was standing next to Curt, one down from Wayne, and had his gloves off and was blowing on his hands. He and McCarthy talked, then he left; at the door he waved at the bar, and Anna waved. She went toward Wayne, then stopped at the two girls: one was Laurie or Linda, she couldn't remember which; one was Jessie. They were still flanked by Bobby and Mark. They all turned their backs to the bar, pressed her hands, touched her shoulders, bought her a drink. She said tequila, and drank it and talked about Sunnycorner. She went to Wayne, told McCarthy to set up Bobby and Mark and Jessie—leaning forward: 'Johnny, what is it? Laurie or Linda?' 'Laurie.' She slipped a hand into Wayne's pocket. Then her hand was captive there, fingers on money, his forearm pressing hers against his side.

'I'll get it. Did you see Ryan?'

'Yes.'

She tried to think in sentences again. She looked up at Wayne; he was grinning down at her. She could see the grin, or his eyes, but not both at once. She gazed at his lips.

'You're cocked,' he said. He was not angry. He said it softly, and took her wrist and withdrew it from his pocket.

'I'll do it in the john.'

She wanted to be as serious and careful as he was, but looking at him and trying to see all of his face at once weakened her legs; she tried again to think in sentences but they jumped away from her like a cat her mind chased; when she turned away from him, looked at faces farther away and held the bar, her mind stopped struggling and she smiled and put her hand in his back pocket and said: 'Okay.'

He started to walk to the men's room, stopping to talk to someone, being stopped by another; watching him, she was smiling. When she became aware of it, she kept the smile; she liked standing at the corner of the bar smiling with love at her man's back and profile as he gestured and talked; then he was in the men's room. Midway down the bar McCarthy finished washing glasses and dried his hands, stepped back and folded his arms, and looked up and down the bar, and when he saw nothing in front of her he said: 'Anna? Another round?'

'Just a draft, okay?'

She looked in her wallet; she knew it was empty but she looked to be sure it was still empty; she opened the coin pouch and looked at lint and three pennies. She counted the pennies. Johnny put the beer in front of her.

'Wayne's got—'

'On me,' he said. 'Want a shot too?'

'Why not.'

She decided to sip this one or at least drink it slowly, but while she was thinking, the glass was at her lips and her head tilted back and she swallowed it all and licked her lips, then turned to the door behind her and, without coat, stepped outside: the sudden cold emptied her lungs, then she deeply drew in the air tasting of night and snow. 'Wow.' She lifted her face to the light snow and breathed again. Had she smoked a Camel? Yes. From Lou. Jesus. Snow melted on her cheeks. She began to shiver. She crossed the sidewalk, touched the frosted parking meter. One of her brothers did that to her when she was little. Which one? Frank. Told her to lick the bottom of the ice tray. In the cold she stood happy and clear-headed until she wanted to drink, and she went smiling into the warmth and voices and smoke.

'Where'd you go?' Wayne said.

'Outside to get straight,' rubbing her hands together, drinking beer, its head gone, shaking a cigarette from her pack, her flesh recalling its alertness outside as, breathing smoke and swallowing beer and leaning on Wayne, it was lulled again. She wondered if athletes felt all the time the way she had felt outside.

'We should get some bicycles,' she said.

He lowered his mouth to her ear, pushing her hair aside with his rubbing face.

'We can,' his breath in her ear; she turned her groin against his leg. 'It's about two thousand.'

'No, *Wayne.*'

'Ssshhh. I looked at it, man.'

He moved away, and put a bill in her hand: a twenty.

'Jesus,' she said.

'Keep cool.'

'I've never—' She stopped, called McCarthy, and paid for the round for Laurie and Jessie and Bobby and Mark, and tipped him a dollar. Two thousand dollars: she had never seen that much money in her life, had never had as much as a hundred in her hands at one time: not of her own.

'*Last* call.' McCarthy started at the other end of the bar, taking empty glasses, bringing back drinks. '*Last* call.' She watched McCarthy pouring her last shot and draft of the night; she faced Wayne and raised the glass of tequila: 'Hi, babe.'

'Hi.' He licked salt from his hand.

'I been forgetting the salt,' she said, and drank, looking at his eyes. She sipped this last one, finished it, and was drinking the beer when McCarthy called: 'That's *it*. I'm taking the glasses in *five min*utes. You don't have to go home—'

'—but you can't stay here,' someone said.

'Right. Drink up.'

She finished the beer and beckoned with her finger to McCarthy. When he came she held his hands and said: 'Just a quick one?'

'I can't.'

'Just half a draft or a quick shot? I'll drink it while I put my coat on.'

'The cops have been checking. I got to have the glasses off the bar.'

'What about a roader?' Wayne said.

'Then they'll all want one.'

'Okay. He's right, Anna. Let go of the man.'

She released his hands and he took their glasses. She put on her coat. Wayne was waving at people, calling to them. She waved: '*See* you people. Good *night*, Jessie. Laurie. Good *night*. See you, Henry. Mark. Bobby. Bye-bye, Mitch—'

Then she was in the falling white cold, her arm around Wayne; he drove them home, a block and a turn around the Chevrolet lot, then two blocks, while in her mind still were the light and faces and voices of the bar. She held his waist going up the dark stairs. He was breathing hard, not talking.

Then he unlocked the door, she was inside, lights coming on, coat off, following Wayne to the kitchen where he opened their one beer and took a swallow and handed it to her and pulled money from both pockets. They sat down and divided the bills into stacks of twenties and tens and fives and ones. When the beer was half gone he left and came back from the bedroom with four Quaaludes and she said: 'Mmmm' and took two from his palm and swallowed them with beer. She picked up the stack of twenties. Her legs felt weak again. She was hungry. She would make a sandwich. She put down the stack and sat looking at the money. He was counting: '—thirty-five forty forty-five fifty—' She took the ones. She wanted to start at the lowest and work up; she did not want to know how many twenties there were until the end. She counted aloud and he told her not to.

'You don't either,' she said. 'All I hear is ninety-five hundred ninety-five hundred—'

'Okay. In our heads.'

She started over. She wanted to eat and wished for a beer and lost count again. Wayne had a pencil in his hand, was writing on paper in front of him. She counted faster. She finished and picked up the twenties. She counted slowly, making a new stack on the table with the bills that she drew, one at a time, from her hand. She did not keep track of the sum of money; she knew she was too drunk. She simply counted each bill as she smacked it onto the pile. Wayne was writing again, so she counted the last twelve aloud, ending with: '—and forty-six,' slamming it onto the fanning twenties. He wrote and drew a line and wrote again and drew another line, and his pencil moved up the columns, touching each number and writing a new number at the bottom until there were four of them, and he read to her: 'Two thousand and eighteen.'

The Quaalude bees were in her head now, and she stood and went to the living room for a cigarette in her purse, her legs wanting to go to the sink at her right but she forced them straight through the door whose left jamb they bumped; as she reached into her purse she heard herself humming. She had thought she was talking to Wayne, but that was in her head, she had told him *Two thousand and eighteen we can have some music and movies now* and she smiled aloud because it had come out as humming a tune she had never heard. In the kitchen Wayne was doing something strange. He had lined up their three glasses on the counter by the sink and he was pouring milk into them; it filled two and a half, and he drank that half. Then he tore open the top of the half-gallon carton and rinsed it and swabbed it out with a paper towel. Then he put the money in it, and folded the top back, and put it in the freezer compartment, and the two glasses of milk in the refrigerator. Then she was in the bedroom talking about frozen money; she saw the cigarette between her fingers as she started to undress, in the dark now; she was not aware of his turning out lights: she was in the lighted kitchen, then in the dark bedroom, looking for an ashtray instead of pulling her sleeve over the cigarette, and she told him about that and about a stereo and Emmylou Harris and fucking, as she found the ashtray on the floor by the bed, which was a mattress on the floor by the ashtray; that she thought about him at Sunnycorner, got horny for him; her tongue was thick, slower than her buzzing head, and the silent words backed up in the spaces between the spoken ones, so she told him something in her mind, then heard it again as her tongue caught up; her tongue in his mouth now, under the covers on the cold sheet, a swelling of joy in her breast as she opened her legs for him and the night's images came back to her: the money on the table and the faces of McCarthy and Curt and Mitch and Lou, and Wayne's hand disappearing with the money inside the carton, and Bobby and Mark and Laurie and Jessie, the empty sidewalk where she stood alone in the cold air, Lou saying: *You'd be good at it.*

The ringing seemed to come from inside her skull, insistent and clear through the voices of her drunken sleep: a ribbon of sound she had to climb, though she tried to sink away from it. Then her eyes were open and she turned off the alarm she did not remember setting; it was six o'clock and she was asleep again, then wakened by her alarmed heartbeat: all in what seemed a few seconds, but it was ten minutes to seven, when she had to be at work. She rose with a fast heart and a head-ache that made her stoop gingerly for her clothes on the floor and shut her eyes as she put them on. She went into the kitchen: the one empty beer bottle, the ashtray, the milk-soiled glass, and her memory of him putting away the money was immediate, as if he had just done it and she had not slept at all. She took the milk carton from the freezer. The folded money, like the bottle and ashtray and glass, seemed part of the night's drinking, something you cleaned or threw away in the morning. But she had no money and she needed aspirins and coffee and doughnuts and cigarettes; she took a cold five-dollar bill and put the carton in the freezer, looked in the bed-room for her purse and then in the kitchen again and found it in the living room, opened her wallet and saw money there. She pushed the freezer money in with it and slung the purse from her shoulder and stepped into the dim hall, shutting the door on Wayne's snoring. Outside she blinked at sun and cold and remembered Wayne giving her twenty at the bar; she crossed the street and parking lot and, with the taste of beer in her throat and toothpaste in her mouth, was in the Sunny-corner before seven.

She spent the next eight hours living the divided life of a hangover. Drinking last night had stopped time, kept her in the present until last call forced on her the end of a night, the truth of tomorrow; but once in their kitchen counting money, she was in the present again and she stayed there through twice waking, and dressing, and entering the store and relieving Eddie, the all-night clerk, at the register. So for the first three or four hours while she worked and waited and talked, her body heavily and slowly occupied space in those brightly lit moments in the store; but in her mind were images of Wayne leaving the car and going into the drugstore and running out, and driving home through falling snow, the closed package store and the drinks and people at Timmy's and taking the Quaaludes from

Wayne's palm, and counting money and making love for so drunk long; and she felt all of that and none of what she was numbly doing. It was a hangover that demanded food and coffee and cigarettes. She started the day with three aspirins and a Coke. Then she smoked and ate doughnuts and drank coffee. Sometimes from the corner of her eye she saw something move on the counter, small and grey and fast, like the shadow of a darting mouse. Her heart was fast too, and the customers were fast and loud, while her hands were slow, and her tongue was, for it had to wait while words freed themselves from behind her eyes, where the pain was, where the aspirins had not found it. After four cups of coffee, her heart was faster and hands more shaky, and she drank another Coke. She was careful, and made no mistakes on the register; with eyes trying to close she looked into the eyes of customers and Kermit, the manager, slim and balding, in his forties; a kind man but one who, today, made her feel both scornful and ashamed, for she was certain he had not had a hangover in twenty years. Around noon her blood slowed and her hands stopped trembling, and she was tired and lightheaded and afraid; it seemed there was always someone watching her, not only the customers and Kermit, but someone above her, outside the window, in the narrow space behind her. Now there were gaps in her memory of last night: she looked at the clock so often that its hands seemed halted, and in her mind she was home after work, in bed with Wayne, shuddering away the terrors that brushed her like a curtain windblown against her back.

When she got home he had just finished showering and shaving, and she took him to bed with lust that was as much part of her hangover as hunger and the need to smoke were; silent and hasty, she moved toward that orgasm that would bring her back to some calm mooring in the long day. Crying out, she burst into languor; slept breathing the scent of his washed flesh. But she woke alone in the twilit room and rose quickly from the bed, calling him. He came smiling from the living room, and asked if she were ready to go to the mall.

The indoor walk of the mall was bright and warm; coats unbuttoned, his arm over her shoulder, hers around his waist, they moved slowly among people and smells of frying meat, stopping at windows to look at shirts and coats and boots; they took egg rolls to a small pool with a fountain in its middle and sat on its low brick wall; they ate pizza alone on a bench that faced a displayed car; they had their photographs taken behind a curtain in a shop and paid the girl and left their address.

'You think she'll mail them to us?' Anna said.

'Sure.'

They ate hamburgers standing at the counter, watching the old man work at the grill, then sat on a bench among potted plants to smoke. On the way to the department store they bought fudge, and the taste of it lingered, sweet and rich in her mouth, and she wanted to go back for another piece, but they were in the store: large, with glaring white light, and as the young clerk wearing glasses and a thin moustache came to them, moving past television sets and record players, she held Wayne's arm. While the clerk and Wayne talked, she was aware of her gapped and jutting teeth, her pea jacket, and old boots and jeans. She followed Wayne following the clerk; they stopped at a shelf of record players. She shifted her eyes from one to the other as they spoke; they often looked at her, and she said: Yes. Sure. The soles of her feet ached and her calves were tired. She wanted to smoke but was afraid the clerk would forbid her. She swallowed the taste of fudge. Then she was sad. She watched Wayne and remembered him running out of the drugstore and, in the car, saying *Jesus Christ*, and she was ashamed that she was sad, and felt sorry for him because he was not.

Now they were moving. He was hugging her and grinning and his thigh swaggered against her hip, and they were among shelved television sets. Some of them were turned on, but to different channels, and surrounded by those faces and bodies and colliding words, she descended again into her hangover. She needed a drink, a cigarette, a small place, not all this low-ceilinged breadth and depth, where shoppers in the awful light jumped in and out of her vision. Timmy's: the corner of the bar near the door, and a slow-sipped tequila salty dog and then one more to close the spaces in her brain and the corners of her vision, stop the tingling of her gums, and the crawling tingle inside her body as though ants climbed on her veins. In her coat pocket, her hand massaged the box of cigarettes; she opened it with a thumb, stroked filters with a finger.

'That's a good advertisement for the Sony,' Wayne said. 'Turning on the RCA next to it.'

She wanted to cry. She watched the pictures on the Sony: a man and woman in a car, talking; she knew California from television and movies, and they were driving in California: the winding road, the low brown hills, the sea. The man was talking about dope and people's names. The clerk was talking about a guarantee. Wayne told him what he liked to watch, and as she heard hockey and baseball and football and movies she focused so hard on imagining this set in their apartment and them watching it from the couch that she felt like she had closed her eyes, though she had not. She followed them to the cash register and looked around the room for the cap and shoulders of a policeman to appear in the light that paled skin and cast no shadow. She watched Wayne counting the money; she listened to the clerk's pleased voice. Then Wayne had her arm, was leading her away.

'Aren't we taking them?'

He stopped, looked down at her, puzzled; then he laughed and kissed the top of her head.

'We pick them up out back.'

He was leading her again.

'Where are we going now?'

'Records. Remember? Unless you want to spend a fucking fortune on a stereo and just look at it.'

Standing beside him, she gazed and blinked at album

covers as he flipped them forward, pulled out some, talked
about them. She tried to despise his transistor radio at home,
tried to feel her old longing for a stereo and records, but as
she looked at each album he held in front of her, she was glut-
ted with spending, and felt more like a thief than she had last
night waiting outside the drugstore, and driving home from it.
Again she imagined the apartment, saw where she would put
the television, the record player; she would move the chest of
drawers to the living room and put them on its top, facing the
couch where—She saw herself cooking. She was cooking mac-
aroni and cheese for them to eat while they watched a movie;
but she saw only the apartment now, then herself sweeping it.
Wayne swept it too, but often he either forgot or didn't see what
she saw or didn't care about it. Sweeping was not hard but it
was still something to do, and sometimes for days it seemed too
much to do, and fluffs of dust gathered in corners and under
furniture. So now she asked Wayne and he looked surprised
and she was afraid he would be angry, but then he smiled and
said Okay. He brought the records to the clerk and she watched
the numbers come up on the register and the money going into
the clerk's hand. Then Wayne led her past the corners and
curves of washers and dryers, deeper into the light of the store,
where she chose a round blue Hoover vacuum cleaner.

She carried it, boxed, into the apartment; behind her on the
stairs Wayne carried the stereo in two boxes that hid his face.
They went quickly downstairs again. Anna was waiting. She
did not know what she was waiting for, but standing on the
sidewalk as Wayne's head and shoulders went into the car,
she was anxious and mute. She listened to his breathing and
the sound of cardboard sliding over the car seat. She wanted
to speak into the air between them, the air that had risen from
the floorboard coming home from the mall as their talk had
slowed, repeated itself, then stopped. Whenever that happened, they were either about to fight or enter a time of shy
loneliness. Now grunting, he straightened with the boxed

television in his arms; she grasped the free end and walked backward up the icy walk, telling him Not so *fast*, and he slowed and told her when she reached the steps and, feeling each one with her calves, she backed up them and through the door, and he asked if she wanted him to go up first and she said No, he had most of its weight, she was better off. She was breathing too fast to smell the stairway; sometimes she smelled cardboard and the television inside it, like oiled plastic; she belched and tasted hamburger, and when they reached the third floor she was sweating. In the apartment she took off her coat and went downstairs with him, and they each carried up a boxed speaker. They brought the chest into the living room and set it down against the wall opposite the couch; she dusted its top, and they put the stereo and television on it. For a while she sat on the couch, watching him connect wires. Then she went to the kitchen and took the vacuum cleaner from its box. She put it against the wall and leaned its pipes in the corner next to it and sat down to read the instructions. She looked at the illustrations, and thought she was reading, but she was not. She was listening to Wayne in the living room: not to him, but to speakers sliding on the floor, the tapping touch of a screwdriver, and when she finished the pamphlet she did not know what she had read. She put it in a drawer. Then, so that raising her voice would keep shyness from it, she called from the kitchen: 'Can we go to Timmy's?'

'Don't you want to play with these?'

'No,' she said. When he did not answer, she wished she had lied, and she felt again as she had in the department store when sorrow had enveloped her like a sudden cool breath from the television screens. She went into the living room and kneeled beside him, sitting on the floor, a speaker and wires between his legs; she nuzzled his cheek and said: 'I'm sorry.'

'I don't want to play with them either. Let's go.'

She got their coats and, as they were leaving, she stopped in the doorway and looked back at the stereo and television.

'Should we have bought it all in one place?' she said.

'It doesn't matter.'

She hurried ahead of him down the stairs and out onto the sidewalk, then her feet slipped forward and up and he caught her against his chest. She hooked her arm in his and they crossed the street and the parking lot; she looked to her left into the Sunnycorner, two men and a woman lined at the counter and Sally punching the register. She looked fondly at the warm light in there, the colors of magazine covers on the rack, the red soft-drink refrigerator, the long shelves of bread.

'What a hangover I had. And I didn't make any mistakes.'

She walked fast, each step like flight from the apartment. They went through the lot of Chevrolet pickups, walking single file between the trucks, and now if she looked back she would not be able to see their lawn; then past the broad-windowed showroom of new cars and she thought of their—his—old Comet. Standing on the curb, waiting for a space in traffic, she tightly gripped his arm. They trotted across the street to Timmy's door and entered the smell of beer and smoke. Faces turned from the bar, some hands lifted in a wave. It was not ten o'clock yet, the dining room was just closing, and the people at the bar stood singly, not two or three deep like last night, and the tables in the rear were empty. McCarthy was working. Anna took her place at the corner, and he said: 'You make it to work at seven?'

'How did you know?'

'Oh my *God*, I've got to be at work at seven; another tequila, Johnny.'

She raised a hand to her laughter, and covered it.

'I made it. I made it and tomorrow I don't work till three, and I'm going to have *two* tequila salty dogs and that's *all*; then I'm going to bed.'

Wayne ordered a shot of Fleischmann's and a draft, and when McCarthy went to the middle of the bar for the beer, she asked Wayne how much was left, though she already knew, or nearly did, and when he said *About two-twenty* she was ahead of his answer, nodding but paying no attention to the words, the numbers, seeing those strange visitors in their home, staring from the top of the chest, sitting on the kitchen floor; then McCarthy brought their drinks and went away, and she found on the bar the heart enclosing their initials that she and Wayne had carved, drinking one crowded night when McCarthy either did not see them or pretended not to.

'I don't want to feel bad,' she said.

'Neither me.'

'Let's don't. Can we get bicycles?'

'All of one and most of the other.'

'Do you want one?'

'Sure. I need to get back in shape.'

'Where can we go?'

'The Schwinn place.'

'I mean riding.'

'All over. When it thaws. There's nice roads everywhere. I know some trails in the woods, and one of them goes to a pond. A big pond.'

'We can go swimming.'

'Sure.'

'We should have bought a canoe.'

'Instead of what?'

She was watching McCarthy make a Tom Collins and a gimlet.

'I don't know,' she said.

'I guess we bought winter sports.'

'Maybe we should have got a freezer and a lot of food. You know what's in the refrigerator?'

'You said you didn't want to feel bad.'

'I don't.'

'So don't.'

'What about you?'

'I don't want to either. Let's have another round and hang it up.'

In the morning she woke at six, not to an alarm but out of habit: her flesh alert, poised to dress and go to work, and she got up and went naked and shivering to the bathroom, then to the kitchen, where, gazing at the vacuum cleaner, she drank one of the glasses of milk. In the living room she stood on the cold floor in front of the television and stereo, hugging herself. She was suddenly tired, her first and false energy of the day gone, and she crept into bed, telling herself she could sleep now, she did not have to work till three, she could sleep: coaxing, as though her flesh were a small child wakened in the night. She stopped shivering, felt sleep coming upward from her legs; she breathed slowly with it, and escaped into it, away from memory of last night's striving flesh: she and Wayne, winter-pallid yet sweating in their long, quiet, coupled work at coming until they gave up and their fast dry breaths slowed and the Emmylou Harris album ended, the stereo clicked twice into the silence, a record dropped and Willie Nelson sang 'Stardust.'

'I should have got some ludes and percs too,' he said.

Her hand found his on the sheet and covered it.

'I was too scared. It was bad enough waiting for the money. I kept waiting for somebody to come in and blow me away. Even him. If he'd had a gun, he could have. But I should have got some drugs.'

'It wouldn't have mattered.'

'We could have sold it.'

'It wouldn't matter.'

'Why?'

'There's too much to get. There's no way we could ever get it all.'

'A *lot* of it, though. *Some* of it.'

She rubbed the back of his hand, his knuckles, his nails. She did not know when he fell asleep. She slept two albums later, while Waylon Jennings sang. And slept now, deeply, in the morning, and woke when she heard him turning, rising, walking barefooted and heavily out of the room.

She got up and made coffee and did not see him until he came into the kitchen wearing his one white shirt and one pair of blue slacks and the black shoes; he had bought them all in one store in twenty minutes of quiet anger, with money she gave him the day Wendy's hired him; he returned the money on his first payday. The toes of the shoes were scuffed now. She kept the shirt clean, some nights washing it in the sink when he came home and hanging it on a chair back near the radiator so he could wear it next day; he would not buy another one because, he said, he hated spending money on something he didn't want.

When he left, carrying the boxes out to the dumpster, she turned last night's records over. She read the vacuum cleaner pamphlet, joined the dull silver pipes and white hose to the squat and round blue tank, and stepped on its switch. The cord was long and she did not have to change it to an outlet in another room; she wanted to remember to tell Wayne it was funny that the cord was longer than their place. She finished quickly and turned it off and could hear the records again.

She lay on the couch until the last record ended, then got the laundry bag from the bedroom and soap from the kitchen, and left. On the sidewalk she turned around and looked up at the front of the building, old and green in the snow and against the blue glare of the sky. She scraped the car's glass and drove to the laundry: two facing rows of machines, moist warm air, gurgling rumble and whining spin of washers, resonant clicks and loud hiss of dryers, and put in clothes and soap and coins. At a long table women smoked and read magazines, and two of them talked as they shook crackling electricity from clothes they folded. Anna took a small wooden chair from the table and sat watching the round window of the machine, watched her clothes and Wayne's tossing past it, like children waving from a ferris wheel.

A FATHER'S STORY

My name is Luke Ripley, and here is what I call my life: I own a stable of thirty horses, and I have young people who teach riding, and we board some horses too. This is in northeastern Massachusetts. I have a barn with an indoor ring, and outside I've got two fenced-in rings and a pasture that ends at a woods with trails. I call it my life because it looks like it is, and people I know call it that, but it's a life I can get away from when I hunt and fish, and some nights after dinner when I sit in the dark in the front room and listen to opera. The room faces the lawn and the road, a two-lane country road. When cars come around the curve northwest of the house, they light up the lawn for an instant, the leaves of the maple out by the road and the hemlock closer to the window. Then I'm alone again, or I'd appear to be if someone crept up to the house and looked through a window: a big-gutted grey-haired guy, drinking tea and smoking cigarettes, staring out at the dark woods across the road, listening to a grieving soprano.

My real life is the one nobody talks about anymore, except Father Paul LeBoeuf, another old buck. He has a decade on me: he's sixty-four, a big man, bald on top with grey at the sides; when he had hair, it was black. His face is ruddy, and he jokes about being a whiskey priest, though he's not. He gets outdoors as much as he can, goes for a long walk every morning, and hunts and fishes with me. But I can't get him on a horse anymore. Ten years ago I could badger him into a trail ride; I had to give him a western saddle, and he'd hold the pommel and bounce through the woods with me, and be sore for days. He's looking at seventy with eyes that are younger than many I've seen in people in their twenties. I do not remember ever feeling the way they seem to; but I was lucky, because even as a child I knew that life would try me, and I must be strong to endure, though in those early days I expected to be tortured and killed for my faith, like the saints I learned about in school.

Father Paul's family came down from Canada, and he grew up speaking more French than English, so he is different from the Irish priests who abound up here. I do not like to make general statements, or even to hold general beliefs, about people's blood, but the Irish do seem happiest when they're dealing with misfortune or guilt, either their own or somebody else's, and if you think you're not a victim of either one, you can count on certain Irish priests to try to change your mind. On Wednesday nights Father Paul comes to dinner. Often he comes on other nights too, and once, in the old days when we couldn't eat meat on Fridays, we bagged our first ducks of the season on a Friday, and as we drove home from the marsh, he said: For the purposes of Holy Mother Church, I believe a duck is more a creature of water than land, and is not rightly meat. Sometimes he teases me about never putting anything in his Sunday collection, which he would not know about if I hadn't told him years ago. I would like to believe I told him so we could have philosophical talk at dinner, but probably the truth is I suspected he knew, and I did not want him to think I so loved money that I would not even give his church a coin on Sunday. Certainly the ushers who pass the baskets know me as a miser.

I don't feel right about giving money for buildings, places. This starts with the Pope, and I cannot respect one of them till he sells his house and everything in it, and that church too, and uses the money to feed the poor. I have rarely, and maybe never, come across saintliness, but I feel certain it cannot exist in such a place. But I admit, also, that I know very little, and maybe the popes live on a different plane and are tried in ways I don't know about. Father Paul says his own church, St. John's, is hardly the Vatican. I like his church: it is made of wood, and has a simple altar and crucifix, and no padding on the kneelers. He does not have to lock its doors at night. Still it is a place. He could say Mass in my barn. I know this is stubborn, but I can find no mention by Christ of maintaining buildings, much less erecting them of stone or brick, and decorating them with pieces of metal and mineral and elements that people still fight over like barbarians. We had a Maltese woman taking riding lessons, she came over on the boat when she was ten, and once she told me how the nuns in Malta used to tell the little girls that if they wore jewelry, rings and bracelets and necklaces, in purgatory snakes would coil around their fingers and wrists and throats. I do not believe in frightening children or telling them lies, but if those nuns saved a few girls from devotion to things, maybe they were right. That Maltese woman laughed about it, but I noticed she wore only a watch, and that with a leather strap.

The money I give to the church goes in people's stomachs, and on their backs, down in New York City. I have no delusions about the worth of what I do, but I feel it's better to feed somebody than not. There's a priest in Times Square giving shelter to runaway kids, and some Franciscans who run a bread line; actually it's a morning line for coffee and a roll, and Father Paul calls it the continental breakfast for winos and bag ladies. He is curious about how much I am sending, and I know why: he guesses I send a lot, he has said probably more than tithing, and he is right; he wants to know how much because he believes I'm generous and good, and he is wrong about that; he has never had much money and does not know how easy it is to write a check when you have everything you will ever need, and the figures are mere numbers, and represent no sacrifice at all. Being a real Catholic is too hard; if I were one, I would do with my house and barn what I want the Pope to do with his. So I do not want to impress

Father Paul, and when he asks me how much, I say I can't let my left hand know what my right is doing.

He came on Wednesday nights when Gloria and I were married, and the kids were young; Gloria was a very good cook (I assume she still is, but it is difficult to think of her in the present), and I liked sitting at the table with a friend who was also a priest. I was proud of my handsome and healthy children. This was long ago, and they were all very young and cheerful and often funny, and the three boys took care of their baby sister, and did not bully or tease her. Of course they did sometimes, with that excited cruelty children are prone to, but not enough so that it was part of her days. On the Wednesday after Gloria left with the kids and a U-Haul trailer, I was sitting on the front steps, it was summer, and I was watching cars go by on the road, when Father Paul drove around the curve and into the driveway. I was ashamed to see him because he is a priest and my family was gone, but I was relieved too. I went to the car to greet him. He got out smiling, with a bottle of wine, and shook my hand, then pulled me to him, gave me a quick hug, and said: 'It's Wednesday, isn't it? Let's open some cans.'

With arms about each other we walked to the house, and it was good to know he was doing his work but coming as a friend too, and I thought what good work he had. I have no calling. It is for me to keep horses.

In that other life, anyway. In my real one I go to bed early and sleep well and wake at four forty-five, for an hour of silence. I never want to get out of bed then, and every morning I know I can sleep for another four hours, and still not fail at any of my duties. But I get up, so have come to believe my life can be seen in miniature in that struggle in the dark of morning. While making the bed and boiling water for coffee, I talk to God: I offer Him my day, every act of my body and spirit, my thoughts and moods, as a prayer of thanksgiving, and for Gloria and my children and my friends and two women I made love with after Gloria left. This morning offertory is a habit from my boyhood in a Catholic school; or then it was a habit, but as I kept it and grew older it became a ritual. Then I say the Lord's Prayer, trying not to recite it, and one morning it occurred to me that a prayer, whether recited or said with concentration, is always an act of faith.

I sit in the kitchen at the rear of the house and drink coffee and smoke and watch the sky growing light before sunrise, the trees of the woods near the barn taking shape, becoming single pines and elms and oaks and maples. Sometimes a rabbit comes out of the treeline, or is already sitting there, invisible till the light finds him. The birds are awake in the trees and feeding on the ground, and the little ones, the purple finches and titmice and chickadees, are at the feeder I rigged outside the kitchen window; it is too small for pigeons to get a purchase. I sit and give myself to coffee and tobacco, that get me brisk again, and I watch and listen. In the first year or so after I lost my family, I played the radio in the mornings. But I overcame that, and now I rarely play it at all. Once in the mail I received a questionnaire asking me to write down everything I watched on television during the week they had chosen. At the end of those seven days I wrote in *The Wizard of Oz* and returned it. That was in winter and was actually a busy week for my television, which normally sits out the cold months without once warming up. Had they sent the questionnaire during baseball season, they would have found me at my set. People at the stables talk about shows and performers I have never heard of, but I cannot get interested; when I am in the mood to watch television, I go to a movie or read a detective novel. There are always good detective novels to be found, and I like remembering them next morning with my coffee.

I also think of baseball and hunting and fishing, and of my children. It is not painful to think about them anymore, because even if we had lived together, they would be gone now, grown into their own lives, except Jennifer. I think of death too, not sadly, or with fear, though something like excitement does run through me, something more quickening than the coffee and tobacco. I suppose it is an intense interest, and an outright distrust: I never feel certain that I'll be here watching birds eating at tomorrow's daylight. Sometimes I try to think of other things, like the rabbit that is warm and breathing but not there till twilight. I feel on the brink of something about the life of the senses, but either am not equipped to go further or am not interested enough to concentrate. I have called all of this thinking, but it is not, because it is unintentional; what I'm really doing is feeling the day, in silence, and that is what Father Paul is doing too on his five-to-ten-mile walks.

When the hour ends I take an apple or carrot and I go to the stable and tack up a horse. We take good care of these horses, and no one rides them but students, instructors, and me, and nobody rides the horses we board unless an owner asks me to. The barn is dark and I turn on lights and take some deep breaths, smelling the hay and horses and their manure, both fresh and dried, a combined odor that you either like or you don't. I walk down the wide space of dirt between stalls, greeting the horses, joking with them about their quirks, and choose one for no reason at all other than the way it looks at me that morning. I get my old English saddle that has smoothed and darkened through the years, and go into the stall, talking to this beautiful creature who'll swerve out of a canter if a piece of paper blows in front of him, and if the barn catches fire and you manage to get him out he will, if he can get away from you, run back into the fire, to his stall. Like the smells that surround them, you either like them or you don't. I love them, so am spared having to try to explain why. I feed one the carrot or apple and tack up and lead him outside, where I mount, and we go down the driveway to the road and cross it and turn northwest and walk then trot then canter to St. John's.

A few cars are on the road, their drivers looking serious about going to work. It is always strange for me to see a woman dressed for work so early in the morning. You know how long it takes them, with the makeup and hair and clothes, and I think of them waking in the dark of winter or early light of other seasons, and dressing as they might for an evening's entertainment. Probably this strikes me because I grew up seeing my father put on those suits he never wore on weekends or his two weeks off, and so am accustomed to the men, but when I see these women I think something went wrong, to send all those dressed-up people out on the road when the dew hasn't dried yet. Maybe it's because I so dislike getting up early, but am also doing what I choose to do, while they have no choice. At heart I am lazy, yet I find such peace and delight in it that I believe it is a natural state, and in what looks like my laziest periods I am closest to my center. The ride to St. John's is fifteen minutes. The horses and I do it in all weather; the road is well plowed in winter, and there are only a few days a year when ice makes me drive the pickup. People always look at someone on horseback, and for a moment their faces change and many drivers and I wave to each other. Then at St. John's, Father Paul and five or six regulars and I celebrate the Mass.

Do not think of me as a spiritual man whose every thought during those twenty-five minutes is at one with the words of the Mass. Each morning I try, each morning I fail, and know that always I will be a creature who, looking at Father Paul and the altar, and uttering prayers, will be distracted by scrambled eggs, horses, the weather, and memories and daydreams that have nothing to do with the sacrament I am about to receive. I can receive, though: the Eucharist, and also, at Mass and at other times, moments and even minutes of contemplation. But I cannot achieve contemplation, as some can; and so, having to face and forgive my own failures, I have learned from them both the necessity and wonder of ritual. For ritual allows those who cannot will themselves out of the secular to perform the spiritual, as dancing allows the tongue-tied man a ceremony of love. And, while my mind dwells on breakfast, or Major or Duchess tethered under the church eave, there is, as I take the Host from Father Paul and place it on my tongue and return to the pew, a feeling that I am thankful I have not lost in the forty-eight years since my first Communion. At its center is excitement; spreading out from it is the peace of certainty. Or the certainty of peace. One night Father Paul and I talked about faith. It was long ago, and all I remember is him saying: Belief is believing in God; faith is believing that God believes in you. That is the excitement, and the peace; then the Mass is over, and I go into the sacristy and we have a cigarette and chat, the mystery ends, we are two men talking like any two men on a morning in America, about baseball, plane crashes, presidents, governors, murders, the sun, the clouds. Then I go to the horse and ride back to the life people see, the one in which I move and talk, and most days I enjoy it.

It is late summer now, the time between fishing and hunting, but a good time for baseball. It has been two weeks since Jennifer left, to drive home to Gloria's after her summer visit. She is the only one who still visits; the boys are married and have children, and sometimes fly up for a holiday, or I fly down or west to visit one of them. Jennifer is twenty, and I worry about her the way fathers worry about daughters but not sons. I want to know what she's up to, and at the same time I don't. She looks athletic, and she is: she swims and runs and of course rides. All my children do. When she comes for six weeks in summer, the house is loud with girls, friends of hers since childhood, and new ones. I am glad she kept the girl friends. They have been young company for me and, being with them, I have been able to gauge her growth between summers. On their riding days, I'd take them back to the house when their lessons were over and they had walked the horses and put them back in the stalls, and we'd have lemonade or Coke, and cookies if I had some, and talk until their parents came to drive them home. One year their breasts grew, so I wasn't startled when I saw Jennifer in July. Then they were driving cars to the stable, and beginning to look like young women, and I was passing out beer and ashtrays and they were talking about college.

When Jennifer was here in summer, they were at the house most days. I would say generally that as they got older they became quieter, and though I enjoyed both, I sometimes missed the giggles and shouts. The quiet voices, just low enough for me not to hear from wherever I was, rising and falling in proportion to my distance from them, frightened me. Not that I believed they were planning or recounting any-thing really wicked, but there was a female seriousness about them, and it was secretive, and of course I thought: love, sex. But it was more than that: it was womanhood they were enter-ing, the deep forest of it, and no matter how many women and men too are saying these days that there is little difference between us, the truth is that men find their way into that for-est only on clearly marked trails, while women move about in it like birds. So hearing Jennifer and her friends talking so quietly, yet intensely, I wanted very much to have a wife.

But not as much as in the old days, when Gloria had left but her presence was still in the house as strongly as if she had only gone to visit her folks for a week. There were no clothes or cosmetics, but potted plants endured my neglectful care as long as they could, and slowly died; I did not kill them on purpose, to exorcise the house of her, but I could not remember to water them. For weeks, because I did not use it much, the house was as neat as she had kept it, though dust layered the order she had made. The kitchen went first: I got the dishes in and out of the dishwasher and wiped the top of the stove, but did not return cooking spoons and pot holders to their hooks on the wall, and soon the burners and oven were caked with spillings, the refrigerator had more space and was spotted with juices. The living room and my bed-room went next; I did not go into the children's rooms except on bad nights when I went from room to room and looked and touched and smelled, so they did not lose their order until a year later when the kids came for six weeks. It was three months before I ate the last of the food Gloria had cooked and frozen: I remember it was a beef stew, and very good. By then I had four cookbooks, and was boasting a bit, and talking about recipes with the women at the stables, and looking forward to cooking for Father Paul. But I never looked forward to cooking at night only for myself, though I made myself do it; on some nights I gave in to my daily temptation, and took a newspaper or detective novel to a restaurant. By the end of the second year, though, I had stopped turning on the radio as soon as I woke in the morning, and was able to be silent and alone in the evening too, and then I enjoyed my dinners.

It is not hard to live through a day, if you can live through a moment. What creates despair is the imagination, which pretends there is a future, and insists on predicting millions of moments, thousands of days, and so drains you that you cannot live the moment at hand. That is what Father Paul told me in those first two years, on some of the bad nights when I believed I could not bear what I had to: the most painful loss was my children, then the loss of Gloria, whom I still loved despite or maybe because of our long periods of sadness that rendered us helpless, so neither of us could break out of it to give a hand to the other. Twelve years later I believe ritual would have healed us more quickly than the repetitious talks we had, perhaps even kept us healed. Marriages have lost that, and I wish I had known then what I know now, and we had performed certain acts together every day, no matter how we felt, and perhaps then we could have subordinated feeling to action, for surely that is the essence of love. I know this from my distractions during Mass, and during everything else I do, so that my actions and feelings are seldom one. It does happen every day, but in proportion to everything else in a day, it is rare, like joy. The third most painful loss, which became second and sometimes first as months passed, was the knowledge that I could never marry again, and so dared not even keep company with a woman.

On some of the bad nights I was bitter about this with Father Paul, and I so pitied myself that I cried, or nearly did, speaking with damp eyes and breaking voice. I believe that celibacy is for him the same trial it is for me, not of the flesh, but the spirit: the heart longing to love. But the difference is he chose it, and did not wake one day to a life with thirty horses. In my anger I said I had done my service to love and chastity, and I told him of the actual physical and spiritual pain of practicing rhythm: nights of striking the mattress with a fist, two young animals lying side by side in heat, leaving the bed to pace, to smoke, to curse, and too passionate to question, for we were so angered and oppressed by our passion that we could see no further than our loins. So now I understand how people can be enslaved for generations before they throw down their tools or use them as weapons, the form of their slavery—the cotton fields, the shacks and puny cupboards and untended illnesses—absorbing their emotions and thoughts until finally they have little or none at all to direct with clarity and energy at the owners and legislators. And I told him of the trick of passion and its slaking: how during what we had to believe were safe periods, though all four children were conceived at those times, we were able with some coherence to question the tradition and reason and justice of the law against birth control, but not with enough conviction to soberly act against it, as though regular satisfaction in bed tempered our revolutionary as well as our erotic desires. Only when abstinence drove us hotly away from each other did we receive an urge so strong it lasted all the way to the drugstore and back; but always, after release, we threw away the remaining condoms; and after going through this a few times, we knew what would happen, and from then on we submitted to the calendar she so precisely marked on the bedroom wall. I told him that living two lives each month, one as celibates, one as lovers, made us tense and short-tempered, so we snapped at each other like dogs.

To have endured that, to have reached a time when we burned slowly and could gain from bed the comfort of lying down at night with one who loves you and whom you love, could for weeks on end go to bed tired and peacefully sleep after a kiss, a touch of the hands, and then to be thrown out of the marriage like a bundle from a moving freight car, was unjust, was intolerable, and I could not or would not muster the strength to endure it. But I did, a moment at a time, a day, a night, except twice, each time with a different woman and more than a year apart, and this was so long ago that I clearly see their faces in my memory, can hear the pitch of their voices, and the way they pronounced words, one with a Massachusetts accent, one midwestern, but I feel as though I only heard about them from someone else. Each rode at the stables and was with me for part of an evening; one was badly married, one divorced, so none of us was free. They did not understand this Catholic view, but they were understanding about my having it, and I remained friends with both of them until the married one left her husband and went to Boston, and the divorced one moved to Maine. After both those evenings, those good women, I went to Mass early while Father Paul was still in the confessional, and received his absolution. I did not tell him who I was, but of course he knew, though I never saw it in his eyes. Now my longing for a wife comes only once in a while, like a cold: on some late afternoons when I am alone in the barn, then I lock up and walk to the house, daydreaming, then suddenly look at it and see it empty, as though for the first time, and all at once I'm weary and feel I do not have the energy to broil meat, and I think of driving to a restaurant, then shake my head and go on to the house, the refrigerator, the oven; and some mornings when I wake in the dark and listen to the silence and run my hand over the cold sheet beside me; and some days in summer when Jennifer is here.

Gloria left first me, then the Church, and that was the end of religion for the children, though on visits they went to Sunday Mass with me, and still do, out of a respect for my life that they manage to keep free of patronage. Jennifer is an agnostic, though I doubt she would call herself that, any more than she would call herself any other name that implied she had made a decision, a choice, about existence, death, and God. In truth she tends to pantheism, a good sign, I think; but not wanting to be a father who tells his children what they ought to believe, I do not say to her that Catholicism includes pantheism, like onions in a stew. Besides, I have no missionary instincts and do not believe everyone should or even could live with the Catholic faith. It is Jennifer's womanhood that renders me awkward. And womanhood now is frank, not like when Gloria was twenty and there were symbols: high heels and cosmetics and dresses, a cigarette, a cocktail. I am glad that women are free now of false modesty and all its attention paid the flesh; but, still, it is difficult to see so much of your daughter, to hear her talk as only men and bawdy women used to, and most of all to see in her face the deep and unabashed sensuality of women, with no tricks of the eyes and mouth to hide the pleasure she feels at having a strong young body. I am certain, with the way things are now, that she has very happily not been a virgin for years. That does not bother me. What bothers me is my certainty about it, just from watching her walk across a room or light a cigarette or pour milk on cereal.

She told me all of it, waking me that night when I had gone to sleep listening to the wind in the trees and against the house, a wind so strong that I had to shut all but the lee windows, and still the house cooled; told it to me in such detail and so clearly that now, when she has driven the car to Florida, I remember it all as though I had been a passenger in the front seat, or even at the wheel. It started with a movie, then beer and driving to the sea to look at the waves in the night and the wind, Jennifer and Betsy and Liz. They drank a beer on the beach and wanted to go in naked but were afraid they would drown in the high surf. They bought another six-pack at a grocery store in New Hampshire, and drove home. I can see it now, feel it: the three girls and the beer and the ride on country roads where pines curved in the wind and the big deciduous trees swayed and shook as if they might leap from the earth. They would have some windows partly open so they could feel the wind; Jennifer would be playing a cassette, the music stirring them, as it does the young, to memories of another time, other people and places in what is for them the past.

She took Betsy home, then Liz, and sang with her cassette as she left the town west of us and started home, a twenty-minute drive on the road that passes my house. They had each had four beers, but now there were twelve empty bottles in the bag on the floor at the passenger seat, and I keep focusing on their sound against each other when the car shifted speeds or changed directions. For I want to understand that one moment out of all her heart's time on earth, and whether her history had any bearing on it, or whether her heart was then isolated from all it had known, and the sound of those bottles urged it. She was just leaving the town, accelerating past a night club on the right, gaining speed to climb a long, gradual hill, then she went up it, singing, patting the beat on the steering wheel, the wind loud through her few inches of open window, blowing her hair as it did the high branches alongside the road, and she looked up at them and watched the top of the hill for someone drunk or heedless coming over it in part of her lane. She crested to an open black road, and there he was: a bulk, a blur, a thing running across her headlights, and she swerved left and her foot went for the brake and was stomping air above its pedal when she hit him, saw his legs and body in the air, flying out of her light, into the dark. Her brakes were screaming into the wind, bottles clinking in the fallen bag, and with the music and wind inside the car was his sound, already a memory but as real as an echo, that car-shuddering thump as though she had struck a tree. Her foot was back on the accelerator. Then she shifted gears and pushed it. She ejected the cassette and closed the window. She did not start to cry until she knocked on my bedroom door, then called: 'Dad?'

Her voice, her tears, broke through my dream and the wind I heard in my sleep, and I stepped into jeans and hurried to the door, thinking harm, rape, death. All were in her face, and I hugged her and pressed her cheek to my chest and smoothed her blown hair, then led her, weeping, to the kitchen and sat her at the table where still she could not speak, nor look at me; when she raised her face it fell forward again, as of its own weight, into her palms. I offered tea and she shook her head, so I offered beer twice, then she shook her head, so I offered whiskey and she nodded. I had some rye that Father Paul and I had not finished last hunting season, and I poured some over ice and set it in front of her and was putting away the ice but stopped and got another glass and poured one for myself too, and brought the ice and bottle to the table where she was trying to get one of her long menthols out of the pack, but her fingers jerked like severed snakes, and I took the pack and lit one for her and took one for myself. I watched her shudder with her first swallow of rye, and push hair back from her face, it is auburn and gleamed in the overhead light, and I remembered how beautiful she looked riding a sorrel; she was smoking fast, then the sobs in her throat stopped, and she looked at me and said it, the words coming out with smoke: 'I hit somebody. With the *car*.'

Then she was crying and I was on my feet, moving back and forth, looking down at her, asking *Who? Where? Where?* She was pointing at the wall over the stove, jabbing her fingers and cigarette at it, her other hand at her eyes, and twice in horror I actually looked at the wall. She finished the whiskey in a swallow and I stopped pacing and asking and poured another, and either the drink or the exhaustion of tears quieted her, even the dry sobs, and she told me; not as I tell it now, for that was later as again and again we relived it in the kitchen or living room, and, if in daylight, fled it on horseback out on the trails through the woods and, if at night, walked quietly around in the moonlit pasture, walked around and around it, sweating through our clothes. She told it in bursts, like she was a child again, running to me, injured from play. I put on boots and a shirt and left her with the bottle and her streaked face and a cigarette twitching between her fingers, pushed the door open against the wind, and eased it shut. The wind squinted and watered my eyes as I leaned into it and went to the pickup.

When I passed St. John's I looked at it, and Father Paul's little white rectory in the rear, and wanted to stop, wished I could as I could if he were simply a friend who sold hardware or something. I had forgotten my watch but I always know the time within minutes, even when a sound or dream or my bladder wakes me in the night. It was nearly two; we had been in the kitchen about twenty minutes; she had hit him around one-fifteen. Or her. The road was empty and I drove between blowing trees; caught for an instant in my lights, they seemed to be in panic. I smoked and let hope play its tricks on me: it was neither man nor woman but an animal, a goat or calf or deer on the road; it was a man who had jumped away in time, the collision of metal and body glancing not direct, and he had limped home to nurse bruises and cuts. Then I threw the cigarette and hope both out the window and prayed that he was alive, while beneath that prayer, a reserve deeper in my heart, another one stirred: that if he were dead, they would not get Jennifer.

From our direction, east and a bit south, the road to that hill and the night club beyond it and finally the town is, for its last four or five miles, straight through farming country. When I reached that stretch I slowed the truck and opened my window for the fierce air; on both sides were scattered farmhouses and barns and sometimes a silo, looking not like shelters but like unsheltered things the wind would flatten. Corn bent toward the road from a field on my right, and always something blew in front of me: paper, leaves, dried weeds, branches. I slowed approaching the hill, and went up it in second, staring through my open window at the ditch on the left side of the road, its weeds alive, whipping, a mad dance with the trees above them. I went over the hill and down and, opposite the club, turned right onto a side street of houses, and parked there, in the leaping shadows of trees. I walked back across the road to the club's parking lot, the wind behind me, lifting me as I strode, and I could not hear my boots on pavement. I walked up the hill, on the shoulder, watching the branches above me, hearing their leaves and the creaking trunks and the wind. Then I was at the top, looking down the road and at the farms and fields; the night was clear, and I could see a long way; clouds scudded past the half-moon and stars, blown out to sea.

I started down, watching the tall grass under the trees to my right, glancing into the dark of the ditch, listening for cars behind me; but as soon as I cleared one tree, its sound was gone, its flapping leaves and rattling branches far behind me, as though the greatest distance I had at my back was a matter of feet, while ahead of me I could see a barn two miles off. Then I saw her skid marks: short, and going left and downhill, into the other lane. I stood at the ditch, its weeds blowing; across it were trees and their moving shadows, like the clouds. I stepped onto its slope, and it took me sliding on my feet, then rump, to the bottom, where I sat still, my body gathered to itself, lest a part of me should touch him. But there was only tall grass, and I stood, my shoulders reaching the sides of the ditch, and I walked uphill, wishing for the flashlight in the pickup, walking slowly, and down in the ditch I could hear my feet in the grass and on the earth, and kicking cans and bottles. At the top of the hill I turned and went down, watching the ground above the ditch on my right, praying my prayer from the truck again, the first one, the one I would admit, that he was not dead, was in fact home, and began to hope again, memory telling me of lost pheasants and grouse I had shot, but they were small and the colors of their home, while a man was either there or not; and from that memory I left where I was and while walking in the ditch under the wind was in the deceit of imagination with Jennifer in the kitchen, telling her she had hit no one, or at least had not badly hurt anyone, when I realized he could be in the hospital now and I would have to think of a way to check there, something to say on the phone. I see now that, once hope returned, I should have been certain what it prepared me for: ahead of me, in high grass and the shadows of trees, I saw his shirt. Or that is all my mind would allow itself: a shirt, and I stood looking at it for the moments it took my mind to admit the arm and head and the dark length covered by pants. He lay face down, the arm I could see near his side, his head turned from me, on its cheek.

'Fella?' I said. I had meant to call, but it came out quiet and high, lost inches from my face in the wind. Then I said, 'Oh God,' and felt Him in the wind and the sky moving past the stars and moon and the fields around me, but only watching me as He might have watched Cain or Job, I did not know which, and I said it again, and wanted to sink to the earth and weep till I slept there in the weeds. I climbed, scrambling up the side of the ditch, pulling at clutched grass, gained the top on hands and knees, and went to him like that, panting, moving through the grass as high and higher than my face, crawling under that sky, making sounds too, like some animal, there being no words to let him know I was here with him now. He was long; that is the word that came to me, not tall. I kneeled beside him, my hands on my legs. His right arm was by his side, his left arm straight out from the shoulder, but turned, so his palm was open to the tree above us. His left cheek was cleanshaven, his eye closed, and there was no blood. I leaned forward to look at his open mouth and saw the blood on it, going down into the grass. I straightened and looked ahead at the wind blowing past me through grass and trees to a distant light, and I stared at the light, imagining someone awake out there, wanting someone to be, a gathering of old friends, or someone alone listening to music or painting a picture, then I figured it was a night light at a farmyard whose house I couldn't see. *Going*, I thought. *Still going.* I leaned over again and looked at dripping blood.

So I had to touch his wrist, a thick one with a watch and expansion band that I pushed up his arm, thinking *he's left-handed*, my three fingers pressing his wrist, and all I felt was my tough fingertips on that smooth underside flesh and small bones, then relief, then certainty. But against my will, or only because of it, I still don't know, I touched his neck, ran my fingers down it as if petting, then pressed, and my hand sprang back as from fire. I lowered it again, held it there until it felt that faint beating that I could not believe. There was too much wind. Nothing could make a sound in it. A pulse could not be felt in it, nor could mere fingers in that wind feel the absolute silence of a dead man's artery. I was making sounds again; I grabbed his left arm and his waist, and pulled him toward me, and that side of him rose, turned, and I lowered him to his back, his face tilted up toward the tree that was groaning, the tree and I the only sounds in the wind. Turning my face from his, looking down the length of him at his sneakers, I placed my ear on his heart, and heard not that but something else, and I clamped a hand over my exposed ear, heard something liquid and alive, like when you pump a well and after a few strokes you hear air and water moving in the pipe, and I knew I must raise his legs and cover him and run to a phone, while still I listened to his chest, thinking *raise with what? cover with what?* and amid the liquid sound I heard the heart, then lost it, and pressed my ear against bone, but his chest was quiet, and I did not know when the liquid had stopped, and do not know now when I heard air, a faint rush of it, and whether under my ear or at his mouth or whether I heard it at all. I straightened and looked at the light, dim and yellow. Then I touched his throat, looking him full in the face. He was blond and young. He could have been sleeping in the shade of a tree, but for the smear of blood from his mouth to his hair, and the night sky, and the weeds blowing against his head, and the leaves shaking in the dark above us.

I stood. Then I kneeled again and prayed for his soul to join in peace and joy all the dead and living; and, doing so, confronted my first sin against him, not stopping for Father Paul, who could have given him the last rites, and immediately then my second one, or, I saw then, my first, not calling an ambulance to meet me there, and I stood and turned into the wind, slid down the ditch and crawled out of it, and went up the hill and down it, across the road to the street of houses whose people I had left behind forever, so that I moved with stealth in the shadows to my truck.

When I came around the bend near my house, I saw the kitchen light at the rear. She sat as I had left her, the ashtray filled, and I looked at the bottle, felt her eyes on me, felt what she was seeing too: the dirt from my crawling. She had not drunk much of the rye. I poured some in my glass, with the water from melted ice, and sat down and swallowed some and looked at her and swallowed some more, and said: 'He's dead.'

She rubbed her eyes with the heels of her hands, rubbed the cheeks under them, but she was dry now.

'He was probably dead when he hit the ground. I mean, that's probably what killed—'

'Where was he?'

'Across the ditch, under a tree.'

'Was he—did you see his face?'

'No. Not really. I just felt. For life, pulse. I'm going out to the car.'

'What for? Oh.'

I finished the rye, and pushed back the chair, then she was standing too.

'I'll go with you.'

'There's no need.'

'I'll go.'

I took a flashlight from a drawer and pushed open the door and held it while she went out. We turned our faces from the wind. It was like on the hill, when I was walking, and the wind closed the distance behind me: after three or four steps I felt there was no house back there. She took my hand, as I was reaching for hers. In the garage we let go, and squeezed between the pickup and her little car, to the front of it, where we had more room, and we stepped back from the grill and I shone the light on the fender, the smashed headlight turned into it, the concave chrome staring to the right, at the garage wall.

'We ought to get the bottles,' I said.

She moved between the garage and the car, on the passenger side, and had room to open the door and lift the bag. I reached out, and she gave me the bag and backed up and shut the door and came around the car. We sidled to the doorway, and she put her arm around my waist and I hugged her shoulders.

'I thought you'd call the police,' she said.

   We crossed the yard, faces bowed from the wind, her hair blowing away from her neck, and in the kitchen I put the bag of bottles in the garbage basket. She was working at the table: capping the rye and putting it away, filling the ice tray, washing the glasses, emptying the ashtray, sponging the table.

   'Try to sleep now,' I said.

   She nodded at the sponge circling under her hand, gathering ashes. Then she dropped it in the sink and, looking me full in the face, as I had never seen her look, as perhaps she never had, being for so long a daughter on visits (or so it seemed to me and still does: that until then our eyes had never seriously met), she crossed to me from the sink and kissed my lips, then held me so tightly I lost balance, and would have stumbled forward had she not held me so hard.

I sat in the living room, the house darkened, and watched the maple and the hemlock. When I believed she was asleep I put on *La Boheme*, and kept it at the same volume as the wind so it would not wake her. Then I listened to *Madame Butterfly*, and in the third act had to rise quickly to lower the sound: the wind was gone. I looked at the still maple near the window, and thought of the wind leaving farms and towns and the coast, going out over the sea to die on the waves. I smoked and gazed out the window. The sky was darker, and at daybreak the rain came. I listened to *Tosca*, and at six-fifteen went to the kitchen where Jennifer's purse lay on the table, a leather shoulder purse crammed with the things of an adult woman, things she had begun accumulating only a few years back, and I nearly wept, thinking of what sandy foundations they were: driver's license, credit card, disposable lighter, cigarettes, checkbook, ballpoint pen, cash, cosmetics, comb, brush, Kleenex, these the rite of passage from childhood, and I took one of them—her keys—and went out, remembering a jacket and hat when the rain struck me, but I kept going to the car, and squeezed and lowered myself into it, pulled the seat belt over my shoulder and fastened it and backed out, turning in the drive, going forward into the road, toward St. John's and Father Paul.

Cars were on the road, the workers, and I did not worry about any of them noticing the fender and light. Only a horse distracted them from what they drove to. In front of St. John's is a parking lot; at its far side, past the church and at the edge of the lawn, is an old pine, taller than the steeple now. I shifted to third, left the road, and, aiming the right headlight at the tree, accelerated past the white blur of church, into the black trunk growing bigger till it was all I could see, then I rocked in that resonant thump she had heard, had felt, and when I turned off the ignition it was still in my ears, my blood, and I saw the boy flying in the wind. I lowered my forehead to the wheel. Father Paul opened the door, his face white in the rain.

'I'm all right.'

'What happened?'

'I don't know. I fainted.'

I got out and went around to the front of the car, looked at the smashed light, the crumpled and torn fender.

'Come to the house and lie down.'

'I'm all right.'

'When was your last physical?'

'I'm due for one. Let's get out of this rain.'

'You'd better lie down.'

'No. I want to receive.'

That was the time to say I want to confess, but I have not and will not. Though I could now, for Jennifer is in Florida, and weeks have passed, and perhaps now Father Paul would not feel that he must tell me to go to the police. And, for that very reason, to confess now would be unfair. It is a world of secrets, and now I have one from my best, in truth my only, friend. I have one from Jennifer too, but that is the nature of fatherhood.

Most of that day it rained, so it was only in early evening, when the sky cleared, with a setting sun, that two little boys,

leaving their confinement for some play before dinner, found
him. Jennifer and I got that on the local news, which we listened to every hour, meeting at the radio, standing with cigarettes, until the one at eight o'clock; when she stopped crying,
we went out and walked on the wet grass, around the pasture,
the last of sunlight still in the air and trees. His name was Patrick Mitchell, he was nineteen years old, was employed by
CETA, lived at home with his parents and brother and sister.
The paper next day said he had been at a friend's house and
was walking home, and I thought of that light I had seen, then
knew it was not for him; he lived on one of the streets behind
the club. The paper did not say then, or in the next few days,
anything to make Jennifer think he was alive while she was
with me in the kitchen. Nor do I know if we—I—could have
saved him.

In keeping her secret from her friends, Jennifer had to
perform so often, as I did with Father Paul and at the stables,
that I believe the acting, which took more of her than our
daylight trail rides and our night walks in the pasture, was her
healing. Her friends teased me about wrecking her car. When
I carried her luggage out to the car on that last morning, we
spoke only of the weather for her trip—the day was clear,
with a dry cool breeze—and hugged and kissed, and I stood
watching as she started the car and turned it around. But then
she shifted to neutral and put on the parking brake and
unclasped the belt, looking at me all the while, then she was
coming to me, as she had that night in the kitchen, and I
opened my arms.

I have said I talk with God in the mornings, as I start my
day, and sometimes as I sit with coffee, looking at the birds,
and the woods. Of course He has never spoken to me, but that
is not something I require. Nor does He need to. I know Him,
as I know the part of myself that knows Him, that felt Him
watching from the wind and the night as I kneeled over the
dying boy. Lately I have taken to arguing with Him, as I can't
with Father Paul, who, when he hears my monthly confession,
has not heard and will not hear anything of failure to do all

that one can to save an anonymous life, of injustice to a family in their grief, of deepening their pain at the chance and mystery of death by giving them nothing—no one—to hate. With Father Paul I feel lonely about this, but not with God. When I received the Eucharist while Jennifer's car sat twice-damaged, so redeemed, in the rain, I felt neither loneliness nor shame, but as though He were watching me, even from my tongue, intestines, blood, as I have watched my sons at times in their young lives when I was able to judge but without anger, and so keep silent while they, in the agony of their youth, decided how they must act; or found reasons, after their actions, for what they had done. Their reasons were never as good or as bad as their actions, but they needed to find them, to believe they were living by them, instead of the awful solitude of the heart.

I do not feel the peace I once did: not with God, nor the earth, or anyone on it. I have begun to prefer this state, to remember with fondness the other one as a period of peace I neither earned nor deserved. Now in the mornings while I watch purple finches driving larger titmice from the feeder, I say to Him: I would do it again. For when she knocked on my door, then called me, she woke what had flowed dormant in my blood since her birth, so that what rose from the bed was not a stable owner or a Catholic or any other Luke Ripley I had lived with for a long time, but the father of a girl.

And He says: I am a Father too.

Yes, I say, as You are a Son Whom this morning I will receive; unless You kill me on the way to church, then I trust You will receive me. And as a Son You made Your plea.

Yes, He says, but I would not lift the cup.

True, and I don't want You to lift it from me either. And if one of my sons had come to me that night, I would have phoned the police and told them to meet us with an ambulance at the top of the hill.

Why? Do you love them less?

I tell Him no, it is not that I love them less, but that I could bear the pain of watching and knowing my sons' pain, could bear it with pride as they took the whip and nails. But You never had a daughter and, if You had, You could not have borne her passion.

So, He says, you love her more than you love Me.

I love her more than I love truth.

Then you love in weakness, He says.

As You love me, I say, and I go with an apple or carrot out to the barn.

EDITOR'S NOTE

Joshua Bodwell

THERE IS PERHAPS no greater double-edged compliment in literature than the phrase "writer's writer." It is at once both high praise and an intimation of authorial obscurity. The phrase inevitably brings to mind writers of undeniable skill and power whose work has not easily or effortlessly found a large readership.

Andre Dubus was a writer's writer. His short stories and novellas have for decades been discussed regularly and reverently among other writers as exemplars of the forms. He was a master of narrative compression, a writer of unyielding compassion, and like his literary mentor Anton Chekhov, an author of far-reaching empathy. And like Chekhov, Dubus deserves to be discovered by generation after generation of new readers.

It was with all this and more in mind that I proposed this project to gather together the vast majority of Andre Dubus's short stories and novellas into three volumes with new introductions by some of those writers who most admire his work.

This volume brings together Andre Dubus's third and fourth collections of short stories and novellas: *Finding a Girl in America* and *The Times Are Never So Bad*.

THE TITLE OF VOLUME TWO

We faced a unique challenge when it came time to title the books in this three-volume project: it was awkward and inelegant to simply merge the titles of two different books, yet Dubus was not alive to offer alternatives.

My challenge then was to find more elegant titles while staying true to Dubus's voice. The solution arrived when I realized Dubus had, over the years, toyed with naming collections after different stories within a collection before settling on an eventual title. Scanning the table of contents for volume two, I knew we had myriad title options for the book, and they were all Dubus's very own words.

The heartrending story "The Winter Father" felt like a perfect title for this volume for several reasons. The title simply and directly touches on two themes that run throughout Dubus's work: fatherhood and family. These were obviously fraught themes for Dubus, and he returned to them time and again in many of his most complex, searching stories.

The title works on another level, too. Somewhat famously, Dubus refused to chase large payments from glossy magazines if it meant ceding the artistic integrity of his prose. "The Winter Father" serves as a perfect anecdote for this sometimes contentious attitude toward publication:

Dubus published three stories in quick succession in the venerated *New Yorker*: "Andromache" (1968), "The Doctor" (1969), and "An Afternoon with the Old Man" (1972); all published, it should be noted, years before his first collection was published in 1975. "The Winter Father" was the fourth Dubus story accepted by the *New Yorker*, but it would never appear on the magazine's pages.

In several interviews in the 1980s, Dubus expressed frustration that famously peculiar *New Yorker* editor William Shawn—who helmed the magazine from 1952 to 1987—deleted several words from "Andromache," including "diaphragm," "horny," and "brownnose". When Dubus was asked to cut the word "fuck" from "The Winter Father," he refused and withdrew the story. His fiction never again appeared in the *New Yorker*; in the late 1990s, the magazine published some of his nonfiction.

"The Winter Father" went on to be published in *The Sewanee Review* in 1980, and was then selected by guest editor Hortense Calisher for inclusion in *The Best America Short Stories 1981*. Of his many appearances in that annual anthology, this may have been the sweetest: Dubus did not receive the large payment publication in the *New Yorker* would have provided, but was likely very pleased to retain something he seemed to value far more than money: artistic integrity.

THE SHORT STORIES & NOVELLAS OF VOLUME TWO

Dubus spent a considerable amount of time contemplating the sequence of the stories in his collections. "The arrangement is important to the reading, and I do take the trouble," he told interviewer Thomas Kennedy. "I learned that from Richard Yates and assume that all short story writers take the trouble. Therefore, when I buy a book of stories, I read them in order." With this in mind, we have honored and retained Dubus's story sequencing here.

Finding a Girl in America was first published in 1980. The collection opens with "Killings," a swift tale of revenge that forces readers to imagine what they might do in the name of family love. The story became the basis of screenwriter/director Todd Field's Academy Award-nominated film *In the Bedroom*. While the film adaptation was mostly faithful to the story, Field decided to make young Frank Fowler an only child, whereas in the story he has a brother. Field told me the change ratcheted up the emotional elements for Frank's parents: "The stakes are absolute for the Fowlers, leaving them just each other, without any other immediate family, to mitigate their grief."

Though it's not mentioned in the acknowledgements of original editions of *Finding a Girl in America*, "The Misogamist" was first published in *Penthouse* in 1976. Like its rival *Playboy*, the magazine was a high-paying venue for fiction in the 1970s. When "The Misogamist" appeared in the magazine, Dubus was furious to discover that without his knowledge, eighty-five changes had been made to the fifteen-page story. Dubus refused to acknowledge the *Penthouse* version of his story, and considered this book version of "The Misogamist" the only true version.

After a fiery letter from Dubus, *Penthouse* returned a second story they'd already accepted: "Killings." That story went on to appear instead in the pages of one of Dubus's earliest supporters, *The Sewanee Review*.

After appearing in the *North American Review* in 1979, "The Pitcher" was selected for the anthology *Prize Stories 1980: The O. Henry Awards*.

"Waiting" first appeared in *The Paris Review* in 1979, making it Dubus's only story to ever appear in that revered quarterly. The story is a particularly good example of Dubus's ability with narrative compression: it took fourteen months to write and was more than one hundred pages in early manuscript form, yet was pared to a mere seven pages by the time it was published. Interestingly, according to Dubus's brief bio note in *The Paris Review*, he considered titling his third collection not *Finding a Girl in America*, but instead simply *Killings*.

Finding a Girl in America closes with the title novella, a story that revisits the lives of Hank and Edith Allison, Jack and Terry Linhart, and closes the trilogy that begins with "We Don't Live Here Anymore" and "Adultery."

Just three years after *Finding a Girl in America*, Dubus's *The Times Are Never So Bad* appeared in 1983. The collection opens with the novella "The Pretty Girl." Writing in the *New York Times Book Review*, Joyce Carol Oates opined the story "... may be the most compelling and suspenseful work of fiction [Dubus] has written."

Taken together, "Leslie in California" and "Anna" show the fascinating breadth of how Dubus's work was read: while the former first appeared in *Redbook*, predominantly read by women, the latter first appeared in *Playboy*, read (or so they say) by men. "Leslie in California" later appeared as a stand-alone chapbook, letterpress printed and hand-bound by Birch Brook Press.

The collection closes with "A Father's Story," which would become one of Dubus's most beloved stories. While Richard Russo's introduction to this volume grapples with his complex feelings of reading Dubus's work over many decades, when it comes to his opinion of "A Father's Story," Russo couldn't be more clear: "I won't mince words. It's one of the finest stories ever penned by an American." When the story first appeared in the *Black Warrior Review* in 1983, the issue included "A Conversation with Andre Dubus," a long interview conducted by Dev Hathaway. Guest editor John Updike selected "A Father's Story" for *The Best American Short Stories 1984*.

EDITOR'S ACKNOWLEDGMENTS

In 2007, Kevin Larimer at *Poets & Writers Magazine* accepted my pitch to write a long piece entitled "The Art of Reading Andre Dubus: We Don't Have to Live Great Lives." Kevin was, as he always is, a patient, shrewd, and thoughtful editor of that piece. The joys of writing that article became the seed of this three-volume project, and for that I will be eternally grateful to the encouragement of Kevin and *Poets & Writers Magazine*.

At David R. Godine, Publisher, the talented team of Sue Ramin and Chelsea Bingham was endlessly helpful, as was the calm, steadying advice of George Gibson, for which I am thankful. Carl W. Scarbrough, designer par excellence, brought his refined touch to the beautiful physical book.

Greta Rybus not only made the photographs for the covers of all three new volumes of this project, but went above and beyond, reading and re-reading Dubus's story, and offering thoughtful, caring, and deeply felt creative ideas about how the photographs might speak in conversation with Dubus's complex stories. We should all be so lucky to have the opportunity to work with collaborators as gifted and generous as Greta.

Many years ago, it was Richard Russo's rich introduction to *The Collected Stories of Richard Yates* that made me begin to read the work of that often underappreciated master. To now have the gift of Rick introducing this volume of Dubus— who was a student of Yates's at the Iowa Writers' Workshop— seems too good to be true. Rick's generosity and integrity are immediately evident to anyone who knows him, and both are on full display in this volume's introduction.

Finally, the last two people to thank are the first two people I reached out to when I conceived of this project: Andre Dubus III and David R. Godine.

David first published Andre Dubus's short stories and novellas more than four decades ago, and for that reason alone, this book simply would not exist if not for the unflagging support of Dubus's work. After every turn, David's enthusiasm and considerable knowledge was invaluable.

Andre III's generosity and big-hearted embrace of this project girded my confidence to proceed. He quickly invited his sister Suzanne Dubus into the process, and both became steady sources of ideas and support. In a world that sometimes seems stymied by a dearth of good men, Andre is one of the very best men I know. *Thank you, brother.*

AUTHOR'S BIOGRAPHY

ANDRE DUBUS (August 11, 1936–February 24, 1999; pronounced da-byüs) was born in Lake Charles, Louisiana to a
Cajun-Irish family and educated in Catholic schools. After
peacetime service in the U.S. Marine Corps, Dubus attended
the University of Iowa Writers' Workshop, where he earned
his MFA in 1965. In 1966, he moved north, settling in Haverhill, Massachusetts to teach literature and creative writing at
Bradford College until his retirement.

Dubus's short stories and novellas appeared in distin-
guished literary journals such as *Ploughshares*, *The Paris
Review*, *The Sewanee Review*, and *The Southern Review*, as
well as national magazines such as *Harper's*, *The New Yorker*,
and *Playboy*. In addition to his many short story collections,
he published two collections of essays: *Broken Vessels* and
Meditations from a Movable Chair. The award-winning films
In the Bedroom and *We Don't Live Here Anymore* were adapted
from his stories.

His prose earned him a MacArthur "Genius" Award, the
PEN/Malamud Award for Excellence in the Short Story, the
Rea Award for the Short Story, the Jean Stein Award from the
American Academy of Arts and Letters, and nominations for a
National Book Critics Circle Award and Pulitzer Prize.

Andre Dubus published just one novel during his career:

The Lieutenant (Dial Press, 1967). After falling under the spell of Anton Chekhov, Dubus would consciously devote himself to the short story and novella for the rest of his life. While his stories were revered when they appeared in literary journals and magazines, after the publication of his novel, Dubus received rejection after rejection when it came to publishing a collection of his stories.

Literary agent Philip G. Spitzer became one of Dubus's earliest and most loyal supporters. During a casual lunch in New York City, Spitzer handed David R. Godine a plain manila envelope with the manuscript for *Separate Flights*. Godine called Spitzer the next day and offered to publish the collection. In the end, Dubus waited seven rejection-filled years between the publication of novel and his first short story collection.

In a 1998 interview with *Glimmer Train*, Dubus recalled "The rejections that really hurt during that period after I published *The Lieutenant* were not the rejections slips that said 'I don't like the collection of stories,' but the ones that said, 'We'll publish this collection of stories if you write a novel.' That hurt. I thought I was being told to be somebody else."

Neither Spitzer nor Godine insisted Dubus write a novel but instead supported his devotion to the short story. Godine quickly realized "there was more punch contained in one Dubus short story than in 99.98% of all the novels being published. I still feel that way."

"I'm one of the luckiest short story writers in America because of Godine," Dubus told the *Black Warrior Review* in 1983. "How many publishers would publish four collections of stories by a writer, without *one* novel?" Indeed, the closest Godine ever came to publishing a novel by Dubus was issuing the long novella *Voices from the Moon* as a gorgeously designed standalone book in 1984; the novella appears in full in volume three of this project, *The Cross Country Runner*.

Dubus's devotion to the short story form—the novella bears a much closer relation to being a long short story than being a short novella—fit him not simply as a prose form, but from a philosophical stance. "I love short stories because I believe they are the way we live," he once wrote. "They are what our friends tell us, in their pain and joy, their passion and rage, their yearning and their cry against injustice."

In 1986, while attempting to aid two motorists on a highway in Massachusetts, Dubus was struck by an oncoming car traveling nearly sixty miles an hour. Dubus stopped at what he thought was a car broken down in the travel lane. The car, it turned out, had become wedged on a motorcycle abandoned in the middle of the highway. As Dubus helped the two motorists—Luis and Luz Santiago, a brother and sister from Puerto Rico—to safety, another car approached. Dubus pushed Luz out of the way. Luis, a young man of only twenty-three, was hit and killed instantly. Dubus was struck, thrown over the car's hood and landed in a crumpled, bleeding mass; a quarter found in Dubus's pocket after the accident had been bent in half by the impact.

While it's startling that Dubus somehow managed to even survive the blow, the accident left him with thirty-four broken bones. He lost his left leg below the knee and his right leg was crushed to the point of uselessness. He would be confined to a wheelchair for the rest of his. After the accident, Dubus was unable to write for some time. He eventually found his way back to writing fiction, in part, by writing a series of powerful essays. In need of money for medical and living expenses, Dubus finally—with the blessing of his longtime publisher, David Godine—accepted an offer from a large New York City publisher. A full decade after Dubus's accident, *Dancing After Hours* appeared in 1996, published by Alfred A. Knopf, and went on to be named a finalist for a National Book Critics Circle Award; the fourteen stories in that collection are his only stories not included in this three volume collection.

On February 24, 1999, at the age of sixty-two, Dubus suffered a fatal heart attack. He was laid to rest in Haverhill, Massachusetts in a simple casket handmade by his sons.

A NOTE ON THE TYPE

THE WINTER FATHER *has been set in Jonathan Hoefler's Mercury types. Originally created for the* New Times *newspaper chain and later adapted for general informational typography, the Mercury types were drawn in four grades intended to be used under variable printing conditions—that is, to compensate for less-than-optimal presswork or for regional differences in paper stock and plant conditions. The result was a family of types that were optimized to print well in a vast number of sizes and formats. In books, Mercury makes a no-nonsense impression, crisp and open, direct and highly readable, yet possessed of real style and personality.* ◆ ◆ ◆ *The display type is Quadraat Sans, a family originally designed in 1996 by Fred Smeijers for FontFont, and subsequently enlarged and expanded into a much larger constellation of types.*